MW01172712

Along Harrowed Trails

Timber Ghost Press

Along Harrowed Trails

Published by Timber Ghost Press

Printed in the United States of America

Edited by: Beverly Bernard, Ashely Cranatas, C.R. Langille

Cover Art and Design by: Carter Reid

Interior Design: Timber Ghost Press

Print ISBN: 979-8-9855521-8-8

www.TimberGhostPress.com

Contents

Behold! The Manifest Age

Maxwell I. Gold

Rickety stagecoaches, dancing on the hinges of tomorrow cried through glass, sandy deserts where bloody hooves from ghoulish horses trampled the dreams and light of the Manifest Age.

Ghost Towns soon bereft and stripped of the golden hope were nothing more than graveyards for the robber barons and steel-gods to dump their rotted, discarded, and used riches to be reconstructed again and again for people to flock to new cities of wood and flack in the hope they'd find gold and treasure, revealed only as ruins of shadow and blood. Still, the fierce pounding of broken hooves echoed across the horizon as the ancient sun crept beneath a yellowed sky and those red, western hills.

And so, by the smacks and whips heralded by dead coachmen on those rickety carriages, they brayed and boomed the dark visions of a world-to-come where all was possible and none were forgotten, but swallowed in a day, and destiny was a pocket commodity. All, in the Manifest Age.

Draugr Gold

Craig E. Sawyer

Luna Falls was once a thriving mining town in the Northern Montana Territory, but now its empty buildings haunted the valley like a ghost that refused to pass on to the next world. The only sign of life left was a tiny coil of smoke from the roof of the only lit building, which had tall windows set in its front that burned like two furious glowing eyes overlooking the muddy main street. A broken sign out front swayed and squealed like a living thing. It was covered with a layer of ice, and barely perceptible underneath were the words *"Sheriff's Office—Closed for the Foreseeable Future."*

The wind mourned coldly, and if a person stood motionless in the middle of main street, they could swear they heard music being played from inside the Faro Hall, but in actuality, it was just the wind that rushed down from the Flathead Mountain Range through the bitterroot trees.

Sheriff Huston was inside his warm office watching the snow fall. His wife was at their home near the edge of town, preparing for their journey to Texas. They were the last family left in this empty town, and they had planned to ride out in the morning. His dreams of raising a family here under the watchful eyes of the great mountain were dead and buried, like those he was supposed to have protected. He was lost in those thoughts of the past when he heard the sound of neighing horses. He could see through the blurred glass that two men were riding up on horseback. He knew the only types of people that rode through here these days were the hunters and the hunted.

He went to grab his revolver, but it was too late.

The front door burst open, and he was hit by a white dervish. In the space stood a gaunt and haggard-looking man. His face appeared chiseled from pale granite, and his attire was more pirate than cowboy. He wore a wide-brimmed black bolero hat that shadowed his narrow eyes and a bright red scarf tucked down into his meaty jacket of furs. His Prince of Wales spurs jangled loud on the hardwood floor with every one of his methodical steps.

"You Sheriff of this iceberg?"

"Who's asking?"

Sheriff Huston could see two horses over the man's broad shoulders. They were tethered to a hitching post out front. Among them was a chestnut mare that still had a man in its saddle and a sturdy smoky colored "bulldog" quarter horse that the gaunt man had just obviously dismounted. The man's horse looked as wild and worldly as its master but had been ridden hard and needed care. The other rider was bound and tied to his own saddle. His stringy hair moved in the evening breeze like it was underwater, and his right eye was just a black socket. "My name is Captain Sidacious Tomlinson."

The name fired a recognition in the Sheriff's blue eyes.

"You were one of the Texas Rangers that killed all those Comanche at the Battle of Walkers Creek."

"Yeesir, but I'm no longer a Ranger. My current profession is that of bounty hunter, and I have dire need of someone who can take me up to the old fur trapper's camp at the top of the Lost Trail. I would travel on my own, but the main trailhead was blocked by an avalanche. I can pay a person handsomely."

"Who's your prisoner?"

"He ran with a group of cutthroat thieves throughout the territory and Texas. They call themselves the Nettle's Gang, and ole One-Eye here told me the rest of them were holding up at a fur trapper's cabin up in the Flatheads."

The Sheriff was sizing up the man and decided he was nothing but trouble. Death circled over his head like a black cloud, and the Sheriff was thinking more about living these days. "I'm pretty much retired and planning on leaving at first light, but you're welcome to hold up here for as long as you need. Nothing blows through here much except for the wind."

The bounty hunter let out a growl of discontent. "But you know a way up to that cabin, don't ya?"

"Like I told you, I'm riding out in the morning. Sorry that I can't be more help," he said, giving a stern nod in hopes of ending the discussion, but he still hadn't discounted the chance that this little meeting might end in violence. He had seen this Captain's type before—a bleak despair and stubborn disposition.

"You see that hole where his eye used to be?" He said, pointing out the window.

The Sheriff shook his head nervously. "Yeah, I see it."

"I took it with the end of a heated buck knife. The act gleaned some fairly pertinent knowledge of where his gang was hiding, and the most important fact—they have a king's ransom of stolen Wells Fargo gold. A fortune I would be willing to split with you."

The Sheriff took a sharp look at the one-eyed man shivering on the horse and then back to the eyes of his visitor. "I have enough to get me where I'm going, but I thank you for the offer."

"No one ever has enough," the colorful bounty hunter said before stomping back outdoors to retrieve his prisoner.

He jerked the one-eyed man down from the horse and drug him inside, kicking the door shut behind them. "Meet ole One-Eye. Tell the Sheriff about all that gold." The captain pressed the barrel of his Colt revolver into the captive's bruised cheek. "Make a single errant move, and I will paint the wall with what little brains you have."

The man drooled like a hungry dog. "Uh, t-two stammar fylld med guld."

"He don't speak English too good—he's a dirty Swede."

"But the odöda, the ghost... won't let you get it," One-Eye added.

The captain pulled off his hat and tossed it on the Sheriff's desk. His head was scarred like a parsnip. "Don't let him scare you with his stories of boogeymen."

Sheriff Huston stared at the captain.

"I'd rather be ugly and alive than pretty and dead."

"I just never saw a man who had been scalped."

"You would think this hairdo was from a damn injun, but I got it at Camp Douglas. I survived that twenty-six acres of Hell on Earth, which wasn't fit for a brokedick dog, much less a human being. Damn every last one of those Billy Yanks who ran it."

"What did he mean, a ghost?" The Sheriff said, in hopes of changing the subject. He could see the strive growing in the man, and he didn't want to have to pull his gun.

"He claims that a ghost killed all his fellow thieves by drinking their blood and eating some of their flesh, and that he barely escaped with his own life in the middle of the night. I feel that's just a damn lie to scare me off from the gold when in fact, he killed them himself. I caught him at the Grinning Dog Saloon in Whitefish."

The front door opened, stopping the captain in mid-speech.

The captain pulled a pocket derringer with his free hand and pointed at the intruder.

"Wait, don't shoot! That's Aiyana, my wife!"

There was a pretty native woman with waist-length hair that looked like it was made from silk. She stood there in a simple blue dress with not a drop of fear on her face, even though death was pointed at her.

"You almost got your guts removed, little lady."

The captain lowered his gun. "You didn't tell me your wife was an injun?

The Sheriff went for his gun, but in his clumsy attempt to draw, he dropped it on the floor.

The captain laughed. "I'll be bloody damned. How did you ever get to be a sheriff? My injun killing days are over if that's what has you wanting to skin that smoke wagon for?"

"I'm a Cree. And you are?" Aiyana said.

"Captain Sidacious Tomlinson at your service, little lady," he said with a look of disdain before spitting a glob of tobacco at her feet.

"The Dade family stole all of our money," she said to her husband. The money she spoke of was their entire life savings and with it any hope of relocating to Texas.

"That–that just cannot be true! They were our friends," the Sheriff said. His face crumpled in disbelief.

The captain slapped his thigh. "Ding it! I guess you will be needing that share of outlaw gold, after all!" Aiyana looked at her husband with a frown. "No one travels up the Lost Trail this time of year and lives."

"God's plans are unfathomable to us mortals. Sometimes we are little more than tiny boats moving in whatever direction the wind blows us," The Sheriff said while wringing his hands and shivering in the night air.

"Didn't you hear? God is dead," the captain said.

The sun had yet to rise over the hulking mountains and open up the valley. The small paddock was still midnight dark, but Sheriff Huston was already in the stable, preparing his horse for the journey. His Friesian named Rough Belly was a magnificent horse and tall for his type of breed, standing at eighteen hands. He was fast with the stamina of a pack mule.

"This is gonna be a heck of a ride, ole Rough," the Sheriff said, patting his horse on the thigh, after tossing a blanket and saddle on.

The horse neighed.

"Early riser?" A gruff voice said from the stall door.

"It's just my nature, I suppose," the Sheriff answered.

"I haven't slept more than two hours straight in years. The slightest twig break or the feathers of a bird flapping has me up with my gun in hand. The years of fighting does that to a–"

The captain doubled over into a coughing fit.

"That's a nasty hack."

The captain pulled a handkerchief from his pocket and placed it to his lips, and when he lowered the white cloth, it was stained with blood.

"You're sick?"

"From the time a person is born to the time they are placed in the clay, ole Death is always nipping at their heels. And one day, that ole pale horse will catch um, no matter how damn fast they can ride."

"Maybe, you should just take One-Eye for his bounty and forget the rest?"

The captain lifted his saddle and placed it on his horse's back. A horse that he loved as dearly as anything in this rotten world. He had named him Hellfire. It was a testament to the fiery spirit of the large hinded and barrel bodied steed.

"What's the fun in that?"

"I don't find any of this fun."

"What happened to this town?"

The Sheriff's head fell. "Bandits rode through, and I failed to protect it. A lot of people suffered horrendously. Most left after that."

The captain's face suddenly wilted like a flower that hadn't seen rain in years. "You still got your wife."

"And I thank God for that every day."

"My sweet wife Matilda May was a school teacher. Her dying wish was for a new schoolhouse to be built in our little town called Conroy, just south of Houston. I wasn't the best husband in the world. I'm gonna honor that with my dying breath."

"You will see her in heaven one day."

"Me and you are as different as dirt and sky."

The Sheriff shook his head and tugged at the cinch on his saddle.

"We'll be ready at first light."

The group had been riding up the Lost Trail for the good part of an hour when they spotted a snow-covered pile of rocks with a giant boulder in the center. It was big enough that it would take at least a dozen men hours to remove it all, and just to the right and the left through a grove of pines were two rougher-looking trails.

"This is how far I made it yesterday," the captain said, and bit off a mouth full from a plug of tobacco.

Aiyana pointed to the left path. "We will freeze to death if we don't make that cabin by sundown. The trail to the left is the faster one."

Ole Rough snorted and pawed the ground.

"What's got you so spooked?" The Sheriff patted her neck before pointing to what appeared to be the top of an overturned wagon buried in the snow. "Look there!" He dismounted and made his way to the overturned wagon.

"We don't have time for this, shit!" the captain yelled.

The Sheriff holstered his gun and plodded with high steps to the wagon.

Once there, he started to claw out handfuls of snow, digging about a foot down. His furious digging abruptly stopped as he reached something horrible.

"Jesus!" he yelled before falling backward into a snow drift.

"What the tarnation is going on?" The scowling captain said as he made his way to the wagon to see for himself. In the snow was the severed head of a man in his late thirties. "That a member of your missing Dade family?"

"That's Moses Dade," The Sheriff said.

The captain walked up and kicked the side of the wagon a few times causing most of the snow on top to fall off to reveal the faces and limbs of other frozen bodies.

"A pack of wolves must have attacked them," the captain mused.

Aiyana had dismounted and was inspecting markings on the ground. "There are no wolf prints, only the tracks of a barefooted man."

"The Dades had three small children," The Sheriff said with a sob in his throat. He started to frantically search in and around the wagon. "They have all been torn apart."

"A man with no shoes would get frostbite in minutes."

"It's no man—it's a Draugr," One-Eye said.

"Keep talking, and you keep living," the grim-faced captain said.

"I speak more English than I've been letting on. That ghost that scared me off from the cabin, I wasn't lying about that, but it's something much worse than the spirit of a person. We were snowed inside that cabin for weeks without food. I ventured out to possibly trade with the natives that had camped for the winter not far from the cabin, but I was taken captive by them. I managed to escape weeks later with a little food. I made my way back to cabin, but I saw no sign of my men. That's when I caught a glimpse of our leader—Sam Nettles, staring at me through the frost-covered window. The look on his face made a cat run up my spine. His appearance was emaciated, like that of a corpse fresh from the grave. His cheekbones jutted out through his skin like sharp rocks, and his eyes were sunken deep into his skull. A tendril of greenish drool poured over his chin as he licked the glass. I could hear his voice in my head saying the same word over and over."

"What was that?"

"Hunger... hunger... hunger...."

"Jesus father in heaven, so he did eat them?" Sheriff Huston said.

"He's just trying to steer us clear from a whole lot of gold," the captain said.

"My people have a name for this too, but we call it Wendigo," Aiyana said. Her face looked frightened for the first time.

"I'm telling you, forget the damn gold! We should turn and go back to town," The trembling One-Eye said.

"If what you are saying is true, then how do we kill it?" the captain snarled.

"I don't know, but father was a hunter, and he would tell me stories of the Draugr. He said they could control the weather. They can even attack you in your dreams, but the main thing is they are always starving for human flesh."

"You can't—it's already dead," Aiyana said. "It is powered by the spirit of greed, loneliness, and hunger."

"You say it's the animated body of a dead person, so that means it has a head like that of a normal man, correct?" the captain said.

Bart and Aiyana nodded in agreement.

"Then, I'm going to blow its goddamn head off, and then I'm gonna take its gold," the captain said. "Mount up!"

The cabin was surprisingly in good shape, considering it had been built over forty years ago. It was a sturdy enough frame, and the snow had been falling heavy enough for the past hour that it was raised halfway up the front door. The sun was nearly extinguished, all but for a few rods of gold and red.

The riders came out of a massive grouping of forty-foot pines, and the weather had suddenly taken a turn for the worse, and the snowfall made seeing more than ten feet impossible.

Aiyana was in the lead, with the captain a few feet behind her with his rifle drawn.

"That's the cabin," One-Eye said, his voice barely a whisper.

The captain rode out in front of Aiyana and came to a stop.

He dismounted and tied his horse to a tree. The others followed suit.

"The captain pulled his long knife and turned to Aiyana. "Here, take my Arkansas toothpick. You stay and watch the horses and

One-Eye, Little Lady. If we don't have those, then we are not making it out of here." The captain handed her the large knife.

She grabbed the giant knife's coffin-shaped ash wood handle and brandished its carbon steel. Its blade gleamed in the weak light. It had been blessed by a preacher in Tennessee just after the captain had saved his son from bandits, but that's a story for another time.

"Sheriff, you post up at the front door. I'll go through the back to flush him out. He probably won't be able to get out the front, but if he does—shoot him."

"I don't want to leave Aiyana out here with him."

"We need you at the door."

Aiyana placed her hand on his shoulder. "I'll be fine. If he tries anything, I'll cut out his other eye," she said and looked over to One-Eye.

"Kiss my ass, you injun bitch! Bullets won't stop it! Only fire hurts a Draugr."

"We'll see about that," the Sheriff said, and if you call my wife a bitch again, I'll shoot you right here and now.

The captain made his way to the back of the cabin, which was partially buried like the front, but a path to the doorway had been dug out recently. The cabin's logs were too solid to shoot through, and the lone window in the back was covered in snow, so Captain Tomlinson knew that at least he wouldn't be shot making his way up on the door.

The captain pushed it open slowly and stuck his head inside to get a look. The barrel of his Sharps carbine leading the way.

Back at the horses, Aiyana tried to keep focus on her husband, who was crouched down near the front door with his gun raised. The snow had let up a bit, but visibility was still bad.

"So, I stashed some of the gold in the woods near a crooked pine that had been struck by lightning. Me and you could live one hell of a life with all that money," One-Eye said from atop the tethered horse. His hands were still bound at his front.

"Shut up," she said through gritted teeth refusing to look at him.

"Just undo these ropes, and I will make you a rich woman."

"I said..."

A branch snapped loudly from behind the horses, which caused them to start to paw the ground in a nervous fit.

"Did you hear that?" One-Eye stammered. "It's that thing!"

"Quiet," she said and turned with her knife at the ready, trying to see anything through the falling white. Aiyana stood close to the horses. One-Eye was frantically looking in a circle for whatever made the sound.

"I think it was just an animal."

But he had no sooner spoken, when a tall figure pulled him from the horse and tossed him to the ground beside Aiyana.

A nightmarish apparition clawed its way onto the neighing horse's back.

Warm blood hit the cold air.

She reached over and cut the panicked animal's reins, and it easily tossed the creature off before bolting into the nearby pines.

Aiyana was now face-to-face with the thing. It was well over six feet tall, and its desiccated skin was pulled like a tight membrane over its bony frame. Its complexion was grey and death-soaked. Something had chewed its lips off, exposing its teeth which chattered loudly.

"Hunger... hunger... hunger," it hissed over and over.

Aiyana was terrified, but she defiantly stood her ground between the thing and the horses.

The creature sniffed the air in her direction before turning and leaping onto One-Eye.

"Help me!" One-Eye screamed as the voracious Draugr devoured his flesh in chunks, and after it had made quick work of the outlaw, it whipped around to his next feast, for the hunger never subsided in a Draugr.

She was scared, but with the heart of a warrior. The daughter of a feared and respected Cree chief called Morning Wind, who was instrumental in her people holding onto their sacred lands much longer than most other tribes.

The Draugr swung a clawed hand at her, which she easily avoided and returned with a slash across the creature's side, exposing even more rib bone.

The abomination hissed, its teeth chattering, and lunged at her with its rotten teeth. The thing's weight landing squarely and pinning her to the snowy ground.

She raised up the blessed blade the moment before the manic beast landed on her, and its razor-sharp blade pierced its black heart and sent its demonic spirit back to Hell.

The creature was heavy, but Aiyana managed to push the thing to her side.

She gasped for air and screamed a Cree battle cry to the heavens. Her people's trade was war, and her ancestors' blood flowed hot through her veins.

Back inside the cabin, the captain could see that the room was in terrible disarray, and very little light could make its way through the snow-caked windows. A cold lantern sat on the table in the center of the room.

He took out a match from his jacket pocket and lit the lantern. Its soft orange glow gave the room a dreamy appearance. However, a gut-wrenching smell assaulted his nostrils. He swallowed hard to hold back the need to vomit. He slowly scanned the large room, which was revealed to be full of paper and stacks of coin scattered among the other trash and dried gore that stained the light wood.

He could hear the chatter of teeth from the shadows.

"Who's there?"

As his eyes settled even more, he could make out piles of blood and bones that led up to a massive stack of half-eaten human and animal carcasses. The captain suddenly had a feeling that he was back in bloody Camp Douglas, the worst Confederate prison camp of the war. He was back inside a five-by-five sweat box and could hear the cries of his fellow soldiers calling out to him to put an end to their misery. He was suffocating and coughing as he tried to move what felt like a hand holding him by the throat.

The captain realized that he had not fallen into a haunting memory, but was being choked by the Draugr. Its body was bloated after having recently glutted itself with kills. Its strength held the suffocating Captain like a full-grown man would hold a small child.

The Draugr opened its lipless mouth, wheezing the words, "Hunger."

The captain reached for his holstered Colt, but the creature stopped his arm, so he switched tactics and pulled out the small pistol inside his breast pocket.

He held it up to the creature's salivating mouth and pulled the trigger.

The blast from the pocket pistol had enough force to make the Draugr release him.

The captain fell to the floor with a hard thud, but in a flash of instinct and self-preservation, he unholstered his Colt revolver and stuck it to the demon's chest. He pulled the trigger and unloaded it in a blaze of fury and smoke. "Die, you bastard!"

The Draugr fell backward against the wall.

The front door opened to reveal the Sheriff with his gun drawn.

He looked down at the deformed creature. "Is it dead?"

The Captain tried to stand upright but fell back down coughing until he spit up a puddle of blood onto the floor.

The Sheriff carefully stepped over the Draugr to help his ailing comrade.

"What are you waiting for—find the gold and run," the wheezing captain said.

Before the Sheriff could reach him, a clawed hand shot up from the flooring and grabbed the Sheriff by the legs. The bony arm with sagging flesh started pulling him under.

The captain reloaded his Colt between violent coughs, which caused him to drop most of the bullets.

The flesh on the Sheriff's face was already being ripped away by the undead creature as the head of the animated corpse extended from the hole to sink its teeth into the screaming Sheriff's side.

The captain raised his gun and made a perfect shot into the center of the creature's forehead.

It screeched and released the Sheriff before retreating back into the hole.

Sheriff Huston managed to pull himself up. He limped over to the downed captain. "Grab onto my shoulder, and I'll get you out of here."

"You *can* shoot pretty good," the captain said and started coughing.

They could both hear others moaning and stirring directly underneath them.

"Sounds like there are a lot more of those evil bastards," the captain said with a weak voice. "Hand me that lantern."

"Why?"

"Just do it, Goddammit!"

The Sheriff placed the handle of the lantern in his hands.

"You never told me if you were Union or a Johnny Reb," the captain said, with a smug look of a man who had resigned themselves to their fate.

The Sheriff was about to answer.

"It's probably best if you just keep that to yourself. Otherwise, I might change my mind and shoot you, myself."

The men both smiled. "I want you to do me a favor," the captain asked.

"What's that?"

"Get the gold and that pretty wife of yours to Conroy, Texas, and make a good life for yourselves. I have a log house just outside of town, there—it's yours now."

The two men shook hands.

Just before the Sheriff walked out the front door, he stopped and turned. "I'll make sure that schoolhouse gets built for Matilda," he said.

"Thank you," the captain said with a nod of respect. "Now get!"

The Sheriff nodded, and vanished into the night.

The captain broke the lantern against the table. A small fire started to grow from its shattered glass and quickly consumed the wood and trash.

He could see the silhouette of the first Draugr standing up.

Other rotted figures started appearing from the hole in the floor, and the sound of chattering teeth could be heard over the crackling fire as they encircled the wild-eyed captain.

"Come and get it—you sonsofbitches!" He roared, and with a satisfaction that he hadn't felt in years, he sent a hail of bullets and Texas fury into the lot of them.

Outside, as the Sheriff reached the pines, he saw no sign of his wife or the horses. "Aiyana!" he yelled, but the words died in his throat once he saw the bloody remains. His thoughts turned to defeat as he fell to his knees and crumbled into tears.

The neigh of a horse made him look up as he saw Aiyana trot out from the snow-covered pines while leading his horse Rough Belly. Her hands were muddy, and she dropped two saddlebags onto the ground in front of him. Etched in their leather was *Wells Fargo Bank,* and gold coins fell from the flaps onto the ground from the two stuffed bags. She slid off her mount, and they embraced.

"Thank God, I thought I had lost you," he said.

They looked out over the mounds of snow at the burning cabin, but each said nothing as they mounted up and rode toward Texas. Their future wasn't completely written, but having a fortune of outlaw gold would help.

Wrath of the Widowed

Winston Malone

Anyone who'd ever meant anything to Elia Worthington had died in her arms. Even the son who had yet to become a man was lost to disease. Some said the Lord had called him to his new home for a better purpose, but she didn't believe that. Her loved ones had been taken, not called. Death was in the business of stealing life, ripping it away indiscriminately to leave those who remain to live on and suffer.

Elia knelt down by the graves at the edge of the ranch to pay her respects. The sun had dipped low, half submerged behind the flat-topped mountains on the other side of the river. Four wooden crosses marked the graves: her father, brother, son, and—

A horse whinnied and halted next to the small graveyard. A man unsaddled and stepped down. He wore a white hat and a black button-up shirt. There was a revolver at his hip. He was handsome, but there were crows' feet at the edges of his eyes. His beard was twice as long as it had been in his youth. It was her husband, and he was alive.

"How are you doing, hon?"

She raised herself to stand before him. His eyes failed to meet hers.

"I'm okay, Cole. Still doing okay. How are you?"

Cole Worthington stepped forward and passed through Elia to kneel by the fourth grave.

"Sorry I'm late. The cattle were unsettled. Not sure what had 'em riled up, but they're calm now."

Tears streamed from her translucent eyes. Elia's shoulders slumped, her weightless form gliding a few inches off the ground. She hated that she would never get a chance to embrace him again, that she could only see him, not be *with* him. Was this yet a curse, or perhaps a blessing to live on like this?

Cole kissed his fingers. Then he touched the cross that marked Elia's grave. "I sure do miss you, El."

"I miss you, too."

Cole rose, went to his horse, and climbed back into the saddle. He seized the reins and guided the horse back to the house. Elia knew she'd appear back at her grave in the morning but returned to the ranch with her husband every night. Even as the horse reached a high-speed gallop, she moved swiftly and effortlessly beside him. It was nearly dark. Cole secured the horse in the stable and went into the ranch house. The house consisted of two stories. There was a porch that ran along the perimeter of the house that was covered with an overhang. Not much had changed since Elia's death, except maybe the addition of a layer of dust. She didn't blame him for his untidiness, though. Running a ranch and taking care of such a large property would be difficult for anyone. Elia had hated cleaning but would have given anything to have a few more hours to interact with the real world.

After eating a can of cold beans, Cole retired upstairs to the bedroom and undressed. He'd grown skinny and had lost much of his muscular tone. Elia slipped into the large bed, on the side once reserved for her. Her spectral head lay on the undisturbed pillow. Cole opened a window to let in the cool night air. He lay atop the sheets since he hadn't bathed. He stared at the ceiling in silence and then turned to Elia. This was her favorite part of the evening, the moment that felt the most real.

His steely eyes melted as he looked at her pillow. He blinked out tears and placed his hand where Elia's cheek would've been. She closed her eyes. His fingers hovered over her, and she could almost feel his touch.

"I wish you were here, hon," Cole said.

"I am here."

"I love you."

"I love you more."

"Good night, El."

"Good night, Cole."

Cole's hand relaxed on the bed, passing through Elia's phantom midriff. She laid her hand over his. She swore she could feel the heat emanating from him. Elia had tried to tap into that strange energy, but after a nightmarish shock that had startled Cole out of his sleep, she hadn't tried it since. Elia couldn't sleep as she had when she was alive. If she lost focus, she simply faded away and returned to her gravesite.

Nights on the ranch were quiet, serene. The Worthington Ranch was ten thousand acres, nestled between the river and mountains on the west side of the property and the vast desert wilderness bordering the east. They were two hours' ride from Cheyenne, and other than the Union Pacific railroad tracks that crossed over the northeastern side of their property, no other signs of humanity marred the pristine landscape.

Elia kept watch over Cole through the nights. That's when it felt most normal, like nothing had changed, like the incident at the bank had never happened. Time passed differently when one couldn't find rest. The torment periodically took its toll over the course of the past two years. It was a period of unending distress that caused her to wail and rage about the house some nights in an attempt to cross over.

As she felt that rage build inside her even then, Elia recognized the warmth spilling out from Cole's chest like a light at the end of a mountain tunnel. She reached out and laid a hand on him. With her eyes closed, she could see his dream, the dream of a haunted man, alone and aimless. Cole stood nearly naked at the center of a parched, cracked wasteland. Buzzards circled overhead. The sky was red like blood and the sun unrelenting in its fury. Elia saw it as if she were there but had refrained from manifesting herself within the dream lest he be awakened.

The spectral landscape warped and blurred. The sun was eclipsed by the moon, and the world was cast into utter darkness save for the fires that floated around Cole's head. The six fires illuminated six Kiowa men. They chanted as they circled him at a staggering pace, faster than he could turn about. Elia had heard stories of the Ghost Dance, a ceremony that reunited the living with the dead.

Cole stopped turning and focused intently on something in the distance. Elia followed his gaze. It was her, or a version of her. Her skin had rotted, and there were empty sockets where her eyes had been. Her mouth hung open in a silent scream, one arm outstretched toward him.

"El? Hon?" Cole whispered, then much louder, "Elia!"

The Kiowa men dissolved, and the fires fell to the ground and burst like lanterns. The flames engulfed Cole's feet and rose over his body. He screamed.

"Elia!" he yelled again, jerking upright in his bed.

"I'm here, my love. I'm sorry, I shouldn't have done it. I just can't stand no longer being with you."

Cole panted, wiping sweat from his brow. The sound of a train whistle pierced the night. Even though she knew he couldn't hear her, she felt compelled to explain what had gone wrong.

"I had to feel you. I had to—" Elia cut off as a strange boom rattled the house. The mirror attached to her desk in the corner wobbled back and forth before settling into stillness.

Cole scrambled over to the window and leaned out to look north. Flashes of yellow flared against the black canvas of night, and the moonlight reflected off rising smoke. "It's the Union Pacific," he said. "It's derailed—my God!"

Elia watched him dress in haste. He pulled on his boots, checked that his revolver was loaded, secured the holster on his hip, and ran out of the door. Elia left through the still open window, slowly cascading down to the ground, studying the fire on the horizon. Cole burst through the front door as she reached the ground. He sprinted past her toward the stable, but Elia had a sinking feeling in her stomach. Something wasn't right, something about the derailment of the train.

Elia Worthington needed to scout ahead and make sure that Cole wasn't walking into a trap. She would protect him at all costs. He was the last thing she had in this world, whatever *this* world was. He was her reason for being.

Elia soared toward the fiery signal on the horizon. She looked back to see Cole exit the stable and saddle his horse. She flew faster, unsure of how much time she needed to figure out the truth of what had happened before Cole would arrive. It was less than a ten-minute ride up the hill if riding at full speed.

She felt the void of death long before she could even make what she was seeing. The engine—or what was left of it—and the first passenger car were toppled over on their sides. The raging flames were contained to the engine, but small patches of fire littered the ground surrounding the crater caused by the explosion that had obliterated the tracks.

Men on horseback gathered on one side of the train. There were half a dozen in all, their weapons drawn and faces covered by black bandanas. They shouted at one another to keep an eye out for survivors.

As she descended, Elia speculated what it was she was witnessing. It seemed to be a train robbery gone wrong, a botched attempt at exploiting the wealthy passengers normally found aboard the Union Pacific. Luckily, at this time of night, the train wasn't as crowded as it might otherwise have been during the day. At least from what she could make out from this vantage point. She neared the group of men below her stepping down from their horses to form a staggered line.

There was movement from one of the toppled cars. A hefty man climbed out of a sky-facing window, now parallel to the ground. He was bloodied and held his hand to the side of his head, eyes wide with fear. He tried to get up but fell to his knees, chest heaving with panicked breaths. One of the outlaws separated from the group and headed toward the uncoupled passenger car.

"What have you done? You outlaws, you fiends. If my wife is hurt, you will pay for this—"

The hefty man went to stand up, but a man in a black hat leveled his revolver at him so he remained on his knees.

"Now, now, that's some big talk coming from the largest criminal among us. Ain't that right, boys?" The three other men in the posse laughed in response. "I assure you, Mr. Bornwallace, that you and your wife won't be seeing the sunrise. So now isn't the time for idle threats."

A gunshot rang out in the night, followed by another. Screams erupted from the uncoupled car that had not toppled over in the crash. Elia could make out shadows of panicked passengers trying to flee the killer who had boarded.

"No, no, no. Please don't do this. I've got money, see?" Mr. Bornwallace produced a wallet chained to his disheveled suit. With bloody hands, he held out several folded bills. More shots flashed in the darkness.

"You see, Mr. B—can I call you that? Hell, why am I asking?—I find it odd that you have money to hand over *now*, but a month ago you didn't. I think your exact words were 'we've gone bankrupt'. You fired us Cheyenne boys helping you build your toy railroad, but then reaped the rewards anyway. No mercy from you then, Mr. B; you get no mercy now."

"Wait, you fellas worked the railroad? I can hire you back. Not a problem, I swear!"

"Too late for that, Mr. B. You should've thought about how your actions might affect our lives and our families' lives. But I'm sure you considered all of that with a heavy heart when you made your choice, right?"

A woman screamed. Elia rushed to the passenger car, phasing through the thin outer shell. She always suppressed the sick feeling she got when she passed through physical objects. There was a man stepping over the dead passengers. He approached a woman crawling at the back of the car toward the door. His feet straddled her, and she weakly turned over to look up at him with one hand raised, the other holding a bloody spot at her side.

Elia tackled the man, or so she tried. She flew directly through him, and he didn't react to her in the slightest. What was worse, Elia hadn't felt any warmth from him, as if he were devoid of the life energy she'd gotten so used to feeling from Cole. She turned to see him looking up at her with dead eyes, the black bandana covering the lower half of his face.

"Well, I didn't expect this," he said, his voice strange and guttural. "Where have I seen you before?"

Elia grew confused, unsure if the outlaw was addressing her or not.

"Please, you don't have to do this," the injured woman whispered.

The outlaw returned his attention to the woman trembling beneath him.

"Sorry, ma'am, I don't make the rules. I just want you to know that it ain't personal."

Elia had heard that from somewhere, but she couldn't quite recall. He raised his revolver and shot one last time before returning his icy gaze back to Elia. She hovered there, feeling powerless that she couldn't stop him from killing the woman. This man was a distillation of pure evil.

"Now that it's just you and me, let's get reacquainted," the outlaw said. Something about his voice was familiar, yet different. Elia looked out of the train window and noticed a figure cresting the hill nearby. If she had a beating heart, she would've felt it skip. The leader of the group, Black Hat, appeared frustrated and removed his bandana. He yelled toward the passenger car.

"Hey, Gust, you all done in there?"

The outlaw standing in front of Elia raised a thumb toward the window to signal back to the leader, who smiled broadly. The heavyset man slumped over and wept. The men unloaded their weapons into him like a firing squad. They hooted and hollered in joyful reverie before one of them noticed Cole on the hilltop.

"Hey, boss, looks like we got a witness," a skinny man yelled next to Black Hat.

"Well, what are you doing? He's seen my face. Kill him!"

Cole reined the horse around and hightailed it back toward the ranch house, a plume of dust rising behind him. The outlaws scattered to retrieve their horses, and the delay gave Cole a head start.

Elia tried to fly to Cole, but the outlaw, Gust, grabbed her by the wrist. Her eyes went wide at the sudden connection of the physical to the spiritual realm. Hot fire shot up her arm and spread through her chest. She screamed when she realized who he was and where they'd met last.

"Ah, yes. That's where I know you from. You're the reason I'm dead."

Elia slashed at his face, but her fingers failed to connect, passing through skin and bone. However, the strike was able to loosen his bandana. When the cloth fell from his face, she gasped and tried to pull away, but he was too strong.

"Hard to look at ain't it?" Gust said. As he spoke, his exposed tongue flapped against the roof of his mouth due to the absence of half of his jaw. "You can thank your husband for that."

Elia grew desperate in this creature's grasp. She thought about the other men catching up to Cole—about never seeing him again, never lying next to him in the bed. The idea frightened her more than the day she had died. Back then it hadn't seemed real; there wasn't time to consider what might happen after death. But after the last two years of pain and loneliness, she wanted her time with him now, in the hereafter, to mean something, to fix the past somehow.

Focusing on this pain, an aura formed around her that brightened the interior of the passenger car. The undead outlaw looked around, uncertain. She was going to have to do the one thing she knew would work. The glow intensified into a blinding white light, and Gust covered his eyes with his free hand. When the light faded, she was no longer in his clutches, or in the train for that matter. Elia had returned to her grave.

Elia flew as fast as her spectral form could manage, meeting up with Cole just as he neared the ranch. He hid the horse behind some bushes at the back of the house. Entering through the back, he retrieved his Winchester lever-action rifle from the living room wall and locked the front door. Then Cole posted up against the wall near the stairs, obscured by darkness, only the moon highlighting the world beyond the window panes.

Five men descended on the ranch house in a fury of hoofbeats and shouts. The leader trotted around in a wide circle.

"Hey there, stranger," the leader shouted at the darkened home. "I don't know what you think you saw, but come on out and we'll talk this through. There's no need for any bloodshed. The ones that deserved it, got it. I think we can come to a common understanding. What do you say, stranger?"

There was a long pause that stretched after the leader had quit talking, the horses making the only noise in the valley. He halted his horse for a moment, a crooked smile on his face. He chuckled and shook his head as looked at his fellow outlaws.

"Looks like we'll have to do this the hard way," he said in a low voice meant only for them.

A crack rang out and glass shattered at the front of the house. Everyone looked around for a moment before regarding the leader who slumped backward in his saddle so far that his black hat fell off. His horse grew anxious at the odd weight change and trotted forward. The leader fell to the flat dirt, a hole in his forehead where the bullet had entered.

"Holy—" another outlaw had started before a second bullet caught him in the throat. The remaining men opened fire on the house in a desperate retreat from open ground. Elia winced as lead splintered wood and ricocheted throughout the living room. Cole overturned the dinner table and ducked behind it. When the men stopped firing, he bolted up the stairs and down the hall into the bedroom. Elia stayed with him, unsure of what she could do to help. From the bedroom window, Cole watched the three men flee behind the barn, shouting and cursing.

"Oh, Elia, hon. What have I gotten myself into this time?" Cole said to himself.

"You just wanted to help. It's not your fault," she said.

"Who are these guys?" he asked aloud.

Elia wanted to show him what she saw. She touched his shoulder. Cole doubled over, holding his head. He gasped and sat upright, blinking furiously to rid himself of the vision. She'd shown him the undead outlaw who'd killed the woman on the train.

"What the hell was that?" Cole said, scanning the bedroom. Cole glanced at his reflection in Elia's mirror and saw a mark on his shoulder that looked like the impression of fingers.

Behind the barn, the men got off of their horses and reloaded their revolvers, huddling against the back wall, out of view of the ranch house.

"He killed 'em, just shot 'em dead," the outlaw with the handlebar mustache said in a quivering voice.

The skinny man grunted. "That feller's gonna die tonight. He knows it. We all know it."

The third man with the sunken, dark-ringed eyes remained quiet, staring at the dirt under his feet.

The undead outlaw arrived on his horse. He'd redone his bandana so as to not frighten the other men in the outfit. "Looks like you boys met good ol' Cole Worthington. You should've known what you were getting yourselves into."

"Yeah, so, what about 'em?" the skinny outlaw blurted out. "He's just one man."

"Well, if that's what'll help you muster up the courage to do what needs to be done, then so be it. But tonight is going to be war. Luckily, we've got Hell on our side."

The other men looked at each other and gulped. "Well, Gust, what do you reckon we do?"

August Buchanan, better known as "Gust the Butcher," dismounted and faced them. "Do you have any more of that dynamite?"

Cole braced himself against the open window. From that vantage he could look down over the entire barn. The strange vision of the man who'd shot the passengers in cold blood was seared into his mind's eye. The man in the vision had resembled his wife's killer, but Cole knew that wasn't possible. He'd already killed that man himself. Hate brewed deep inside of him—a hate that made him want to hunt the outlaw down and put a bullet in him. But Cole was done with all the killing. That's why he'd moved out here in the first place. He'd seen enough of it in the war, not to mention the jobs he'd taken before he met Elia. Was it too much to ask to live alone in peace to cherish the memory of his wife?

Movement came from the left side of the barn. A tiny flash illuminated a running figure. Cole aimed down his sights and shot three times. The figure fell to the ground in a heap, the flickering light laying at the dead man's side. Another man rounded the corner of the barn and rushed to the downed outlaw. Cole centered his aim and was about to fire when a hail of bullets shattered the window frame, sending chunks of wood about the bedroom. Cole ducked, catching a glimpse of someone standing at the opposite end of the barn. He cursed and slid over to his box of ammunition to reload.

A slender object thudded against the window sill, emanating a distinct hiss. He turned and saw the stick of dynamite teetering on the window's frame. He smacked it out but knew that it wouldn't be enough to protect him. Cole scrambled to his feet, charged through the bedroom, and dove into the hallway as the front of the ranch house evaporated in a violent churn of splinters and shards.

Elia heard the explosion but didn't see it. She'd floated behind the outlaws, seeking to gain an advantage for her husband. If she could transmit her sight to him, she could show him where each of them was.

But they had executed their assault far quicker than she'd expected. And she was upset with herself for not being with Cole. Three men approached the front of the property. Elia flew through the air, screaming shrilly. She intentionally avoided the undead outlaw, his obsidian eyes watching her as she passed through the mustached man who shivered and ducked, looking around hysterically for the cause of the icy sensation he'd just felt.

As she entered the hole in the front of their home, her anger dissolved into sadness at the sight of their obliterated bedroom. Small fires had erupted in several areas and would soon be too large to put out. Elia scanned the debris, bracing for the worst when, finally, she saw Cole's legs moving in the hallway. He groaned and sat up, leaning against the stair rail, blood from the wound on his forehead streaming down the right side of his face. She rushed to him.

"Cole, are you okay?"

He coughed and shook his head, but it wasn't in response to her question. He was just dazed. Elia touched his knee. He sat bolt upright like a man just dipped into an ice bath. The strange vision returned and the image of the men closing in on him made him realize he didn't have much time. Cole rechecked his ammunition and saw he only had three .44-40 rounds left, one for each of them if he didn't miss. The ammo box had been lost or destroyed in the explosion. However, he still had the Colt Single Action revolver in his holster.

Cole got to his feet and moved to the upstairs library at the back of the house. It had been Elia's passion to read, not his, so he rarely entered the room. A layer of dust covered nearly every surface. Cobwebs clung to the bookshelves. He reached the back window and opened it. He leaped out, landing in a crouch on the roof of the porch that ringed the entirety of the home. His horse behind the bushes down below grew restless, and Cole clicked his tongue to calm her. It worked momentarily, but Cole heard the scrape of boots on the porch directly underneath him.

Elia descended to find the man with dark circles under his eyes creeping along the back of the house. The man was peering through the windows. Elia waited in his path and let him walk through her. This made him shiver.

The horse whinnied and caused the man to jump. He angled his revolver toward the animal in fright. He cursed, shaking his head, then pulled back the hammer. Elia flew up through the overhang and passed through Cole to give him the exact location of the man beneath him.

Cole aimed his repeater rifle down and fired. The bullet tore through the thin wood like paper. A scream came from below, followed by a thud. Retaliatory shots blasted upward, missing Cole completely. Cole adjusted his aim and pushed the lever forward to chamber the next round and fired. Another yell. He repeated the action, firing a third time. When he heard the man's revolver slam against the porch wood, he knew the threat was eliminated. He'd used all three bullets for one target. He tossed the empty weapon down into the bush by the horse, then crept along the overhang, unholstering his revolver quietly as he moved.

Elia phased through the back wall and saw black smoke filling the upstairs completely. Pockets of fire popped and raged, forming bubbles along the walls and spreading down the hall. She found the mustached man crouched in the living room, watching the staircase for Cole to descend to escape the fire. Mustache's attention was drawn to something overhead. Elia followed his gaze and saw Cole's silhouette passing by one of the large windows.

With a lunge, Elia barreled through Mustache. He wobbled backward on his heels. She wondered if her strength was growing the more she connected with the physical world.

"What in tarnation," he yelled. "The stories must be true. This land *is* haunted."

Elia was about to fly toward Cole and alert him of the enemy's presence, but the man turned and dashed out the front door. She watched as he bolted toward the barn for cover, but two shots rang out overhead and the man dropped face first, the plume of dirt cast up by his fall blown away by the wind.

A third shot erupted, the blast sounding slightly deeper than the others. That was because it wasn't from Cole's gun. Elia heard Cole collapse and roll off the overhang. Through the large windows in the living room, she saw her husband hit the ground. Pain and desperation overwhelmed her senses. It overflowed from her and rippled across the living room in a wave of energy. A chair by the overturned table moved. The cabinets shuddered.

Simultaneously, wood panels broke through the wallpaper, as flames spilled out in a violent regurgitation. The fire was hungry and consumed everything in its path. There was no stopping its wrath. There was no stopping Elia's either.

Gust the Butcher stalked up to Cole, keeping his revolver trained on him. Cole rolled onto his side and reached for his gun.

"I don't recommend doing that, Worthington," Gust said, his voice low and throaty. He removed his bandana to reveal his hideously mutilated face, the result of a shotgun blast at close range.

"You should be dead," Cole said, holding his stomach.

"Well, I guess I don't take kindly to dyin'."

"What are you?"

"Honestly, I haven't quite figured that out yet." The blazing ranch house illuminated Gust as he squinted at Cole. "But despite it all, I just want you to know that this ain't personal."

Gust pointed the revolver and froze. His finger twitched on the trigger, but he didn't pull it. He grunted and twisted his head to find Elia behind him. White tendrils of spectral energy exuded from her outstretched hands, piercing into his body. His eyes burned bright with the fires of Hell. With energy counter to hers, he dispelled her hold on him in an instant. Elia faltered. She felt out of breath despite not needing to breathe.

The undead outlaw turned and fired two shots, but these simply passed through Elia. He snarled and holstered his weapon. Then he leaped forward. He grabbed her by the throat, the evil spirit within him able to connect with the ethereal realm just as easily as with the physical one. She squirmed but saw Cole getting to his feet and heading to the barn. The raging flames of the ranch house rose ever higher behind her.

"For two years, I've wondered what it felt like to burn for eternity in the underworld," Elia said.

He gazed past her toward the collapsing house. "Lucky you. I can show you."

Gust stalked forward, holding her in front of him as they neared the house. He made to discard her like an empty bottle of whiskey, however, she clasped onto his arm with all of her strength. He couldn't rid himself of her, and he yelled as a sharp pain shot through his skull. The images imposed themselves onto his mind. Elia showed him the events from two years prior in the Bank of Cheyenne. She gifted him the paralyzing fear she'd felt that day as she begged him for mercy and he'd said it wasn't personal. His grip on Elia's throat weakened.

"Please, please, don't do this," Gust coughed up.

"Hey, Gust," Cole said, wrenching the undead outlaw from the terrifying vision.

Gust the Butcher turned to find Cole standing at close range with a shotgun.

"I want you to know that it's definitely personal," Cole said.

The subsequent blast removed the rest of Gust's face. He staggered backward yet still stood upright. Cole fired again, aiming for his chest this time. The force sent Gust careening backward into the flames, his body igniting like oil-soaked tissue paper. His screams echoed and then degenerated into the otherworldly moans of a spirit getting its first taste of eternal damnation.

Then, all was quiet, save for the crackling of burning wood.

Cole fell to his knees, then collapsed. Elia rushed to him. He touched his side and felt the blood from his fatal wound. She cradled his head in her arms. She felt his warmth fading. Then the edge of his lips curled into a grin.

"It was you all along," he whispered.

"I never left, Cole."

The first rays of sunlight peeked over the horizon and dispelled the shadows of the night. She didn't have much time left with him. Elia focused all of her pain and anguish into her palms and held them over her dying husband. She prayed to the Lord that He wouldn't call him home like this. She prayed that Cole would live to know that she'd loved him and had clung to this world for him and him alone.

Then she vanished. Elia awoke the following evening, the familiar sound of the babbling water moving down the river in her ears. The sun sank behind the flat-topped mountains. As she turned and looked at the graves, she was reminded that anyone who had ever meant anything to her had died in her arms. Why was she still here? What could be so important that the Lord hadn't called *her* home?

"How are you doing, hon?"

She glanced up to find Cole standing there. Elia raised herself to stand in front of him. She noticed that his eyes met hers. He could see her.

He smiled.

She couldn't help but to smile back.

Cold Spring

Deborah Cardillo

San Francisco. 3rd March, 1857

"Frances, I'm cold."

"I know, Ma. I'm sorry," Frances said. "We'll go home soon."

The thick, white fog crept up California Street like a wall of snow. Frances was cold too. In California, spring always seemed to be slow in coming, if it came at all. She hardly remembered what it was to be warm.

Frances buried her hands deeper into her wool and quilted cotton muff. She had made it herself from scraps from an old coat of her mother's. One day, she hoped, she could get a fine fur one, but this one would have to do for now.

She remembered warm springs in Missouri and hazy childhood afternoons picking flowers and bringing them to her mother. Her mother would press them between the pages of her journals and write long notes alongside. She didn't know then that her mother was interested in botany. She was just happy to bring pretty things to her Ma.

"I'm hungry," her mother said. Frances sighed as the almost-lost memories fled. She was cold and tired. These days, her mother didn't take care of her. She took care of her mother.

"We have to shop first," Frances soothed. "Once we've done our shopping, we'll go home, and I'll make supper."

A chill wind swirled the fog. It crept under her wide skirts. Her cage crinoline, a contraption of spring steel and cotton tape, held her skirts out to a fashionable width but let in the bitter breeze. Her mother's many starched petticoats were ten years out of fashion, but at least the raw wind didn't twine up *her* legs.

Nonetheless, her mother's weary voice still came. "I'm cold."

Frances bit back a sharp retort. It wasn't her mother's fault. California was cold, but there was no way back to Missouri now. There wasn't the money or the will.

"Just let's finish our shopping, Ma," she said softly.

Frances paused at the window of a haberdashery. She looked past the spools of ribbons and the daintily folded gloves. Inside, colorful bonnets almost glowed on their stands. Two ladies were fussing over feathers and silk flowers. One even brandished a taxidermy pigeon wing. She didn't know either of them. They wouldn't come and walk with Ma and her.

"Frances," her mother complained.

"Yes, all right. I've not forgotten. But we must go farther to get something for supper."

California Street's wide, dirt expanse had little horse traffic, only people walking like Frances and her mother. Men tipped their hats to her. Ladies gave her nods or smiles. San Francisco wasn't very crowded except down at the piers. Down there, sailors and stevedores, fishermen and travelers made the town boisterous and strange. Up here, it was easy to know who someone was, even without a proper introduction. No one disappeared up here, but down there by the big ships, anything could happen. A man could be shanghaied. Or worse.

"I'm cold," Ma said again. Poor thing was always cold now. Ever since they got to California.

"Hush now, Ma," Frances crooned. "We'll go home soon."

A handsome young man paused and lifted his hat to her. "Why, Miss Donner, what are you doing out all alone this time of evening?"

"Oh, Dr. Edwards, how nice to see you. I'm afraid I've lost track of time."

"Do let me escort you home," he said kindly.

Frances closed her hand around the straight razor she hid in the quilted lining of her muff. "Thank you. That would be very kind."

"I'm hungry," Tamsen Donner hissed in her daughter's ear.

Doctor Moratelli's Music Machine
Matt Bliss

"The soul sings," Dr. Moratelli announces to the gathering crowd while struggling to button a two-sizes, too-small coat. "This, my friends, is the key."

He paces around the dusty clearing, pulling braces from the covered cart and snapping them in place. It's still bright despite the haze. This may play well for him. "Your soul does not *live* inside you," he says, squeaking knobs underneath the tarp. "It is a sound. A voice. A song that resonates within each and every one of us with its own unique melody of the heavens."

He leans against the covered machine as it lets out a hiss of breath and scans their faces. "The souls of the dead are among us. No more than vibrations, singing to our deaf ears."

These faces, Moratelli thinks, he's seen before. Faces smudged with hardship and dust. Faces the same as every other town in this new *frontier*. The people hungry for something new. People heading west to find their hopes and dreams gleaming gold in the hills, but instead find only dust and desperation.

"But only when we understand that can we hear their music... with this," the doctor pulls the tarp off the device with all the showmanship his slouched form will allow. Brass cogs and gears gleam in the high noon sun. Machinery assembled around tubes and hammered copper in a chaotic nest of metal. Some gasp, while others grumble about the haphazard appearance before them.

Dr. Moratelli moves to the cherry wood handle sticking from an oversized sprocket. "You can see with your own eyes... hear with your own ears... as I call up the souls of the lost to speak in the voice of beyond."

Moratelli pulls his hat down snug over his brow and hunches over, wrapping his eight good fingers around the wooden piece.

Hushed voices and chatter spread throughout the crowd. Still, they press closer.

Moratelli's back flexes and heaves, turning the crank, and clicking the gear teeth faster until they rise to a sharp hum.

The machine begins to turn. Its center mass rotates clockwise while its entirety shifts closer to the crowd, then further away.

Moratelli huffs with the effort, using his whole body to turn the crank faster. Sweat channels down his nose, clinging to the tip in one droplet that refuses to fall.

The machine turns faster. Its colors melding into one rusted hue. Thin wisps of steam rise from the smokestack before falling around them like fog.

The crowd holds their breath between the whirring of parts. Even the horses held quiet. Each heartbeat stuttered to fall in sync with the machine's hum.

It starts as a thrumming in their gut. Something pulsing with unseen rhythm.

Moratelli turns his head, still swelling with each turn of the handle, but now he watches their eyes grow wide and their fingers cover wordless lips.

Shrieks sound around them like expelled breaths. High notes, sliding in and out of existence like the drag of a bow. Each sound cuts through the fog in a swirling gust of wind.

The machine puffs more mist into the sky, filtering the surrounding sunlight into amber beams.

A bass note rises from the ground, rattling teeth as it moves through them. Notes flutter down from separate spaces. Chattering, dancing like fingers across ivory keys. Each voice twisting around one another before its fleeting departure. They stack on top of each other, a symphony of souls, playing their unearthly song at the sway of Dr. Moratelli's baton.

The crowd drifts with the sway of sound. Mouths open, some stretching their hands out wide, some reaching to the haze above, but all are lost in the wonder of Moratelli's machine. All but one that is.

Moratelli glances past the sea of marveling faces to find the only gaze not floating upon the sound. Instead, it focuses on the doctor. His eyes are cigarette burns below a misshapen hat, still and deep, pointed at Moratelli.

He releases the slick handle, letting the machine coast while he unfolds the kink in his back. The parts pause slightly, warping the sound flickering above them before slowing in haunting effect. Sounds creep like dripping molasses. Freezing their song in time before the last turn of the brass wheel snuffs them out.

The fog retreats at once. Pulled back into Moratelli's machine with a wave of silence, and he quickly moves to cover it again with the tarp.

Shuffling to the front, Moratelli takes off his sweat-soaked hat, slaps it against his thigh, and bows. He smiles among the jeers and applause that erupts around him. He passes the hat to the nearest man before leaning back on the frame of the cart and studies the crowd for those same unwavering eyes.

The hat travels among the crowd, coins clinking inside, but it never makes its way to the man in the back. Moratelli watches and waits as the people stream out, or move in for a closer look at the machine, or just want to shake the doctor's crooked hand, but the man in the misshapen hat... is gone.

Dr. Moratelli shakes out two coins and clatters them onto the bar. "Two whiskeys," he says, holding up his pointer finger and pinky to keep the crooked ones hidden. A habit he now repeats with his good hand as well.

The bartender licks the front of his teeth and tosses two glasses between them. They're stained brown at the bottom with spotted pale flakes. He glares at Moratelli while splashing the brown liquid into both.

"Thank you," Moratelli says, raising the first to his lips.

"You got some nerve there, pal," says the bartender.

"Oh?" Moratelli asks. He tosses the drink back and breathes out its fire.

"The way I see it," the bartender says, leaning closer. "Either you put on a hell-of-a show, or you're playing God out there. I just can't figure out which."

Moratelli runs a hand across the stubble of his beard and then raises the second glass toward the man. "I assure you," he says, "it's neither."

The bartender folds his arms and glares.

Moratelli shrugs and sinks the second shot.

"Then what is it? Those are good people out there... hard-working people. People who came here looking for a better life. A fresh start, and you're here drinkin' on their coin. I don't like it, and I'm sure I'm not the only one who thinks that way."

Moratelli grunts and pulls his already crooked bowtie further from center. He turns away and glances over the bar. "Look," he says, nodding his head. "I'm the same as them. Just trying to get by with the only thing I know. Some people just want to be entertained. Some want to learn more about how it all works, *the afterlife,* and what-have-you. And some... well, some just want what I have."

He sees him then. The man with the misshapen hat. The man with holes for eyes sitting in the shadows, watching him from the back of the room. He knew he would be there—they always are.

The bartender speaks louder. "Some say it's men like you that give this place a bad name. Men like vultures, sniffing out their next meal. Men selfish, who get a thrill off drinking on someone else's tab."

Moratelli cocks his hat back and turns back to the bartender. "Really? Because someone else might say, *shut your damn mouth and pour me another goddamned drink.*" Moratelli stares through him while dropping another coin from his *good* hand. It lands heavily between the two.

The bartender grabs a glass, coughs up a wad of phlegm, and spits into it with as many throaty sounds as he can muster. "Enjoy," he says, pouring the whiskey on top.

The doctor grumbles to the man's back and eyes the slime floating on the surface. He wipes a finger across top and places the glass to his lips. *I've had worse,* he thinks and sucks the dark liquid down.

Moratelli turns back to the man watching from the shadows, but when he sees an empty chair, he smiles. It's a wide smile, thanks to the liquor-loose lips, but a warm one just the same. He rights his hat and stumbles toward the door, letting his fingers ripple across the dusty out-of-tune piano as he passes.

Dr. Moratelli jumps awake at the sound and is even more startled by the preceding silence. He knows full well that the snapping didn't come from his campfire outside. He opens his eyes and raises his hands, palms out except for the bent two fingers that couldn't straighten further, and turns to see what is behind him.

Standing over him in his tent is the man with the misshapen hat, glaring with colorless eyes down the barrel of a shaking pistol.

Moratelli freezes, recognizing then that the sound was the cocked hammer of the pistol held in his face.

"How do you do it?" the man asks. The corner of his mouth pulls backward between each word. His teeth are black as coal and smell of rotten fruit.

The doctor remains still.

"How... do you do it?" he asks again, more forcefully.

Moratelli watches the man for a moment before speaking. "Would you mind if I sat up?" he asks, pointing his raised hands at himself.

The man nods and readjusts the revolver's grip in his hand.

Moratelli eases himself up from his sleeping roll, making sure to keep his hands raised throughout. He positions himself upright and wets his lips before speaking very slowly. "How... do I... do what?" he asks.

The man shivers with anger. "You know! You know damn well what I'm talking about!"

"Okay, okay. I'm not playing games with you, see? I'm not trying anything funny."

"Tell me how you do it!"

Moratelli carefully twists his legs over to the dirt floor in a more comfortable position. "It's just like you heard me say out there. *The soul* is a sound. And that machine, *out there*, makes it so we can hear that sound. So we can hear *them*. No more than that, really, I—"

"I heard *her*. Out there, when you did it. I heard her voice... *singing*."

Moratelli let his hands fall sluggishly to his side. "Who was she?" he asks.

"My wife, I heard her."

"Really? I did not hear—"

"Don't you say that!" the man presses the barrel closer. "I heard her! I would know her voice anywhere, and it was hers!"

Moratelli widens his eyes. "Listen, I believe you, really, but why are you *here*, pointing a gun at me now?"

The man's face contorts as if the question is bitter. "Show me how to do it. How to work the machine."

"I can't."

"Why?" he asks, grabbing the neck of the doctor's pajamas.

"Because it only works for me."

The man drops him and looks at the covered machine outside. "And why should I believe you?"

The doctor can't help but smile and fumble around for his hat. "Well," he says, pulling it onto his head. "I'm tied to it. It's a part of me—so to speak. Of course, you could kill me now and give it a try for yourself, but I assure you, it will *not* work."

"Then... then... I want you to do it!"

This time, Moratelli doesn't ask, only raises an eyebrow at the man.

"Bring her back. Do it," the man says, stepping out of the tent.

Moratelli follows.

The fire pit is only an orange glow of embers now. The night is dark and still. Even the crickets and bugs of the night are smart enough to keep quiet then.

Moratelli says, "I know what you want, but I can't bring her back."

"I heard her—"

"Not like she was. You heard her from the beyond. We can only *hear* her. I can't bring her back, or at least not in the way you remember her."

"I don't care. Do it!" The man slams the heel of his pistol against the frame of the machine. Tears roll from the dark space of his eyes.

Something shifted in Moratelli then. Life out west was a hard one, and Moratelli knew more than anyone how the souls of the ones lost along the way can haunt you. A constant reminder of how alone you truly are.

"Okay," the doctor says. "I'll do it."

The man lets his pistol fall to his side, but his hand still shakes with unease.

Moratelli pulls the tarp off his machine, and even in the night, the metal of its parts gleam. He circles to the front and grips the cherry wood handle of the crank, all without taking his eyes off the man before him.

"Are you sure you want this?" Moratelli asks.

"Please," says the man.

The doctor braces his feet in the dirt and bends at the hip. He lets out a grunt as he jerks the handle up and away, slowly at first.

The machine begins to turn. It spins clockwise while shifting on its orbital path.

Moratelli cranks faster. Already he feels beads of sweat clinging to his back. It moves faster as it gathers speed. The whir of gears grows louder with each turn.

The man steps back. His eyes drift to the smokestack as it exhales slender strands of white. The smoke slithers down around him like a snake coiling around its prey.

Something escapes the mist and moves with the breeze.

Music...

Hushed tones at first, moving in and out like strings changing pitch.

The man's jaw drops. He holds his hands out at his sides, turning. Searching for a familiar voice.

Moratelli cranks the machine faster. Pulling and pushing with muscles burning for a pause.

Sharp notes scream out around them. They move with the fog in a spectral cadence. They move like playful puppies, pawing at chords from high to low.

"Baby?" the man asks. "Is that you?"

Something rattles through him like the bass of a cello before twisting into an incomprehensible voice. It steals the man's breath, leaving words stuck in his throat to choke on.

The man smiles at the sound, however. He raises his chin and closes his eyes, letting his whole body slump as his muscles relax. Moratelli knew then that he had found the voice he was looking for and is lost within its song.

The doctor releases the crank and quickly reaches inside his shirt.

The man turns toward him, mouth agape, eyes closed, still lost in the wonder, lost in the music. Moratelli removes a pistol no bigger than his hand and presses it to the man's chest.

The weapon rings out its tune with a pull of its trigger. A crack that stops the voices among them—sending the otherworldly sounds back to the machine at once.

Sound stops. The man looks down at the hole in his chest and lets out a growling gasp before he falls to the dirt.

"Yes," Moratelli says, walking closer. He works a toe underneath the gun at the man's side and flings it far into the desert. "I think you will fit in nicely with the orchestra."

The man lets out a moan, deep and low among gurgled wetness. He holds his hands to the hole in his chest as his blood pools around him.

"A bit of baritone," says Moratelli as he moves back to the machine. He wraps his eight good fingers around the handle and starts cranking the machine in reverse.

The man lets out a shaking breath as his movements grow still.

"Vibrato... This will be a pleasant touch."

The machine moves backward, turning counterclockwise as it picks up speed. Sounds patter out among them. Whumps and chatters cut short and repeat in a disturbing rhythm.

Dr. Moratelli turns his head while continuing to turn the crank. He watches the crumpled body of the man. Watches the fragile tendrils of smoke rise from the bullet hole in his chest. He watches them trail to the smokestack above. And when nothing but a pale coldness remains, he stops. He lets go of the handle and wipes his good hand over his sweaty face, leaving a smile in its wake.

In a way, Moratelli reasons as he pulls the tarp back over the machine. It is almost poetic. *He* got what he wanted, and so did Moratelli. After all, the man was with *her* now—well, with Moratelli too, and all the others inside the machine, but they were together again, no less.

He pats the hammered copper tank on the machine before walking toward the tent. The eastern skyline rises in layers of gray and violet.

He doesn't have long to pack up camp before the sun would be up, bringing that unbearable heat along with it. He unfolds a map and measures the distance with a thumb. The next town couldn't come soon enough. He could use a good drink. Performing twice in one day is no easy task, and he figured he deserved a whiskey or two.

Doctor Moratelli gathers his things and loads them on the cart. He heads south as the sun peeks over the horizon, where he hopes for enough people there to perform for—*enough coin to pay for those drinks.*

It shouldn't be hard, he presumes. After all, he just added an entire new instrument to his ensemble, and together... *they would sound marvelous.*

Steer Head Steeple

A.L. Davidson

"That him?"

"Yup."

Marcus exhaled tobacco-filled smoke. It billowed out between his lips and disappeared into the breezy morning air. He took another drag and studied the figure across the way with intensity in his earthen-colored eyes. He flicked the dead cigarette stick to the dusty ground and stamped it out with his boot.

"Wasn't expectin' a priest," he noted.

"Nope," his boss replied unenthusiastically.

"He's kinda purdy."

"You need to head to the brothel, boy. You've been out here too long."

Marcus groaned, "I'm just sayin', he's... delicate lookin'. What the hell's he out here for, anyway? That's definitely a city boy if I've ever seen one."

The ranch owner stroked his beard and spit out his chewing tobacco onto the ground. He turned to his young employee, "He says he needs a guide, so you're gonna guide him. Ain't that complicated, Marcus. He ain't from around these parts, and it's easy to get lost."

"I know, why else you think I'm packed already? I'm just sayin', it's weird to see folks like him out here, especially on their own. Usually they got a whole damn city with 'em. Man's as pale as a sheet, looks like he ain't never seen sunlight."

"May not have. You know how them holy folks are. Holed up in their chapels all damn day while the rest of us are out here bakin' in the sun."

"Surprised you okay'd it, boss."

The gruff old ranch owner threw him an unenthused look as he leaned on the porch railing. He pulled his heavy cowboy hat from atop his head and wiped the sweat from his brow before he acknowledged the younger man's remark.

"Look at him. He'd be dead before sundown if he went out on his own. You ain't got nothing better to do," the older man grumbled.

"True... Guess I'll get goin' then. Don't miss me too much," Marcus snickered as he began his walk across the homestead.

He approached the shorter man with the reins of his horses clutched tight in his hand. The priest was dressed fully in black, a pop of white beneath his collar, and a light pack trembled in his unsteady fingers. He had merely a scarf around his neck to ward off the low temperatures. Golden curls, like wheat at the peak of harvest, fell over his bright blue eyes, eyes that quickly shifted toward the approaching ranch hand.

"Howdy, padre," Marcus said with a whistle.

"Hello. I'm Father Strauss," he said as he fumbled his hand free of his pack's strap.

Marcus took his hand, "Marcus Santiago. I'll be guiding you through the wilds."

"I appreciate it, sincerely."

"You've ridden before?"

Father Strauss nodded. Marcus took the pack from the priest and secured it to the straps that adorned the smaller of the two horses.

The spotted Appaloosa stomped the dusty ground as he ensured the leather saddle was properly affixed. Marcus noticed the unease in the expression of the young clergyman and extended his hand for him. The priest took it and allowed the seasoned guide to help him mount the animal.

Marcus handed him the reins, "You good?"

"Yes, just... start slow, if you'd be so kind. I'm afraid it's been a while," he replied.

"Can do. Where we headed?"

"Steer Head Steeple."

Marcus stopped mid-motion and turned back to him with a look of concern on his scruffy face. He tipped his hat back a bit to get a better look at the shifty priest. It was obvious the newcomer was uneasy. It was an expression that did not match his features, a troubled visage betrayed by the shimmer in his blue eyes.

"You realize that place is gone, right? A ghost town?" Marcus inquired as he fixed his supplies over the back of his trusty steed, "We've plenty of other chapels to visit, padre."

"It's a sort of... pilgrimage. I must go; it's non-negotiable. If you do not feel comfortable with it, I can find another escort. I do not wish to burden you," Father Strauss replied.

"No, no, it's fine. Just wanted t'be sure you knew what you were gettin' into since you seem a bit uneasy. Steer Head Steeple ain't a place people want to go to, and it ain't been up and running for a long time. Just a bit of a shock is all. Stick close to me. The terrain is rough, and we'll be headin' into mountain territory. I'll get you where you need to go safe and sound so long as you listen."

Father Strauss nodded and watched as the muscular ranch hand mounted his darkly colored mustang and fixed the strap of his rifle across his back. Marcus settled himself in the saddle and urged his steed forward. An unsettled feeling crept into his marrow as he felt the forward momentum roll through his body. He looked back over his shoulder, his face half-hidden behind the fur lined collar of his coat, and watched the young priest send up a silent prayer for their journey. The skies turned grey above them.

This didn't feel right.

The escort's queasiness over the situation did not cease. His stomach was in knots, somersaulting in his abdominal cavity as they quietly made their way into the forests at a steady pace and small incline. Those grey skies turned a sickly color, and the mountainous terrain brought a chill that was as bitter as it was relentless. He felt like he was being watched.

Father Strauss shivered atop his horse; his pale cheeks were brushed a tinge of red that looked painful. Their casual conversation turned quieter with each passing hour. It was apparent the journey wore on the stranger.

Out of the corner of his vision, Marcus noticed a small clearing and diverted his horse away from the path. They came to a stop, and Marcus softly patted his mount's neck. The horse whinnied in response.

"Is everything all right?" Father Strauss asked, tone quiet.

"No, it's not. You need a break, and it's gettin' late. This seems like a good enough place to call it quits for the night," Marcus replied as he opened one of the packs hooked to his saddle.

"Are we unable to reach the chapel tonight?"

"No, it's still a ways off, and those skies are gettin' angry."

He could see a heavy level of distress fall over his companion's face. He smiled reassuringly as he unfolded a canvas tarp. He found the rope that was bundled up inside of it and pointed to the nearby tree.

"Do me a favor? Can you guide this 'round the tree for me?" Marcus requested.

As Father Strauss dismounted his horse, his legs buckled beneath him, which caused Marcus to nearly fall off his own steed to catch him. The clergyman's limbs were numb. He grabbed hold of the rope that Marcus extended out for him and did as he was asked. He met the ranch hand on the opposite side of the trunk.

"Thanks," Marcus said gently as he began securing the rope. "You got a first name? Feels strange callin' you *Father* when we're practically the same age."

"Johann," he replied through chattering teeth.

"Well, Johann, help me get this set up so our overworked mounts don't get pelted by the rain on the horizon and we can get you warmed up. That little scarf ain't doin' much."

The men went about securing the tarp and their horses. Marcus handed each of the trusty steeds an apple and rummaged through his packs for his tent. He removed his heavy coat and handed it to the priest. Johann took it with his frigid fingers and wrapped himself up before he sat down beneath the tarp.

He watched in silence as Marcus set up the tent atop another stretch of canvas tarp. It was apparent he had done this on numerous occasions. The way he moved was graceful and mindful. Not a second was wasted, and the pace he held was as natural as breathing to him. His arms were strong and sure, his face contemplative and focused. He was well acquainted with this terrain and its hostilities.

"Padre," Marcus said quietly, snapping the priest from his thoughts.

"Yes?" Johann inquired.

"Your lips are purple. Get inside while I set up your shelter."

"I... don't have one."

Marcus blinked his whiskey-hued eyes slowly, "Pardon?"

"I didn't realize I'd need one, I thought it was only a short ride."

"Get inside."

"But—"

"Johann, get inside."

Marcus extended his hand for Johann to take. The priest wearily stood, thankful for the support. Marcus escorted him to the shelter and held open the flap for him. He sat outside and set his pack in between his legs. He rummaged through the contents and found a folded blanket. He gently offered it to the freezing man across the way before he grabbed his canteen.

"Did you bring *any* necessities? Your pack is awful light," Marcus asked.

"I have my bible and a spare pair of socks, some civilian clothes, but they aren't heavy," Johann replied.

"What the hell? Sorry, I'm just... most people who decide they want to wander into the wilderness come a bit more prepared. You're lucky I'm a worrier and overpack."

"I was a bit rushed."

Marcus looked at his newfound companion and noticed a twinge of distress run across his eyes. The priest hadn't removed his gaze from the world outside, as if he expected someone to come walking up. As if he were afraid of the possibility.

"Not blamin' you, only concerned. It's cold up here this time of year, and you don't even have a coat," Marcus said quietly.

"How much longer until we arrive?" Johann asked.

"Not sure. It'll depend on if this rain turns to snow and whether or not I want to leave at first light. We'll get there by end of day tomorrow, I promise, but the biggest priority right now is food and gettin' warm and lettin' you rest. Here, drink."

Marcus handed over the canteen. Johann took it and sipped the refreshing water. He watched as Marcus headed back outside, closing the tent flaps as he went. When he was sure the brave, confident ranch hand was out of sight, he brought his knees up to chest and buried his face into his arms. The encroaching fear of the setting sun burrowed into the back of his mind. He felt guilty. He had doomed the kind soul outside to a horrible fate with his neglect. All he could do now was wait and pray that morning came quickly.

Dropping several small pieces of wood into the pile he hastily threw together, Marcus lit a fire and warmed his cold fingers over it. He emptied a mason jar of pre-made soup into a small pot and let it heat up over the increasing flame as he surveyed the area for threats. He spent an hour prepping the area for the night, mostly to settle his own anxieties. His tan skin was covered in goosebumps; the hair on his arms stood on end from the chill. He could feel the wind picking up, and his chestnut-hued locks rustled in the breeze. They were losing daylight.

He headed back to the tent. He lifted the flap and smiled softly to himself. Johann was bundled up beneath the blanket, his messy mop of golden curls lay limply on the ground, face obscured by the heavy fur lined collar of Marcus' jacket. He hated to wake him.

"Johann," he called gently, "Come eat."

Johann lifted himself from the floor and rubbed his eyes. "What?"

"Soup's on. Come eat before we lose sunlight."

Johann covered his yawn with his slender fingers and slowly crawled himself out of the tent. He sat down near the fire and handed Marcus his coat back. The escort happily slid it back on over his body before he ladled some soup into a heavily dented bowl. He handed it over to Johann.

"Do you do this often?" Johann asked as he fixed the blanket around his body.

"Yeah, s'pose so. Most of my days are spent helpin' the boss 'round the ranch, but every so often we get folks like you who need help navigatin' the terrain. Gettin' easier for folks with all them railroads comin' in, less need for guys like me, but sometimes it's just easier t'pack up the horses and ride. Real purdy out here in the fall. The trees turn gold and shimmer for miles," Marcus explained with a smile.

"I suppose I picked the wrong time of year, then."

"Sure did."

"I'm sorry."

Marcus lifted his eyes as he grabbed a portion for himself, "Not your fault. Just means you'll have t'come back 'round these parts so I can show you the sights."

Johann set his spoon back down. It was hard to tell if the red in his cheeks came from embarrassment or the wind. He smiled sheepishly and went back to eating. Marcus smiled a lopsided grin and turned his attention back to his soup.

As darkness fell, so did the rain. Marcus lay beside Johann in the cramped tent with his coat laid over his upper half. His wide-brimmed hat was set over his head, and a soft snore crept out of his lips. The rain pelted down atop the canvas tarp above them. The sounds of the forest around them were drowned out by the storm.

One sound, however, pulled the escort from his slumber with a thunderous resound.

Marcus shot upright and fumbled for his rifle. His hat fell to the ground behind him, and his eyes struggled to adjust to the darkness within the confines of the tent. The heavy weather had darkened the environment around them. He saw the impression of a hand quickly pull away from the side of the canvas tarp.

As he cocked his rifle, a scared noise pulled his attention away. He looked down and saw Johann curled up with his hands trembling by his lips, mumbling the Lord's Prayer with panic in his tone. Sweat dripped from his golden curls and his rosary shook in his unsteady hands.

"Johann—"

Another slapping noise hit the exterior of the tent. Marcus swallowed hard as he finally focused on the situation. He fumbled for his oil lamp and lit it with a tremble in his fingers. He watched the small space grow warm with orange light and gasped.

Hands, large and powerful, pressed into the canvas, buckled the frame. Fingers clawed at their small shelter. Marcus steadied his rifle and tried to move forward when he felt something brush his leg. He turned his eyes down and saw the priest gripping tight to his thigh. Johann shook his head nervously, though he did not lift his gaze to acknowledge the escort at his side. He continued to frantically recite the prayer; tears rolled down his cheeks onto the ground. His voice was hoarse, dry, and weak.

Marcus kept his rifle steadied ahead of him, aimed at the tied tent flaps. The relentless shadows continued to paw at the tent. Through the echoing sounds of the storm, unnatural moans became clear. Voices called out with raspy tones, beckoning the priest to step outside, to come into the chaos and join them in the darkness.

"Come to us."

"Johann."

"Hell's waitin' for ya."

Thunder crashed above them. Lightning rippled through the sky. The illumination of forms, lanky and twisted, appeared for a brief moment. They were utterly surrounded. Marcus swallowed hard. He heard Johann finish the prayer with a terrified *amen* before he inhaled painfully.

The escort gently set his hand on the priest's back. His shirt was soaked through with sweat. Marcus could feel his exhaustion, feel his frame weakening, his prayers growing quieter.

Johann swallowed hard and began gain, "Our Father—"

"Our Father who art in heaven, hallowed be thy name."

Johann's deep blue eyes opened and looked up at the ranch hand as he fumbled over his own words. He watched as this stranger spoke in tandem with him, reciting the prayer with fervor and heightened tones, loud enough to make the figures outside step away. Marcus nodded.

"Take a break," he whispered. "Give us this day..."

"Don't... stop, *never* stop. Not until you see daylight," Johann mumbled.

The priest clamored his way to his side and laid down on the ground for a moment to catch his breath. Marcus reached for his canteen and handed it to Johann, then gripped his shoulder tight to let him know he was still present, never once letting his words falter. His rifle rested in the crook of his arm, and his voice remained steadfast.

Johann's body trembled as he downed the water. The emptied canteen hit the ground, and a satisfied gasp fell from his lips. He relented to his exhaustion. He fell asleep beside Marcus, limbs limp and splayed out on the ground.

The figures came back with the snap of lightning. Looming. Hungry. The hands rested across the top of the canvas and drug downward with the flow of the rainfall.

Marcus kept his hand on Johann's body and his eyes straight ahead, "Amen."

Sunlight. Johann woke with a start. He inhaled sharply and looked around the tent, only to be met with the tired, heavy eyes of Marcus. The escort tilted his head to the side and smiled.

"Howdy," he said gently with a yawn.

"What happened?" Johann asked as he brushed his damp curls back.

"Dunno. Was hopin' you'd tell me."

Johann turned his eyes down to his body. His priest's collar was askew, the top few buttons of his shirt had come undone, and his rosary limply hung between his fingers. He sat back on his haunches and stared at the cowboy with the loaded rifle in his lap.

"I'm... so sorry," he mumbled.

"You gonna tell me what's goin' on?" Marcus inquired.

The priest nodded weakly, "I—"

"Hang on, padre. It's all right," Marcus said gently as he set the back of his hand against the priest's face. He softly wiped the tears away. Johann nodded and tried to compose himself. He carefully removed his collar and tossed it toward his pack.

"I'm cursed," he stated wearily.

"Cursed?"

"Possessed. Cursed. I don't know. They follow me *everywhere*. Whenever the sun goes down, they come for me."

"And you think goin' to Steer Head is going to help?"

Johann looked at him with shock on his pale face. Marcus smiled and yawned a bit before he laid back. He set his rifle to the side and picked his hat back up.

"All right. We'll get goin' in a bit. I'm exhausted. See that glimmer of sunlight through the flaps there?" Marcus asked.

Johann turned his eyes to the front of the tent, "Yes?"

"Watch it rise. When it disappears, you wake me up, all right? Don't leave the tent. You're safe, padre. I'm right here."

Marcus set his hat back over his head and tried to let his body relax. Johann watched him for a moment before he slowly unbuttoned his shirt. He crawled to his pack and opened it quietly, looked for his spare shirt tucked beneath his sparse belongings. Marcus lifted his hat for a moment, took note of the prominent crescent moon shaped birthmark upon the priest's shoulder, and smiled to himself before he drifted off to sleep. The sun would be high enough sooner than he'd like. His rest would be short-lived.

All Johann could do was sit in silent prayer, watch the sun, and try not to break down as the cold morning air seeped into their shelter. He sat in silence and listened to the soft snoring of the kind-hearted ranch hand as he slept. He wasn't used to being awake during the daylight hours. It had been so long since he'd heard birds chirping, since he saw the sun creep up around him. It was pleasant.

When the time came to wake him, Johann felt guilty for doing so. Marcus was exhausted. It was apparent in the trembling of his fingers against his chest. He approached carefully, quietly. He set his hand on Marcus's shoulder and gently shook him awake. The ranch hand yawned and pulled his hat off of his head.

"Time already?" Marcus asked with a yawn.

"Yes. We need more water," Johann said quietly.

"Yeah, we do. There's a stream up ahead. We can refill the canteens then. I have some jerky in my pack if you're hungry, though."

"I'm a bit nauseous. I'm all right for now."

Marcus nodded and propped himself up on his elbow. He smiled and looked at the confused, trembling priest. He felt horrible. He couldn't imagine how scared he must have been, how long the horrifying situation had plagued him. He needed to protect this man.

He slid his coat back on and grabbed his rifle. He untied the tent flaps and poked his head out into the breezy, snowy morning. The bitter chill hit him in the face like a harsh punch. He exhaled and watched as his foggy breath rolled up into the sky.

"Oh... hell..." he mumbled as he stepped outside.

He looked at the tent, took note of the bloody handprints that littered the canvas' exterior. He shifted his eyes to the clearing around him, at the mounds of snow that had been kicked and moved with fervor. He saw the spotted Appaloosa on the ground, motionless, with its blood pooled over the pure white snow. It had been eviscerated, head set against the trunk of the tree it had been tied to. His mustang was gone.

He set his fingers between his lips and whistled, "Rusty!"

A few moments passed before his horse trotted out of the woods, neighing with a huff. The big horse had a few surface-level wounds across his side but was otherwise untouched. The reins around his neck were tattered. Marcus sighed with relief and softly stroked his head.

"Glad you're safe," he whispered as he looked back at the mangled horse across the way. He walked toward the tree where the tarp was tied and undid the ropes. The canvas fell over the corpse, hiding it from view. He went back to the tent. Johann jumped and exhaled when he realized it was only his escort.

"Sorry. You ready t'go? I need to clean up the tent," Marcus asked.

"Is everything all right?" Johann asked as he grabbed his pack.

"Uh... Betsy got killed. Rusty's okay, though."

Johann's blush pink lips parted, "Oh. I'm... I'm sorry. I'm so sorry."

"Let's go. Wrap yourself up with the blanket, okay?"

Johann did as he was asked. He handed the packs to the escort and picked up the blanket. The priest grew ghastly pale when he saw the blood. Marcus took his hat off and set it atop Johann's head, tilted it down to hide his eyes, and quickly packed up the shelter.

Within a few minutes, their gear was loaded and secured safely to the remaining horse's saddle. Marcus set his hand on Johann's back.

"Go on," he urged.

"Go... where?" Johann asked.

"Go... on the horse? Saddle up?"

"Oh. Sorry."

"Stop apologizin'."

Marcus helped Johann mount the horse and fixed the blanket around his body. He handed him the small burlap sack of jerky and urged him to eat to keep his strength up. The escort slid his foot into the stirrup and swung his leg up and over. He leaned back and exhaled before he plucked his hat off of the priest's head. Johann looked over his shoulder at him with confusion in his expression.

"Let's get some water and get goin'. You, sir, are goin' to tell me exactly what's happenin' while we haul ass to this church," Marcus said as he reached around Johann's body and grabbed the reins. He urged his horse to start walking.

Johann turned to look back at the path ahead as they began to make their way back toward the trail. He fixed the scarf around his neck and held the ends of the blanket closed around his body. He tried to relax but felt himself stiffen up whenever the muscular ranch hand's arms brushed his own.

"Relax, padre," Marcus said gently. "I know this ain't optimal, but we've got no choice."

"I know."

"You gonna tell me what's goin' on?"

"I'm cursed. I already said that."

Marcus fixed his hold on the reins, "You sure 'bout that?"

"Yes. Maybe... I don't know. Not for certain."

"Well, judgin' by what happened last night, I can definitely say somethin' strange is goin' on with you."

Johann nibbled on the jerky and nodded, unsure of what else to say or how to address the strange situation. Marcus let him ruminate for a while. Let his tired mind process and try to formulate the things he seemed desperate to say. To share. To get off his chest and let his poor, suffocated lungs breathe. Let his soul take some time to ease the burden and pass it on to someone willing to help lift the weight.

They stopped by the stream, filled their canteens, and embarked on the last leg of their journey. Johann sipped the water, savored the brutal, ice cold chill of it against his worn down, tired throat

"I'm from this area," Johann stated quietly.

"Really now?" Marcus inquired.

"Yes. I was born here, but I didn't stay. My mother took me in the night and fled to the east when I was young. She was afraid of the call of the wilds, of the west, and how it drives men to do unthinkable things."

"I think men inherently do unthinkable things. It's in our nature."

"Is slaughtering your congregation and attempting to set fire to your church to hide the crimes inherent?"

Marcus looked at the watery, weary eyes of the priest who was bundled up in his arms. Johann looked at him expectantly, as if he were desperate for confirmation that he was not insane, that he was allowed his concerns and worries.

"No. No, it's not. However, I don't believe the sins of a father should be a burden for their children. Even if the father happens to be Hacksaw Helmut," Marcus said gently. He felt his companion stiffen with fear.

"Hard to not feel that burden," Johann replied with a yawn.

"Ain't nobody sayin' you don't have t'feel it, Johann. *I'm* sayin' you don't *need* to. Lots of people died that day. It was decades ago, and this damn area ain't used to lettin' things like that go. Gossip keeps the bars and brothels goin', and Hacksaw Helmut is a wellspring of rumors and chitchat, seein' as nobody ever found him. Guessin' you think appeasin' those souls will stop whatever's happenin' to you?"

"That's my hope. Every time the sun goes down, they come for me, screaming his name and calling me toward them as if my soul will be enough penance for his mistakes. I can't blame them. I can't. I'm just tired of them coming for me. I'm tired. I apologize, I'm used to sleeping during daylight hours, and these last few days have been hard."

Johann yawned again and rubbed his eye gently. Marcus tightened his grip around his body and urged him to lean into him.

"You can sleep. I'll keep you safe," Marcus promised.

"I shouldn't."

"You should. Sleep, Johann. You'll need your strength when we arrive. Sounds like we've got some spirits to exorcise."

Johann looked up at him. Marcus smiled and tightened his hold, pulled him into his frame. The priest finally relaxed and let his weary back rest against the escort. Marcus felt his cheeks grow warm and turned his eyes back toward the path.

The old husk of a church sat tucked between several large, charred trees off in the distance. The surrounding cabins and little general store were decaying from the pull of time and the elements. The ghost town sat hushed under a blanket of snow, nary a track or footprint to be seen atop the shimmering blanket of white.

Marcus stirred Johann with a gentle motion and set his chin against the shorter man's shoulder, "Hey, you ready?"

Johann blinked a few times and focused on the area. It was a hazy memory, drowned in his subconscious, one he was unsure was wise to conjure. Some of the buildings looked familiar, but he was far too removed from adolescence to truly place anything of importance. He blinked the sleep from his eyes and looked at the handsome cowboy who smiled warmly at him.

"Will you wait for me?" Johann asked.

"No," Marcus replied with a shake of his head.

"Oh... I—"

"We're doin' this together. These devils killed my horse and frightened my new friend. You think I'm gonna let them get away with it?"

Johann smiled sheepishly. Marcus patted his arm and hoisted himself off of his horse. He fixed his rifle strap and extended his hand for the priest. Johann joined him on the ground and grabbed his pack. He quickly changed back into his priest garb. Marcus affixed his collar for him and draped the rosary over his neck, then fixed the scarf around his shoulders to keep him warm. He grabbed the lantern and held it in his hands. He lit it and lifted it up to light their path.

Father Johann Strauss, scared and uncertain, picked up his bible and his cross and turned to the steeple that pierced through the darkened skies like a sword. The cross atop the sharpened point loomed like a beacon, calling the sinners and maddest of men to its embrace. The front door creaked in the wind, wheezing out like an elder in pain from the movement of brittle bones. The call of death echoed, beckoned him forward.

He felt a soft hand on the small of his back and turned his eyes upward. Marcus fixed his hat upon his head and gave a confident nod before he cocked his rifle. The two men trekked up the short pathway through the drifts of snow. The old wooden sign swung softly; the words had faded with time. Remnants and ghosts of a place once full of hope, decimated and covered in a coppery color. It was haunting.

Johann mustered up his courage and stepped inside the charred innards of the once holy place. He approached the pulpit, sitting at a slant from the sagging of the floor, worn from the elements and mold. He set his bible atop it and opened it to a bookmarked passage, then gently placed his cross to the side. Marcus approached, turned on his heel, and waited. He set the lantern down beside him. They watched the sun drop through the broken windows and gaps in the burnt back walls.

"Are you a believer, Marcus Santiago?" the priest inquired.

"I wasn't up until about fifteen or so hours ago. Now... I can't say for sure. It's been a strange day," he replied honestly with a shrug.

"I could use your prayers."

"Then you'll have 'em, padre."

Marcus whipped his rifle up and steadied it. He unloaded a shot through the doorway. The shuddering black, spindly frame that crept into view was pierced and vanished into a wisp of smoke. The hordes of hell screamed out in anger in the forest as a bullet casing hit the wooden floor beside his worn down cowboy boots.

Johann began to recite his scripture.

Marcus exhaled slowly and took aim once again. The creaking of the wraiths' bodies echoed like gunshots through the silence of winter, their large horned heads cast angry shadows in the moonlight. Their frames moved in unnatural ways. Their hands left trails of blood across the surface of the church. Their harrowing calls were mournful and angry, begging for the son of the priest who desecrated the land with corpses to come hither. Come to the halls of hell as recompense.

Not today. Not if Marcus Santiago had anything to say about it.

Clang! A handful of bullet casings hit the ground. Marcus quickly reloaded and continued to hold the front line. The nearby window shattered, spraying glass into the building like rainfall. Johann clutched his wooden cross to his chest and lifted his eyes. He felt every bit of oxygen slip from his lungs as a black mass writhed and spiraled into view. The winds picked up and took wood, glass, and nature with it.

"Johann! Now would be a good time t'do somethin'!" Marcus shouted as he fumbled his ammunition. He took a step back and grunted out in pain as a wayward piece of glass sliced his face.

"I'm sorry," Johann said quietly. "I'm sorry!"

The black mass resembled his father, and fear swelled within him. The moonlight vanished, blocked out by the wicked forces that surrounded the decaying building. The darkness felt all consuming.

Johann dropped the cross and raced toward Marcus. He grabbed the lantern from the ground and held it up. The wraiths hissed but refused to stop their slow forward march. They filed into the church with taunts and anguished cries. Johann's hand trembled. He held the lantern up higher.

Marcus shifted his eyes to the rafters above . He whipped his rifle upward and unloaded a shot. With great strength, he wrenched Johann away from the pulpit. A resounding *crash* echoed through the building as a burlap sack tumbled to the floor. The rope that once held it to the rafters was split by the bullet, and the horrendous sound of bones shattering filled their ears.

The ranch hand raced toward the bag and ripped it open. Inside were the decayed remains of a man. Broken bones and decayed flesh lay in a crumpled heap. In his mangled hands, the corpse held a hacksaw. Everything was stained in the remnants of blood. The severed rope had taken his life, a tight noose crushed his vertebrae.

Marcus picked up the hacksaw and tossed it down the aisle. It came to a rest by the pews. The largest black mass slithered its way to the corpse and wormed its way inside of the burlap sack. With angered, heated cries, the wraiths descended upon their tormentor. Hellish wails reverberated out into the night.

With quiet but hastened movements, Marcus took Johann's hand and pulled him out of the church. Johann took the lantern and tossed it into the decrepit building and watched the warped, brittle old wood finally succumb to the touch of flames. The spiraling black smog of the demonic forces seeped out through the wood paneling until everything fell still. The framework collapsed, and the once tall steeple came crashing to the ground like a weapon piercing a heart.

Marcus grabbed hold of Johann's arm and pulled him away. They silently made their way down the hill. The ranch hand's grip slid down the priest's forearm until he was able to interlock his fingers around the trembling stranger's. Johann grabbed hold of his priest's collar and ripped it free from his neck. He tossed it to the snowy ground, tightened his hold on Marcus' hand, and breathed out a sigh of relief.

The voices were gone. The silence was sweet as sacramental wine.

Somehow, the thought of seeing the sunrise beside this man brought him more peace than his bible ever did. He was greatly looking forward to that sight.

On the Salt Flats

Jennifer Crow

All of heaven's grief crystallizes
on the flats, blank white surface
reflecting the sun into burning eyes
as raw dust settles on reddened
skin, the body giving up its water
moment by moment, sundown
forever too far ahead as the oxen
bend and fall, bend and fall. Relics
we tossed from the wagon bed
kick up puffs of poisonous salt
where they break the featureless
surface, a memory of oceans
past. Midday we pass bones
crusted and vividly pale, curved
eye sockets staring blankly
at the sky, a few shreds of cloth
the only sign that a human life
ended here, withered and defeated.
Our last ox lows, but heaven remains
too high and hard and distant
to hear it and show mercy.

We learned in our youth to fear
the dark, ignorant of the pitiless
eye of the sun, the blank face
of lands parched to bone.

Candelaria and the Red-Eyed Bunch Gang

KC Grifant

From between fir tree trunks, Candelaria Hernández watched the Red-Eyed Bunch Gang, their drunken laughter heightened by the bag that sat close to the bonfire. Her left hand curled around the musket she had fired exactly eight times in her sixteen years, all on men who didn't seem to listen unless a bullet was whizzing by their ear.

Her gaze fell on the leader, Elliot "Snowman" Carson, whose gaze was always bloodshot. He'd earned his nickname during his thirty years, so the legend went, for his tendency to shoot his victims in the eyes and along the mouth, as well as down the torso. Waste of bullets, but worth its weight in gold for his reputation, he had explained. Candelaria's gaze drifted down to the leather satchel next to him, that she herself had lined with treated paint two days ago to hide the precious cargo within.

Candelaria stepped out past the trees into the clearing. The seven gang members, with beaten hats and crooked grins, took in her dusty face, gleaming darkly against the bonfire. She tried not to look at Jake, Carson's righthand man. Somewhere in the distance, coyotes yipped at the slowly sinking sun, along with the much fainter hint of rumbling deep in the forest.

They ignored her, steadfastly talking after a beat. A tactic to make her feel small. Jake was the only one who stayed silent. He blinked, pain and longing clear in his eyes.

She fired the musket into the tree behind Carson.

That got their attention. The others shut their traps, pistols appearing in their hands, all except Jake and Carson. Carson stayed reclined as if he hadn't a care in the world, his pasty and pockmarked skin glowing mottled against the flick of the fire.

"Smile sweetheart, or that puckered look is going turn you into a worn-out boot," Carson greeted, drawing a finger through his scraggly beard. "Found us faster than a bloodhound." Bastard smiled as if she were an old friend, but she didn't let that faze her. If there was one thing she had learned growing up, it was how to manage a man.

Candelaria crossed her arms over her long jacket, hanging over a stained cotton shirt and split skirt, and looked at him coolly. The others relaxed, holstering their guns.

"You leave all your gals to fend for themselves?" Candelaria said, letting her voice boom into the air. People often seemed startled at how loud she talked, but she found being a girl of her age she had to speak twice as loud to be half as heard. "Big fancy outlaw like you?"

Irritation flashed across Carson's face like lightning before it smoothed over.

"Pretty face like yours seems to get along just dandy," Carson replied and shot her a smile full of yellow teeth and malice.

"Lucky for you, or you'd miss out on the opportunity to give me my cut," Candelaria said and saw Jake sit up a little straighter. Jake "Hustling" Pickett was the one who had approached her on Carson's behalf in the market not even a week ago. He had offered a generous cut if she helped them plan out a heist at the "bank" she worked at—really more of a storage building in the leading mine camp of Irons

Flat. It was a vault even she didn't have access to, but if she could help the gang plan out the theft, their dynamite would make sure they got the goods. It had taken Candelaria all of two minutes to consider and say yes. Ever since she landed the job, the building owner had gotten more and more handsy and loved to comment that she would be better suited working at the saloon, even though she was faster at inventorying than any other employee there.

Plus, she had liked Jake's face, his penetrating gaze blacker than the tons of coal she inventoried. Even though he was an obvious grifter, she thought he was someone she could trust.

"Boss, maybe we ought to—" Jake started.

"Shuddup," Carson said and squinted at Candelaria. "You know what they say: Don't let your yearnings get ahead of your earnings." Two of the other outlaws smirked; one outright leered at her.

Candelaria ignored them. She kept part of her attention listening for sounds behind her, where she had left a trail, while the satchel burned a hole in the corner of her eye. Nestled in the bag were raw unhatched lizotiy eggs, creamy and more luminescent than pearls, a rare and favored material that miners in Irons Flat had the luck of unearthing. The lizotiys were violently paternal monsters, possessive even of their unfertilized eggs, thought to bestow their wearers exceptional health. Any stolen eggs eventually had to be treated with a chemical mixture to mask their scent so they'd be safe to wear before setting into jewelry or adorned into hats for the wealthiest of the wealthy. She had spent a full day mastering the chemistry to mix up the anti-lizotiy paint that now coated the inside of Carson's bulging satchel, making it safe to transport until they could treat the eggs directly.

With just a handful of the stolen raw lizotiy eggs, Candelaria would have a fortune that would last years.

Finally, the silence—and her undeterred stare—got to Carson, who shifted.

"What's a little orphan girl like you need them for anyway?" Carson mused, picking at a hangnail. "Take it from me, sweetheart: mosey onto town, find a nice man, pop out a baby or two."

Ambitions tied to sudden wealth flooded her mind; foremost of all was going back to the orphanage that had protected her so she could likewise watch out for kids who weren't as strong as she had been. She could fix up the building, maybe construct a few more. Buy a business, set herself up so she'd never have to work for anyone again.

"You wouldn't have the eggs without me," Candelaria said flatly, a simple fact. Some of the outlaws shifted. She knew she made people uneasy. Plenty of folk didn't like a serious girl.

"Candie, sugar pie, since we lost a bag in the shootout, we just don't have enough to split." Carson shrugged like the conversation was over. "Things happen. Besides, what are you gonna do? Shoot us?" He laughed at that, and everyone except Jake joined in.

Things happen. She didn't need to remind him that *she* had distracted the front guard before the gang ambushed him, that *she* had let the gang in after hours and directed them to the vault. And when the next two guards appeared, *she* had given them pause, holding out her hands and shouting. The guards hesitated at seeing a young, seemingly upright young woman caught in the middle, giving Carson enough time to fire an obscene number of bullets, carving his telltale snowman pattern into the first guard, blood pouring out of his face in a grotesque mask as he tried to scream.

The second guard had got off a shot, ripping apart one of the lizotiy egg bags in Carson's hand. She'd never forget the sight of splinters of the iridescent gleaming eggshells, now worthless, mixed with blood underfoot.

"Things happen," Candelaria echoed thoughtfully and took a few steps closer to Carson. The second guard had grabbed her skirt as he fell, moaning, when Carson made him a second 'snowman.' Before she could wrench him off, the gang had shoved out the door and escaped, echoes of shouts and a single gunshot outside. She had glimpsed Jake glancing back, saying something, before another outlaw yanked him out the door.

Most men weren't strong enough to do the right thing right away, she knew.

But now—now she could see the storm brewing in Jake as easily as if it were a tornado. She had kept him at arm's length as they got to know each other over the last week, and she sensed him become enamored, in awe of her even, quick to recognize the intellect that made it easy for her to predict how people would act before they did.

He was almost on her side; she could feel it. That was the thing about grifters. They'd turn as quick as the wind.

She met Jake's eyes.

"Fair's fair, Carson," Jake piped up, the storm in him nearly crashing to the surface of his tense face. "She can split some of my—"

"I said, *shut your trap*," Carson growled.

Jake jumped up, and Carson pulled two pistols on him just as quick. The other five of the Red-Eyed Bunch Gang stared, guns waiting, ready to shoot at his command.

"Now, now, lover boy," Carson laughed. "Such a sucker for a pretty face."

"She just wants what's hers. Gimme my cut and we'll leave you be," Jake said.

"How bout I make me another snowman." Carson's eyes glittered.

"Before you both get yourself into a tizzy," Candelaria said. "There's one thing you ought to know."

A rumbling rose behind her, a sound Candelaria had been waiting for.

It was time.

"Most folk make the mistake of underestimating me," she said, hearing the sharp bite in her own voice. She controlled her emotions most of the time, but there was one thing she would never abide.

Betrayal.

She reached into her side pocket to pull out a wrapped handkerchief. Carson and the others half watched her, still skeptical until she unfolded the cloth. Crushed lizotiy egg shells she had scooped up from the building's floor, still sticky and speckled with blood, rested in the cloth.

Jake registered it the faster than the others, looking behind him in a panic. "You'll get us killed," he gaped.

"You stupid cow," one of the gang shrieked. "The damned monsters will find us."

"Too late," Candelaria said over the hisses of the lizotiys that seemed to echo around them.

"Fan out," Carson barked and loomed over her as if to strike. "Your death sentence too, sweetheart."

She opened her coat where the shine of the black anti-lizotiy material paint gleamed and rendered her all but invisible to the monsters. Carson's eyes narrowed greedily—right before she smashed the shell bits into his beard.

He howled and grabbed her, trying to rip off her coat. She kneed him in the side as he shoved her. She staggered back but rebounded quickly, catching sight of Jake scooping up the satchel and pointing toward the far side of the clearing.

The dirt erupted next to Candelaria. She stepped back as a smooth, white, maggot-like body half the size of her burst out of the ground.

Everything in her tensed to flee, but she reminded herself that the coating should hide her from their scent.

She still had to bite down a scream as the lizotiy twisted higher up, its body ringed, scaled and stinking of something unburied and fecal. In its face rested puckered eyes and a mouth the size of a wheel, gaping and dark. It hissed, the rippled white skin on either side of its face moving to make a sound between a rattler and a steam train.

"Shoot every damn one!" Carson shouted as he wiped his beard, flicking the egg shells away. Bullets sprayed up dirt against the blue twilight, and Candelaria stepped back to watch the carnage unfold.

Two of the gang members hightailed it toward the trees despite Carson's hollers. A pair of lizotiys burrowed out of the dirt and swallowed up the legs of both gang members like quick-drawn knapsacks. Except these knapsacks were lined with teeth and closed with enough force to make a sickening crack. The outlaws screamed as their torsos caved and their bones crushed. Both monsters yanked the men down into the ground, out of sight.

Candelaria scanned for Jake but saw Carson had him frozen in place, gun pointed. He wretched the satchel from Jake's hand.

"Gimme your coat or I shoot lover boy," Carson said as the ground shook. "Throw it over. Now."

It's not like she loved Jake—not yet—but she hesitated anyway as the gunfire behind her stopped and the remaining posse's muffled screams cut off. Jake had potential, and he cared for her, she could feel it. But she couldn't—*wouldn't*—take the risk. Not for someone who betrayed her once.

She met Jake's eyes and saw the realization hit one second too late. Everything crossed his face at once: fear, shock. Then resignation.

Carson rolled his eyes and fired. Jake twisted away, but the bullet shot through his left eye. Candelaria swallowed back a shriek. A flap of skin hung loose next to Jake's nose, blood pouring out of the hole like water out a loose spigot. Jake moaned and collapsed.

Carson stumbled back as the ground shook harder, dirt spraying up around him. That was her chance—she darted forward to wrench away the bag. Carson swung his free fist, and she ducked, yanking harder, but he held tight.

Until the ground burst.

She dove backwards, clutching the satchel and watching Carson shoot the lizotiy through its gaping abyss of a mouth once, twice, three times. He was more focused than the other outlaws, firing steadily. Finally, the lizotiy screeched and collapsed, a giant slug of white twitching against the ground. Before Carson turned toward her, a second lizotiy burst out between them. She clamped down a screech. Carson jumped out of the way—too slow. The monster bit down onto his leg and held on.

"Damn you!" Carson hollered. Carson cursed and fired again, but this monster shook him hard, making his shot go wide.

Candelaria paused. She aimed the musket at Carson's heart, but there wasn't a clear shot through the dust and his squirming. As much as she wanted to stay and see his demise, she couldn't be sure that the lizotiy might not detect her after the others were gone, since the coat didn't fully cover her.

She glanced at Jake's still form a few feet away. She started toward him but stopped herself.

"Brought it on yourself," she said quietly. Maybe if he hadn't betrayed her, things would've turned out differently for him.

She had what she wanted, she reminded herself, and squashed out any inkling of remorse like a beetle underfoot. She took off into the woods, leaving Carson's muffled shouts and gunfire behind her. When her breath steadied and the sounds had fallen away, she thought of the orphanage again, the one place that had felt like home, where people didn't always try to take advantage of her.

Maybe she could make a difference. For other girls like her.

She hurried against the dying light, the satchel of eggs heavy and warm against her side and the monsters gone. At least, for now.

The Word for Goodbye

David A. Elsensohn

It was not that the dead rose in Clarkson County, for they did so every
year at the beginning of May, clawing up from frail wooden prisons,
dragging themselves across the sodden ground to devour the living.
No, it was that the dead rose on Dennis Gilman's birthday. He knew
it had nothing to do with him personally, but he couldn't help but feel
it was his fault.

Gilman was a loner but could never get the hang of living alone.
Mary hailed from Boston and didn't like him but married him anyway;
her bonnet had been set in some goal of reform, to make him a mirror
of the tinhorn gentlemen she usually liked. She failed, and therefore
he failed. She didn't like the child she bore either, and as Katherine
grew into a shy young girl, her mother grew thin and grim. When Mary
began sitting for hours before the ashy fireplace with wool blankets
over bony shoulders, shuddering and coughing, blonde hair hanging
in strings over her face, Gilman asked Lucille to come and help with
everything.

Lucille, who lived nearby, had moved in without a word, washing
Mary's clothes, combing her hair, mixing her gruels of grasses and
roots that Mary wouldn't touch. Lucille would shake her head, her
necklace of bone hairpipes and beads clacking, but would say nothing
to the white woman. Mary had plenty to say to her, though, blaming
her husband and Lucille for her lot in life. Gilman's head lowered daily,

accepting her venom, but the Comanche woman stoically shrugged it off. When Mary died, Gilman mourned almost all the year. He had never said goodbye to her. Lucille had stayed, and Gilman was quietly relieved, for he had no idea how to raise his daughter.

"Don't eat so fast, Kate," he said.

"Sorry, Pa." She looked like her mother but was quick to take blame like her father.

Lucille scraped the last of the fried corn and bacon onto their plates. "You know today, Dennis Gilman? What it is?" She rarely bothered with more than a hand's worth of words but always called him by his entire name.

"Yeah, I reckon I do," Gilman sighed. He knew she hadn't meant his birthday. "I'd best go out and collect all the tools. Never know when one of 'em will figure out how to use weapons." He rose from the table and stumped out while Lucille put on coffee and began to sing Katherine one of her gourd dance songs. Lucille had a dulcet voice, but they only discovered that a few months ago; Mary hadn't tolerated any language but English spoken in the house.

Gilman had only just dropped the heavy oak bar across the door when the birds went quiet. The sun would soon touch the tops of the pines, stretching shadows like cobwebs across uneven hills. Darkness would chase over the ridges. He hated this time. From this moment, the night would proceed in silence, crickets and forest creatures wisely hiding from whatever walked among them. Gilman felt the distance from town more than ever.

Lucille scrubbed the iron skillet. Kate huddled on her bed in the corner, blonde ringlets swaying, preparing a stack of oil-soaked torches. Gilman lined up paper-wrapped cartridges along the dinner table and took a brush to the bore of the Sharps .52 carbine. Maybe nothing would find them tonight, but it was best to be ready. Tomorrow morning, there would be bodies littering the roads and fields, to be collected in wagons and reburied. It was a somber tradition in Clarkson County, and in other places Gilman had heard of.

They waited.

"Help! Halloo in the cabin!" came a man's voice. Gilman already stood with a hand to the shuttered window, having heard the hoofbeats. The dead did not ride, nor did they speak. He opened the shutter and peered out. The night was lit in flickering uncertainty by the torches planted in the ground around the house.

"Help, there!" The man was grey-mustached and stocky, and he lay down over the horse's mane, holding just barely. His face shone with sweat. The horse was lathered.

Gilman unlatched the door and looked around the property before handing the Sharps to Lucille. "Kate, get his mare into the barn, quickly now. Take off the bit and saddle and throw a blanket over her, but come right back after." She went pale but ran outside with him, grabbing the reins.

The man fell into Gilman's arms, and together they labored into the cabin. Lucille and the Sharps stood guarding the doorway, waiting for the young girl to return. Kate dashed back in the doorway, whimpering as Gilman got the man lying down across his bed.

"You'll be safe here tonight, sir," Gilman said. "Let's have a look at that leg, if you can bear it."

By the time they cut through the twill of his pant leg, the older man was gasping and nearly unconscious. There was a good deal of blood, and Gilman kept the man talking to keep his mind from it.

"I'm Dennis Gilman, and this is my daughter Kate. And this is Lucille."

"Good... good evening, miss. Ma'am." It somehow did not sound inane.

"*Maruawe*," said Lucille quietly. Kate bobbed, wide-eyed but remembering her courtesy.

"I'm Hill. Franklin Joseph Hill, Texas Ranger, and am I glad Lizzie found her way up here. I was gearing myself up for dead." He whooshed out shaky breaths from under his grey mustache as Gilman and Lucille washed the wound. "I'm surveying down from Lubbock. I didn't realize it was the end of April. Damned stupid of me, oh, apologies, miss, ma'am... some of them are already about. One of them caught me, almost pulled me out of the saddle."

"Coffee, Franklin Joseph Hill?" Lucille said.

"It's black, I'm afraid, and we've got no sugar or milk, Mister Hill," said Gilman.

"Black is just fine, and I don't need sugar or milk, but if you have some whiskey to put in it, I'd be sorely grateful," Hill said.

They rushed to comply, and soon the two men were blowing over tin cups of tongue-varnishing black liquid.

The moon was a splinter this time of month, and the stars hid behind swaying pines. Hill lay on his back, snoring fitfully, leg bandaged and poulticed. Such wounds became a danger if they infected, but Lucille knew her remedies; he would heal. Kate huddled on her bed, twirling her hair around a finger. Lucille sat at the table across from Gilman, who looked up occasionally to see her gazing at him. He would look down quickly, for her eyes were black pools, too peaceful and knowing for his conscience. Neither of them was young, but Gilman sometimes felt both too old and too young when near her. When Mary was alive, she overwhelmed their lives with her presence; now, Mary did so with her absence. He swallowed, thinking of how life would be without Lucille there, without her soft-shouldered brawn and her confident vigor.

He started up suddenly. A branch crackled in the dark beyond the torchlight.

Gilman went to one window, Lucille to the other, peering between the slats of wood. Nothing, yet. Hill coughed behind them, now awake and struggling to sit up.

"There, Dennis Gilman," Lucille said.

The sound was tiny but stomach-churningly familiar: a wet shuffle and thump on the grass. Gilman went to her window and peeked at the dark shape leaning forward, walking slowly toward them, aimless like a mad dog. It looked male, once, but was too far gone to tell for certain. It paused just outside the circle of torchlight, swaying, as if mesmerized by the snapping yellow light.

Gilman went to the table, Sharps in hand, and scooped up cartridges.

Sometimes they wouldn't try to get in, but just shuffled around the cabin, bumping into the wood, gurgling and clucking. Other times a dim memory burned in their heads, and they tried to enter, rotten hands hammering the door; it was then that guns had to be brought to bear.

"Another one, Dennis Gilman."

"Hell."

"Here, take this, folks. It's all I've got, but it's sturdy. Extra bullets are in my belt," urged the Texas Ranger, his shaking hand holding a pistol butt-forward. "I'm afraid I can't do much from here, but I'll be right here with you, be certain of that.

"And don't you cry none, miss," he said, nodding at Kate, who shook on her bed with arms wrapped around her knees, eyes squeezing away tears. "Soon it'll be all over, and tomorrow the sun'll be bright and warm."

Wounded as he was, the older man would be of little aid if they couldn't hold the door, but Gilman was glad for Hill's presence. He glanced over at Lucille, glad of hers, too.

Then something gave a thump on the wood next to the door. The walls rasped as something rubbed against them. It thumped again, harder. Gilman threw down the Sharps' lever, snapped a cartridge into the chamber, and closed the breech. He squeezed a thick finger into the slim trigger guard and raised the dark walnut stock to his shoulder.

Lucille went to the tiny square panel in the door, through which one could see visitors, and pulled it inward. A stench of soil seeped into the room, and a white face filled their vision, teeth parting. Gilman pushed the carbine's barrel into it, squeezed, and the cabin shook with thunder. He stood back from the shove of the recoil, then leaned to see the result. The head was mostly gone, and the body lay still upon the dirt. The dead did not suffer much from hits to the body, so it was best to remove as much as possible from the top.

"Sure is noisy, miss, ain't it?" the old Ranger said to Kate. "Your ma and pa will have things cleared up right soon; that's how it all works around here."

Gilman stole a glance at Lucille, who for once lowered her head with a quiet smile. He grinned and shot the lever down to load another round, preparing for the next figure who stumbled toward them in the night.

The darkness wore on, broken by bright flashes and thunderous booms from the Sharps carbine. Lucille had also put Mr. Hill's Colt to use, aiming the long barrel between the wooden slats. She was teaching Kate the words to another song, about a red wolf.

The dead were more numerous than ever tonight, lurching from the darkness of the pines and into the firelight as if drawn by the warmth and life of the house. Sometimes they were people Gilman once knew or knew of, but he could not afford to hold back. He and Lucille struggled to repel them, pushing steel through the shutters and door panel and filling the air with smoke and shot. Kate kept busy reloading for them and putting more coffee on the iron stove.

Another body was thrown backward by a heavy bullet. Despite the unearthly happenings, Gilman was almost enjoying himself. Things were under control. "Boom! What's the Comanche word for goodbye, Lucille?"

"There isn't one."

"Up in Lubbock," Hill said, sipping at a steaming cup, "they make it a celebration. They gather round on the rooftops, or around big bonfires on the hills, drinking and dancing. They hold tournaments, and give out blue ribbons for the most dead put down."

Gilman nodded. Here in Clarkson, where neighbors couldn't see each other without an hour's ride, the event was more somber, more careful. There was no comfort of solid buildings and many townsfolk. There was only one's family and whatever provisions one could store up.

One would think that people would figure out some means to stop it all. He'd heard that in England, they'd started something called cremation, but figured it wouldn't catch on here; people held fast to tradition.

Lucille had told him once that the Numinu packed up and walked as a group all night, shooting those who approached. Only when the first rays of the dawn began to pull its way through the trees and grasses did they stop and sing thanks.

A banging was heard outside, then a wooden crash, and they began to hear the screams of animals. The barn. Gilman spun toward his daughter, eyes wide.

"Kate... Kate, did you latch the barn door?"

"I'm so sorry, Pa!" She flew into her bed, overcome with sobs.

Gilman and the Sharps started toward the door, and they stopped him: Kate with tearful pleas, Lucille with a strong hand. Hill shook his head.

"You can't go out there, son."

Gilman sat down and placed his head in his hands as the screams of horses and pigs filled the night.

"Mister Hill, I must apologize to you," he said.

Hill whooshed out a breath from his mustache. "Well, son, that's what God decides sometimes. Lizzie was a good mare. It wasn't your fault, miss." Kate wept into her pillow.

Another wooden crash sounded. There came a horse's high-pitched whicker, then hooves pounding the moist earth. Hill chuckled despite the situation.

"That's Lizzie, for certain," he said. "Should have figured she wouldn't stand for that kind of predicament. She'll get away for sure. Mr. Gilman, seeing as you took me in, when I make it back to Lubbock, I'll see what I can do about replacing your poor creatures."

Kate remained inconsolable. Gilman sat next to her and rubbed her back with a calloused hand. It wasn't her fault. None of this was, and it wasn't his, either. He was beginning to understand that.

Gilman sat wearily, head hanging almost to his knees. A few hours remained until dawn. Lucille sat next to him, composed, Hill's pistol in her lap. She had undone her hair, letting the black waterfall descend her ample bosom. The night had been quiet for a time, but the Sharps was nearly out of bullets. They would soon have to use shovels and pickaxes. His thoughts sank into darker places.

A scratch sounded outside, and he rose wearily to his feet and threw open the little panel. He stared, then fumbled at the heavy bar across the door, letting the carbine knock against the wall.

"Mr. Gilman... what are you doing, son?" Hill rasped.

"Pa, no."

Gilman did not hear them. He threw open the door and stumbled into the torchlight.

Mary stood there solemnly, wavering in the utter stillness. She stood in silhouette before the guttering torches, dressed in the same grey dress. Her face was drawn and streaked as if with tears, and pale strands of hair hung over her face. The months under the soil had not been kind to her. Her girl-thin arms hung at her sides.

"Mary," he whispered. She dragged a foot closer to him, silent.

Her arms reached for him in a frigid embrace. He shivered, and then she was on him, gripping with hideous power, skin sloughing from her bones as her teeth neared his face. Blood streamed where her bony fingers clawed his arms. Gilman tried to howl and could not, gasping and hiccupping from the foul air. He fell to the dirt, and she fell with him. He swallowed and waited to die.

There was a click, and a cold cylinder of steel pressed against the side of Mary's head. Gilman finally did howl when the bullet exploded into the fair-haired skull, spraying him with black fluid and bone and dirt and memory.

His dead wife's body slumped away from him, and he looked up at Lucille standing tall as clouds above him, pistol smoking, bead necklace swaying slightly. Through the horror rampaging in his mind, he looked at her broad face with its shining black pools.

He struggled to his feet and regarded the figure in the grey dress.

"Goodbye, Mary." He had finally said it. He wiped old blood and tears from his eyes and staggered into the cabin where Lucille and Kate were waiting. Hill shook his head.

"Thought you'd left us there for a minute, Mr. Gilman."

Gilman sat heavily in a chair and buried his face in a cloth. Lucille put more coffee on and pulled out the whiskey bottle.

"Happy birthday, Dennis Gilman," she said.

West for Its Own Sake

Dermott O'Malley

Reuben turned and unfurled the bedroll in the manner one would shake open a paper bag. The horse, Fox, shook and whinnied.

"Easy, girl," he said. He laid the bedroll down and approached her side. "What's wrong?" He stroked the side of her neck, but she shook again and shied away from him. Reuben's hand was now covered in a chalky layer of red dirt. The horse's gray coat hid it well, but up close he could see the iron-rich dust from their trek through the Red Desert had filled her coat, even caking up around creases. "Phew, we gotta clean you up. Is that what's botherin' you, Foxy?"

He unbuckled the saddle and began to remove the load from her back. As he lifted, he accidentally glanced again at the dark wagon in the distance, now just a blurred, dark figure standing perfectly still in the silhouette of the sinking sun. "Yeah, that's what's wrong. C'mon, girl, we'll getchu cleaned up."

He tried his best to slap and comb the dirt out of the horse's hair with his fingers, but the dirt was too fine and deep for even a proper brush. He promised the horse she could enjoy a bath the next time they found water, lying and saying he was sure they would come across a nice stream soon.

Dinner was a slab of salt pork and a tin cup of whiskey and water. Dipping the salt pork in the liquid helped, but he wanted something fresh. Some white fish or apples that weren't sun-dried would do nicely, but he didn't lie to himself like he did Fox; there wouldn't be an apple tree or fruitful river for many miles.

Soon, the stars were brighter than the embers of his fire, and Fox's heavy breathing was louder than the crackle of buffalo chips and dry firewood. Reuben listened to the horse; he knew she was sleeping by her breathing, which was good. The horse was tired. She hadn't slept nearly as much as she should have in the week they had been traveling together. She seemed to be aware of the wagon following them as well, and it made her as uneasy as it made him.

In the morning, Reuben gathered his things and rolled up his bedding. He fed Fox a handful of dried apples and scratched her nose as she ate them from his palm. He tied his belongings onto the horse but made sure to focus on the task, not letting his eyes glance up to see the dark wagon sitting in front of the rising sun. He didn't need to, because he knew it would be there in the same direction and distance as it was the day before and the day before that.

As a child, Reuben had ridden in a similar covered schooner with his family. His father, a banker, thought there would be more money in the mountains of gold out west than there was in his old bank out east. They traveled west in a caravan of strangers, all on the same hopelessly hopeful journey as them. Reuben was just a child at the time, and the excitement of adventure lasted even beyond Independence Rock, when cholera and dysentery began weakening and thinning their caravan. Reuben didn't really understand the danger they were in at the time.

His father had been scarred from helping pull women and children out from wagon wrecks and clearing limbs from bloody spokes, and the diseases jumping from wagon to wagon turned him into a recluse. The last few days Reuben spent with his family, they were forbidden from leaving the safety of the wagon. Reuben and his family were prisoners of wood, canvas, and paranoia.

His father hadn't been wrong; safety and health were the primary concern at the start of the trip for good reason. What nobody on their caravan knew was that the Shoshones had finally grown tired of the less-than-peaceful travelers that came before them. They had been organizing retaliation by way of small war parties with goals ranging from blockades to robberies, and sometimes, massacres. Word of the danger along the well-traveled paths wouldn't reach east for another few weeks, but since they were on the trail, that word would never reach them.

One morning, and without warning, gunshots and whooping sounded off outside, seemingly all around them. Before the banker could even gather up his rifle and ammunition, a stray bullet ripped through the wagon and his throat with more blood than sound. He clutched his throat and collapsed to the floorboards as asphyxiation and blood loss raced each other to claim him. As Reuban's mother and sister cried and held their dying patriarch, Reuben struggled to load the rifle. His father had never actually gotten around to teaching him how to properly use it.

A young warrior tore open the canvas back, and Reuben's mother and sister both cried out, begging mercy from a warrior who may or may not have even understood English, let alone mercy. Reuben raised the rifle and pointed it in the general direction of the Shoshone. He closed his eyes and squeezed the trigger, but only heard the sound of the hammer striking blank steel. When he opened his eyes, the warrior was smiling. Reuben dropped the rifle and curled up in a corner, covering his head with his arms. He heard the screams from his mother and sister as they were dragged out of the wagon. The tribe finished collecting their spoils—including his father's rifle, scalp, and women—but spared him. He never knew why.

But the wagon following him now looked different than the schooners of the old pioneers. He couldn't allow himself to look at it when he rested, but once he was moving again, he allowed a glance over his shoulder. It was far away, only able to be seen on flatter stretches like this one, but close enough to make out a few distinct differences: It was led by three large horses, not a yoke of oxen like the old pioneers steered, and instead of white canvas protecting the passengers from sun and weather, this wagon appeared to be dark in color. But not just dark; the heat waves above, around, and below the wagon rippled and waved faster than the desert around it. Reuben told himself it must be because of the sun heating the dark material, but in order to convince himself of that, he also had to actively deny that the waves were flowing the wrong way, as if it wasn't radiating heat, but rather, sucking in the light around it.

The early morning sun cast stretching shadows of the three massive horses' heads, which were bobbing up and down as they trotted forward. They moved in sync with each other, but also always in sync with Reuben and Fox. When he first spotted the wagon, a week ago now, he and Fox took off running at a full sprint. The pursuing horses matched their gallop, but when Fox's exhaustion forced him to slow, so did the dark wagon. When he rested, they rested. When he continued, they followed. It had been seven days since he first spotted the wagon and eight days since he met Fox. He leaned forward and stroked the side of the horse's neck. She responded with a sharp exhale through her nostrils and shook. "Sorry, girl," Reuben said to the horse. The horse shook again.

He rode west, to the spot he and his previous companions had called camp for the past several months. They were like him, mostly all products of other failed pilgrimages—widows and widowers, orphans and the abandoned—though some were folks who made it all the way west to find there was nothing there for them. They lived off stickups and robberies and wagon wrecks, living their lives somewhere between a pack of coyotes and a wake of vultures. When they took him in all those years ago, they taught him their way of life. As a child, he became an expert pickpocket and could swipe a whole camp meal worth of food from a shop and walk out without so much as a bulge showing in his shirt. As he got older and became a man, he learned more useful skills from the gang. By his twenties, he was an expert marksman, hunter, fisher, trapper, and highwayman.

But they were a dying breed by the time train cars started volleying across the completed Pacific Railroad. As if the scarcity of travelers—and the supplies they carried with them—wasn't enough, the few that they did come across were usually others like them, too seasoned or well prepared to be caught with their pants down. Their doings became focused on the sparse surviving towns built up along the paths of the old pioneers and prospectors, and as it did, so did the need for law. Most towns were known to be off-limits already, and the few that weren't were becoming too risky between the lawmen and townsfolk who had all been around long enough to see their way out of scam or scuffle.

Others took all of these changes and responded with brash, desperate moves, eventually getting the wrong bounty hunter or lawman sicced on them; but not Reuben's crew. They sunk their camps deep into the land and traveled out to do their hunting and fishing and robbing. They passed through towns in small groups, stealing what they could and trading for the rest. Sometimes, they could pose as regular God-fearing travelers and win some tips from the locals. It was one of those tips that led Reuben and the others to Mr. Martin.

Someone brought word back to camp that in three days a man from a local town was packing up his things and moving somewhere further west. The thought of a man putting all of his worldly possessions on one wagon and riding out by himself seemed as foolish as telling the stranger sitting next to him at a bar, so they couldn't resist. On the day the man was to travel, Reuben and three others went into town. They let the man's wagon round the horizon before following. They followed for the first day, slow enough to make sure they wouldn't end up getting spotted, and that night they only rested a few hours before continuing their trek. They traveled under the dim light of the moon, so their approach was mostly covered in darkness. The plan was, as it always was, to approach the wagon at dawn and take their spoils with the rising sun to light their escape.

They were spotted early and could see the man trying to pack up camp and strap in his horses. Reuben and the others spurred their horses hard to catch him before he could escape.

"We ain't gonna hurt ya!" Reuben called out. By the time they reached the campsite, the man had barricaded himself inside. One of his horses was half-strapped into the two-horse harness while the other was still loose.

"We know you're in there, Mr. Martin," shouted Gillam, the organizer of this particular robbery. "Why don't you just come on out now, ain't nobody gonna shoot ya," he said. Reuben smirked. He knew Gillam would fire as soon as Mr. Martin exited the wagon. Gillam held his aim on the wagon with his rifle, Big Mike. Big Mike was a beautiful and ornate custom Henry repeater, named for the message, "For Mikael," etched into the receiver cover. Gillam was as vain as he was ruthless, and he was an excellent shot—a dead man named Mikael would attest to that, as would a dead man whose custom leather riding boots he wore.

After a lot of silence and looks exchanged amongst the crew, Gillam gave Reuben a nod. Reuben climbed down off his horse and started walking towards the wagon. He only got four or five steps before a shot rang out, and a lead slug whizzed past Reuben's head. The rest of the shots fired were only in the direction of the wagon, at least a couple dozen between all of the men, and then there was silence. Reuben discovered the bullet that had missed him had struck his horse in the neck, and it had run off to die out in the prairie.

"Bastard almost shot me," Reuben muttered, brushing the spot on his temple where he had felt the gust of wind from the bullet blow across. Gillam gave another nod, this time to Stanley to take point and check the wagon. After finishing reloading his revolver, Stanley made his way to the back, weapon drawn. The rest of the crew watched as he ripped open the canvas wagon, looked inside, and lowered his weapon. "We settled?" Gillam shouted.

"Well. In a manner, yes," he said.

The rest of the crew approached and looked at the inside of the wagon. Mr. Martin lay dead on the floorboards alongside what must have been Mrs. Martin. Crouched and crying over the woman was a boy, probably only nine or ten years old. This was a problem. Their gang had rules, and failure to abide was not taken lightly. One of the rules was that women and children were off limits; killing either drew too much attention.

Per Gillam, the men dragged the bodies out and laid them next to the wagon. The boy didn't even protest as they did; he followed his dead mother out and sat next to her in the dirt. They went through the wagon, took what they could, and left the rest, deciding that stealing the whole wagon was against good judgment.

"What about the boy?" Reuben asked.

"What *about* the boy?" Gillam said.

Reuben looked at the child. He sat in the dirt with dried tears and dust streaked down his cheeks. His emotionless gaze was fixed on something, or perhaps nothing, far across the open land.

"We can't just leave him," Reuben said.

Gillam made it clear that not only *could* they leave him, but that it was exactly what they were going to do. He had organized the robbery, so he knew he would be accountable if things got out of hand. Killing the woman was bad enough, it was against the rules, but at least they could plead ignorance to the bosses and move camp further out until things blew over. Having a child involved complicated things, but knowingly executing him would only complicate things further.

Reuben looked at the child, and it became very obvious to him he was staring at himself through the eyes of the young Shoshone warrior all those years ago. He had always wondered why the warrior had not killed him, and realized, in that moment, the truth. Killing is wrong in the eyes of the law, but in nature it is natural. Killing a child, however, is against the laws of both. They could claim they were leaving the child for moral reasoning or camp codes all they wanted, but that wasn't any more true than the idea of Shoshones leaving him out of pity or malicious intent. It was cowardice.

Gillam demanded a response from Reuben. Reuben responded by walking over to the boy, putting his pistol to the back of his head, and pulling the trigger. The rest of the crew had rushed to try and stop him but were miles too late. They tackled him to the ground and ripped the gun from his hand.

After some heated debate that Reuben did not participate in, the crew decided they had broken enough rules for the day, and that killing one of their own would be one rule too many. *More cowardice*, Reuben thought to himself. Despite Gillam's objection, they instead opted to leave him stranded. Gillam warned him, should he survive being stranded, not to follow them back. When they got back to camp, they would tell everyone it was Reuben who made the robbery go wrong.

"They'll all hear how you went crazy and just started shootin' up the place," Gillam said. With a story like that, should he return, he would surely be shot on sight.

After they left, it took the rest of the day to track down the strayed Martin horse that had run off when the first shots were fired. He brought the horse back and finished rifling through the wagon's contents for whatever undesirable food and supplies the crew left behind, packing up slabs of salt pork and a few cans of preserved foods on the horse. He patted down the dead Martin family for anything else useful but found that only the boy had anything on him. The man's rifle and a pistol found in the woman's hand had both been taken by the crew, along with Reuben's weapons of course, but he found a small double-barrel derringer in the boy's pocket, probably given to him by the father before the shootout. In his vest pocket was a small notebook, which Reuben discovered was a diary. Thumbing through it, he saw the child wrote quite well. Better than Reuben, at least. The last few filled pages talked about packing up their home and how excited his father was to go out and live off the land. It included a crude drawing of their wagon with the names "Scout" and "Fox" written above the horses.

As he mounted the horse and readied himself to leave, he glanced east and saw the dark covered wagon lingering in the distance.

Riding a week later, Reuben was doing his best to ignore his tail while he continued in the direction of camp. He considered that if the wagon was the law, or some do-gooder that found the Martins, or even another gang, he would be leading them right to camp. But then again, if he allowed himself to think his actions all the way through, he knew the camp would already have been packed up and moved somewhere else. That was the rule after any botched job. Because of this, he was not surprised when he rounded the ridge that oversaw the campsite and saw no opened-up chuck wagons and tents where they had previously stood. He was, however, surprised to see a single horse grazing in the grass off to the side of the site.

Before he could get any closer, a plume of smoke emerged from the grass more than seventy-five yards away a moment before the bullet struck him. Fox bucked, sending him toppling backward and crashing to the hard ground. The horse ran off, and blood seeped through his shirt. He ripped it open to see the fresh open wound in his chest. He balled up the shirt and pressed it over the gushing wound, making his eyes water and teeth grind as he pressed harder to try and stop the bleeding.

"I told you not to come back here," he heard a voice call out, and he didn't need to look to know it was Gillam. Gillam was probably the only one in the camp both cocky and competent enough to make that shot on the first try. "It really was a shame, what you did to those poor Martin folks," he said as he approached Reuben, who was now curled up on the ground. "I told the others what you did," he said. Reuben looked up at him through wet eyes and saw him grinning down at him. "Now you know how they are about us takin' the life of one of our own, but after we told the boss about what you did, he agreed, of course."

Reuben spat out blood on the ground.

"Can't have you blabbin' about what we've been up to, can we?" he said with a smirk, now looming over Reuben. "Took you longer than I thought to get here," he said. "I've been campin' in that grass for three days, ya know. I was startin' to think you were gonna make me have to hunt you down like an animal."

Reuben drew another mouthful of blood mixed with snot and spit, and this time, spat it out across Gillam's black leather boot.

"Damn it, boy!" he shouted. He stepped back and tried to rub the cocktail of bodily fluids off in the dirt, giving Reuben the opening he was hoping for. He pulled the little derringer out of his pocket and fired the first round into Gillam's stomach. Gillam hunched over, clutching his belly and dropping his hat in the process. Reuben fired the second round into the top of his bald skull. Gillam collapsed to the ground, twitched twice, and died.

Reuben lay on the ground fading into the space between consciousness for what very well could have been hours before the triad of pitch-black horses finally rounded the ridge. Other than the sound of their feet punching the dirt like anvils being dropped from the sky, the horses made no sounds of any kind—not a whinny or a snort amongst them. They dragged behind them a covered wagon unlike anything Reuben had ever seen before. It was considerably larger than the old schooners or even Conestoga wagons, and instead of white canvas stretched over the bows, the whole thing was loosely draped in countless layers of black silk that flowed majestically in the still, windless air. The body of the wagon was the gray color of centuries-old petrified wood, and the wheels looked to be carved from solid stone.

Nobody sat on the driver's bench up front, yet the horses stopped the wagon abruptly when it came up alongside Reuben. The black silk parted as a figure emerged. "Hello, big brother," the figure said.

Reuben rubbed his eyes and focused on the girl. It was his sister, looking no different—nor older—than the day she was taken. "Sarah?"

"Yes, it's me," she said with a smile. "We've been waiting for you."

"Who?" Reuben asked.

"All of us," a new voice said from within the wagon. The silk parted again as his mother stepped out alongside his sister.

"I thought they would've killed you," Reuben said.

The silk parted for a third time, and Reuben's father stepped out and placed his hand on Sarah's shoulder. He looked at Reuben and smiled, but Reuben couldn't look away from his father's hair. The image of his father's scalped head in the wagon had overwritten the memory of his tidy, parted black hair so fully that he had forgotten what it looked like.

"They did, Reuben," his father said. "But we can all be together now."

"I don't understand," Reuben said. "You're all dead. Father, I watched you die."

"You did. And here is where we rest," he said, gesturing to the silk-covered wagon. "Isn't it beautiful? A pioneer's Valhalla. It welcomed us all those years ago, and it has chosen to welcome you, too. It's been following you for a very long time, Reuben. Are you ready to come aboard?"

"I don't think I can," Reuben said. "I'm hurt pretty bad here."

"It's okay, Reuben," his mother said. "Look down."

Reuben looked down and saw that he was now standing, and on the ground in front of him was his own discarded body, bloody and limp.

"Do you understand? It's okay, now. We can all be together here," his mother told him. "All you need to do is climb aboard. Come along, Reuben."

"I'm afraid," he said.

"Don't be," she said. "Come with us, Reuben. It will be just like when you were a boy. We can leave everything in the past behind you, to the east, and ride toward the never-ending horizon. We can ride west. Forever."

"West to where?" Reuben asked.

"We don't know," his father said. "And I don't know if we'll ever get there, but I reckon that isn't the point. It's about the journey, Reuben. A journey free from fear. With no pain, no hunger, no fear, not even a destination. Come along, we'll show you," he said. Reuben walked up to the sidestep of the wagon, and his father stretched his hand out to him.

"What if I don't want to go west?" Reuben asked.

His father frowned and furrowed his brow. "Don't be foolish, Reuben. There's nowhere else to go but west," his mother said. "Everything we ever desired is just inside this wagon, let me show you. Just come aboard, Reuben. Please?"

Reuben looked at his family, and glanced over his shoulder to the nothingness behind him. His body and the bloody ground it laid on had disappeared. "I'm sorry, Mother. I just don't think I can. I'm not the same boy you knew, and I stopped desiring anything a long time ago."

"But where will you go?" his mother asked.

"I suspect nowhere," Reuben said. "I think I'll just stay right here."

The wagon hesitated for a moment, but eventually, the horses started slowly walking forward. Reuben watched and said nothing as his family disappeared into the wagon, their souls swirling into the flowy fabric of the silk sheets to join the hundreds of other swirling souls in each of the infinite layers. After it disappeared, he remained where he was. He did not go west, nor any of the other three cardinal directions. He felt the ache of death and longing for life as he floated in the nothingness in between. He felt all of this, but he felt no regret.

Ladies After Nightfall

Kathryn Tennison

The best whiskey in town is what gets you there,
The ladies are what make you stay
In that rickety place by the old boneyard
That's all boarded up in the day

By sunlight it's quiet and dusty and dead
By moonlight it all comes to life
The satin-draped dames beckon you with a wink,
Their skin lily-white in the night

And if you awake with a bite on your neck
And vague recall of pleasure and pain
The thought of their eyes and their bloodred smiles
Makes you want to go right back again

Home-Grown Resistance

C. H. Lindsay

Granny Gertie kept one eye on her cards and one eye on the back door of the saloon. The unease she'd felt all day kept distracting her. So far, she'd washed her granddaughter's white dress with her red skirt, pulled up half a dozen flowers instead of weeds, and almost ruined the latest batch of moonshine. And now, she couldn't focus on her regular card game. Maximillian was coming back—and this time he'd be coming for Lily.

Reverend Bill picked up the card she discarded and laid his on the table. "Three tens. That's the third time you discarded the one I needed. Something bothering you tonight, Gertie?"

She wouldn't lie to a man of the cloth. That was the surest way to go to hell, and she'd seen enough hell for two lifetimes. But she could tell him a partial truth. "Sorry. Guess I'm feelin' a storm comin'." She rubbed her knee for emphasis. It just wasn't the type of storm he'd think it was.

He nodded his understanding. "That's three rounds you owe me." He nodded toward her knee. "Want to call it a night?"

With the way the day had gone so far, she shouldn't tempt fate. "Lily's last number's done, so best be goin'. Next time, it'll be your turn to pay."

She barely heard the reverend chuckle, feeling the sudden call echo in her bones. He found them. "Bill, will you do an old lady a favor?" She pushed her nearly full pint in his direction. "Bless my beer."

Gertie saw her granddaughter enter the saloon from backstage, her attention on the front window. By the expression on Lily's face, she felt the call, too.

"Your beer?" Bill gave the mug a puzzled frown, then looked back at Gertie. "Why?"

She blinked, pulling her attention away from her granddaughter. "My *bunica* once told me it eases rheumatism. It's better hot, but this will do." There were too many people around to use her slingshot, and if she pulled out her Jerusalem olive wood knitting needles and stabbed him in the heart, people would think it was murder. She learned long ago they only saw what they wanted to see.

The scent of extreme age and old blood became stronger than beer and cigar smoke. He had to be just outside. She mentally urged the reverend to hurry. If this didn't work, someone could die—or worse.

Reverend Bill shook his head and chuckled. "I don't think blessing your beer will help with that, but it shouldn't hurt." He made the sign of the cross with two fingers and muttered a few words over her drink.

"Thank you, Bill." Gertie's hand began to tremble. Her granddaughter was moving in short, stiff bursts toward the swinging doors, her hands clenched at her sides.

A gut-wrenching fear made Gertie feel nauseous. She was too old—and too unprepared—for this.

All conversation in the saloon stopped as a tall, pale man dressed in a black top hat and frock coat walked in, his dress indicating he came from Europe. His cold gaze scanned the room until he saw Lily. He inhaled on a slow hiss. "At last."

Reverend Bill's hand reached for the crucifix around his neck, looking from the man to Lily and back. Everyone else in the room continued to watch the stranger.

Except Gertie. The old woman grabbed her glass and stood. "Leave Lily alone, Maximilian! You are not welcome here."

"*Buna* Gertruda. I can't say it's a pleasure." He didn't look at her, his attention locked on Lily. "Your granddaughter is even more beautiful than you were."

Maximilian held out his hand to Lily. "It is time. Come with me."

Lily looked at her grandmother in a silent plea for help. Her knuckles were white as she fisted them in her skirts.

"I said leave her alone," Gertie growled, her grip on the beer tightening.

Maximilian's hand was still extended imperiously to Lily as he glided toward her, his gaze intent on his prey. "You know I come for her. Do not interfere again."

He was only a few feet away now—but so was Lily. "Go to hell." Gertie said a silent prayer—for help or forgiveness, she wasn't sure which—and flung her beer, glass, and all, at Maximilian.

He turned his hand and blocked the glass, but a good portion of beer splashed on it and his face, sizzling where it hit. He swore in a language Gertie recognized from her childhood and was gone before anyone else got a good look at the beer burns.

"Gertie...who was that?" the reverend asked, still holding his cross as the doors stopped swinging.

"Not here. Come by in the morning," she said, picking up her bag and tossing a few coins onto the table. "I'll explain what I can." Right now, she needed to get home with Lily where it was safe—if anywhere could be truly safe now.

Gertie tossed and turned until she gave up on sleep. She'd finished the mending, washed the dishes, cleaned the cottage, swept the front porch, and had a kettle of water heating on the wood stove before the reverend arrived.

"Good morning," he said after she let him in. He removed his hat and looked around the room. "That's an odd combination." He nodded to the string of garlic and the cross on the mantle of the fireplace

"The garlic is an herb my *bunica* used to ward off evil, and the cross is because this is a Christian home." Her tone was a little brusque as she was unsure if he meant it as a criticism.

He held a hand up to prevent further explanations. "I was merely curious, as it was not here the last time I visited." He continued to look around the cottage, pausing at the knitted shawl dotted with silver beads that draped over one of two rocking chairs beside the fire.

She wondered why he was so curious about her protections this time; but if he wasn't going to ask, she wasn't going to explain. "Tea's almost ready." She led the way to the kitchen at the back of the room, still unsure what to say to him about Maximilian.

The reverend glanced around again. "Where's Lily this morning?"

"She's working in the garden. Best to do it before it gets too hot." Gertie tried to sound nonchalant, but she could hear the tightness in her voice.

"Is that wise?" He raised an eyebrow as his gaze focused on the older woman. "Won't her gentleman accost her there?"

"He's not her gentleman!" She grabbed the kettle and thunked it on the trivet. "She wants nothing to do with him. Besides, he won't come until full dark."

"Why?"

Gertie straightened, taking a moment before she responded. "That... man... is a creature of darkness."

Bill put his hand to his cross. "What do you mean by *creature of darkness?*"

She took out a ball of tea and dropped it in the kettle with a bit too much force. "He's from the old country, same as my family." She wiped up the water that splashed on the table to keep from looking at him, then took another moment to inhale the scent of chamomile and peppermint tea "His kind are called vampyr."

Bill made a quick, guttural noise. "Vampires do not exist, except in old wives' tales."

"They're real, and they've existed for centuries." She plunked a plate of molasses cookies on the table. Folding her arms, she glared at him. "You felt the darkness last night. I saw you hold your cross. Like everyone else, you couldn't stop watching him. Didn'ya think somethin' was wrong when all the talkin' stopped? Even Lily couldn't resist, and I've been teachin' her how to protect herself since she was ten."

His lips tightened. "You're mistaken. You must be mistaken."

The door to the garden opened, bringing the scents of wild roses and lemon grass into the cottage. "She's not. Everything she said is true." Lily paused in the doorway, sunlight casting a halo around her for a moment before she went over to the reverend. "If you won't help us, then give us sanctuary in the church. It's the only place we can be completely safe."

"No." Gertie shook her head with enough force that a gray strand came loose from its bun. She unfolded her arms and watched her granddaughter for a long moment. "If you do, he'll be furious, and someone will die. Someone always dies before he leaves."

"Why would someone die if I give you sanctuary?" he asked Lily.

"Because Maximilian wants Lily at any cost." Gertie took out three cups and poured the tea, setting one in front of the reverend. "He'll need to heal after what I done to him last night. That alone may cause him to feed. If he can't have her, he'll go after others 'til she gives in or we stop him."

"You only threw your beer at him. How could that possibly cause him harm?" Reverend Bill shook his head, denying what she said. "And there are no vampires."

"Didn'ya see the burns on his hands an' face?" Gertie waved for Lily to sit down. She hoped with them sitting around the table, she and Lily could make him understand. "That's why it needed to be blessed. It's one of the few things that hurts him."

"No!" He shook his head and stood. "That's preposterous."

"Please." Lily put a hand on his arm. "Believe her... us. We don't want anyone to die this time."

He pulled away and turned back to Lily, his eyes wide. "This time?"

"He came for me forty years ago." It was Gertie that answered. "Because I was hiding in the church, four people died before he was driven off. One of them was my mother."

The reverend clasped and unclasped his hands. "I've lived in these parts for most of my life. Surely I would have heard... something."

"It happened up north in Dry Gulch. The newspaper said a foreigner made everyone in the house sick. Truth was, the priest didn't want people to know it was on account of all the blood being sucked out of their bodies, so he said it was a plague and had the house burned down." She picked up a cookie for something to hold. "I left as soon as I could get away without bein' seen."

Reverend Bill made the sign of the cross as he backed away. "I will pray for both of you, but I cannot accept this... nonsense." He turned and strode out the door.

Lily wound a lock of hair around her finger and turned to her grandmother. "Were we wrong to tell him?"

"No. He needs to understand. I just hope he sees sense before it's too late."

To keep herself busy until nightfall, Gertie made yeast-free rolls peppered with chunks of garlic—far more than she would ever use if she was going to eat them. But these were for Maximilian. She brought a wooden bench outside and set the balls of dough in the sunlight to harden.

Lily turned from weeding beneath the wild rose bushes that covered a wooden cross near the back door. "We have three dozen already."

"May not be enough. We gotta be ready if Maximilian comes after you—us—tonight." Gertie had no intention of sacrificing her life for Lily if she could help it. She put a hand over her stomach to ease the knot inside and breathed in the familiar scents of roses, hawthorn, and herbs. Definitely getting too old for this.

"Do you know where he sleeps? Can we find his coffin and stop him first?" Lily stood and dusted dirt off her long skirt.

The old woman shook her head. "No. 'Sides, it's too dangerous to go searchin' for him." She looked at the cottage. "I sure wish Reverend Bill would see sense. Could use his help with all this."

"You wanted him to bless the moonshine, didn't you? Will the garlic infusion be enough?" Lily dumped the weeds in the composting barrel, added a layer of soil, and sprinkled them with water.

"Ain't never tried garlic-infused moonshine on a vampyr before." Gertie adjusted the tray of garlic rolls. "Dunno if it'll work the way I hope. But I did use holy water in the batch I'm makin'."

She flashed her granddaughter an impish grin. "Maggie met a travelin' minister at the hotel. Knew I was lookin' for more holy water. She only wanted three jugs of moonshine and my chocolate cookie recipe for it."

The younger woman stopped pumping water into a bucket to face her grandmother. "How much holy water did you get?"

"Ain't sayin'." Gertie smoothed her gray hair, tucking the loose strand back in the bun. "Just gonna say he had a powerful thirst for local brew."

"But what if he asks Reverend Bill about it?"

Gertie laughed and slapped the side of her leg. "As much as he drank, he ain't gonna remember comin' here at all." It was the first time she had been able to share the story. She continued chuckling as she went into the grove of trees to check on her still.

Granny Gertie sat in the garden beside the rose-covered cross, the silver-beaded shawl draped around her shoulders. Every few minutes, she glanced up from her knitting to the lanterns, wondering when Maximilian would come. It was late, and she'd felt his presence in town for a while. She put a hand to her throat, tracing the small silver chain and cross. It cost her a pretty penny, but it would be worth it if she and Lily survived the night.

Lily rubbed garlic and lemon grass oil on her neck for the third time. "Are you sure he'll come?"

"Yes. Ain't sure if it'll be tonight or if he'll wait to catch us off guard." She finished and slipped the knitting needles into her skirt pocket before draping a silver-beaded scarf around her granddaughter's neck. "That'll help."

In return, Lily put a handful of garlic bread balls into her grandmother's pocket. "You'll need some of those."

"You'll be needin' 'em more." She walked around the perimeter of the garden, hoping this wasn't the last time she'd see it. She was getting anxious, and that would do her—and Lily—no good. She had to remain focused and calm.

The sound of a twig snaping and something brushing past the bushes at the side of the cottage startled both women. Gertie slipped a hand into her pocket and wrapped it around a knitting needle for protection.

"Is it...?" Lily whispered.

"No. You'd feel him, like before." Even so, she wondered if it was one of his acolytes. She let go of the wood and grabbed three garlic balls so she could keep her distance.

"Gertie? Lily?" a voice called from beyond the gate.

"Bill. What're you doing here?" If he came to apologize, it should wait until morning.

"I knocked, but you didn't answer. So, I came around back to see if you were well." He stared at Lily's scarf over the gate.

"Why?" Her gut told her there was something wrong, and she didn't care if she sounded cantankerous.

"We're fine. Come on back, Reverend." Lily moved to the gate to greet him.

"No. Stay back, Lily!"

"Oh, for heaven's sake, Gertie." He put a hand on the latch and opened the gate. "I came to talk with you on behalf of a suitor."

"At this time of night?"

Just then, Lily gasped and put a hand to her scarf, moving closer to her grandmother.

Gertie felt him, too. Following her gut, she turned and threw all three garlic balls at the bat that flew into the garden, clipping its wing.

Before it could hit the ground, the bat became Maximilian.

"Bill, help or get out of the way!" Gertie didn't wait for his answer, throwing three more balls of garlic bread at the vampyr.

The reverend was visibly shaking, but he put one hand on his cross and stepped forward. "I command you to return to whatever hell spawned you."

In two strides, Maximilian was in front of him. "You haven't the power to command me!" He backhanded the reverend, who hit his head against the cross and slumped to the ground.

Gertie couldn't think about Bill right now. She used the distraction to grab her granddaughter's arm and run into the woods.

"You can't hide from me, Lily. I know your scent." Maximilian taunted from the garden. "If you love Gertruda, come to me now."

Lily hesitated.

"Don't listen," Gertie hissed, grabbing her granddaughter by the ends of her scarf, and pulling her toward the still at the edge of a clearing. "Get your slingshot ready."

Lily fumbled in her pocket and pulled it out, along with three balls of garlic bread.

Maximilian followed them through the trees, nonchalantly stepping on twigs so they would hear him coming. "You will never get away from me. It is useless to try."

But that wasn't Gertie's plan. She closed off the steam valve on the still and picked up the end of the hose attachment. She had one chance to make this work—as long as she didn't miss.

Lily turned once she got far enough into the grove and loaded a ball into her slingshot. As soon as she saw Maximilian, she shot him in the chest. She loaded it again and hit him on his cheek. He hesitated just long enough for her to grab three more balls. She hit him with two of them, but he continued to come after her.

Before she could grab more balls, he caught her by the arm. "Enough games." With his other hand, he reached for her scarf. As soon as he touched the silver, he cried out and stepped back.

Just then, a blast of hot, garlic-infused moonshine soaked his face and clothing. He lunged for Gertie, but she stepped aside. Instead, he fell into her still, knocking it over and spilling the rest of its contents.

"Help me," Gertie called, slipping in the mud as she tried to roll Maximilian over.

It took both of them, but they soon had him on his back. His exposed flesh was covered in blisters.

"One more thing." Gertie took a minute to catch her breath, then pulled out her two knitting needles and plunged them into his heart. Black blood oozed from the wound as his body jerked once then lay still.

"Is he dead?" Lily bent over him, curious at his reaction to both the holy moonshine and the knitting needles.

"He's not completely dead, so best stay back." She looked at Maximilian. "I wonder why he barely reacted to the garlic balls." But she knew she wasn't going to get any answers. "Come on, we have to get him into the open. We won't be safe until the sun rises."

Once he was sprawled in the middle of the clearing, Gertie made sure the olive wood needles were properly staked into his heart. "We hafta keep watch 'til dawn."

They heard someone coming along the path through the trees and stood, blocking the view of the body. "Hallo?" Gertie called.

Reverend Bill stumbled out of the trees, rubbing the back of his head. When he saw Lily, he stopped. "Where is your fiancé?"

She looked confused. "My what?"

"Maximilian. He came to the church in search of you."

"The two women glanced at each other and turned back to the reverend. Gertie frowned. "He ain't her fiancé."

"I know arranged marriages aren't common, but he had a letter signed by Lily's parents. The document is legally binding."

"Lily's folks've been dead for more'n ten years." Gertie was surprised the reverend didn't remember that.

"What are you trying to hide?" He moved to look past the two women and froze. "You killed him?"

"Not yet." Gertie put her hands on his arms and pushed him back. "He hit you and tried to kill us. It's our right to protect ourselves."

He shook her off and turned to Lily. "We have to get the sheriff. I'll explain that you felt threatened by him. I'm sure you won't hang."

Lily huffed and punched him in the jaw, knocking him out again.

"Lily!" Gertie ran to make sure the reverend hadn't hit his head again. "Nicely done. You clean him up, and I'll put the still to rights. Then we'll take him inside and..." She hesitated, not sure exactly how they were going to make it look like he imagined the whole thing.

"No." Lily grinned. "I have a better idea. Help me move him over by the still."

Lily directed her grandmother to lay the reverend in the underbrush next to the still, so it looked like he'd been there on purpose. Then she carefully drizzled moonshine into his mouth and onto his clothing so he'd have the taste and smell of it. "Now we wait until sunrise. Then there'll be no sign of the body, just the reverend who came by to sample your new batch."

Gertie chuckled. "That's my girl. There's a few jugs set aside for emergencies. We'll drink to you not gettin' hitched and leave the rest with Bill."

The reverend woke with the first rays of sun. It took him several tries before he could sit up. "What happened?"

Gertie was playing a game of solitaire on the bench that was now by the still. She turned when she heard Bill. "Guess I made that batch a bit too strong. That, or you lost your head for hootch." She chuckled at her joke.

He shook his head once, then put his hand to it and groaned. "I never drink moonshine."

"You did last night." Lily came into the clearing and held up a half-empty jug. "You wanted to try Grannie's new garlic flavored brew."

"Garlic?" Bill turned toward Lily, then stopped halfway, staring into the clearing. "Is that Maximilian?" He stumbled to his feet to get a better look. Just then, the sun broke over the trees and bathed the clearing in light. Smoke began to rise off the vampyr. He burst in to flames and then turned to dust.

"Impossible." Bill put his hand to his head again.

"It's not impossible. The sun rises every morning." Lily slipped her hand through his arm and led him back to the grass.

"Not that... Oh, never mind." He took the jug from her, sat on the ground, and got quietly drunk.

The two women removed what was left of Maximilian, scattering the ashes across the stream at the back of the property. When they were finished, Lily checked that the reverend was asleep.

"He won't remember none of this once he's sober." Gertie looked at the deck of cards and began to chuckle. "I think we should go to the saloon tonight to celebrate. Bill promised me another game of cards, and I'm feeling lucky."

Lily grinned. "I think I'll join you. After this, I'm feeling lucky, too."

Forty Miles From Hell

Robert DeLeskie

Nevada, 1869

The man chained to the post had no fingers. According to Charlie, the big orderly, Walter Biltmore had done the work himself.

"Dynamite?" Henry Solms felt a sympathetic pang in the stub of his ring finger, mangled by a Minnie ball during the rout at Manassas Junction in '61.

"Teeth." Charlie spit a dark spume of tobacco then dragged the sleeve of his Federal blue sack coat across his mouth. "His own. But you needn't worry. Dentist took 'em all out."

Biltmore grinned, revealing a pink hole.

"Can't eat nothing but grits, thanks to you lot." He waggled his crudely cauterized stumps at Charlie, then at Solms.

Solms adjusted his hat. There was no shade in the dirt yard. Still, the commandant had insisted the conditions for parley would be more genial outdoors than inside the Warm Spring Hotel, as the Carson City prison was known.

"You know Gerloff Van Oordt." A statement not a question. Biltmore showed no reaction to the name or to the fat fly making its way across his forehead. "He hired you to transport his belongings to California."

"I reckon he did."

"But you didn't."

"No sir, I did not. Calamitous circumstances prevented me from doing so." Each plosive sent a spray of spittle arcing from Biltmore's lips.

"What calamitous circumstances?"

"I'm not at liberty to discuss. I signed an agreement of confidentiality."

"With who?"

"Mr. Van Oordt."

"*I'm* working for Van Oordt. *You* were supposed to deliver his possessions to San Francisco by September 1st. You didn't, so he hired me to find his things. I want to know where they are."

"Can't say I rightly know."

"Can't or won't?"

Biltmore's face twisted, eyes rolled up to the whites, his body straining against the chains with such force that Solms expected his shoulders to pop.

"He does this," said Charlie. "He'll be okay in a moment."

During the war, Solms had watched men try to match physical strength against agonizing or shameful memories, a contest as vain and futile as wrestling with the wind. But defeat and the humility that followed sometimes loosened their lips.

The fit subsided, and Biltmore's eyes sharpened. "Guess the grits don't agree with me." His gaze fixed on Solms like he was staring down the iron sights of a rifle barrel. "Now let me ask you a question. You ever meet Mr. Van Oordt? I mean in person."

"No." The contract had been arranged by telegram between the Pinkerton offices in Chicago and Sacramento. From what little Solms managed to glean before setting out, Van Oordt was some eastern bigwig heading West like half the country seemed to be. He'd sent his chattel ahead by wagon, no doubt planning to make the journey in greater comfort on the new railway.

"Oh, he'd like you. Straight-to-the-point, no fancy talk or messing around. He likes that sort."

"I don't give a rat's ass what he likes. He's paying my boss who's paying me to find his things. That's why we're both standing out here melting in the sun."

"You think that's the reason?" Biltmore giggled. Unperturbed, the fly crawled along the swollen ridge of his lip.

"What else would it be?"

Biltmore fixed him once more.

"When the word is given, every man must put his back to the harness. But men aren't mules or oxen, are they? They are sheep. And what do sheep require if not a shepherd?" Biltmore's slug-like tongue darted out and enveloped the fly.

"You're gonna make me ride out into that goddamn desert, aren't you?"

Biltmore snickered, swallowed.

"I'm done here." Solms tossed Charlie a half-dollar and started towards the gate.

"Where's my recompense?"

"You didn't give me nothing."

"And for that I will be richly rewarded. But let me offer you a word of advice, free of charge."

"What's that?" Solms slowed but didn't look back.

"Quit this job while you still got something worth quitting for."

Solms kept walking, thinking of Biltmore's missing fingers, his missing teeth.

Solms despised anything that sent him eastward. Riding out of Carson City in the crimson stillness of dawn, trailing two horses and enough provisions for a week, he feared some current might sweep him up and convey him across the desert, past the mountains and plains and forests, all the way back to Connecticut, to the scrap of land where his father, mother, and sister lay buried, all ghosts now, or at least he hoped they were. But he'd never allow himself to be transported thus. He'd shoot the horses—and himself if need be—first. Of course, there'd be no need to waste the ammunition; the waterless tract of the Lahontan Valley would devour him first, without urging or compunction.

And yet, Walter Biltmore had wandered out of that shadowless vale, the stretch of hell-on-earth between the Humboldt Sink and the Carson River that emigrants called the Forty Mile Desert, and so Solms rode there now, reassuring himself that *into* was not the same as *across*.

The border of hell was Ragtown, where the worst of the desert ended at the banks of the meandering Carson River. Cresting a rise, Solms gazed down at the figures scattered along the riverbend like so much flotsam and jetsam after a storm. Yellow with dust, tongues lolling like dumb cattle called to pasture, they moved with the gait of stiff-legged revenants, splashing into the shallow, silty stream, drinking and bathing in eerie silence, as though incredulous to still be alive. The discarded clothes that carpeted the bank, limp and lifeless as victims of a battlefield slaughter, lent the place its name. A fog of stench lay over the valley—unwashed bodies, the stale reek of exhausted people and animals, and something worse. Not all the unmoving heaps were empty rags.

Hand me the light, son.

The carrion reek cast his mind backwards. He was thirteen, his breath misting the November night air. In the ghastly flicker of an oil lantern, his twin sister Rose's face, unsunken despite a month underground, a paler shade of white than the snow that surrounded her disturbed grave, radiated an unearthly beauty. Were it not for the smell, he'd have sworn she was just sleeping.

Hand me the light, son. His father traded him an antler-handled hunting knife for the lamp. It took Solms a moment to understand the significance of the exchange. Afterwards, he never blamed his father for making him undertake the grisly task. How could anyone butcher the body of their own child?

"What's your business here?" Two men on horses approached. Their freshly starched shirts set them apart from the wretches on the riverbank.

More than two. A third man sat straight-backed on his horse near a shack two hundred yards from the river, a rifle resting across his forearm. That was likely to be Asa Kenyon, who allowed the emigres to use his stretch of the river, the better to sell them horses and supplies at usurious prices. Where and how he acquired his inventory was a question no one dared ask him.

"I'm looking for a train that might have come through here. The Wilkins party. Ten wagons, maybe a month ago. One of the wagons had a red bonnet."

"Never heard of 'em. But lots don't make it through."

"You think Asa might know?"

"Who's asking?"

"A man with money. But he'll pay for his possessions, not information."

The two men exchanged a look.

"He might," said the smaller of the two, removing his bowler and picking at the bald pate beneath. "But I wouldn't ask him right now. He's in a particular foul mood."

"On account of what?"

"That wouldn't exactly be your business, would it?"

Kenyon didn't have Van Oordt's things, Solms decided. If he did, these men would have sent him chasing a false trail to the Sierras. Still, they had the aspect of men who knew more than they let on.

"I'll be riding back through here a week from now. Maybe Asa will remember something. Or maybe you will. Like I said, I have a man who wants his things and doesn't care what it costs."

"You sure about that? Things can cost an awful lot out these parts."

"He'll pay. Be sure to let Asa know." Solms wheeled his horse around in the direction of Carson City. Best let them think he'd given up.

Two miles outside of Ragtown, he doubled back, cutting a long arc to carry him past the fence line north of the Kenyon ranch. He was headed to the desert to have a look for himself.

It took two days of hot, dusty riding to find what remained of the wagon train.

Heaped wood and tattered canvas formed a crude circle, like rotted, ground-down teeth embedded in the baked earth. Feeding insects and desert dryness had done their work, the carcasses already starting their slow, putrefying melt into the landscape. The air was still, and absolute silence prevailed, as if life itself would not brook the place. Even the sun hid behind a tombstone grey bank of clouds.

The Wilkins party did not die easily.

Solms began in the middle of the corral and worked his way outwards. A night attack, the charred remains of campfires told him. Overturned tin plates and cooking utensils testified to a surprise assault, a night of smoke and flame.

Two dozen corpses lay scattered around the inside of the circle, matching the number of men, women, and children belonging to the Wilkins party. The bodies that weren't burned were in an advanced state of decay, tanned skin pulled tight over bones. On the north side of the corral, a smashed and trampled wagon testified to where the penned animals had broken out, no doubt in a wild panic spurred by the conflagration, the jumbled trail pointing deeper into the desert. Curiously, he saw no indication they'd been rustled by the attackers.

Also curious were the arrows scattered like matchsticks around the camp. Paiute design, fashioned with enough skill to convince naive travelers stumbling over the scene to dutifully report an Indian attack to the first soldiers they met. But Paiutes raided to capture flocks and herds, relying on stealth, not siege. These attackers were bandits, perhaps even Asa Kenyon's men, after whatever valuables they could haul away, and indifferent to what price the fire demanded. But then how to account for the pay chest, half sunk into the earth, blackened but intact?

He counted nine wagons. One missing—the one with the red bonnet that carried Van Oordt's cargo. So, the story didn't end here.

It didn't take him long to find the ruts, a solitary trail headed westward. He thought to follow, to hasten things to a conclusion, but the sun was already high. Even in October, it was foolish and perhaps deadly to travel in the full heat of day. Still, he wanted to put some distance between himself and the scene of the massacre.

When blue dusk fell and shadows obscured the trail, he made camp in a gulch. The dry desert air gave up its heat, and he shivered next to the little fire he made from scraps of wagon wood.

His reflections turned to Rose, his sister, his bright star. Sparrows would alight on her outstretched hand, and strange dogs calmed their barking and bowed in her presence. She entered the world mere minutes before him, and thenceforward was the first in all things; the first to talk, to walk, to read. And when consumption tore through Jewett City like a wildfire in their unlucky, thirteenth summer, she'd been the first to die.

And the first to come back.

Now, she stood on the dark plain before him, her white shift glowing in the moonlight.

Turn around, she said. *This is not the way for you.*

"Rose—"

Go back. Then she transformed into the vile thing she had become after death. He woke up screaming.

At the first sight of dawn, he resumed his course, following the wagon tracks. When the sun was midway along its morning rise, he spied a wound slashed into the desert. A red bonnet, splayed over sun-bleached bones that thrust from the sand like a ruined chariot from mythological times, harnessed to the mummified bodies of men, twisted in a tableau of misery, bent like beasts of burden straining at the leather.

He examined the corpses with grim curiosity. Eyeless wrecks dressed in breechcloths and leggings made from sagebrush bark. Their post-mortem beards betrayed them; these were white men who died in their make-believe costumes. What threat of punishment or promise of reward could have compelled them to take up the harness and kept them tethered until death? Solms counted, finding an odd number and an empty yolk. Biltmore?

When the word is given, every man must put his back to the harness, the madman had said. But how had Biltmore found himself hitched to his own wagon? And who had been the driver?

In the half-sunken remains of the schooner, he found boxes filled with Midwestern finery—wool suits and dyed-cotton shirts, boxes of silk hats, crystal glassware packed in straw, cases of silver flatware, bone china wrapped in pages of *The Tribune*, a French table clock, a stack of rosewood chairs. He matched each item against the crumpled bill of lading he pulled from his pocket.

Near the front of the wagon he discovered what the waybill described as "a great wooden chest." Peering over the lip, he saw a layer of rich, dark earth lining the bottom. Then the smell hit him, and he recoiled, practically rolling over himself to escape. He vomited, but the crypt smell, rank yet sweet, still filled his nostrils.

I tried to warn you. Maybe it was Rose, or maybe just his own mind mocking him.

To hell with the job, with Van Oordt, with Pinkerton too. He'd tell them he went to the desert and found nothing. Let the Lahontan keep the wagon and its secrets and let him keep his.

It was an hour past sunset when the moon-shadow passed over him. A buzzard, happy to keep him company in case he or one of his horses should stumble and provide it with an opportune meal. He craned his neck to track it, but the shape vanished into the indigo fabric of the night. Perhaps he wasn't destined to be a meal anytime soon. Just as this auspicious sign began to lift his spirits, the shape reappeared, gliding across the face of the moon, larger than any bird he had ever seen. Then it descended.

All around him was a confused fury of leathery wings and glimpses of a screeching, mammalian head. His horse screamed, and then Solms was lifted from his saddle. Below, his animals scattered in terror, growing small on the moon-dappled plain. An instant to appreciate the view, then he was falling towards a pool of quicksilver, weightless for a moment, the earth rising up fast as a fist, and then everything went black.

He came to in the cold night, the moon already past its zenith in the velvet firmament. Pain lanced through his side when he pressed his palms against his knees to stand; his ribs were sprained or dislocated, but through some miracle nothing was broken. He could still walk.

A glint of silver, thin as the edge of a knife, hovered in the distance; the moon reflecting off the angled roof of a barn. Soon, he came upon a fence that curved in a long bend towards a clutch of buildings. The odor of sheep shit caused his heart to swell. He might not die out here after all.

The buildings were dark silhouettes against the crest of a moon-dripped rise—on a cloudy night he would have walked right past the farm. He made his approach slowly but without trying to conceal himself. A lone stranger wandering at this ungodly hour was as likely to get shot as offered shelter. He'd slip into the barn to sleep, wake before sunrise, then fall on the mercy of the ranchers.

The wind stirred, carrying a whiff of fetor and the wordless murmur of dumb animal grunts. The smell ripened into a stew of sweat and sewage as he approached the barn. It was a strange farm that locked in the sheep at night.

You should leave. The voice sounded like Rose; he was sure this time. But he had nowhere to go. Without map or compass or water, death lay in every direction.

Solms lifted the length of raw timber that barred the barn door. Hands reached out and grabbed him, pulling him into the stinking darkness, smothering him in a nearly lightless void made of flesh, reeking blasts of breath, and witless moans. A mad, shuffling procession around and around. His feet tripped over something that lay on the floor, and he grasped wildly at hair, pliant skin, anything to keep from falling to the ground, slick with offal. A small, soft hand slid into his with an almost obscene familiarity. In a narrow shaft of moonlight, he glimpsed a child, a girl of no more than eight years.

Around and around they went. He glimpsed the pale silver of the doorway and pushed towards it, eliciting idiot shrieks and growls from the shambling mob. Reaching the door, he glanced down at the girl's pallid face, her dull, dead eyes. He tore his hand free and threw himself outside. Quickly, he barred the door, though none of the wretches made any move to escape. Perhaps the very concept had passed beyond their comprehension. He staggered away from the barn.

From somewhere behind him came the soft crunch of gravel. Turning, he saw a silhouette glide into a poured patch of spectral light, and with fear-fueled clarity, Solms focused on the image of a man. A hairless pate gleamed above porcine eyes, a soft nose, and plump lips. Thin shoulders and spindly arms and legs seemed at odds with the bulbous, distended belly. He was naked.

"Hello, friend. There's nothing to fear." The man spoke with an accent Solms guessed was German or Dutch. "Why don't you put away your pistol and we can talk like civilized men, yes?" Solms had drawn his gun from instinct. He lowered his aim but did not holster the weapon.

"Who am I speaking to?"

"My name is Van Oordt, lately of Chicago, Illinois. I am newly arrived in these parts. And who would you be?"

Solms' mind reeled. "Henry Solms. I work for you."

"I don't recall hiring anyone by that name."

"Your lawyer contracted the Pinkerton Detective Agency to find and retrieve your possessions. I've done more than that it seems."

"How fascinating! And do you have a means of transporting my things away from this ghastly place?"

The grim absurdity of the situation nearly caused Solms to laugh, yet he knew he was in grave danger. He tried to ready his gun, to raise it, but his arm felt leaden with fatigue.

"I—I'll need to come back with men and horses. But it's doable."

"I must commend my lawyer. You seem a very capable fellow. Are you equally discreet?"

"People pay me to keep my mouth shut. No one's ever asked for their money back."

Van Oordt was suddenly beside him, his hand resting softly on Solms' shoulder. "I apologize for my biblical state, but my belly seems to have outgrown my clothes. I have overindulged."

"It—it's of no matter to me." Solms wanted to shrug off Van Oordt's clammy hand, but his body wouldn't obey.

"A fellow sophisticate, how refreshing. Well, you see, I'm in a bit of a jam. You see how pale I am?" He held out his arm, white like a fish's belly. "I am albino. Do you know what that means? I must avoid the sun."

"Then I reckon you came to the wrong goddamn place."

"Don't be rude. I'm offering you a job. Excellent pay, too."

"What is it you want me to do?" His tongue felt thick. He thought of Biltmore's toothless lisp.

"I would still like to go to California and require someone to make arrangements for my conveyance, and to help me get established once I arrive. I hired a man, but he went mad. I understand the desert does that to some people. I would like you to replace him as my attaché."

"I—I might need some time...to think about that." Solm's own words seemed distant, as though he was merely a bystander to a conversation taking place at the limits of his perception.

"Time? There is nothing here but time." Van Oordt waved his hand towards the vast nullity that surrounded them. "Do you feel it? This is an old, old place. Eons ago, it was the bottom of a lake. Can you believe that? More recently, there was an Indian encampment on this very spot. A rancher murdered the inhabitants. Then he killed the men who came to avenge them. He built his house here, right over their bones. He was very proud of himself. So, I slit his belly and bid him meditate on the subject of hubris. I fed and watered him for three nights to give him more time to reflect. Then I grew bored and ate half his family. I don't know where he is. In fact, he might still be alive somewhere. Not that I care about the poor Indians he slaughtered, you understand, but I consider myself something of an ironist. Am I boring you?"

"It's—it's been a long day." Solms could barely keep his eyes open.

"Understandable. Then we have an agreement?"

Solms' tongue was frozen. He tried to speak, to utter the single word that would reject Van Oordt's proposition, but the only sound he produced was a dull groan.

"Let us consider that a 'yes.' And now we seal the deal."

Van Oordt pressed him into the dust with the ease of a parent laying an infant in a crib. Teeth opened his neck. Stars occluded his vision, and the world grew dim. The only sounds he heard were Van Oordt's low, satisfied moans as he nursed. Finally, Van Oordt rolled off him.

"You think me foul and grotesque. But we are no different. Your kind came to fatten yourselves off this land like hungry ticks, taking what isn't yours, leaving ruin and carnage in your wake. But even ticks have ticks. And I do not waste a drop."

Van Oordt towered over him. In the darkness, he seemed a shadow inside a shadow.

"When you wake, you will go and find as many men as you need and promise them whatever they ask for. Work with haste. Each passing day we are separated will grow more terrible for you. You found me through that fool Biltmore, no doubt. His future awaits you if you stray from our pact."

The unnatural heaviness lifted, and Solms knew at once he was alone. He tried to stand, but anemia set his head spinning and the earth pulled him down. Pressing a hand to his neck, he found the wound already sticky and clotted. He curled into a ball against the cold and lay this way through the waning hours of the night, time seeming to stagger forward through dreamless ellipses, until the sun rose high enough to limber his arms and legs. When he stood, his pockets were weighted down. Inside each, he found a handful of gold coins, stamped with the likenesses of kings and queens he didn't recognize.

His horses were tied to a nearby post, tack heaped next to them. As he expected, Van Oordt had no interest in the contents, and the sheathed knife was still lashed to his saddle. Ever since his father had traded him for the lamp, Solms had kept the antler-handled blade close.

Though he was not a religious man, the circumstances in which he found himself and the uniqueness of his ability to respond made him question whether providence had indeed played a role. Had some divine hand guided him, subtly directing his affairs until the moment he walked into the Pinkerton Detective Agency in Sacramento and received this assignment? Ultimately, it didn't matter whether fate or fortune had delivered him to this moment. The actions he would take today were not merely those of self-preservation. An opportunity to right the balance of the cosmic scales had been afforded him by some power beyond his comprehension.

Solms intended to make the most of it.

He deduced Van Oordt was a different order of creature than what his sister had become, something greater, though they were clearly related. A week after Rose had died from what the doctor diagnosed as consumption, he accosted her leaving their mother's room, lips dripping with gore, eyes wild as a hungry animal. She seemed incapable of speech. In that way, she resembled the poor creatures Van Oordt kept for food in the barn rather than Van Oordt himself. But undoubtedly Van Oordt, or something like him, had been the source of her affliction. Whether or not he was the monster who had transformed his sister, Van Oordt had to be killed, and Solms had some thoughts, and—he hoped—knowledge about how that might be accomplished.

The morning was already gone. There were perhaps six hours of full sunlight left, but they would go quickly, and he would get no second chance.

Some distance behind the farm house, he located the roof of a root cellar; an obvious place to start. A half-dozen uneven wooden steps led him down to a latched door that opened into a pitch-black chamber. He dug a box of matches from his pocket and struck one against his heel. The chamber was cryptlike, the walls re-enforced with roughhewn stone and wood, shelves burdened with baskets of parsnips, potatoes, and rutabagas. Leaned against the wall was a shovel. He used it to poke at the bare earth floor, but there was no sign it had been disturbed. Van Oordt was nested elsewhere.

The front door of the farmhouse was unlocked. Inside, a fine layer of sand covered the floor; the desert had already begun its work of reclamation. There were no footprints, but Solms knew that meant nothing; his sister had left no prints in the snow. Everywhere he searched, he found signs of life interrupted. A pot of rancid stew on the stove. Playing cards scattered beside the fireplace. A child's blanket hooked on a floor nail. An empty crib.

Positioning the point of the shovel between two floorboards, he levered up a plank, then another, and another, turning the house into a ruin of splintered lumber. It was like laboring inside a coke oven. The work took hours and yielded nothing.

He next visited the farmhand's quarters and gave it similar treatment, proceeding with frantic haste and using an axe instead of a shovel. When he emerged, the sun hung low in the western sky, already well along its shortened autumn path.

He tipped over the outhouse and probed the stinking cesspit with a long beam. Next, he followed the fence that encircled the main portion of the homestead, hopeful he might discover a shed or hidden cellar. He came across a corpse, fixed in a frozen crawl, its belly slit from sternum to crotch, the cavity hollowed out by carrion-eaters. The rancher, no doubt. Further on, he found two wooden crosses. The ground looked unmolested, but he had to be sure. He worked the shovel until he uncovered two simple pine boxes, a woman in one, a bundle of rags in the other. Dead at least a year, but he couldn't take chances; he severed the heads of mother and child and turned them face down. If he survived, he swore he would rebury the bodies with proper ceremony.

Blood boiled on the horizon; the day was dying. There was no place left to look. Except—had he checked the barn? Yes, the very first place he'd searched. Or was it? From his position, it looked undisturbed. Was his confusion simple exhaustion or one of Van Oordt's tricks? And if it was a deception, was the point to make him waste time in fruitless repetition or to keep him from discovering the truth?

Ride out now, a voice said. *Try to get ahead of Van Oordt before night falls.*

A solid-sounding plan, but it wasn't his, and the voice wasn't Rose's either.

He started towards the barn.

The building was silent. Perhaps the creatures inside were sleeping, if indeed they slept. He walked the perimeter, using his shovel to probe the spaces where the wooden slats met the dirt ground. On the side furthest from the house, he discovered a dugout, stopped and disguised with soiled cloths. Hastily, he pulled out the rags, uncovering a narrow passage, barely wide enough for a man to slither through on his stomach. There was no way in hell he was going to crawl under there. He'd get to Van Oordt another way.

Ride out. Ride away—it was Rose's voice this time, he was certain. But it was too late to turn back.

He dug a pit, filled it with kindling, and lit a fire. The old women in Jewett City had told his father how to do things right, and his father had instructed him. Once things started, there wouldn't be much time.

The day had lapsed into grey dusk; it would be darker still inside the barn. He took an oil lamp from the house and lit it. Then he unbarred the barn door and stepped inside.

In the lamp's sulphurous glow, he counted seven men and four women, what remained of the rancher's family and hired hands. Their eyes were dull and ovine, and they ignored him as he walked through air thick with human stench. He was careful not to look at the little girl who had taken his hand.

Mapping out where he believed Van Oordt lay, he set the lamp on the dirt floor and rested his knife next to it. Then he thrust the spade into the packed earth and started to dig.

A murmur rippled through the barn's occupants. They rocked from foot to foot, emitting a low whine as if with a single voice. Keeping a careful eye on them, he dropped the shovel and began to clear the hard-packed soil with his hands. The ground rose and fell as if it were a living, breathing thing. It was nearly frozen to the touch.

A face appeared beneath his fingers.

Solms reeled back. The eyes were open but as lifeless as black stones. Unsheathing his knife, he steadied it over Van Oordt's Adam's apple.

He had a butcher's job to do.

"Hand me the light, son."

The memory lasted but an instant; long enough for icy hands to wrap around his neck and squeeze, crushing his windpipe, choking off the flow of blood and oxygen to his brain. He would be unconscious in seconds, and dead—or worse—shortly after that.

Don't fight. Let it happen. The monster spoke to him. Solms leaned forward and pressed his chest against the antler handle. If this was the end, so be it. Let the darkness claim him... let his dead weight force the knife down, down, the tip piercing cold, unliving flesh. Just as everything went black, the point lanced Van Oordt's throat. The monster released his grasp and thrashed wildly, feet kicking like a steer that had survived the sledgehammer's first blow. Solm's ears rang with cannon fire. His vision was down to a single point of pale light, but he pushed, pushed. Now bodies pressed against him, tearing at his hair, his arms, his hands, grasping his clothes, but still he forced the blade down. Van Oordt gurgled a single word.

"Wait—"

Blood spurted on Solms' cheeks, cool like deep cave water, and the struggle was over. The human livestock fell back. Solms collapsed on top of Van Oordt.

The job wasn't done.

First, he sawed off the head. Then he inserted his knife under Van Oordt's sternum, slicing deep into flesh and muscle, opening a passage so he could dig his hands into the frigid cavity. Something inside still pulsed with life. He pulled until he could see the beating heart, cold like a fish caught from a winter stream. He used the knife to pare around the edges, severing veins and arteries, mindful of his four remaining fingers.

The headless corpse reached out—not for him but the precious organ he held. Van Oordt's jaw worked like it was chewing, rattling a single word:

"*Mine...*"

Solms turned the head face down and stamped it into the dirt. Then he ran out of the barn and barred the door.

The organ exploded like a sack of black powder when he tossed it into the fire. He saw white and felt heat, felt and smelled his hair burning. As he beat out the flames, a chorus of screams rose behind him. He blinked until his eyes cleared.

The barn was ablaze.

The voices that cried out were not those of mindless animals but living men and women, their senses restored, begging for deliverance. Solms struggled to lift the beam, but fire bit his fingers. He searched for a length of lumber to batter in the door, but when he returned the barn was completely engulfed. The cries for help had become shrieks of agony. He could do nothing but watch. When the roof collapsed, sparks shot into the night sky like a column of stars returning to heaven. The night grew silent.

Something moved at the edge of his vision, a wraith, emerging from behind the burnt hulk of the barn. Solms fell to his knees. He had no strength left to fight.

I gave it a go, Rose. It would have to be enough.

The clouds parted, and moonlight cascaded onto the ash-strewn farmyard.

Her dirty face and earth-stained dress told him she had managed to dig herself out of the barn using Van Oordt's tunnel. Her eyes, wide with shock, told him she was freed from whatever spell had held her. Wordlessly, he approached and offered his hand. When she took it, it was as light and delicate as a bird. The coldest part of the night had come, so he wrapped her in his cloak.

After he buried the bodies, Solms started in the direction he believed Carson City lay. Neither he nor the girl spoke. He didn't know what fate awaited them when the sun rose, but he'd do what he could to see that they both survived the coming day.

The Wind Witch

Rachel Horak Dempsey

Come closer to the fire, children, and I will tell you why you must never ever touch the tumbleweeds.

A man who rambles, without roots or chains, is free. A woman who wanders is dangerous.

No one could say exactly where she came from or how long she'd been living on the outskirts of our small desert town. We all knew old hags and whores who dabbled with herbs, crystals, and bones, but this one was different. This witch didn't read tarot cards or trade in curses and cures.

She spoke a language none could understand, in an accent harsh and throaty as a Slav's. Her very scent was foreign—damp, brackish like the kelpie Pa warned me against back in Scotland when I was a lad no older than you are now. Even if one of us screwed up the courage to ride past her adobe hut on our way to the creek, we dared not linger for fear of the tumbleweeds.

Some say the plant carcasses followed her all the way from the Russian Empire. I imagined her sailing across oceans on a barge made of thistles. She could have landed in New York or California. Brined in salt water, the weeds would have twisted round her wrists and ankles, and slithered through her long, inky hair like serpents. By the time they reached New Mexico Territory, though, both plant and woman were desiccated husks.

But they carried a horde of seeds.

The first time a lass went missing, we searched all the usual places. Well bottoms, dry wash canyons, and caves. Years passed. More disappeared. Sisters, daughters, wives, and mothers. We found no tracks. No bodies. Not one returned.

As if they'd been swept away by the wind.

I forbade my wife to leave our home alone. The tumbleweeds, or wind witches, as we'd begun to call them, kept their distance when men were around. Every time another woman vanished, reports followed from folks who'd seen her a day or sometimes mere hours before, stalked by a bundle of thorns. We kept our doors closed, but herds of them pummeled the walls, stacked as high as our flat roofs. When we tried to roll them away, the prickly branches tore our flesh, and soaked up our blood. And when we burned them, they rose in a flaming dust devil, crackling and moaning in the voices of our lost loved ones.

My wife—your mother—was the last to disappear, along with the witch. Those evil plants though, they stayed.

Weeds thrive in degradation, my sons. Someday our women will return. When they do, we must hold them tighter so their roots will grow strong and choke out the devil's vagrant seed.

And the Godless Shall Come to Dust

Keith Anthony Baird

The Town of Barren Dust, New Mexico, 1854

"In the name of the Father, the Son, and the Holy Ghost, I cast you out, unclean spirit. Give up this girl... for she is pure of heart and a follower of Christ the Redeemer."

Father Devlin kissed the cross on the rosary about his neck and doused the restrained Hiscox girl with holy water again. She arched off the bed and hissed as the thing inside her felt the scald of divinity it carried.

There'd been hours of this, but days and weeks of it before, as the priest brought in from New England by frantic elders had battled long for the child's salvation. He was weary. The dark agent in possession of her inner throne was one, yet legion the same.

Smallpox had come a-calling on the township the year before, claiming many, and the Hiscox girl had fallen sick with a sinister malady in its wake. Her father, John Byron Hiscox—JB to the locals—had established his cattle ranch, built the church, opened the gold mine and brought the railroad to the town he'd put on the map. But for all his wealth and good fortune, he was powerless to rid his daughter of the thing which plagued her soul.

The priest, JB, and Sheriff Kincaid kept the vigil in the upper east wing of the Hiscox ranch. Visibly shook, the lawman was at the threshold of what he could endure. The scene was utter madness. Never before had he witnessed such infernal damnation. The girl, Eleanor, was bound by her wrists and ankles to the bedframe. The piece of furniture itself had lifted clear of the floor and clattered repeatedly upon it. Horses whinnied in the stables while a storm the likes they'd never seen raged in constant roar upon the Hiscox residence. It was as if the Devil himself had laid claim to the hapless child.

By now, Devlin was ailing. Drained by repeated attempts to wrest the child from dark forces by performing the sacred ritual time and again. Each battle had prematurely aged him. His crop of dark hair was now streaked with grey, and the eyes of a once outgoing man were mere coals in the hollows of an ashen face. He leaned in once again to continue the recital of the hallowed texts. And it was then that the cord restraints gave way, allowing the thing inside poor Eleanor to have her levitate off the bed and scurry across the ceiling into the darkened corner of the room. Phantom eyes flickered green in the shadows, and a howl of the many poured scorn upon the holy man.

Kincaid made the sign of the cross, and JB near collapsed as Devlin pursued evil to the far side of the room. Presenting his crucifix, he shouted a Latin verse above the raging storm but was floored as the girl dropped wildly upon him. Now somehow face down, he tried to rise, but she crawled onto his back, grabbed his hair, and flicked her tongue into his ear. "Your God is a worm in the dying earth of your church."

Straddling him and keeping him pinned, she urinated on the man of the cloth. The sheriff was done. Friend or no, JB would now have to suffer this alone. Taking flight from the Hiscox homestead, he took the thunder road into town, seeking solace in the spirit of the corn.

Whiskey steadied the man but also set his tongue to wagging. Rumours were rife in Barren Dust—simply Dust to the locals—of strange happenings at the Hiscox place. Ranch hands, too much under the influence, had let slip their accounts in the smoke-filled saloon on many a day. Now, with their sheriff preaching hellfire, it was enough to push a town in fear over the edge. A posse assembled, flaming torches in hand, and they took themselves a cart and coffin to the outskirts. They'd rid the community of the scourge in their midst and the Lord's work it'd be, child or no.

At the ranch, JB was a man at the end of his rope. Devlin had failed for the last time. All hope of bringing peace to the parlour was gone. Alone in his study, while the cacophony of torment still raged on the next floor, he put lead and flesh together and scattered the brains which had forged what should have been his legacy all over the redwood timber panelling. His wife, Clara-May, was simply too far gone to notice, having lost her grip on sanity some ways back. Only a broken priest now stood between a baying mob and a haunted little girl. They came with force and purpose, and though Devlin threw the ire of a desperate man against them, he was little match for their will and number.

Riding hard through dead weather, they took the girl and the thing inside her to the cemetery which sat on the bluff overlooking the township. On consecrated ground, they dug a plot in driving rain whilst a braver few man-handled the Devil's wastrel into the coffin. Nailed shut, with a frenzy of screams, growls, and scratches beneath the lid, they buried Eleanor alive in an unmarked grave. So powerful the fury of the thing inside her, they heard its venom bringing down a hex on all Dust folk as they rode off through the fire and brimstone of God Almighty's hell-storm.

Barren Dust—Modern Day

An aching wind moans across this empty highway. Hitch-hiking, I've been a drifter out of Death Valley with no particular purpose since leaving California. I'd decided I would simply go where the road took me. Across Arizona and into New Mexico, the landscape is pretty much the same in the shimmering heat haze. The last ride left me in the middle of nowhere, but that's right where I want to be after my crisis of faith. Maybe I'll find God again out here. Maybe not. Perhaps I'll be Godless for the rest of my days. One thing's for sure, I'll be damned if I know.

There's just walking and hitching here. Walking and hitching. Plenty of time for soul-searching in this sprawling, sun-parched wilderness. The hours pass, and the shadows grow long. Eventually, a truck pulls up. He's going *somewhere*. What does it matter? Anywhere is good for me. I get dropped off after a few hours. The tail lights disappear around a bend, and I'm left standing in the beam of a low, full moon. I can almost see everything, and it feels good to be carefree and alone in the desert at night. Thinking back, I was never going to cut it as a priest. There's a need to be selfless, which, being honest with myself, I don't possess.

For the first time on the road, it feels cold tonight. I do a 360, and then I hear it on the breeze. A mournful dirge coming from a few pinpoints of bokeh lights to the west. Civilisation. A bar, no doubt. A comfortable bed someplace until it's time to move on. It's all the lure I need. Ten minutes walk down what seems an old cinder track gets me to the shanty town's faded sign. That's sure an odd name, but undoubtedly apt given the location.

Even in the dark, I get the sense of a place stuck in a time warp. The music, louder now, is fiddle and banjo and pretty maudlin minor key stuff. It's a ramshackle town. There are cars and trucks parked up, but none on the move. Passing a line of them on Main Street, it seems a fair number are quite an age. The bar's called *Ye Ole Prospector,* and the neon sign has failed on the letters P, r, and o, to read '*Ye Ole spector*'. As I cross the street, the music stops abruptly, the sign flickers, then dies, and the door gets bolted. I guess they don't welcome strangers. Damn... and I have a thirst like my throat's been cut.

Sighing, I turn my attention to finding a room for the night. In the silver moonlight, I can make out that much of the place is either gutted or boarded up. Even the gas station looks like a relic. I drift. There's the odd piece of garbage on the wind, which tumbles by and dances over whatever it encounters. It's eerie still. Not a dog barking or even a cat prowling the rooftops. And then there's the cold. A bite I've not felt for some time. I blow into my hands and keep moving. Overhangs create ink-black pitches in the latticework of streets. A sign for lodgings proves fruitless, as closer inspection reveals the site as one of those of the abandoned.

It feels like a long, drawn-out hour of wandering. Whatever was here that catered for the traveller seems long gone. I'm going to have to rough it—find myself somewhere in these empty homesteads to give a measure of comfort and at least a little shelter from the chill. Morning will bring the chance to find something better. Half a dozen tries, and I get lucky. A former residence in the heart of the place is unlocked, and a brief search uncovers a stout, wide sofa in a back room. Somewhat dusty, it will serve my needs on a hasty clean, and the house itself stands tight against the elements. *Good find, Brandon. You're bossing this open road thing.* But hell, it still feels like a meat locker in here.

Despite a long day, I'm not weary for some reason. Sleep will come eventually, I guess. Lying here, time seems a meaningless device, but it's a chance to reflect on a lot of things that have happened. The most haunting is the path from the priesthood, but I've been over it a thousand times and know I won't find the answer now, either. It's just tumbleweeds in my head—desiccated brush in motion which induces a slow descent into restfulness.

Something acute cuts through... again, like the clang of metal on metal. It's still dark as I come to a waking which doesn't feel like I've even been asleep. Again it cuts through, though it's distant, and now I understand the source. A bell. Tolling... way off from the broken bowels of the township. Its rhythm is slow and deliberate. I rise, go to the window, but can see nothing except the silver dollar of a moon, which makes angular darkness of the buildings beyond the pane. On and on it hammers out in steady dismal timbre. I walk the rooms and unlatch the front door. Residents in number drift through the warren of roads. In their hands, pale lights they hold, all of which converging to a route out of town.

It climbs out of the timber maze, carrying a procession which now sings in sombre unison en route to a church atop the bluff. I follow. As I walk, I realise I've heard this song before. The very same spilling from the bar on my arrival. I'd have to run to catch up with them before they summit, so I'll keep a distance and eyes on what unfolds. I see now they carry lit candles, none of which snuff out on a dead-of-night breeze. The bell still tolls its summoning. Each peal seems a doom as opposed to a call, but I heed it not and continue my ascent.

The church begins to fill with light. I assume those crossing the threshold are passing flame from wick to wick within. *Why all this at this ungodly hour? What sense lies in a post-midnight gathering?* I'm a tad fearful but intrigued. The last of the throng disappears inside, and the bell ceases its chiming. Approaching the gates, I see a mass of grave markers in stark contrast to the pale illumination spilling from the House of God. Many are crooked, broken, or sunken in the earth, and their plots haphazard in arrangement. The double doors stand open—maudlin song a-spilling. I clear the gates and walk the final steps to the entrance.

The congregation lines the pews. Heads bowed, they sing a hymn I now come to vaguely recognise. It's a requiem piece that brings my focus from the flock to the rough timber coffin on stands in the sanctuary in front of the pulpit. The church being small, I can see from here the box lies open. I don't know why, but it calls to me, and I'm drifting down the central aisle without thinking. As I walk, the hymn seems to grow faint, and looking back, I see those gathered begin to fade from view. Facing forward once again, those in the front rows fade in similar vein. All that remains are lit candles, this visitor, and an eerie silence that knows the change in me.

I should be terrified. I am not. I should flee, yet something draws me closer to the bone repository. Tentatively, I lean from the position I've taken up and cast a look inside the box. There's no flesh. No dead. No soul at rest... only the trinkets of an austere existence. And then the crush of a moment comes barrelling in. Everything centres, and I know why I'm here. Those belongings are mine. My watch, wallet, cell phone, rosary, and bible deliver the news my mind struggled to understand. I'd drifted off in that truck. Succumbed to sleep and was never to wake. He'd cut my throat—the driver—and taken my pack and possessions before dumping my body by the roadside.

That I've passed over is a cruel revelation, yet one quickly quelled by a raking wind that howls at everything around me to suck out light and lost grace from votive candles. I feel that bitter, deep chill in my core now. The very same that welcomed me to this godforsaken township. All is dark. All is... menace. All is emptiness and final sorrow. There's something here. Something which preyed on my passing. I am beyond God. Beyond favour. Locked here, in perpetuum, to its unhallowed intent. And then there comes a child's laughter. A guise that only masks the true corruption of the thing which taints this holy space. Spectral eyes flare into being in the corner, and in a chilling tone, it speaks.

"Ever it is said, that man shall wander lost upon the left-hand path, and the Godless shall come to dust."

The Last Train out of Calico

Pedro Iniguez

The train's headlight cut through the night like a phantom flame. If there had been a voice of hesitation in Felix Hidalgo's head, it was drowned out by the thundering roar of the cranks and wheels rolling across the mountain pass.

It was just as well. There could be no room for doubt. Not now that they had grown frail, their reflexes dulled by time.

"It will be here soon," Luis Villareal said. He adjusted his eyepatch and loaded his revolver with a slow, shaky hand, his one good eye struggling to account for depth. Satisfied, he snapped the cylinder shut and scowled.

"I wonder if our bodies are still up for it," Nails Benson said, pulling his duster in tight as a gust blew in. "Ain't done this in a long time, fellas. My bones are achin'."

Irving Thompson fastened his wrinkled Union Army kepi over his balding head. It was a relic from his glory days long ago. "If the spirit is willing," he said, "there is nothing a man can't do."

Warren Blackhawk sat quietly atop his horse like a statue. The veteran Lakota warrior's sagging eyes squinted as the light shining through the windows of the passenger cars flickered like fireflies.

Jake Emery tied a red bandana over his face and followed Blackhawk's gaze. "If we mess this up," he said, his voice gruff, "we'll be strung from the gallows and buried at Boot Hill cemetery like the other banditos."

Hidalgo licked his cracked lips and patted the side of his horse's neck, more for his own reassurance than the horse's. "No point talking like that," he said. "We will pull this off. And if we don't, it won't matter because we will be dead long before the gallows, amigos."

"The Jefe's right," Thompson said. "Besides, what awaits us on that train will be enough to have us living comfortably 'til the end of our days. That is worth the risk in my estimation."

Emery shook his head. "How can we be sure? Don't none of us know what's in there."

The train plowed west through the darkness, curving along the base of the Calico Mountains. A jet of steam billowed into the wide, obsidian sky, briefly veiling a small swath of stars.

Benson folded his arms over his chest. "All that talk about the miners finding something inside that mountain means whatever's in there's gotta be big. Why else ship their cargo off on the last train out of Calico in such a hurry?"

"And under the cover of night, no less," Thompson said. "They must have hit a silver vein. They're sending some off to Los Angeles to procure more supplies."

Emery nodded.

The train blasted its horn, sending birds darting from the Joshua trees like scattershot.

"It is time," Hidalgo said.

Villareal reached into his saddlebag and dispersed five sticks of dynamite; one for each other man. He slid his own stick into his bandolier. "This will scare them good, no?" he said smirking as he twirled his grey whiskers.

Under the moonlight, the men looked worn and gaunt, like pale blue corpses. They'd shed their youth like a snake sheds its skin. Yet, in spirit, they remained the same bastards he'd always known them to be. Hearts of steel and fire. Hidalgo knew he wouldn't do this with anyone else.

"Expect some hired guns on that train," Thompson said, pulling his old cavalry gloves over his hands. He carefully unsheathed his old saber and gave it a lookover before sliding it back in the scabbard. "Do not hesitate to shoot every last living man if it comes to it. Just like the old days."

"Amigo," Hidalgo turned to the young, red-haired kid he'd picked up at the saloon earlier that day. The young man, not older than eighteen, shivered atop his horse, a lasso spooled around his right shoulder. "You know the plan. We will stop the train down the track. You will meet us with the horses, and we'll split our earnings with you. *Entendido*? Understand?"

The kid nodded. "Y-yes, sir."

Hidalgo smiled. "*Muy bien, muchacho.*" He faced the rest of the men and tipped his hat.

The men whooped and hollered, bolting headlong towards the train. As they galloped through the desert, the wind ripped across his face. Hidalgo felt alive again. Like when he still had his teeth and his back didn't ache every waking moment. Like before he'd given up his old ways and long accepted the life of an old ranch hand in his home country.

Hidalgo knew they didn't belong in this time. Their brand of mischief was archaic, suited for a crueler world. They were creatures from a bygone era best put to pasture. He could see it now. A new age of marvels and miracles awaited, and men like him were not part of that equation. And it was probably for the best. In his heart he knew this would be their last ride together, win or lose.

The men lined up their horses along the broad side of the first passenger car. The train—a locomotive anchored by four passenger cars, a single boxcar, and a caboose— chugged across an empty stretch of track along the Mojave Desert. Besides the Calico Mountains and the mining town that carried their namesake, nothing existed out here for miles. The only witnesses to their transgressions this night would be half-starved coyotes and God himself.

A furious gust swept across the valley, chilling Hidalgo's bones. The warm amber glow radiating from the kerosene lamps swaying in the windows looked particularly inviting. One by one, the men struck their matches and lit their fuses. Hidalgo gently pressed off his stirrups, raising himself into a standing mount. He swung his left leg over the saddle and waited until his horse was level with the passenger car's entryway. He took a breath, timed his jump, and leapt over the gap. He clung to the railing and pulled himself up the narrow steps. Winded, he drew his revolver and waved the men over.

As each man clambered up, the horses fell away one by one, fading into a veil of dust and darkness until it was just them and the train.

Hidalgo nodded. Villareal and Thompson drew their revolvers. They kicked the door open and charged inside, screaming and waving their dynamite. Benson and Blackhawk followed next. Hidalgo and Emery brought up the rear.

The six of them stood there for what seemed an eternity, unblinking, unmoving.

Apart from the rattling of the car, the hissing of dynamite fuses was the only sound within its confines.

"Put those out," Hidalgo said nodding at the dynamite in their hands. The men snuffed the fuses and gazed at the carnage.

A wealth of viscera painted the passenger car. The upholstery on the chairs was draped with organs and splattered with yellow fatty tissue. The carcasses of what were once men and women lay slumped on their seats and on the floor, the rags of drenched clothing beside them nigh impossible to distinguish from shreds of meat.

Emery bent over, pulled his bandana down, and heaved on the floor.

"What in God's name happened here?" Villareal said crossing himself.

"This is unnatural," Blackhawk said, kneeling beside the torso of a woman. Her lower half had been lost somewhere within the tangle of severed limbs decorating the car. With a gloved hand, he gently turned her trunk over flat on its stomach. Small serrations marked the length of her spine all the way up to the base of her skull.

Thompson removed his kepi. "Not during war have I seen something like this."

"Nitroglycerin," Hidalgo said. "I have seen the remains of exploded railroad workers like this when they hollow out the mountains."

"This ain't no explosives, Jefe," Emery said standing back up again. He wiped his mouth with the back of his hand. "The rest of the car is unscathed."

The men inspected the car. Walls, windows, the floor, all intact. Not so much as a splintered beam overhead.

"Someone beat us to the punch," Benson said. "A botched robbery."

Blackhawk shook his head. "Nothing botched about this. There is intent in this mayhem."

Hidalgo faced the hallway that coupled the next carriage. Darkness stretched all the way down the train. Only small glints of moonlight pierced the windows, catching on the silhouettes of lifeless, bobbing heads. "The lanterns are all out. Whatever did this may still be here," Hidalgo said. "Toward the rear."

Thompson sighed and raised his revolver as he peered into the stretch of infinite black. "Shall we take a look, amigos?"

The men stared at one another in silence, faces pale.

Hidalgo nodded. "I'll go first, muchachos," he said, unhooking a lantern off the wall.

In silence, the six of them moved single-file down the narrow aisle toward the back of the train, their boots trudging over wet, creaking floorboards and shards of glass. Car after car, it was all the same: slumping piles of meat and blood; the flickering light of Hidalgo's lantern reanimating the departed as their shadows danced on the walls, mocking their passage.

A foul odor permeated the air toward the back of the train; a stench of rot and sulfur that burned the sinuses. Emery groaned and pulled the bandana over his face.

A trail of blood and excrement led directly to the last compartment. Hidalgo lifted the dimming lantern to the splintered door.

"Help me," a woman's voice called from within the boxcar.

He leaned forward and pressed his ear against the door.

"Help me!" cried a man's voice, this one louder.

He raised his pistol.

A cacophony of pleas erupted within. "Helpmehelpmehelpme-helpme!"

Hidalgo kicked the fractured door inward and charged inside, the rest of the men storming in behind him.

"Jesus Christ," Thompson said.

Within the lantern's feint glow, Hidalgo could scarcely discern what he was seeing. The floor, walls, and ceiling were besieged with inky, fluid movement. He brought the lantern against the nearest wall. A sea of arachnids the size of armadillos clambered over one another, their long, shelled legs the color of rust. Their carapaces were rocky and speckled like granite. Like stars, the lamplight shimmered off the multitude of black eyes dotting the top of their shells. At his boots, the things scurried fervently over the defiled remains of the passengers, their mandibles snapping through bone and meat. He jumped back, slamming into the men. Blackhawk caught him and straightened him up.

"What in the hell are these things?" Emery said just as one dropped from the ceiling, smacking down in front of him.

The thing tilted its body upward and opened its mandibles. A small tongue-like appendage slid out from its maw. "Help me," it said in mimicry of a human voice. "Help me."

The swarm on the floor paused their feeding frenzy and followed its lead as they turned toward the men. Like feelers, they pushed out thin, fleshy tongues and waggled them up and down. "Helpmehelp-mehelpmehelpme!"

"Aw, fuck!" Emery drew on the nearest one and fired a shot. The top of its shelled head exploded, sending up grey bits of meat. The thing collapsed, its legs falling limp at its sides.

In the shadows, something half hissed, half burbled. Hidalgo swung the lamp toward the source of the sound. A large head reared itself from the darkest depths of the boxcar. In appearance it was like the others, only larger. Hidalgo surmised it was on par with a large steer. This one was different though. Its rocky shell was marbled with silver veins. A few flayed strands of rope were still tied around its carapace. The thing's legs, gangly and rugged, pushed it forward.

"What is that?" the spider-thing said, its mandibles open as it thrust its tongue out. "What is that? What is that?"

"Holy shit," Benson said.

"Get back," Hidalgo said, waving them away.

"Load it on the train," the thing said. "Load it on the train. Load it on the train. Load it on the train."

The spider-thing lifted a long, pointed leg and thrust it at Hidalgo. Villareal grabbed him by the scruff of his coat and threw him toward the men. The leg came down on Villareal's chest with a resounding crack. The thing withdrew its leg sending up a spurt of blood from the fresh cavity. Villareal offered a single gurgle before he began to topple forward. The spider-thing opened its mandibles and clamped them shut on his torso, splitting him in half.

"No!" Hidalgo screamed, hurling the lantern at the floor beneath the spider-thing's legs. The lantern smashed open. A swell of fire engulfed the floor, splitting the car in half and separating the men from most of the swarm. The spider-thing shrieked, the sound like iron scraping against iron.

The light of the raging flames revealed the extent of the horrors inside. The things were bigger in the light. Uglier. They were akin to something between a crab and a spider, their shells and craggy legs seemingly made of granite or limestone.

A swarm of the things began to drop from the walls and ceiling, scaling over each other on their path toward the men.

As the flames lapped up the corpses, miniature arachnids began to spawn from their remains, their tiny mandibles shearing through pale, rancid meat.

While it was distracted by the flames, Thompson opened fire on the large spider-thing, sparks flying where the bullets chipped at its rock-like exterior. Spurned by his courage, the rest of the men fired a volley at the gangly nightmare. The thing reeled and shrieked, swinging its two front legs across the air like scythes.

Amidst the fire and smoke, Hidalgo crouched and gripped Villareal by his bandolier, hauling him backwards the way they came. He stopped when he noticed his friend's entrails unspooling on the floor.

A rough hand rocked Hidalgo's shoulder. "He's gone, Jefe," Blackhawk said. "We need to fall back!"

Hidalgo frowned and released his grip on Villareal. He stood and emptied his revolver into a pair of approaching spiders. Their shells ruptured as they toppled over, their legs curling in on themselves.

"Fall back!" Hidalgo yelled over the fire's roar and the crack of gunfire.

Thompson and Emery darted past the screen of smoke and back toward the passenger cars. Benson emptied his gun and followed close behind. Hidalgo shuffled backward as he reloaded his revolver. Blackhawk covered him, picking off some stragglers scurrying past the flames. Once the things stopped coming, Hidalgo and Blackhawk sprinted toward the first car.

Regrouping with the rest of the men, Hidalgo leaned against a wall and exhaled, his heart thrumming against his chest like a piston. He slammed the butt of his pistol against the wall. It was his only way to fight the tears starting to pool under his eyes. He'd known Luis from their time in Guadalajara, deserters of the Mexican Army both fleeing to a new country in search of plunder and riches.

"What in the holy hell was that?" Benson said, his revolver trained on the hallway.

"I don't know," Hidalgo said, trying to compose himself. He sucked in a deep breath and felt the fire in his chest spread through his limbs. His body had protested every ounce of exertion.

"Spawn of the Devil," Blackhawk said, reloading. "Those things are not of our world."

The shrieks of the spider-thing had ceased as the fire continued to blaze inside the boxcar.

"We've gotta get out of here," Emery said. "I don't intend to end up torn to ribbons or slumpin' and swollen like these people." He peered over the remains of some of the still-intact passengers as their bellies bulged into their laps.

"The dead don't bloat so quickly," Hidalgo said stepping away from the seats.

"He's right," Blackhawk said. "You all saw what came out of the bodies down there. Hatchlings. Swarms of them."

"They're going to reproduce soon," Thompson said.

"Well, fuck me," Emery said.

"Jefe," Thompson said. "We can make our way toward the locomotive and stop the train just like we planned. We'll get off and ride the hell out of here."

Hidalgo kept his eyes on the dead passengers, watching for any sudden movements. They had died horrible, undeserving deaths. What awaited humanity if those things were to escape? He took off his hat and ran a trembling hand through his moist, grey hair. He turned his hand over. It was wrinkled and mottled with liver spots, veins, and broken blood vessels. He thought about the creature's carapace, its rocky, speckled exterior. "That thing down there. It is old. Like us."

"What do you mean, Jefe?" Thompson said.

"They dug that thing up deep in the mountains, amigo. It must have been there for years. Dormant under all that rock. That thing is ancient. Prehistoric. Beyond the reach of time."

"What are you saying?" Blackhawk said.

"That its time has passed. Like ours. There is no room in this world for evil things like us anymore. We can't let it escape," Hidalgo said turning to the men, his eyes sharp, focused, the fire of his youth returned. "Let it be the only good thing we've ever done."

The wind rattled the window panes. Hidalgo spared a glance and saw his reflection staring back. His face was a dry riverbed, carved out by wrinkles and scars. His beard had silvered liked the veins on the spider-thing. *Not long left in this world*, he thought.

"I'm with you, Jefe," Blackhawk said. "Those things cannot be loosed upon the world."

"Life was gonna be downhill from here anyways, fellas," Benson said. "I'm with you."

"Shit," Thompson said. "I'll follow you hombres to the depths of Pandemonium itself."

Emery sighed and nodded. "What do you suggest?"

"We could derail the train," Thompson said. "Speed it up, stick some dynamite between the cranks and wheels..."

Hidalgo shook his head. "No. The creatures would flee into the desert and multiply. We have to destroy the train."

"Hell," Emery said. "How?"

"We have to move down this train and blow every car one by one. We make sure every corpse and creature is destroyed."

"Let's see," Thompson said. "We can uncouple the locomotive, leaving us six cars including the caboose. We have five sticks of dynamite amongst ourselves. Shit! We'll need Luis's stick."

A shriek reverberated down the entire length of the train. The men turned toward the boxcar where Villareal had fallen. A hoard of dark shapes scuttled toward them, dousing the flames with their bodies.

"Emery, Benson," Hidalgo said. "Uncouple the locomotive. We can't lead them to civilization. After that, we won't have long before the train comes to a stop. We'll need to blow the rest of the cars before they can escape."

Emery and Benson hurried to the front of the car, squatted, and lifted the coupling bolt that connected the locomotive to the rest of the train. They watched the backside of the tender car as the locomotive sped off into the night without them.

The rest of the train rolled forward on sheer momentum, its rattling beginning to slow.

Hidalgo drew his revolver as the wave of rolling blackness approached. "We fight together and move up together. Emery, Light your fuse."

Emery lit his stick. Together, they moved up, crossing into the second car.

"I can't see a damn thing ahead of me," Benson said.

"Shoot at the darkness," Hidalgo said stepping forward. He opened fire at the onrushing surge as it occulted every sliver of moonlight shining through the windows. Every gunshot lit the car for a fraction of a second, revealing the orgy of teeming terrors crawling across the train. The men at his back opened fire, sparks flying off the walls around them. The moisture of blood and brains misted the air, mixing with the odor of gunpowder and smoke.

In the pitch of the darkness, Hidalgo felt their spindly limbs brush against his legs. He stomped his boots, digging his spurs deep into their shells. Every crack urged him on, every shriek restored another year of his youth.

As soon as they reached the middle of the second car, Emery tossed his stick toward the farthest corner of the first carriage.

Hidalgo held his breath.

The explosion rocked the train, hurling everything and everyone into the ceiling. The men came down on the seats and floor, the impact knocking the breath from Hidalgo's lungs.

Darkness filled his world again. He offered a look at his back. The car was gone, blown open and exposed to the desert, the moonlight painting the empty remains of the car. What hadn't been destroyed outright was already ablaze.

A choking veil of smoke wafted through the carriage. The groans and hacking coughs of old men filled the car.

He pushed himself off the wet floor, the muscles in his arms and legs straining as they contracted. There came a quick sizzle and a new fuse lit the car, the creatures now partly visible in the flicker of its light.

"I got this one," Benson said. In the light he looked weathered, tired, white dust caked on his face. Like a ghost. "Keep it moving, fellas!"

The spiders, now scattered on the floor of the aisle, twitched before springing over onto their legs. "Helpmehelpmehelpmehelpme!"

"Shit!" Hidalgo said. "Move up!"

He ran. Some of the things not directly under his boots crawled back up the walls, their legs swiping at his arms, slicing through his coat and skin.

He took aim at one and fired. *Click*. Empty. No time to reload, he swung the butt of his revolver in a left-to-right arc, like a club. A few blows connected, shattering their heads, their brains spewing on his face. He kicked and swung his way through the third car, his men firing point blank into the terrors still lingering at his flank.

"Ahhh!" Benson cried out, his light barely afloat amidst a swarm of spiders already on top of him. By his side, Emery fired off the last of his ammunition before they cut him down, his silhouette dissolving into the obscurity of the floor. As Thompson and Blackhawk reached the third car, Benson's light sank into the carnivorous mound.

The blast at his back ripped the second car apart, the thunder booming across the train once more. The force of the explosion flung Thompson into Hidalgo's side, knocking his face into the back of a leather-padded seat. Blood and teeth poured freely from his mouth and down his chin.

"Godamnit," Thompson said, the moonlight now settling on his own bloodied mouth. Thompson prodded the floor. "I can't find my gun."

Hidalgo checked for his own revolver, which was now also lost.

"We have to keep moving," Blackhawk said, hooking an arm around each downed man's armpit. He lifted them up, standing them against the wall. He retrieved a matchstick and lit his fuse. "Run," he said, dropping the stick at his feet before starting for the next car with a wounded gait.

Hidalgo sprinted past the pricking legs and snapping mandibles, Thompson at his heels. They leapt into the fourth car, scuttled into an empty nook to either side of an aisle and took cover under a seat.

The car detonated, flinging the spiders in every direction. A downpour of wood and limbs and shells rained down on the desert floor.

Hidalgo pulled himself up out of cover, wiping the dust from his eyes. As far as he could see, the darkness continued to roll toward them. A never-ending nightmare. He peered around. Thompson was already up and lighting his fuse. Behind them, a trail of fire and debris and nothing else. Not even Blackhawk.

"Come on, Jefe," Thompson said drawing his saber. "Almost there."

Thompson screamed as he stormed down the passenger car, swinging and hacking his way into the boxcar like a soldier leading a charge. The things screeched in the dark. His blade sliced through every leg and carapace it came into contact with, their shelled bits flying every which way. Hidalgo followed him, limping past the smoldering floor and into the ruins of the next carriage.

Inside, the walls and ceiling had nearly burned away along with most of the arachnids, which were no more than ashen rock. On the floor of the entryway, Villareal gazed at an open patch of starry desert sky.

The faint beams of moonlight piercing the perforated roof revealed the giant spider-thing to be gone. Past the cloud of smoke, the entire front face of the caboose had been torn open. Something large and hideous moved within the shadows of the car.

A chorus of shrieks came from their flank.

Thompson flung his stick back into the passenger car and dove onto the charred floor, covering his head. Hidalgo quickly reached into Villareal's bandolier, snagged his dynamite, and slid it into his belt. He then dropped and curled up beside Thompson. The detonation sent up a wave of searing heat, the vibration rocking the train off the track and sending it pummeling into the earth. The train careened and flipped over onto its side. Hidalgo felt himself being thrown into the air before hitting the ground, his body rolling over sharp thicket.

The iron horse screeched and moaned while it skidded along the dirt. Its burning frame uprooted a number of Joshua trees until it came to a stop.

Hidalgo screamed as he pushed himself off the cold desert floor. Like hot coals against his flesh, his left arm burned in the worst way. The skin from his palm had degloved all the way down his elbow where he'd tried to break his fall. He tucked his arm against his belly just as the chill winds began to sting his open wound. He grimaced, limping past a cloud of dust. "Thompson?" he called out. "Where are you, mi amigo?"

He shuffled toward the boxcar, now a shattered pile of smoldering wood and mangled iron. What remained of Thompson jutted out from under the train's frame from the chest up, the rest of his self, pinned under its massive weight. Hidalgo closed his eyes and heard the gravel at his boots swaying on the breeze. He wanted to say a prayer for his men, but no words came.

The familiar burble and clatter of the spider-thing's mandibles broke the silence somewhere in the vicinity.

"Thing's gotta be worth a fortune," the thing said somewhere beyond the veil of dust and ash. "Thing's gotta be worth a fortune."

Hidalgo turned away and retrieved his friend's saber, lying just out of the reach of his curled fingers. He shambled away from the wreckage hoping to get a clear view of the scene.

Once he got enough distance between himself and the train, he trekked up a slope that overlooked the chaos. From here the stars shimmered again, and the Joshua trees swayed softly under the moonlight. Below, the haze had swallowed up everything near the burning rubble. There were no discernable signs of movement.

Eastward, the sound of hard galloping approached. *The kid.* "Shit," Hidalgo grumbled.

"Help me!" the spider-thing yelled, its pointed legs emerging from the smoke. It crawled past the wreckage and scuttled east atop the train tracks. "Help me!"

A plume of dust hung in the air where the kid had been running the horses in the distance. Hidalgo stuck the saber in the ground and pulled a match from his belt. He struck it against the trunk of a Joshua tree and lit his stick.

"Hey," he called out. "Over here!"

The spider-thing stopped and turned toward Hidalgo.

Hidalgo flung the stick. The spider-thing swung a craggy leg, knocking the explosive out of the air. The dynamite detonated just up the track, spitting up dirt and fire.

The stomping of hoofs wasn't too far off now. The poor kid would have no chance.

"Damnit," Hidalgo said under his breath, wincing. The pain in his left arm began to spread through his body like a brush fire. What few teeth he had left began to chatter inside his skull. He didn't know anymore if it was from the cold or the pain. Or both.

He retrieved another match and hobbled toward the spider-thing. "Hey!" he called out. "Come get me. I killed your children. And you killed my friends."

The thing charged at him.

He stood there, his left arm tucked into his belly, his right holding a single match.

When it neared, the spider-thing raised a leg and speared Hidalgo through the solar plexus. He huffed as the air was extinguished from his lungs. The thing lifted him off the ground and pulled him toward its snapping mandibles. Where there had been stars, there were now black spots filling his eyes.

He struck the match against the thing's stony face and lowered it toward his belly, where Villareal's stick of dynamite lay in his left hand's trembling grasp. The fuse ignited, casting both their faces in a warm red light. Hidalgo smiled at the old thing, blood seeping from his gums. It was all there was left to do in the face of death.

The fuse burned down into the blasting cap. Before the light engulfed them both, Hidalgo thought one last time of his friends and felt peace at last. *We did it muchachos.*

Tombstone, the Town Too Tough to Die — Cochise County, Arizona

LindaAnn LoSchiavo

In Tombstone, Arizona, dead men don't
Lie still. They reenact old gunfights, won't
Stop flying those Confederate flags, grow
Outraged at the suggestion dynamo
Robert E. Lee surrendered, lost the war.

They're placing bets about shoot-outs before
The outlaws threatened Wyatt Earp that day
At the O.K. Corral. Doc Holliday,
Though undefeated, killed a dozen more
By doing dentistry twelve years before.

Their tourist board decided the deceased
Had best stay buried. Sightseeing decreased.

Despite their bravery, it's time for three
Earp brothers to enforce all death decrees.

Since corpses don't vote, they can't sport buckskin.
With tombs nailed shut, eternity moved in.

The White Horse
Richard Beauchamp

He entered the tavern, grateful to be out of the icy winds that cut through to the bone regardless of the many fur layers he wore. It was loud inside; no one seemed to pay him any special attention as he walked up to the bar, which was good. Last time he entered such an establishment, he'd been there for all of a minute before he saw gun barrels trained on his person.

He got the attention of the harried barmaid as she appeared from the bustling amalgam of drunken miners that filled the place, and she froze when she saw him, several near-empty mugs of ale hugged to her bosom.

"Help ya?" she asked, depositing the glasses in a wash basin, her hair tied back in a sweaty red horsetail, eyeing him with an unreadable expression.

"Whiskey, please."

"Five cents," she replied curtly as she removed a glass from the pile of dirty dishes in the wash basin. He noticed there was a row of sparkling clean glasses on the shelf behind her, but that was all right, the drink was more for posturing than anything. After giving his visibly smeared glass a perfunctory wipe down with a dirty dish rag, she filled it with a finger of Dickinson and slid it over to him.

He gave her a whole dime, insisting she keep it. She inspected it closely to make sure it wasn't a fake. Seemingly satisfied, she tucked it away, then gave him a side-eye glance as she began to clean dishes.

"Don't be makin' no trouble now, or you'll get shot dead," she said as she went back to her business.

He turned and surveyed the room once more, looking for men of a particular trade that might be able to help him with his inquiries. He looked for the telltale fur coats and fine garments that tended to be of substantially higher quality than the soot-smeared rags most of these folk were dressed in. He looked for hard-edged, often scarred, faces that were a complete dichotomy to the threads they adorned; visages that, even with a cursory glance, you could tell were chewed on by years of hot sun and winter wind.

The newcomer spotted a large man in a beautifully stitched lynx coat; a flowing, patchwork-colored beard sprouted from a craggy face with a jagged pink valley of scar tissue crawling down one side of his forehead. He looked soused; the bristles around his lips and chin glistened with spilled ale. He sat alone at one table, was one of the few in the place who wasn't engaged in some animated form of conversation. The fur trapper fixed the newcomer with a hard, unblinking gaze as he approached. Without being invited to, he sat down across from the man.

"Fuck is a redskin doing in a place like this? You lost, boy? Or you lookin' to trade?" he asked, his voice all gravel and grit.

The interloper shook his head and pulled out the folded piece of paper he'd been showing people for months now, the piece of paper that showed the ghastly visage of a man who looked feral, with one eye shadowed over, his mouth drawn up in a crooked sneer—the result of getting kissed with the corner of a tomahawk—and his clothes that of a distinguished Union officer. He placed the detailed sketch on the table, whereupon a gnarled, hairy hand grabbed it. The trapper stared at the sketch silently.

"Have you seen this man? Formerly known as First Officer Douglas Richards. He goes by something else now."

Gun metal gray eyes flitted from the sketch to him, and back.

"What's your name, son? You speak good English for a native."

"Kawaska."

At this, bushy black eyebrows crawled up a leathery forehead.

"White Horse, huh? The hell is an Osage doing all the way out here in Ute territory? You're far from home, boy."

Kawaska was surprised this man knew his tribe. To most whites, their names all sounded the same, like so much gibberish. He must've been extremely well-traveled to be able to differentiate between such dialects, which meant he had good knowledge of this foreign land. Kawaska was eager to continue the conversation.

"I'm looking for that man. He calls himself—"

"The White Wolf. Been hearing a lot about this feller recently. Thought it was some kind of Indian folktale to scare away us traders from the mountains, till I saw the wanted posters and seen the villages after he was done with 'em. Reckon you're after the bounty on his head?" he asked, handing the sketch back to Kawaska. He shook his head.

"No. I'm hunting him, but not for money."

The trapper nodded sagely, as if he expected this answer.

"Yeah, reckon a lot of people would like to put that crazy bastard down. He moves quick, though. Bout two weeks ago I bought a load of beaver pelts off a band of Utes I do a lot of commerce within Pike's Peak, fifteen miles south of here. Village looked like it'd seen the wrath of god. He came in the night, set fire to anything that would burn, screaming nonsense—moved like the Devil, they said. Them southern

Utes are tough, not people I wanna cross, and even *they* spoke of the White Wolf with fear. Came in like lightning, they said. Killed whoever stood up to 'em and ate the ones they killed. Heard that exact same story through the grapevine a few days ago, some people come running into town from a small mining outpost up near Thunder Butte, not even five miles from here. For a man to get to Thunder Butte from Pike's Peak in a week, he'd have to ride like a madman, day and night, no rest." He concluded this crucial piece of information with a long pull of ale and a belch.

Kawaska stood up, a sense of urgency overcoming him. For months he'd been tracking this monster down, leaving behind what he thought was the whole of the world to fulfill his destiny. Now, after following old breadcrumbs and dead ends, his destiny finally seemed within reach.

"Thank you," he said, and knocked back the firewater, relishing the blaze of warmth in his belly as he turned to venture back out into the frozen maw of night.

"Careful, ain't no one whose tried to hunt that bastard down has ever came back to tell their tale," the trapper said to his back.

Kawaska tried to see past the whirling tempest of shifting white all about him, the twin gouts of steam that erupted from his horse's nostrils not helping in the matter of visibility. He'd been heading due north for two days now, his investigation into the mining outpost of Thunder Butte leading him this way, far off the main trade routes, deep into feral land. Though he was near frozen through and exhausted from having gone two days without sleep, he did not stop. This was the closest he'd gotten so far to the monster his father had created. From the abhorrent tales of depravity and violence relayed to him by the miners he'd interviewed, it sounded like Richard's descent into madness was only accelerating. What was once a simple plan to extol revenge on the white men who'd kicked them off their own land had grown into a deadly problem.

Kawaska shivered underneath his makeshift shawl of coyote skin, but no amount of fur in the world could keep out the sheer mountain wind. He longed for the mild, temperate winter season of his homeland. He could make out the vague shapes of the jagged mountain peaks to either side of him like he was inside the vast jaws of the Earth Mother, the sight of which never ceased to amaze him. Before this odyssey, he'd never left the rolling green foothills and large, slow-moving rivers of the Ozark Upheaval; he hadn't known a world vastly different than his own existed outside of it. Here, the mountains were bigger and meaner, as were the animals who roamed them. Bobcats and whitetail were replaced by cougars and wolves.

He longed deeply for his village, for what remained of his family, for plump catfish and elderberry and other delicious things that this place of sharp earth and teeth did not produce. He closed his eyes for a second and tried to transport himself back to the large brown vein of the Missouri River, feeling himself sweat through the humid heat as he and Anawago piloted their canoes through the fast-flowing water, eager to catch the delicious gar and flatheads that called the river home.

Something whistled past his ear, shocking him out of his daydream. Just as he began to register the lancing pain in his ear, he felt something else fly over his shoulder. He had just enough time to make out the fletching of an arrow as it flew past in a blur.

"Ho!" he screamed to his horse, digging heels into ribs to stop it. Just as he did, two more arrows materialized out of the white abyss; he could feel one of them sink into his beloved mustang, his *non'nunge* jumping and neighing in outrage as the shaft stuck out from her neck. Kawaska was thrown back and into the cold, white powder that cushioned his fall. He stayed buried in the snow, not daring to get up as he watched two more arrows sink into the horse's belly as it rose up on its hind legs in protest.

It staggered for a second as it came down, then collapsed forward, its sides heaving and the wet, harsh sound of its breathing heard over the tearing roar of the wind. Steam rose from it as it lay some five feet away, dying, and soon Kawaska could smell the blood as it began to melt the snow between them.

It let out one last indignant, gurgling snort, and the horse stilled. Kawaska slowly grabbed the obsidian gutting knife from a pocket on his deer skin tunic and held it in a saber grip close to his chest, the blade honed sharper than any bone utensil his tribe could make. He traded six whitetail skins and a beaver pelt to a white trader named Eustace for the blade, who'd claimed it'd been forged from the earth-glass of a volcano and was the sharpest non-metal blade in existence. He'd had to use it three times on this journey so far, and it did indeed part flesh from bone with wicked efficiency.

He waited, his body slowly regaining warmth as he lay in the insulating snow and out of the sheer winds that cut through just above him. He waited, slowing his breathing, watching as the shapes materialized, slow and low, out of the white veil. He waited as they approached with *mindses* drawn, their bows as big as their small bodies, which were clad in drooping layers of wolf skins.

At first, he thought he'd stumbled upon the corrupted pack of white devils he'd been searching for, until one drew close enough that he could see the dark face that poked out from under the sundered jaw of a wolf's head. No, these were first nation peoples, Sioux or perhaps Dakota tribe. He'd heard to be wary of these fierce, warring brothers of the north from the traders and trappers he'd accosted along the way, their grief strong and their hearts filled with hate as they too were evicted from their mother grounds. They would not care that he was first nation; if he was not an immediate member of their tribe, he was an enemy.

He waited until the foot of the nearest man was only a few inches away from him, the wolf's head scanning the horizon, not thinking to look down at what lay at his feet. Kawaska's arm moved with the speed of a viper striking, and he felt the blade sink into the Achilles. He pulled back savagely and felt the blade sunder tendons easily. With a high-pitched scream, the man fell to one knee, and Kawaska pulled him down, the black blade moving in a blur as it went in and out of the body in rapid succession.

More arrows soared through the space he'd just occupied, but now he was back on the ground, pulling this thrashing, bleeding person atop him, cherishing the warm blood that spilled over him and thawed his frozen fingers. The body trembled as arrows sunk into it and not Kawaska, more blood erupting from it with each shaft. These people must've had the eye of the eagle to shoot with such accuracy through this hellscape of ivory; equal parts fear and respect entered Kawaska as more of them drew closer, converging on the two prone bodies.

A foot shot out and kicked the body away, which now resembled a porcupine with all those arrows sticking out of it, and Kawaska lashed out again, the black glint of blade honing in on more cuttable meat. He felt the blade glance off calf muscle, but the person was quick, kicking out with his leg and pinning Kawaska's arm to the cold earth. Kawaska lashed out with his other hand, meaning to grab and pull the man off balance, but soon they were atop him, pinning him to the ground.

Kawaska was then looking at the fine points of two spearheads that hovered an inch away from each eyeball. He unfocused from these and instead looked at the people yielding them. Kawaska blinked in disbelief, for the faces he saw adorned in wolf's head hoods and pelts were not those of men, but boys. He looked over with incredulity at the corpse he'd used as a shield, and saw the young, almost cherubic face poking out from a bundle of wolf skin.

The one who had his arm pinned down spoke, but Kawaska did not know Sioux or Cheyenne or whatever tongue it was that rattled off his lips. When incomprehension remained on Kawaska's face, the boy switched to severely stilted English.

"You...You are not *wasichu*. Why here? Where from?" he asked, almond-shaped eyes unblinking as he knelt down to examine Kawaska closely. Small hands reached for the pendant Kawaska always wore around his neck, a sigil made by his father, the now-exiled shaman who was responsible for this whole mess. The boy examined the sigil, which was comprised of the fangs of a copperhead lashed together with hair from both himself and his mother to signify the blood ties to his tribe.

"NO!" he screamed as the boy ripped it away and pocketed it. He tried to overpower them, for they were just children, and he was a full-grown man. But before he could even struggle, he saw the high arcing blow of a war club for a split second before it cracked into his head.

He awoke with a throbbing ache in his skull, ghostly images of fire danced across his vision as he vacillated between wakefulness and death. Unable to move his legs or arms, he understood he was bound. He lay prone on a stone floor, and as he finally came fully awake, he saw he was in a large cave; the air around him did not bite at his exposed flesh, but warmed it. Kawaska groaned as he slowly raised himself to a sitting position, eyes squeezing shut to override the blinding thunderclaps of pain that shot through his head with each slow beat of his heart.

His tongue felt and tasted like a lump of dry moss in his mouth; his stomach groaned. He looked up to see a tall figure sitting across the fire from him. Through the dancing flame,s Kawaska could see this was no child, but an elder; a deeply lined face was poking out from a beautiful ornate ritual dress made of bone and bear skin, the feathers of a red-tailed hawk lined his hood, and the reflection of the fire cast onto eyes glazed over with cataracts. He'd been grinding something in a large wooden bowl; the sound of vegetation being ground against wood in a steady rhythm played in counterpoint to the crackle of the fire.

When he saw his prisoner had come fully awake, he arose slowly, and without looking at anything in particular, the blind man crossed the cave and knelt in front of Kawaska.

"Evoohta," he said, his trembling voice deep and guttural, sticking a gnarled, arthritic hand into the green paste that filled the bowl. He presented a glistening lump to Kawaska, an earthy but sweet aroma wafting up from the mass. Kawaska hesitated only slightly before opening his mouth in reflex, his empty stomach telling his body to consume anything that appeared even remotely edible. The elder delicately pushed clumps of the green mass into his mouth, and Kawaska chewed, his eyes watering with the bitter, sour taste.

But he ate anyway, taking every offering until the hand stopped coming and, instead, the elder began to help himself. He finished what was left of the bowl, and then grabbed a water skin that had been hanging off his side. He presented it to Kawaska in inquiry, and Kawaska nodded gratefully, as the matter he'd just consumed left on his tongue a filmy, sour residue and stung his throat. As he drank deeply of the leathery-tasting water, he realized his mouth had begun to go numb, starting with his lips and proceeding down his throat. He tried to say something, but it came out as gibberish, drool spooling from numb lips.

The elder called out loudly, his voice echoing off the high cavern walls. He sat next to Kawaska, glazed eyes staring in his general direction. Kawaska got the sense that despite his physical blindness, this man could see with the vision of his soul, like Kawaska's father had. His own vision began to alter, the dancing flames growing in brightness and vividness. Small shapes flowed into the room like smoke, lining the walls around him. Small wolves that walked on two feet sat next to the fire, their tiny hands filled with green leaves, the sounds of their chewing tickling his ears as his hearing became profoundly sensitive; he could hear every leaf being crushed between molars, could hear his own blood flowing through his veins, the spitting of pine knots in the fire.

One of the little wolves presented the elder with a shining black blade, and Kawaska realized it was his obsidian knife. He tried to rear back as the elder approached him with it, but he found his mind and body had become detached at some point. He could only produce a deep glottal sound in his throat as the blade approached. He felt his hands and ankles become untethered, felt them fall uselessly against the ground as he lay in a heap.

The elder began to chant, his guttural baritone rhythm a pleasing sound to Kawaska. Then, leathery hands were upon him, sitting him upright. As soon as he was sat up, he felt his gorge rise in an acidic bulge, and geysers of green sludge erupted from him. He stared down in amazement at the swirling veridian puddle in his lap, the glistening mucous-filmed surface catching the firelight and creating dazzling prisms of light.

The wolves began to chant in unison with the elder, an invisible pulse filling the cave as he felt the cadence of their words in his bones. He felt leathery fingers cup his chin. He looked up at the elder, his face sporting deep arroyos and valleys of ancient flesh, his eyes two portals into the ether. He pressed his forehead to Kawaska's, and with this intimate form of physical contact, Kawaska felt a current form between them, a binding of minds. And as he saw himself in the reflection of two white orbs, he felt himself gazing into the other plains, where the tree of life planted its roots, where all things living grew and died and were reborn. He felt himself leaving his body, leaving this cave, leaving everything.

He watched with the dizzying, omniscient bird's eye view of the all-father as First Officer Douglas Richards and the 34th infantry battalion razed what was left of his village to the ground. Ornate sabers slicing through flesh, horses trampling women and children to pulp, muskets breathing their dragon's breath into the night as lead flew and tore apart flesh and shattered bone. The view zoomed in on the man leading the charge, a regal figure with combed and parted brown hair, shaped muttonchops, piercing blue eyes, and a blue uniform adorned in all matter of service medallions. He stood atop his war horse, surveying with pride the damage he'd wrought on one of the last stubborn villages that'd refused to acknowledge the emancipation of their own land.

There came a high-pitched ululation, and Kawaska watched his own self appear from the smoke and mist of that morning's slaughter, his lean body flying through the air as his tomahawk soared. He watched an event he'd lived through in this profound new perspective as the weapon cleaved off the officer's nose and caught the corner of his mouth, tearing his charming grin into something crooked and ghastly.

The all-seeing eye followed him as he ran, musket shots whizzing past as union men screamed for their fallen officer. He'd raced back to his yurt, which was on the outskirts of the village, farther into the tree line than the others, where he'd instructed his sister and mother to hide, their status as a shaman's offspring allowing them to live apart from the main sprawl so that his father could focus on meditation and praying.

It was there he'd found two infantrymen atop his sister, trying to perform unspeakable acts upon her. His mother lay slumped in a corner, her skull caved in. His father was held at gunpoint, weeping and cursing these men while his sister was violated. Kawaska only remembered seeing red after that, his rage so great that the primal spirits of the *Meen-tsoo*, the war bear, came forth, and in a blur of motion and blood, he'd stabbed the two rapists, dual-weld tomahawks decapitating one and the other quickly sliced to ribbons.

The man with the musket had just enough time to turn around before Kawaska leaped upon him like something feral, teeth bearing down on the exposed throat, hot bitter blood flooding his mouth as teeth sundered jugular and arteries.

The scene changed. A cave similar to the one Kawaska's physical body was currently in. With the flesh of white men still stuck between his teeth, he helped his grief-crazed father perform the forbidden ritual, using blood magic long banned by his tribe, the People of the Upland Forest. With the body of his sister wrapped in a ceremonial shroud nearby, her life taken from her by subsequent infection from her injuries, the two men cast forth an ancient, elemental demon to haunt the soul of First Officer Douglas Richards as revenge for his slaughter. Kawaska saw the demon emerge from the fire, a roiling cloud of black that erupted from the flames and flowed through the roof of the cave.

It shot like a meteor through the night, the all-seeing eye following it effortlessly as it crossed miles of foothills in seconds, where it angled sharply down and slammed through a canvas tent and into the infirmary where Richards was held. No one saw this specter, of course, those around the officer only saw the man shoot upright from his bed, eyes going skyward, his torn mouth gibbering in an ancient tongue not spoken for a millennium. This same madness infected the men of his battalion as well, the conditions of the curse applying to all those who'd been part of the raid on his father's village.

From there on out they did not sleep, did not walk or talk like mortal men. The demon found Richards a most suitable vessel, and the entity that was supposed to render him a useless, gibbering invalid instead turned him into a warrior with unquenchable blood lust, one that constantly ran stolen horses to death and flowed unstoppably through the countryside as Richards and his men attacked and raided in random, chaotic patterns of battle, their only needs to kill and to sup of the flesh from those they slain.

Another scene change, this time in a vast canyon village surrounded by the sharp, massive mountains that had so awed Kawaska upon first seeing them. He saw the elder cowering among these children, hiding them in a cave deep underground as their parents and grandparents were systematically slaughtered and masticated above. The soldiers materialized out of the night, coming through the dense pine forests and loping on all fours like animals, their uniforms long shredded to tatters and the miasma of their rotting, unwashed flesh could be smelled before they were seen. At the head of the pack was him, Douglas Richards, who rode in on a black steed whose mouth was caked with foam and whose nostrils ejected bloody plumes as Douglas ran this recent acquisition far past its breaking point.

He leaped off the horse just as it collapsed, moving with the speed and grace of the lithest and youngest of the Cheyenne warriors that surrounded him, his once neatly combed hair and prim beard grown into long, matted tendrils caked with blood and mud, his mouth open to bellow in the tongue of the one who inhabited him. He fought, feasting on the warriors as they fell, needing the blood fresh and hot as it spurted from arteries.

Kwaska was jolted awake without realizing he'd been asleep. He looked around; the fire smoldered, producing a weak glow, and in it he could see the frozen faces of the cubs staring at him, the shaman's scabrous visage locked in a state of horrified awe.

"It...was...you...Your tribe is...responsible for this..." he said, and Kawaska found he could understand what the shaman said, though he still spoke the highland language.

"We didn't mean for it to happen like this. We did it to ruin him, not empower him," Kawaska said in his mother tongue as the cubs rose, and they began to howl, a sound of rage and grief. They took up their spears and closed in on Kawaska, but the shaman raised a trembling hand and their war cry stopped instantly. Still, they stood with weapons poised, eyes glinting in the low light.

"It must be you who stops him then. Binding rites of blood magic can only be undone by those who are foolish enough to perform them. I will instill within you the true guidance of the North Star, and it will show you where the one who calls himself White Wolf resides. I shall grant you safe passage through my land, but just this once. Go, White Horse, son of all-seer Imperial Eagle. Go, and remove this stain from your tribe, bring honor to the People of the Upland Forest, and peace to the rest of us."

Kawaska's knife and his sigil were placed firmly into his palm; the spears lowered.

The desecrated corpse lashed to a ponderosa pine was the freshest evidence he'd seen yet. Further inspection showed the person—sex was unidentifiable given that the breasts and groin had been eaten away—was bound to the tree using their own intestine and sinews, and the skull of a stag elk hung in place of a human head, its antlers draped in frozen viscera.

He understood now why the horse the Cheyenne had gifted him with for his quest had staunchly refused to proceed any further up the steep mountain track he'd been following. The creature nearly bucked him off when he tried to spur her further and had grown steadily more skittish throughout the day as he let the instinctual compass the shaman had bestowed upon him guide him. She must've smelled the corruption long before he.

The ride out from those strange caves had seen him through terrain beyond his wildest imaginings. The White Wolf seemed intent on spreading his abhorrent language of violence and depravity to the very ends of the earth as Kawaska ventured down narrow, barely navigable trails with sheer hundred-foot ice walls to one side and drop-offs to torrential white water rivers far below.

He saw evidence with each day that he was growing closer to his quarry. Human bones gnawed to nubs discarded along the trail, piles of viscera that not even the wolves or bears would touch, occasional odd symbols whose very geometry made one sick to look at scorched into the various species of pine that dared grow in such a barren tundra.

He walked past the corpse, his blade drawn. He had been gifted thick wolf skins that did a much better job at keeping the cold at bay, and he moved freely through the forest, trying to summon forth the clarifying rage and courage of the War Bear. He'd begun to pass odd, super-heated pools of water that occasionally shot geysers of steam into the air, and it was around the caldera of one of these hot springs he saw the first of Douglas's men. He bounded down the almost-vertical cliff wall ahead and landed on all fours like a cat.

White skin long gone the shade of catfish belly, this particular man was missing an ear and had a nasty dent in the side of his head, and that was all Kawaska had time to take in before the man pounced like a cougar, covering some ten feet and closing the ground between them in seconds. Kawaska had just enough time to bring the blade up and felt it punch through breast bone as they were both knocked to the ground.

Kawaska gritted his teeth as he slammed into frozen stone but leaned into the momentum and kicked the gnashing, hissing man with yellowed eyes up and over him with all his might. The man was all stringy sinew and bone, it felt like he was kicking away a doll. He flew high, his limbs flailing, and landed right in one of the bubbling cauldrons.

A sound like pork fat spitting in a fire came to him, and Kawaska rolled to his feet just in time to see the abomination clawing itself out of the hot spring, boiled flesh sloughing off bones as it staggered towards him, steam rising as it collapsed in the snowy ground, melting into it.

Kawaska turned as he heard a commotion behind him and saw another from the battalion, this one hairless and naked, looking more like an imp than a man, stare at him with something like confusion before it let out some guttural slew of consonant growls and bounded off up the slope, running away from him. *Using itself as bait to lure me in?* he thought, and could feel the adrenaline and rage flood him at the remembrance of his people's genocide. He ran after the loping feral thing, hoping the creature would lead him to White Wolf.

The closer he grew to the mountain's peak, the more he was sure this was an ambush, and he breathed deeply, preparing for the final fight of his life, preparing to die if it meant vanquishing this abomination from the earth.

He reached the summit and looked down to see a large bowl-shaped caldera stretched out before him. He saw the barren remains of a primitive village similar to his own, the air here much warmer than below.

The imps surrounded him, unmoving but crouched to strike. The White Wolf stood tall among them, chewing on a human arm like it was a turkey leg. The bodies of the original villagers lay strewn about, half-eaten, and some with their limbs rearranged into grotesque mockeries of the symbols seared into the trees. One crawled towards Kawaska, trailing entrails behind, her body crudely ripped in half.

He stepped forward and promptly slit the woman's throat, ending her misery as he strolled boldly toward the line of abominations.

"You..." White Wolf said, the voice deeper than any human register could go. He did not immediately attack as Kawaska expected him to, but instead let him draw closer, until he could see the ruined body of Douglas Richards, the feet worn down to the bone, skeletal phalanges webbed with maggots. His hair was tied back in a mockery of a tribal war chief, braided with bones, his face smudged in a war paint that looked like a mixture of shit and blood. The very sight of him appalled Kawaska.

"I've come to put an end to your reign, demon." Kawaska called, his voice strong and unshaken, the spirit of the War Bear flowing through his veins. White Wolf began to speak just as the first of his minions lunged at Kawaska.

"End my reign? But it was you who called forth my soul from the ether—"

Kawaska ducked and rolled, opting for the war club tucked away on his back, breaking femurs and shattering humeruses, understanding these things couldn't truly be killed but only debilitated.

"You and that other, I heard you call my name."

"A mistake! You were sent to haunt this man, not sail him like a ship!" Kawaska roared as his club stoved in a skull, his flesh taking bite wounds and stab wounds, but the pain was distant, unimportant.

"Ah, such hubris, to think you could control the likes of me. I was a warrior long before your ancestors were semen in the balls of weak men. I do the bidding of no one!" White Wolf roared, sending his men onwards.

But Kawaska cut through them all, no longer fighting as one man now, but as a vessel piloted by an energy as pure as the demon's within Richards was evil. His weapon sailed true and every strike to his enemies was either crippling or lethal. The White Wolf saw he fought with the veracity of those he'd shared the earth with long ago. Watching the young warrior shirking off the physical trauma unheeded, a primal excitement filled the demon—the possibility of a true fight worthy of its kind, something more entertaining than systematic slaughter.

White Wolf called off its demons and approached Kawaska, the young warrior's body sheened in blood and sweat, his club caked in the flesh and hair of many men.

"Fight me, White Wolf, and be sent back to the hell from which you came!" Kawaska roared, charging at the corrupted shell of a man.

White Wolf dodged and weaved, his desecrated body moving with impossible grace, but soon even he could not keep up with the flurry of relentless blows Kawaska delivered. The demon did not realize until it was too late that the crazed warrior was beating him back and back, edging him closer to the steaming, bubbling lake right behind him.

Finally, White Wolf saw his opening and grabbed the war club in mid-swing, pinning it to his battered body and ripping it from Kawaska's grasp, his other hand shooting out to wrap around Kawaska's throat. He thought the warrior would panic, but Kawaska did something no mortal had ever managed to do.

He surprised White Wolf.

"You think I'm not prepared to die to end this? You are wrong!" he screamed.

Kawaska moved forward, bear hugging the wretched, smelling bag of bones, and together they plunged into three-hundred-degree water. Kawaska kept his arms wrapped tight around White Wolf even as he was boiled alive, ensuring the demon whose true name only Kawaska's father could speak would be trapped in a ruined, boiled body forever.

Boundary

Morgan Melhuish

Boundary remembers sweat. There was so much of it at its birth. Salt slick flicked from wiped brows. Sweat gathered kiss me curls, plastered cow's licks, fringes stuck fast on foreheads. Beads of perspiration ran down a nose, the back of an ear, a grubby red neck.

Planks of wood, the bones of Boundary, were flecked with it. Clammy damp palms gripped saws, hammers, spades, and planes.

The town absorbed the sweet swelter like a varnish, quickly sucking it within itself before it could evaporate in the bastard heat of those grimy days.

Boundary collected that sweat and toil, the blood sacrifice of the ram, the iron stench of ichor filling foundations. It took the spit and gobbets of phlegm cast into golden dust; it took all they had to give.

Boundary remembers the men cursing, heaving, grunting, erecting, bringing it to life.

Boundary was christened.

It was the most remote point across the frontier. Until it wasn't, and someone went further....

But they were glory days. Gold fever ran rampant, driving men crazy as mercury fumes. First, there were panners before the town even got started, then a stamp mill processing ore. Another followed. Mines were dug. Seams blown.

The general store was stacked with cans and jars of apricots and pears, squash, and corn. Pies and tarts. Razors and soap, medicines and rubs, roach killer. Slices of bacon. Little luxuries ready to be added on tick in the grocer's ledger.

Sears catalogue men brought deliveries of paint, a gramophone, cheap boxy furniture, lime lights, and a barber's chair.

The saloon's bar flowed with whiskeys called Tarantula and Tanglefoot, gut rot all, and the few streets in Boundary coursed with people.

The town's lifeblood pulsed with prospectors, fixers, hunters, engineers, planners, schemers, lovers, dreamers, the desperate of all kinds.

Boundary saw it all. Triumph and tragedy. Winners at cards and blown stakes. Cat house women gasping at rough disregard. It saw fights and brawls. Laughter and prayer. Dead men walking and martial law being dished out.

Then the stagecoach would rattle through, depositing more fortune hunters at its door.

Boundary boomed.

And just like that, it was abandoned to the heat and dust.

They raped the earth, plundered each rock and crevice until there was nothing left.

Smart men read the signs and skipped town in moonlit flits, their debts unpaid. It was the slow on the uptake, and the hopeful, that suffered most. The townsfolk cut their losses, headed off, their tails between their legs. American dreams crushed.

Boundary swallowed tears then. Its first true taste of despair.

It could do nothing but offer shelter to comfort, but no one wanted to stay.

Without its people, Boundary was half dead.

Where once there was Humanity, now spiny lizards hid from hawks, scuttling into broken homes. Packs of coyote roamed empty streets, and kangaroo rats scavenged without much success.

A poor substitute for the life people had brought to Boundary.

Tumbleweed caught on porches. Lonely swirls of sand, whisked up by the wind, rattled window panes, knocked at doors. The rusting sign hanging from the saloon squeaked eerily.

Ashes to ashes.

Dust to dust.

Boundary longed for the past.

Look!

Here's Jim Anson, died of a snake bite; finest moustache in town.

Here's Ma Fowler, who worked the general stores. They say her heart overflowed with kindness 'til it burst, and she passed on clutching a handful of dimes.

Here's Shade Jackson and Phineas Baxter drunkenly reenacting their fatal pistol duel, both too full of liquor and bravado to back down.

Boundary has shaken their bones free of the grit they were interred in. It has stirred their souls, brought them back to listlessly wander the earth.

It only wants company.

Boundary didn't realise the ghosts would bring others.

The wails, the howls, the spectral gunshot—the calls echoed across the plain like kestrels screeching.

This twisted siren song lured the curious, the self-proclaimed fearless; they rode up to Boundary's streets to sate their spirit of inquiry.

It wasn't like before, but Boundary took what meagre pickings it was given, the brief warmth of a body.

It remembered men without names riding into town, how they never stayed long.

Boundary couldn't let that stand.

And so the disappeared brought more. One or two on a moon-lit night, faking bravery or scientific curiosity, a misguided reporter searching for a story, buoyed by a nip of Dutch courage.

The town tried to keep them all: to wall them up, have them tumble into an abandoned cellar, trip and smack their head against a jagged stoop.

Just as it had tasted sweat and tears, Boundary wanted blood. It wanted to make them pay for leaving. It wanted people in its streets again.

Boundary got its wish.

A mob rode into town.

It had forgotten how men lash out at what they don't understand. How they rage.

Boundary was shunned again. The band of angry men smashed in windows, shattered glass, and splintered the doors of what had once been a sanctuary.

Not content with wanton vandalism, they razed the town to the ground, cheering at the flames, buoyed by their good work.

They believed the place excised of its ghosts, fire purifying the desert dirt. They slapped each other's backs and rode back home to friendlier places. They kicked off boots and went to their beds, content with a job well done.

The men had fought against an empty place and won.

Boundary was broken, smouldering embers, charred stumps. It burnt, and it hurt....

Yet something remained. The sweat, blood, and tears, the dreams and the despair and the life... it was still there. Desire and greed blazed within.

But it was Boundary no more.

This nameless thing was unleashed, unfettered by cartography, unfixed to a place or name.

It bounded away, wild and free.

And hungry.

In Pursuit of the Navarino Nobody

Aristo Couvaras

Palomino Digest Presents:
In Pursuit of The Navarino Nobody,
An Account by One Elijah Jacob Delaney.

Chapter One
A Tall a Tale as Any...

"A tall a tale as any..."

"A tall a tale as any? Why if it ain't the tallest, most preposterous spouting of manure I ever heard!" a man at the bar said.

From the table nearest the bar, another man leaned back in his chair, keeping sure to hold his hand of cards close to his chest, and said to the man who had spoken, "See, I don't recall having told you no story, and I certainly don't recall asking none on your opinion."

The man at the bar spun about, one hand still on the counter, cradling his glass of whiskey, the other hanging low by his holster. He said, "Best you recall, friend. Best you recall."

The card-playing man, who had been regaling the other poker players at the table with his tall tale, asked the dealer for another card. All the while he kept his gaze fixed on the man accosting him from the bar. He placed his hand down, cards face-up, excepting for the one he recently accepted from the dealer. That one, for some reason, he stuck in the band of his tattered hat.

One of the other poker players let out a low whistle. Another whispered, "Ace of spades, ace of clubs, eight of spades, eight of clubs."

"Dead Man's Hand," said the lone man at the bar, grinning wickedly. His thumb flicked the catch of his holster with practiced ease.

"Well, go on then, gunslinger," said the man with the card in the band of his hat. There was a twinkle in his eye, akin to the sun catching a drop of rattlesnake venom hanging precariously from deadly fangs. He made certain to show that his hands were both on the table.

The barkeep said, "Easy there, gentlemen. If'n y'all got some business to settle, why don't y'all go and conclude your affairs outside my establishment."

A gun went off.

The barkeep's head painted the mirror behind him in vermillion and pink scatterings, adding to the grimy patina of the glass. Right about then, the mirror itself cracked, making a spider's web of the reflection, which was showcasing the broken skull of the barkeep. Glass shards fell, taking bottles on display with them, and crashing to the floor where the barkeep's body slumped.

The men at the poker table cleared themselves from there in a hurry, all save the one with the Dead Man's Hand. "As I told you," he said, "Go on then, *gunslinger*."

The man at the bar had not yet drawn his revolver. He was petrified, thinking at the sound of the gun, it must have been aimed in his direction and that he should, by all reasonable accounts, be dead. He took notice of the man with the Dead Man's Hand. An ebony-handled revolver was now atop the cards, a ribbon of smoke presently dancing upwards from the barrel.

"See I won't be asking you a third time, on account of three being a holy number, and myself being only recently at odds with the Divine, I do not wish to incur any more of His wrath than I may already have done. But I do solemnly wish to incur yours...*gunslinger.*"

The gunslinger's eyes went to the pistol atop the cards. The man at the table smiled, a grisly countenance, all teeth and no joy. All the other patrons were watching, breathing shallow breaths, hands going to their own holsters. Another fragment from the mirror fell, singing as it shattered on the hardwood floor.

The gunslinger cleared leather. Fired once. Twice. Three times. The smell of cordite mingled with blood and spilled liquor. The gunslinger trained his iron on the man at the poker table—who was now slumped forward—ready to dispatch more shots. His hand trembled. Blood pooled on the floor beneath the poker table.

"I'll go and get Sherriff Wycombe," somebody said.

The man slumped at the poker table said, "Now, why you wanna go bother your ol' sheriff over a little misunderstanding as regards the authenticity of my story? It's not as if anybody died over it." He laughed and sat up. Spat blood onto the floor.

The gunslinger shot him three more times, still depressing his trigger when the gun reported an empty series of clicks and his bullets were spent. The man who had drawn the Dead Man's Hand went over backward like a dead man.

The gunslinger said, "Well, I'll take that as your admitting to it, in fact, being a tall tale, then." He shakily tipped his glass to his lips and took comfort in the bite of the whiskey.

It quickly became apparent, however, that the dead man was less than dead, as he rose and pulled himself to his feet, laughing like a hellion as he did so. Where one bullet had put out his eye, there was no bloody wound, rather a gaping aperture whirling with mist, like smoke on the water. He reached for the ebony-handled revolver and shot the gunslinger's shooting hand, cackling like a man possessed. He shot the gunslinger again, in the knee, bringing the man down, and mounted him and began beating the man with that ebony handle. Blood leaped as high as the glass recently drained on the bartop. Through the squelching of blood and the noises of meat being tenderized, there finally came the unmistakable echoes of bone being broken. Of brains being tossed about like pig feed.

"Reckon y'all can go call on your Sheriff now, if'n you're still inclined."

Panic ensued as patrons made their way from the establishment.

The storyteller, gambler, and self-confessed man at recent odds with the Divine drained the drops of blood from the gunslinger's glass, licking the rim and his own palms when he was done. He picked up his hat from the floor and took out the card in the band. He smiled viciously at what he saw. Then he took his fair share from the poker table and walked on over to a solitary man at a table in the corner, too terrified to move.

"You a free man?" he asked.

"I am, sir," the free man stammered.

"And here's me thinking they weren't civilized in these parts...What's your name, son?"

"Elijah Jacob Delaney, sir."

"You didn't think mine was a tall tale did you, Elijah?"

"Can't say I heard too much of it from here."

"Perhaps a day may come where I tell it to you. I thought it was a tall tale, for what it's worth. Though I suppose there ain't but a few who won't say the same if'n you recount this here day to them," the man who should have been dead said, his eye and wounds still smoking with a shroud like nothing borne from the flames of a fire. "I sincerely did think it tall." And he placed the card face-up before Elijah.

It was a tarot card, and inscribed on it were the words: *The Hanging Man*.

"Wonder how that got mixed up in the deck," he said and grinned something that made Elijah's blood run as cold as rivers in winter. The infernal smoke leaked out from between the man's teeth and out the hole where his eye had been.

"Between us," he said to Elijah, "I thought it was just about as tall a tale as I ever heard…"

– E. J. Delaney.

Chapter Two
The Shootout for Calico's Soul

A stick was held over the fire and used to light the tip of a cheroot.

"You reckon we'll make it there by midmorning tomorrow?" Elijah asked.

The man on the other side of the fire drew on the cheroot and let the smoke trail like a river out from his mouth. As it drifted over his face, casting an opaque pall over the man's eye, Elijah felt the frosty fingers of remembrance clutch his heart.

"*Sí*," the man said. "Reckon we will. Reckon he'll still be there, his bones will be picked clean, but he'll be there." The man chuckled, a wheezing sort of sound. "What you gonna call it? This dime novel of yours?"

"Well, I ain't set on a title just yet. But I'm pondering on something akin to 'A Verified Account of the Exploits of the *Vaquero* Villa.'"

The light of the fire danced on the man's bared teeth. "The *vaquero* Villa," he mused. "It's better than a host of names I've gone by. Of course, any man who ever called me one I didn't take to, didn't call me it but more than once."

It was Elijah's turn to offer a smile. "Well, Mister Villa, I can only then count myself lucky you're partial to the title."

"Partial," Villa echoed the word. "They let you go to a fancy school, one of 'em like I've heard about in Boston? What with all your reading and writing?"

Elijah set about unrolling his bedroll. He said, "I'm fairly certain my exploits and story won't excite a man who's led a life such as yours."

"Well, why do it then? Tell tall tales making out killing is such a wondrous thing?"

Tall tales. Elijah felt the icy grip again. He let the moment pass and asked Villa, "Why do you want your story told?"

"Well, that's easy, you paying me. Anyhow, it's safer showing you the bones of a man I've killed than having to kill again."

"Didn't reckon a man whose walked the paths you have gives too much thought to safety."

Villa exhaled smoke and looked up at the moon. "A man who walks those paths doesn't walk them too far if he don't have a care for safety."

"Well if that ain't the God's honest truth. That bit is for sure going in the book," Elijah said as he got into his bedroll. Within it, he felt the notch on the handle of his own pistol. He said, "Well then, goodnight, Mister Villa."

"Goodnight, Elijah. Reckon I'll be up a while longer, call it first watch. Even out here it's best to be cautious, have one pair of eyes open. Besides, men with notches on their guns don't sleep well, and don't let no one ever tell you different."

"Oh, I'll take your word for it," Elijah said and behind closed eyes, he saw a man leaking smoke like oil afire.

The morning sun beat down upon them as if it were a smith's hammer striking red-hot steel; the air was dry and dust clung to them as they led their mounts up the narrow path of the mesa.

"We should hitch the horses here," Villa said, pointing to a slim crevice in the cliffside. "Through there we'll get to the top and you can set your eyes on the bones of ol' Jesse Calico."

After squeezing their way through the gap and following the rise to the flat summit of the mesa, Elijah halted. His eyes fixed on the solitary tree growing atop this dry, arid spot. Hanging from one of the boughs was a frayed and weathered rope fashioned into a noose. It hung there, dancing with the breeze, no longer a simple length of cord but a viper still coiled and awaiting the prey it had been denied.

"You want I should tell you the story now?" Villa said, walking towards the tree. He kicked some sand aside at the base of the trunk, exposing a sun-bleached skull. Villa said, "Calico steel and calico eyes. Hm, the first did him little good when called upon, and the eyes...well, they ain't as blue as the sky over no prairie no more."

"The noose there," Elijah said. "Was it here when you and Mister Calico had your encounter?"

Villa pushed the brim of his sombrero up over his eyes, he fixed his gaze on the dangling open jaw of rope. "*Sí*," he said. He blew out air, Elijah saw the motion of Villa's hand drop to his holster, saw the *vaquero*'s eyes dart down to the open pits of Jesse Calico's skull.

"This is what you pay for, eh?" Villa said. "I'll tell you the story. Just as I said I would. Here where I can see he's still dead."

Villa regaled Elijah: "I heard it was the girls in the Madame's house which started calling him Jesse Calico, on account I'm sure you know of, his eyes. Certain you heard all sort of talk about him, roguish and handsome, quick on the draw. But before we had our differences, I knew Jesse, and he were a strange one. Face like his or not, it was the coin which brought him the attention of all those workin' girls. See, before Jesse became... business minded... he was strange. Had a belief in all sorts of devilish things. Used to wake at odd hours and look at these cards beneath the moon. Not playin' cards, mind you, ones with pictures on 'em. Grim things they were. Sure, I ain't no saint, but I knew well enough there are some things of an occult nature, things best left to a *bruja* and kept well away from. Things a man should never dabble with. Jesse Calico, well, his eyes may have been blue, but his soul was black..."

Elijah was scribbling madly in his journal, asking Villa to repeat parts of the tale.

"So," Elijah said. "This wasn't over revenge or money?"

Villa shook his head. "It was to save the soul of a man I once called my friend. He said it all on this very spot to me. I should leave him to become a hanged man on this tree, and then after this noose, no bullet would ever harm him."

Hanged man. Elijah looked up at the noose; it suddenly felt far too cool beneath the searing sun. "Where do you think he came upon such a notion?"

Villa said, "Told me he met a man who drank rattler whiskey out on the trail. Said the fella did it there before his very eyes, squeezed the venom right out of a live one, straight into the bottle, and drank it down like it weren't nothing. Just afore sunrise, the strange man took off, leaving the bottle with Jesse. Jesse were too scared to drink it, but he thought this might've been the place the man had come to, so as to become...whatever he was."

"So you shot Jesse to stop him from hanging himself?"

Villa shook his head. "I came up here to *stop* Jesse from hanging hisself. I shot him on account of him reaching for that calico steel of his."

– *E. J. Delaney.*

Chapter Three
The Bordello Bruja

"She was sweet on Jesse," was what the Madame had told Elijah. "O'course it ain't unheard of for working girls to go sweet on a handsome fella. And she weren't too popular with the rest of the clientele at the time. Heard tell most of the men 'round these parts were too scared to *conduct business* with her."

Presently, Elijah came to understand the Madame's meaning as he looked at the woman through the bars of the local sheriff's cell. Dried blood caked her lips and chin.

"Wouldn't get too close, if'n I were you," the deputy said. "Be mighty difficult to do that writing of yours with no fingers."

The woman bared her teeth; it wasn't a smile, not exactly.

"Then again," the deputy continued. "I try not to even look in her eyes, let alone talk to her."

"Ma'am," Elijah began, "You wouldn't mind telling me, would you?"

"Oh, I truly wouldn't, sir. They tasted good, each and every young man. The blood's always sweeter when their innocence is all riled up."

"Yet," Elijah said. "I've heard tell you never tasted the blood of Jesse Calico?"

She bared her teeth once more, grinning and licking her lips. "Oh, I did, Ol' Blue Eyes. And he mine."

"Yet no lawman ever found you stripping the flesh off Jesse's bones."

"O'course not," she replied. "Used to call him my Bordello Beau, and I was his Bordello *Bruja*. If'n he were still about and hadn't run off looking for nobodies and rattler whiskey, why—" she paused, attempting to taste what dried blood was still on her lips— "Why, then them Comanche wouldn't have dared bringing me in. Right scared of me, they was, same as any Chris'ian man or woman ought to be. But Jesse weren't."

"Way I've heard it told, Jesse Calico weren't exactly a God-fearing man," Elijah said.

She laughed dryly at his comment; the sound was like shed snake skin blowing over desert sand. "S'pose all depends on which gods it is you mean."

Elijah rose and placed the chair he had been sitting upon near the deputy's desk.

The woman said, "Is that all, mister? Sheriff said you'se a story man, you gon' put my tale in one of 'em dime novels of yours? How you think it ends for me, mister— end of a noose or burning at the stake?"

"How it ends," Elijah said, as he put his hat on and headed for the door, "ain't all that important. For what it's worth, it's the 'why' of how it ends for you. And that'll be the same as it was for Jesse, with you gone from this plane on account of you chasing after things no sane man or woman should ever seek."

She cackled before Elijah departed, "You're lookin' for him same as Jesse was, ain't you? You so desperate to drink rattler whiskey, mister? Or you just want to look in that smokin' eye o' his?"

Elijah stepped outside.

"Mister Delaney," the deputy said, following on Elijah's heels. "Hope it ain't impertinent of me to ask, but I got a copy of your latest dime novel, the *Vaquero Villa* one. You wouldn't mind signing it for me, would you? That is, while we wait for the sheriff to return with word on whether the Kwahadi—them what's known as Western Comanche—that brought her in will meet you too?"

The sun was dipping in the west, and the first breaths of winter blew across the prairie. On the outskirts of the town, where the Kwahadi had set up camp so as to trade but primarily to see the execution, Elijah waited to be granted an audience. A grizzled Brave, who spoke English, said to Elijah, "The sheriff may have told you she is a medicine woman, but this does not speak to the heart of what she truly is. You will treat her with respect and when she says the audience is over, you will leave."

"Understood," Elijah said, and began to unbuckle his gun belt. The Brave said, "You may keep your weapon. She has said that one who tells tales will not harm her. That you have but the life of one man taken and will not make her your second."

Elijah halted; his fingers caressed the notch on his pistol. The Brave nodded knowingly and led Elijah within the low tent.

The wizened woman had one eye shining like a full moon on a clear night, her other as milky as the patina of grime on the surface of aged milk in a pail. She spoke and the Brave translated for Elijah.

"Your concern is not for the woman and her witchy ways," the Brave said after listening to the elder. "Though her crimes are of the flesh, and it is for these transgressions she will be punished, we caught and brought her here for her crimes of the soul, for we would not have her spirit linger about our people. You know this to be true."

"I believe...well, I'm not sure what I believe," Elijah said, pausing so the Brave might translate. Elijah continued, "I have listened to those who sought to explain their actions with answers of the spirits. My concern, I suppose, is for one man who, over the years, I believe may have had some influence on those with unnatural beliefs."

The Brave and the elder spoke to each other for a time. After their parlay, the Brave said to Elijah, "This man you seek is no man. For all men owe a death; we all must let our spirits return someday from where they came." The old woman tapped the Brave and gestured with her hands. The Brave said, "Do you have the portrait? A small painting like the one men in a saloon might gamble with?"

After all this time, Elijah slowly withdrew the tarot card, holding it with a trembling hand. The Brave pointed to the elder and Elijah placed the card in her palm.

The elder began speaking and the Brave gave voice to the words so Elijah might understand. "Once a man, yes. One who lost a great deal, for whom no medicine could dull the pain. But a man no longer. More a snake that has shed its skin and allowed something else...something wicked, to inhabit the scales. You, the weaver of tales, would stare into an eye brimming with smoke. To know what you once saw, you truly did. But this will bring you no comfort. You have looked into the burning eye before. Why search to meet what was once a man again?"

Elijah could not trust himself fully to speak; he felt as if he were back in that saloon, watching a man rise impossibly after being shot. It surged through his bones and his teeth, this sensation that he was once again party to something beyond the realms of rationality.

"All you have said is true," Elijah said. "Is there no more you can tell me?"

"The plains are vast and the mountains high. There is much land in this world for a man with no name to stay hidden. Even with the expansion of this nation of railroads and new towns, a spirit cloaked in the flesh of a man has many leagues west to journey."

"Do you know where he is? Where he might be?" Elijah heard the insistent fervor in his voice.

The woman licked the card, where specks of aged blood had stained the picture.

"Where he has blood still, what has not become all smoke yet," the Brave translated. "Came from a great distance in the east, it is old blood of an old world, from across the great waters. Where a great battle was fought..."

Elijah and the Brave both waited.

The last word the woman spoke was, "Navarino."

– E. J. Delaney.

Chapter Four

A Grave Undertaking

In pursuit of this nobody from Navarino, this man—who was apparently not a man—who drank rattler venom and poured smoke from open wounds, and whose witnesses were all either dead or soon to be, Elijah found himself, months later, chasing rumors and hearsay to the town of Robinson. The former town of Robinson was perhaps the more apt descriptor. For even as Elijah rode through the hinterlands with the town on the horizon, a pall of smoke hung over the place.

Flies busied themselves, buzzing and bloated, over corpses until they were a miasma, an affliction of the flesh, a pox of parasites. Elijah covered his mouth and nose with a kerchief, so pervasive was the malodorous stench of rot and death. Flames still cavorted within one establishment, bringing a beam down in what had once served as a haberdashery, sending embers out of a shattered windowpane. Elijah's horse became skittish and he had to soothe his mount as he drove her onwards to the ruins of a gallows, still standing outside the offices of the local sheriff's building.

Two men in funereal attire, one with grey whiskers and both scarlet in their countenance from the heat, were in the process of heaving a coffin onto a wagon already laden with the charnel stock.

As Elijah approached, the younger one said to the other, "Mister Calloway, looks as if we have ourselves a visitor."

Mister Calloway turned to face Elijah, dusting his hands as he did so. His eyes were misty with mourning. "Well, hey there, friend. Sure hope you are such. As you can see, Robinson has had just about enough of unfriendly folks of late. And, uh, not too many friends left."

Elijah said, "G'day, Mister Calloway, my name's Elijah Delaney. Sadly, I can see the tales of your unfriendly visitor and the effect he had upon your town were not as embellished as any honest man might have hoped they would be."

Calloway and his apprentice shared a look. Calloway took out a kerchief and wiped sweat and dust from his face. After a moment of contemplation, he said, "I ain't certain what you heard, Mister Delaney, and I can see you ain't been knee-high to a grasshopper for some time, but I'll tell you this, you don't want to be on the trail of this visitor we had. No more than you want to grab the tail-end of a rattler."

"No, I suppose I don't," Elijah said. "However, I received correspondence from an acquittance of mine well acquitted with the Pinkerton Detective Agency. Well, the details of which left me both intrigued and horrified. It's not often, I wager, a man wreaks this sort of havoc *after* he's been hung."

"Mister Calloway, he knows!" the apprentice said.

"You just hush now, Jedidiah," Calloway barked.

"But, Mister Calloway, this fella knows already!"

Elijah said, "You mind awfully telling me about just what happened?"

"Jed," Calloway said, "Get these good folks over to the funeral parlor. We can parlay, Mister Delaney, but if it's all the same with you, I prefer to discuss such matters in the chapel over yonder."

Within the cooling shade of the chapel, Calloway pried a loose floorboard beneath the frontmost pew. He retrieved a bottle of clear liquid. "God forgive me, the chaplain ain't with us no more, but the Good Lord, well, he watches still...He sure has tested us of late. Jed's the one who makes this. Never used to touch the stuff myself, but the last few days it's been about just the only thing that can help me get to sleep. That can help quiet my thoughts." He indicated Elijah should join him on the pew and passed him the bottle.

"How long ago did he ride into Robinson?" Elijah asked.

"Can't rightly tell you," Calloway said. "Reckon he's been gone from here some three days passed.

"First I heard tell of him was the night a whole ruckus was kicked up in the saloon. O'course there was talk of a stranger in town, always is in a place this size, so rarely visited by the outside world. Some folks used to say Robinson was a boom town just a-waiting for its boom...well, we sure enough got more than we could handle, more than we deserved, I reckon."

"What happened in the saloon?" Elijah asked, taking a swig, then passing the bottle back to Calloway.

"Way I heard it, some ranch hands from Granger's was pressing this stranger on what he's doing in town, if he were up to no good, sitting and skulking in the corner of the saloon, way he was. Type of thing young men all liquored up is wont to do on occasion. Apparently, this stranger weren't too prickly, he even invited the ranch hands to play a game of cards with him. They was all getting pretty well on with the bar, if you catch my meaning, and mind this is all as Jed told it to me. This stranger kept dealing them cards, the ranchers kept betting, and Jed said he even inched closer to hear the yarn this stranger was spinning.

"At some point, the stranger quits on his story, looks up at William Mathews. Says he believes William has a good hand. Well, the rest all fold, until only the stranger and William is in—all in—and the stranger says it's William's turn to show his hand first."

Elijah interrupted, "And this young William Mathews puts down the ace of spades, ace of clubs, eight of spades, eight of clubs, and one other card."

"Dead Man's Hand was what Jed called it," Calloway said slowly, looking straight at Elijah. His hand jittered as he lifted the bottle to his lips, then he said, "And then, quick as lightning, or so Jed said, this stranger breaks a bottle and stabs it right into William's throat. Now keep in mind they don't allow no guns into Granger's. Nevertheless, I had all those ranch hands in my parlor the next morning.

"By the time the law came through, Granger's was well afire and the ruckus had spilt out onto the street," Calloway continued. "Strangest thing, at that point in any case, and even the sheriff attested to this, the stranger didn't put up no struggle. Just let 'em take him away.

"Circuit judge arrived and weren't long before the stranger—who never gave 'em no name, only said in court his daddy had seen the war in Navarino, and took off from a war-ravaged country to come to America, how he'd then grown up to fight a war in America— was sentenced to be hanged."

Calloway looked up to the crucifix and muttered a prayer before carrying on with his testimony. "I watched him laugh as they put the noose around his neck. It weren't no madman's laugh either. It were earnest laughter. I heard his neck snap. And...*I saw*..."

"The smoke pour out of him," Elijah whispered. Calloway looked at him with eyes big as saucers. He nodded.

"We all watched him then pull the noose off his broken neck, rubbing the flesh of his face raw. We were all so stunned. Seeing something so *unnatural*. Even the lawmen near him. Of course, once he grabbed one of their repeaters from 'em, well, you've seen the result of all the bedlam. Were like the whole town lost their minds. On account of one man not losing his life."

Calloway took a mighty swig of the shine and hunched over. "Now I'm about as busy an undertaker as I ever been. And ain't many left who can pay. Got to be done, I suppose. It's a grave undertaking, burying most all a town, grave undertaking indeed."

"I have a grave undertaking myself," Elijah said. "Do either you or Jed have a clue as to what direction this stranger from Navarino rode off in?"

– *E. J. Delaney.*

Chapter Five

The Approach of the Midnight Stagecoach

Note from the editor of Palomino Digest: As with all Elijah Delaney's writing, he would periodically post to our offices chapters he had completed whilst continuing his travels and research. The previous chapter was the last manuscript we can be assured was sent by Elijah himself. What follows is a transcript we received most recently, which the editor can assure our readers was most certainly not penned by the hand of Elijah Delaney.

His whereabout have been unknown for quite some time. Whilst we cannot attest to the veracity of the more fantastical elements accounted herein, we at Palomino Digest, *along with our readers, can only hope and pray we will hear from and see Mister Elijah Jacob Delaney again in due time.*

His eyes were trained on the edge of the light where the glow from the fire only faintly touched the shadows, the way young lovers might dare to let their fingers meet for a passing moment before they invited unwanted attention. He was wondering, that shape in the night, was it naught but brambles and brush stirring in the breeze, perhaps a coyote skulking closer for some scraps to make away with? Then again, perhaps, he thought, it were a man, some no-good bandit itching to slit his throat. Perhaps, he thought, it was no man at all.

When the voice spoke, he thought the speaker didn't notice him gripping that iron of his 'neath the bedroll. "You're a teller o' tall tales, Mister Delaney. Best be cautious you don't find yourself wound up in one; one that's more cautionary parable than quick-drawin' drama to excite folks who ain't hardly been farther west than the Mississippi."

Elijah answered, "We're a might further west than the town of Robinson. I've taken note, over all these years, you always move further west. I've wondered if you believe America will ever catch up to you? If you worry that one day the only thing on the western horizon for you will be the Pacific? A man who can't die must reckon the day'll come when bright city lights cover the whole continent."

"Shouldn't worry yourself on my account. In any case, I been out further west than the sunset and back. Yet, you keep lookin' for me. And I wonder if you got in your head to gun me down and see that I don't rise."

Elijah said to the shadows, "I harbor no illusions as to what will happen. Once, I did; doubted that I could've seen what my mind recalled. I don't reckon I can stop you. But you ain't pulling heists on banks and trains all over the territories, ain't running with a posse of wild gunners, so I do reckon you're hopin' I got some silver bullet as it were."

The stranger, the man Elijah had been seeking all this time, made himself comfortable by the fire. "Rattler whiskey?" he offered Elijah, who expectantly declined.

"I was raised on stories," the stranger said unbidden. "On tales that Charon would come and take your soul on his ferry at the moment you pass. O'course one must pay for passage. At the moment when I wished very much to ride his ferry, I learned two things. One, in this land, Charon don't steer no ferry, he drives a stagecoach. And two, if'n you got the right type of payment, he can take you further."

Elijah interrupted, "To a tree where if you hang yourself, Charon would bring you back and promise you'll never again have to ride his stagecoach."

The stranger tipped his hat to Elijah and sipped his drink. He said, "I appreciate your precocious and inquisitive nature, as I said, I was raised on stories. Stories older than what they call America, but I appreciate every land, and people need their mythologies. And you work damned earnestly in aiding to create one here." Here the stranger was now aiming his iron at Elijah, the flames dancing on the ebony handle. Elijah had his pointed at the stranger, and he wasn't dissuaded by the wicked grin, nor smoking stare, of the man across the fire.

"Can you hear the hoofbeats?" the stranger asked Elijah. "The rattling wheels of the Midnight Stagecoach?"

"I'm quite certain I do not," Elijah replied.

"That's on account of you still havin' a choice."

"Why does it worry you so? Who would believe this tale?" Elijah said.

"Ain't one I ever asked to be told," the stranger said.

"Yet it is one you share from time to time. To unburden yourself, I suppose, assured that any who survive the telling wouldn't lend it any credence. And if they did, well, not a soul they told it to would put much stock in it. Matter of fact, on the day we met, I do believe you said it's one you might share with me someday," Elijah said.

"It is a tall tale."

Elijah replied, "A tall a tale as any..."

The stranger laughed and, holstering his pistol as he rose, said, "Might be you deserve to have it told. All the same, you know how this ends. Now, why don't we do like they do in your dime novels? Only we'll be beneath the full moon, by the light of a fire, and you draw when you hear the approach of the Midnight Stagecoach..."

–The Navarino Nobody

A Respectable Kind of Woman

Samantha Kelly

The cicadas sing to each other as the sun goes down.
A susurrus,
you need not decipher.
It isn't for you.

It is for the long grass,
waving as the wind picks up.
For the oppressive heat
and the darkening clouds overhead.
A storm approaches.

You lift one foot
then the other—a release of pressure.
But only temporary.
The smoke from your cigarette curls up
into your eyes as you wait.

For the town to appear, almost as one.
A regular mob.
They whisper, about how
they didn't expect this

of a schoolteacher.
A respectable kind of woman.

He wasn't a good man, the man she shot.
But that mattered none.
They say,
she smiled as she did it.
The gun was still smoking when you arrived.

You climb the steps to the gallows
that the O'Reilly boys have built
so diligently, these past three days.
Your body is slick with sweat,
even though the heat is dry.
Expectant.

You wipe your hands on your thighs
to better hold the list of charges.
It's your job to read them.
She taught you to read, once.

Now, she's led up after you
and asked by the sheriff for her final words.
Ever the teacher, she tells a story.
About those who lied and believed the lies
about her.
A respectable kind of woman.

As she lists their names,
you think you understand.

This is a morality tale.
And those only end through penance.

She begins with Miss Higgins.
The schoolgirl rival (only in her own mind)
It's a funny kind of pain,
to live your whole life in second place.
Worse, in some ways, than last.
To know with certainty that you would prosper,
given a little pruning.

Perhaps it was that certainty
that caused Miss Higgins, through her lies
to turn a husband to a jealousy that could not be quieted,
to turn a schoolteacher into a wife with a smoking gun.
In two months' time, Miss Higgins will be found
dead, from consumption.
And you'll learn that a curse can sound like morality.
If it's said by a respectable kind of woman.

But she was not the first. There were others.
The storm broke that night, once the hanging was done.
The worst any can remember.
And once it's over, the wreckage examined.
You find the O'Reilly boys, crushed
by the remnants of their own gallows.

Rumours are like a fire,
With nothing to stoke them, they die out,
their embers lying dormant.

But all they need is a spark. Like the sheriff
who caught a stray bullet as bandits rode through town.
He was on the list too.
That's a pretty big spark.

Finally, she says your name.
You might have let her go. There was time.
But you had weighed it up
and judged that you wouldn't get away with it.
You won't get away with this, either.
She'll come for you, like she will the others.

It takes six minutes for her to die.
She never stops smiling.
And when it's done, you let the charges drop to the floor.
And light another cigarette on your way down the steps.

The Awl
Levi Hatch

"Masks up, boys," Smiles whispered and hiked his own bandana up over his nose.

He didn't have to look to know Hogtrough and Doughboy obeyed. They were good boys. Always did as they were told. If they didn't, they wouldn't even be on his crew. He wouldn't have allowed it.

With the sun long gone and the land as dark as the devil's soul, the three men crept along low on their haunches through the tall dry grass towards the farmhouse. Any movement not calculated perfectly would crackle the dying blades, and in the still air of the night, those small sounds were as betraying as a gunshot. Their progress was therefore slow. Painfully so. But old Smiles didn't get to be who he was without considerable helpings of patience and caution.

The old cabin they stalked towards stood alone in the middle of the wide and flat prairie without so much as a single shrub around it they could have hidden behind. There was a rundown wagon nearby and a single ox out grazing, but that was hardly enough for any kind of real cover. To try and close in on the place in daylight would have been as stealthy as trying to hide a buffalo in a chicken farm. So the three had laid low all evening, watching the place with hungry eyes until dusk spread its blanket over the world for the night.

Low candlelight flickered just inside one of the cabin windows, and its glow cast an orange rectangular beam onto the ground outside.

When a shadow moved across it, Smiles instantly threw out a hand to signal his men to halt. They did so.

The figure stayed in the window, blocking the light, and Smiles almost started to panic that whoever was in there was staring out at them hiding in the grass like children, although it was impossible to tell because the person's silhouette was nothing more than a black and featureless outline to them. Eventually, the person left the window and the light returned. Smiles strained his ears towards the cabin. A few heartbeats of silence later, he knew they had not been discovered.

"Okay," he whispered. "Let's move."

Hogtrough turned to Doughboy. "I told you there'd be somebody in there," he said.

Doughboy spat into the dirt, leaving a trail of saliva clinging to his thick gray beard, and said, "Shoot. Well, when you don't see no sign of life all day, you start to wonder, is all!"

Doughboy's whisper could be described better as a rasping cough and was anything but quiet. Smiles snapped around to the two of them.

"Shut up!" he hissed. Smiles could just barely see them both latch their jaws closed in the darkness.

Rolling his eyes, Smiles turned back to his goal, the cabin. They were good boys but often got to bickering which tended to run Smiles' squirrel right out of his tree.

Smiles motioned to the two of them, and the trio once again continued forward, inch by inch. It was almost another hour before they actually reached the cabin. Like highly trained soldiers that needed no command, Hogtrough slithered through the grass to the far side of the cabin's low doorway, and Doughboy took up a position on the close side. When Smiles got into place directly in front of the door, he nodded to his men, and all three of them drew their six shooters.

Hogtrough gave a silent three count on his left hand for the other two to see. When his last finger finally closed into a fist, Smiles leapt forward and drove the heel of his boot into the door.

The small door burst inwards much easier than Smiles had been expecting, and the extra force he had put into his kick ripped the door part way off its hinges. Half a second later, all three of the large burly men were inside.

The cabin's only occupant, a slight woman somewhere in her mid-thirties with long dark hair, dropped the book she was reading and fell out of her rocking chair when they stormed in. With eyes wide, she yelped and scrambled away on her hands and knees towards what Smiles guessed to be the bedroom.

"Hands up! Stop!" Smiles shouted, but she ignored him.

Halfway to the door, she managed to get back up to her feet and almost made it, but Doughboy was on her like a wild dog on raw meat. He wrapped his arms around her waist from behind and lifted her, kicking and screaming, off the ground. Doughboy was laughing wildly as she threw elbow after elbow back into his stomach and face.

Hogtrough was snickering too. Both him and Smiles holstered their guns and watched. They both knew Doughboy had been in far too many tavern brawls for the tiny arms of this little prairie sprite to do any real damage, and so they stood back and watched as the large man wrestled her down. When she showed no signs of tiring and began to throw heel kicks into her captor's groin, Doughboy quickly lost his sense of humor.

"That's enough!" he barked. "Quit!"

She wouldn't listen.

"My husband will be home soon! You'll be sorry when he gets here!"

"I said, that's enough!" Doughboy yelled, and in one quick movement, he whipped her around to face him and plowed his fist right into her jaw. Her screams cut off instantly, and she collapsed in a heap onto the cabin floor. Panting and obviously trying to play off how much his manhood ached, Doughboy whirled on his companions.

"You could've helped, 'stead of just settin' there!"

Hogtrough, who was wiping away tears of laughter at the skirmish, staggered forward, holding his stomach.

"It looked like you had it all under control!" he said between giggles.

Smiles was actually wearing an involuntary grin, though he hated the way it made his cheeks feel. The woman on the floor was weeping, but the fight, it seemed, had been taken out of her at last. She just lay crumpled where she fell in the blue nightgown she was wearing, her body quivering with sobs.

"Alright, boys," Smiles said. "Search the place."

"You really think she's got anything of value after all this?" Hogtrough asked incredulously while looking around the simple un-adorned room. "I hate to say it, but I think we struck a dud on this one."

"She'll have something," Smiles said. The cabin was blistering, and he removed his hat to wipe the sweat from his brow. He wished he could remove his bandana from his face as well but didn't dare. "New settlers like her, they always bring some kind of valuables from wher-ever they come from."

Hogtrough shrugged, and he and Doughboy set to work. They emptied every drawer and cupboard they could find, bagging silver-ware, fine china, a gold pocket watch, and Smiles even found a small wad of cash hidden in a tiny dugout in the wall behind a hanging picture. The woman made no protest. It was like she had decided to just ignore their presence while they ransacked. At one point, however, she did sit up and glare at Smiles while he emptied her hidden stash of money.

"My husband will be home soon!" she spat. Doughboy had obviously broken her jaw. It hung loose and the words she formed were slurred and barely intelligible. "Trust me! You don't want to meet him! You better go before he gets here!"

Smiles licked his fingers and began thumbing through the bills, not even bothering to look at her.

"I mean it!" she said. "He'll kill you! He'll kill you all for what you've done!"

Still not looking up from his new money, Smiles said, "Lady, you got no husband. There ain't a single thing in this house that makes me believe that you ain't the only one living here. There ain't no men's clothes. No guns. No nothing. You're alone. Face it, there ain't nobody coming to save you."

Just then, Hogtrough entered the second room the woman had been trying to get to.

"Well! Looky here!" Hogtrough said.

Smiles turned. Through the opening he could see in the next room a large four poster bed complete with drapes. In the rough built cabin, the bed looked very out of place. It looked like it should belong in a princess's room in a castle somewhere.

"Looks like a pretty little honeymoon nest," Smiles said. Then, turning to the woman, "I confess. Looks like you had a husband at one point. Some pretentious little sap from the looks of things. But I bet you he's long gone now. Probably went and got himself killed. Hogtrough, go through them dressers and see if there ain't any man's clothes in there."

Hogtrough tore out each drawer, each one filled to the brim with lady's clothing. When the bedroom was searched thoroughly without turning up any evidence of a man's habitation, Hogtrough shook his head at Smiles.

"There's nothing but this pointy thing I found in the dresser." Hogtrough held up what he was talking about.

"That's a leather worker's awl," Smiles said, shaking his head at his man's ignorance, but he reminded himself that as long as Hogtrough could shoot a gun then that was all the intelligence he needed.

"Oh," Hogtrough said, looking down at the tool with curious eyes before tossing it back onto the bed.

"But that's it?" Smiles asked.

"Yep."

"Thought so," Smiles said triumphantly. "Sorry little missy. Your bluff's been called."

"You'll be sorry." She said the words so low that Smiles was barely able to hear them.

Hogtrough stepped back out of the bedroom and said, "What do you want us to do with her, boss? Kill her?"

Hogtrough's grin widened, showing a row (if it could even be called a row) of black weathered teeth as he looked down at the woman who was still kneeling on the floor where Doughboy had thrown her. She did not cower from Hogtrough's words but returned his gaze with a defiant sneer.

For several moments, Smiles stood still watching the woman. She had fight in her, that had been proven in her scrap with Doughboy. But there was something else about her. Something hidden that made Smiles uncomfortable.

"No. I don't think so," Smiles said. "Not her. We don't need to be calling down any more bad voodoo on us than what we already got coming!"

Hogtrough's smile vanished. "But boss, I—"

He was cut off by a howling screech outside the cabin. It was a shattering cry that broke the stillness of the evening air with a sharp and vengeful resonance. The sound seemed to sink into every one of Smiles' pores, sending a shiver running down his frame.

Doughboy dropped a ceramic teapot he was examining and which he was about to stuff into his sack. It exploded into a hundred little fragments when it hit the floor, but none of the room's occupants seemed to notice. The hair on Smiles' arms and neck stood up as taut as piano wire. The howl lasted for several whole seconds, and it swept through the cabin like an icy wind that gripped Smiles' heart with long arresting fingers.

"What..." Hogtrough spluttered, "What was that?"

No one answered.

There was nothing outside but darkness. Smiles glanced at the broken door hanging on torn hinges and began to regret kicking it so hard when they first entered. He found in that moment he would have given half his acquired fortune for a solid steel door to shut out the night and the nefarious occupant it had produced. He turned and looked back down at the woman and thought he saw, for just a second, the tiniest spark of a malicious grin. However, as soon as he looked, it vanished.

"What was that?" he said to her. His voice cracked when he spoke, losing all authority in his tone.

"I warned you," she said.

For the second time that night, the three men drew iron and aimed their revolvers through the open doorway. With the lamp and firelight inside the cabin, they could see nothing of what was outside. The entrance was only a still, black rectangle to their eyes.

All of them jerked their aims violently to the right when the same ungodly howl once more shook the night, and a small window which hung in the adjacent wall shattered inwards. Smiles felt the blood flee his face when he just barely caught a glimpse of what looked like a monstrous claw retracting from the freshly broken window. The creature, whatever it was, continued to squeal and scream like a possessed thing. Obviously, it was not overly concerned with stealth because they could hear it scuttling around the backside of the cabin, screeching and pounding on the walls as it went.

"It's playing with us!" Doughboy said. His rasping voice came out high pitched. Like a stuck pig. In any other setting, the noise would have been downright comical. No one was laughing then, however.

When they could hear that the creature was almost around to the open doorway, Smiles decided he'd had enough.

"Deal with it!" he squeaked, and he grabbed the woman by the arm and dragged her into the bedroom. She didn't resist. Smiles came down with an awful suspicion that she was enjoying their fright. He was almost sure that she loved seeing them squirm like little children. Smiles told himself not to worry about whatever the woman was thinking as there were bigger things to worry about at the moment than his pride.

As he was slamming the door, Doughboy and Hogtrough made to follow, but they were too late. Smiles was grateful to find the door had a bar which he threw down the instant the door was closed. He ignored his men's screams as they banged their fists on the other side of it.

"Boss! Wait!"

"Don't do this!"

"Let us in!"

Smiles didn't even act like he could hear them. He threw the woman backwards onto the bed and then turned to face the door, weapon in hand.

"You're a cruel man," the woman said.

"Shut up!" Smiles shouted. He spat a curse at her.

His men continued to shout with frenzied voices.

"They won't be able to stop him," she continued. She *was* enjoying this!

"They're good boys," Smiles said. "They'll—"

A monstrous roar vibrated the cabin. Smiles even saw a small cloud of dust drifting down, shaken from the rafters by the noise. The pounding on the door quickly ceased as suddenly as it began, but his men's screams doubled in volume and franticism. Smiles felt a small stream of urine run down his leg as he listened to the unmistakable sounds of tearing flesh and snapping bones.

"Help us!" they both shouted. A vicious snarling accompanied their screams.

"Let us in!"

"Please!"

Smiles didn't move. He couldn't move. Not until the cabin once more fell completely silent. He strained to hear anything above his erratic pulse which thumped in his ears.

The creature began scraping and beating on the other side of the door. As if roused from a trance, Smiles retreated, pulled the woman off the bed to her feet, and held her in front of him with his arm around her neck. He placed the muzzle of his revolver to her temple.

"You call off your hound monster, you hear?" he hissed into her ear.

"He's my husband," she said.

"Bull!" Smiles spat. "That thing is—"

The door to the bedroom, bar and all, burst inwards, splintering into a thousand small fragments. The woman let out a soft yelp—out of surprise, not fear—and held up her arms to shield herself from the flying debris. Smiles ducked down behind her back.

When everything had settled and Smiles discovered that they were both still standing, he mustered what little courage he had left, swallowed a large gulp of nothing, and peeked over the woman's shoulder.

What he saw made him think that even if he survived the night, he would never sleep again.

Hunched over in the doorway was a monster unlike anything Smiles had ever seen. With over a dozen legs and giant, snapping claws, the thing looked to the burglar like an unholy blend of scorpion, crab, lobster, and spider. It had long black hairs that stood on end, two enormous claws, three long tails with what appeared to be stingers on the ends, probably thirty different black eyeballs, and gigantic fanged mandibles still dripping with his men's blood. On the floor behind the monster, crumpled up like discarded newspaper, were the corpses of Hogtrough and Doughboy.

"S-s-s-stay back!" Smiles tried to command, but it came out more as whisper.

One sticky pedipalp at a time, the creature inched towards them, greedy pincers clacking.

"Stay back!" Smiles said again, this time a little more forcefully. "I'll shoot her!"

"He doesn't understand you. He's just an animal," the woman said.

"Shut up!" Smiles shouted. Then back to the creature, "I'm warning you!"

The beast lunged. Claws snapped. Jaws smacked. Smiles didn't even think. He only reacted. Taking his weapon from the woman's head, he stabbed it forward and fired. The shot was deafening in the confined space, but Smiles' adrenaline was pumping too hard for him to notice. The beast fell back from them, wailing and writhing miserably. Black gore oozed from a newly made hole in what Smiles thought of as its thorax.

Taking courage, Smiles threw the woman aside, recocked his gun and fired a second time. Then a third time. He shot over and over, and with each bullet fired he took another, more confident step forward.

The beast backed away from him, whimpering and moaning until, when Smiles' revolver cylinder was finally empty, it collapsed onto the floor, seemingly lifeless. Blood poured from the monster's perforated hide, and all Smiles could do was stand there in shock.

Was it really dead? Had he really survived?

The night was once again silent. Not even the breeze blew through the ravaged cabin. Still unbelieving that it was really over, Smiles took one more step towards the beast to inspect it closer.

When it twitched, he jumped backwards and retrained his smoking gun on it. The beast started to convulse, flopping from one side to the other. It was a couple seconds before Smiles even noticed that the beast was changing as it twitched. Legs began to pop from their sockets, eyeballs rolled away on the floor. The entire creature continued to morph and mold until Smiles recognized a human head growing out of its thorax. The two claws became hands. Smiles had to keep rubbing his eyes, not believing what he was witnessing.

Halfway through the transformation, the convulsions stopped, however. A beast, half scorpion, half man lay on the cabin floor, wheezing gargled breaths in and out. His hair was dark brown, and he had a thick handlebar mustache. Just before he died, he looked up at Smiles who was still holding the gun. Smiles shivered when he saw that the man's eyes were still the soulless ebony eyes of a spider.

The man choked, coughed once, and said, "Thank you."

He then expelled his last puff of air and lay still.

"What the—" Smiles began to say, but he was cut off when something sharp stabbed him in his neck.

"Agh!" he cried and staggered to his feet, whirling.

There the woman stood, awl in hand, a single drop of his blood about to fall from its prick. That same grin he saw before was once more on her face.

Smiles reached his hand up to feel the wound. She had broken the skin, but that was it. Why hadn't she driven it in deep when she had the chance? He felt blood, but when he brought his hand back to his eyes to examine his fingertips, his stomach sank into his feet. The substance running from his neck was not blood. It was a black, tarry substance. Sticky to the touch.

"What?" he began, looking up at the woman. "What did you do?"

Her smile drilled through him. Suddenly feeling queasy and wobbly, he pointed his revolver at her and pulled the trigger. *Click.* He pulled it again. *Click.*

He had forgotten his weapon was empty. The colors in the room sharpened, and his field of vision grew wider. He felt his forehead to discover he had sprouted a third eyeball!

"What have you done?" Smiles screamed.

The woman, still smiling as ever, sat back onto the bed. "Don't fight it," she said. "You can't fight it." He looked down at the awl still clutched in her fingers. Of course. A conjurer's awl! He had heard many frightening stories as a child about the awful things but had never before seen one nor witnessed its awful power. He cursed himself for his own stupidity.

Frantic, he reached down to his gun belt to fish out more bullets but was dismayed to discover his fingers had been replaced with scorpion-like claws. He yelped and then heard a *clunk.* He looked over to see that his other hand was a claw as well, and without fingers, he had been unable to hold his gun from falling to the floorboards.

"No!" he screamed. "NO! PLEASE!"

The woman just sat there, watching it all as calmly as one watches an entertaining opera.

Smiles felt his point of view shrinking as he was forced to hunch down onto all fours. Or rather, all sixes—all eights. Like his legs, he was also sprouting eyes like dandelions, taking in more and more of his surroundings at once. His smell was sharpening. Instead of just the simple odor of smoke which pervaded the cabin, he was beginning to pick out all kinds of different scents. He could smell the musty pages in the book she had been reading. He could smell beetles and insects in the walls. He could even smell the woman's fingernail polish and immediately knew it had been applied two days earlier. Most of all, he could smell the corpses' blood, so strong and sweet, and found himself lusting for a taste.

The last human characteristic to leave him was his mind. Words disintegrated into base emotions. Then emotions disintegrated into instinct.

When at last the process was complete, Smiles existed no longer. There was only the creature, identical to its predecessor.

Contained in those instincts he developed was a strong and loyal devotion to the woman that was sitting on the bed. He knew she was master. He just knew it. And like the good loyal pet he had become, he scuttled forward and knelt before her, awaiting her command.

"Good boy," she said and stroked his thorax. "Good boy. Now. Enjoy your feast."

She bandaged her own broken jaw and got ready for bed while Smiles, the monster, buried his newly grown fangs into the savory meat of Doughboy and Hogtrough.

Three Nights with the Angel of Death

Emily Ruth Verona

Arizona, 1884—Day One

The people of Vulture City are calling him the Angel of Death. But that makes no difference to us. There's a one-thousand-dollar reward on him, and that kind of money never comes easy. No. It comes soaked in blood. Wet and slippery. Not that it matters when all is said and done. Bloody money buys a hell of a lot more than empty pockets. I can tell you that much.

Most of the Arizona territory knows him by the name of Tom Radley, the same Tom Radley who robbed five banks in five coal mining towns in 1882. The law managed to catch up with him after that last bank in Comstock; he was rotting in Yuma Territorial Prison until about six months ago. The son of a bitch escaped. Got all the way to Clayton, New Mexico, before they snapped him up again.

That's where the Angel of Death comes in. You see those lawmen—the ones tasked with bringing Radley back to the prison—they didn't make it far. Started dying off one by one... in real peculiar ways too. The kind that make the skin on the back of a man's neck shrivel and prune when he hears tell of 'em. One fella was said to have strangled himself to death, if such a thing is possible. Another was found with his throat slit but not a drop of blood in his body or even on the ground around him.

By the time they got Radley to Vulture City, there was only one lawman left on his escort, and he was raving. Refused to take Radley any further. Said his last remaining compatriot had vanished in the night—just up and disappeared in the desert somewhere west of Wickenburg. Of course, being a mining town, Vulture wasn't too keen on keeping Radley around for long. Put a group together as fast as it could to get him gone.

Guess that's how we ended up here, in the very belly of the Sonoran, between Vulture City and Yuma Territorial Prison with nothing but the sky above and hell below. It's a four-day journey, and there are five of us besides Radley, each desperate enough or stupid enough to think we can make a buck off Radley's hide.

There's this fella from Wyoming who keeps calling Radley a living gold mine. *Gotta protect the gold mine*, he says. The others exchange looks uneasily every time. We don't like Bill Henry—that's his name, lord knows he's reminded us often enough—and I suspect there are one or two men who wouldn't mind seeing him the first to be struck down out here in the desert.

It seems Bill's a better talker than he ever was a miner, jumped at the chance to join our group when he heard what Tom Radley is worth. But Bill Henry is poorer company than a dead man. Every time he cracks a joke or slaps one of us on the back, the kid from Vulture City grimaces like he's poked at some fantom bullet hole in the boy's gut. The kid from Vulture City does not want to be here, more so than the rest of us. His daddy—who lost a leg in an accident at the mine and has at least six mouths to feed—was said to have beaten him into it. That's what the ranch hand says. You can still see a bruise swelling beneath the kid's left eye. He will make more in these four days than he ever could in town. And he knows it. But that don't stop disdain from bubbling on his sweaty face underneath this sweltering sun. He pulls his hat down, pats his horse on the neck, and keeps to the back of the pack so as to avoid having to say much. I don't blame him. You never know what you're gonna get in a group like this, and Radley—hell, you'd have to be hell-bound from the start to want anything to do with him.

Day Two

The ranch hand is dead. He was the only one who could tolerate Bill Henry's jokes, shrug them off with a smirk and a nod, but now his head is lying in the short grass beneath the early morning light like a head of cabbage ready to be picked. Mouth half-open and blonde hair fluttering in the wind. Blood from the stump of the neck has seeped into the dirt, giving the thirsty earth a dark red hue.

He wasn't even meant to be here in the first place. The sheriff knew a rancher said to be a crack shot, asked him to join our party. Pleaded with him, in fact. The rancher went and sent the hand in his stead. Don't know if he could shoot. Don't know anything about him save for the fact that he's dead now. That makes four of us left, not including the Angel of Death.

Radley hardly even blinked when he saw the head, wasn't impressed by it in the least. Not that he would be. He's seen worse. Once or twice now, Bill Henry has gone and tried to get him to talk about the last prison escort he'd been on, the one that had ended with a man disappearing altogether. Radley won't say a word about it though. No. He just sits on his horse and minds his own business, eats when we say and sleeps when we say and pisses when we say. He probably thinks nothing else matters. The way he sees it, he'll be free soon enough.

The sheriff ain't pleased by what's happened. It's plain on his face. He's a good man, I hate to say it. Honorable maybe. Or whatever counts for honorable in Vulture City. But he's kept our party in line without waving his pistol around or swearing himself into a rage, which is more than I can say for most men in his position.

We were all standing 'round the head this morning when the kid spoke up for what was surely the first time since he kissed his momma goodbye. "We should bury it," he said.

Bill Henry let out a spittle-ridden laugh. "What about the rest of him?"

That was the question. See, the head was there waiting for us under the eastward sun, but the body—hell, there was no body. It was as if the ranch hand's body had gone and rode off without him. No. Not rode off. Run off. His horse is still here, after all. How far could a dead man get on foot without a head?

No one has asked how it happened—who did it. I don't think anyone wants to know. They just want to pretend it's nothing. Let it be forgotten. Except for the sheriff. He doesn't seem rattled by it like you'd suspect. I think he would've been more surprised if we were somehow able to deliver Radley to the prison without incident. Walk him up to the gates, collect our money and be on our way.

The sheriff is insisting we ride on though. Doesn't want to lose daylight. Right now, the kid from Vulture City is digging a hole below the long, rigid blades of a sotol shrub. We don't have a shovel, so he's digging it with his knife. Would be an impossible task if there weren't so little of the ranch hand left to bury. Bill Henry and the sheriff are readying the horses. I've been tasked with keeping an eye on Radley, who is lying flat on his back staring up at the big blue sky like it's the darndest thing he's ever seen. He's got an ankle up on one knee, and one of the hands tied at his wrists is holding his hat. He should put it on—that fair skin of his is all freckled under patches of red hair—but Radley don't seem bothered. The look on his face, I'd call it wondrous. I would. Like the sky is a thing of rare beauty and we should all stop to appreciate it. He probably ain't wrong. But all that sizzling blue up there means something different to a man damned to prison than it does for other men. Men who've got time to look up at it whenever they please. I don't care much for it, one way or another. It's just the goddamn sky.

Day Three

The kid from Vulture City hasn't even finished vomiting last night's dinner into the dirt, and already I can smell it. Beans and stomach rot. This'll be a long day, no question. The sheriff hasn't said anything yet. He's just standing there with his fingers in his beard and his eyes narrowed so tight the crow-footed lines of his face are liable to up and fly away. "We press on," he says at last, then looks up at me like he expects an argument.

I give a shrug. "We press on," I agree. The kid, wiping his mouth on his sleeve, is pale, skin slick and pasty. He looks scared but won't say a word about what's happened. Not if no one else is going to. Hell, he hasn't said anything at all since he went and buried what was left of the ranch hand.

I'd be lying if I said I wasn't relieved. I'm not saying Bill Henry deserved what he got, but if one man had to be cut open and strangled with his own innards, that loud-talking son of a bitch got what was coming to him. At least now it'll be quiet. As for Radley? Well, he could look a little less pleased with himself. The sheriff seems just about ready to accuse him of something, with that smug twinkle in Radley's eye, if not for the fact that we tied Radley up twice over to a Mesquite tree last night before we put out the fire. He's still there as a matter of fact, boots perched on those big, gnarled roots, shaking his head and chuckling to himself. Not like a madman or a man who knows his days are numbered. He's grinning almost like a bemused father watching his little ones running 'round, playing at something they won't understand until they're old enough for it to kill 'em.

The sun is hot today. Too hot. The kind that makes it hard to swallow. The horses are restless, breathing in and out too fast. I don't blame them. I feel the same. As if to apologize, I pet my mare's neck—whisper in her ear, which flutters understandingly. When I look up, I see the sheriff staring out at Radley. One of us will have to untie him soon. Unless we leave him here. Something tells me our party wouldn't mind doing a thing like that now. Only, if we do then what's the point? The dead are already dead. And there's still money left to be claimed. "You think he's cursed?" I ask suddenly.

The sheriff snorts, doesn't look at me. "No such thing as curses," he says.

"Then how do you think he's doing it?"

There's no answer right away, and the longer the quiet stacks itself up between us, the more I begin to notice that the sheriff ain't looking at Radley at all. No. He's looking through him—past him—out into the dessert. At last, he turns his head towards me. "Tom Radley hasn't done a damn thing."

This is why the sheriff has been so eager to make use of daylight—get as far as we can as fast as we can. He thinks we're being tracked. Only, tracked ain't really the word for it. Hunted. He thinks someone—likely more than one someone—is hunting us down. Picking us off one by one, just like how they killed the lawmen bringing Radley back from Clayton. "Whoever's out there hasn't been building a fire," I point out. "We would have seen that."

A quiet nod from the sheriff. The boy from Vulture City joins us by the horses and notices straight away that something ain't right. He looks worriedly from the sheriff to me to the sheriff again, hoping one of us will answer his unasked question. "Come on," the sheriff says, nodding towards Radley. "Let's get him on a horse and get moving."

It's nearly sunset when we stop for the night. There's only ten miles to go, but the horses won't last another five. So, we go through what's beginning to feel like routine now. Throw our packs on the ground, water the horses, find somewhere to stick Radley. No trees around, but we've set up camp alongside the edge of a rock formation—fewer points of entrance that way—and have him with his back up against the rocks and his wrists bound too tight. You can see where the rope's slowly burning through the dirt and down to the flesh. He don't complain though. No. He looks content as can be.

The one thing we don't do is get a fire going. The sheriff thinks that's how whoever's following has been able to spot our camp. The deepening dark is making the kid from Vulture City twitchy. Nervous. I can tell he wishes we could strike something up, not just for the warmth but for the light. Never mind that it could get us all killed.

That's man for you—clinging to the known, the familiar, even when it's as straight and true as a nail in your coffin.

Even without that fire, we're seated 'round like we got one. A right trio we are—might as well be the Father, the Son, and the Holy Ghost. The kid's nibbling on a biscuit like a mouse, eyes wide and alert despite the fact that he looks about ready to fall over from exhaustion. That bruise under his left eye ain't healing right. It's still too swollen.

All there is to eat with no fire are biscuits. The sheriff has already had three—we've got extra, after all, without the ranch hand and Bill Henry. I don't have much of an appetite for anything, not in this heat. I've got a rifle out and ready across my knee, mostly to put the kid at ease. We've decided to sleep in shifts, and I already offered to take the first watch. I steal a swig from my canteen, look over at our prisoner who is dozing quietly, still seated upright with his hands bound. Men like that, they sleep through goddamn cannon fire.

When I turn back, I see the kid looking at me for reassurance. Like I'm the one who can give it. Not the sheriff. Me. I don't mean to sneer at his meekness, but I do. Can't help it. That kid shouldn't be here, and I'm starting to hate him a little for it. There's enough to worry about as it is. "Maybe we should blindfold him," says the kid, glancing in Radley's direction. "Stick a sack over his head. I don't like the idea of him waking up and watching us."

I snort. "Who says the Angel of Death needs eyes to see?"

Day Four

There's something about the way stars pierce the night sky that almost makes them worthwhile. Almost. I set the rifle down in the dirt and gaze across the moonlit desert towards the mountains. It's well beyond midnight, finally cool enough to breathe right, and it's nearly time to wake the sheriff for his shift.

It's been quiet all night, except of course for Radley's snoring—but the kid and the sheriff are so dog tired, it don't seem to trouble them none. I rise to my feet, muscles sore from sitting still for so long, and roll my neck in circles until it feels less stiff. Push up my sleeves. Yawn. The kid is asleep in front of me, the sheriff opposite him facing towards Radley.

Quietly, I go over and kneel beside the sheriff. He looks younger now in the dark than he does with his hat and his duster on under the desert sun. Pity. That's what it is. A damn pity.

I break his neck quick—it's the least I can do, and because I'm too hungry to make a fuss. Spilling Bill Henry's guts didn't leave much blood left for feeding, though it had felt more than warranted at the time.

With my knife I cut a clean slit through the sheriff's jugular and press my palm to the wound. My skin absorbs the blood with an eager hunger I know too well. It feels something like the opposite of sweating, water returning to your body instead of leaving it. My body takes blood cleanly, efficiently—not wasting a drop. It comes in useful out here, where there'd be nowhere to wash bloody hands or hide bloody clothes. I can drain a man without leaving a stain on me.

"What's happened?"

Damn it. Feeding rattles the senses. Keeps you from noticing things you should notice. Like the kid from Vulture City waking up to take a piss.

"What's going on?" he asks again, this time more cautiously. It's hard for him to see even in the moonlight, which helps me some but not enough. He has my rifle. Must've picked it up off the ground.

I slide my bloody knife beneath the sheriff's body to hide it, turn towards the kid. "He's dead," I say, trying to sound surprised.

"W-what? How?" he sputters, forgetting himself and dropping to his knees beside me. When he sees the cut across the sheriff's throat, he shakes his head. "No… no." I can hear his heart racing from here. "That can't be right. Where's—where's the blood?"

I guess he can see enough to know the wound in the sheriff's neck is fleshy, pink, not red or wet. Something is wrong. And he knows something is wrong. And he has my rifle. So, it's got to be done. *Damn it.* "I'm sorry," I tell him.

He looks up at me with those sad brown eyes, that bruise unchanged beneath the left. He's waiting for an explanation. Because even now he still thinks I can help him. With both hands I lunge at him, pin him to the ground, and rip his eyes out. No need to worry about keeping my shirt bloodless no more. My skin takes in some of the mess, but he's still alive—still screaming. I snap his neck, just like I did the sheriff's, and drain every last drop of blood from each of their bodies before reclaiming my knife and rising almost drunkenly to my feet, stumbling under the fading moonlight. Being this full brings a stupor on, but I push through it.

Radley's awake. Watching. Lord knows how long he's been doing that. When I get to him, I bend down beside him, cut his ropes, and drop breathlessly onto the ground. He rubs his gritty, bloody wrists. I can smell his blood, but it doesn't bother me. I've already had my fill. "About damn time," he says before grinning. "And to think they were calling *me* the Angel of Death."

He laughs. I don't. "The kid didn't have to die," I tell him.

"Of course, he did."

I'm scowling, and I know it.

"You think he would have fared better going back to the mine? You're getting soft on me, Lucas."

"I'm getting tired is what I am."

He stands up, and even though I want to sleep, I know I can't. Not here. So, I stand up with him. "There would have been no need to kill this kid if you'd killed the last one."

That's how we ended up in Vulture City to begin with. I hadn't wanted to kill that baby-faced lawman, the one who kept talking about a newborn son and getting back home to him. So, after the others were dead, I took off—left him and Radley alone in the desert. Hoped the kid was smart enough to cut his losses and save himself, but that's not what he did. No. He managed to get Radley as far as Vulture City all on his own, even if he refused to take him one inch further than that. That meant I had to come back and clean up the mess I'd made. "You'll have to sell the horses," says Radley.

"I'm keeping Adelaide," I say, nodding towards the mare I've been riding since Clayton. Radley laughs but doesn't argue. "Your sister still up in Montana?" I ask.

He nods.

"Good. Can't stand the desert. Too damn hot." Fellas like me—creatures like me—prefer dark, cool places after all. Not hot, blinding deadlands.

"She'll pay you when you get there," he says.

Five hundred dollars. More than I would have gotten once we split that one-thousand-dollar reward five ways. Of course, I was never interested in the reward. Radley put me on his payroll early. Soon as he got out of Yuma. Had heard tell of what I could do and how I could do it. Said he might have work for a fella like me. *You could make yourself some easy money*, he said. That was the selling line.

But this kind of money never comes easy. No. It comes soaked in blood. Wet and slippery. Not that it matters when all is said and done. Bloody money buys a hell of a lot more than empty pockets. I can tell you that much.

The Last Free Ride

LH Michael

She browbeat her horse forward, glancing back all the while
   It was darkening, not fully dark
   On the flat ground ahead
   Appeared three shadows

   They rushed her
   Kicking aside what the ground put in front of them
   They were horses, running as a pack
   All had saddles, none had riders

   She thought they'd separate
   Instead, they huddled together
   A battalion set to run her down
   She lifted her gun and fired at the sky

   One startled horse stepped on another's leg
   They buckled in agony
   The third galloped away
   The moon was out now, lighting a lantern over what she'd done

   She circled the two broken horses
   As they brayed against all they'd seen since becoming transportation

She stepped down and judged their prognosis
One snapped at her, almost bit her knee

She shot that horse first
Though the other was more deserving of a bullet's reprieve
Their saddles were immaculate
Apart from the blood she'd spattered on them

She continued on, glancing back all the while
The moon, now veiled in clouds, showed her nothing
Straight ahead, a man stood up, arms stretched out
His wingspan nearly matched his height

She changed direction
But another man jumped in front of her
His arms were just as long
She shot him in the heart

Her horse pulled up, refusing to move
It bucked around, as though determined to eject her
The other long-armed "man" tracked her down
In each hand he held a heavy stone

She steadied her gun as the first rock flew wide
Her horse flipped around, she couldn't aim
She fired, she missed
He held a hand over his face, looking like a human tarantula

She fired again, caught his neck this time
He fell back, like a collapsed fence

Her horse brayed against all it'd seen since becoming transportation
It had seen enough

The horse sent her flying
When she landed, her leg bent against her joints' wishes
She thought she heard a gun shot
It was the sound of snapping bone

Even in the gloom, she saw the bone sticking out of her skin
She bit her shirt to mute her tongue
She had no one to scream to for help
Screams would only tell those listening she was helpless

She dragged herself along the ground
Glancing back all the while
It was cold, not cold enough to cool her breached leg
The wound was already sucking in dirt

She reached her limit near dawn
Shivering, panting, freezing
Within hours she was burning up
And pining for shade

She wormed behind a rock
The shape and size of which offered respite
She needed the rock's cover
Because tromping in the distance was something with very long arms

It stopped and bent down

Then slammed its hand against the ground
It raised a writhing snake up to its mouth
And tore off a bite

Ever since they'd arrived
With their long arms slapping their ankles
Stability had deserted
Gone from the town, the valley, the river

The "man" looked in her direction
And flung away the partly devoured snake
He stretched his arms wide
And barreled towards her

She had no remaining bullets
Why had she spent two on the horses?
All she had left was her knife
And a good stab requires good legs

His shadow spilled across her rock
She hoisted her blade
He charged right past her
Towards a teenager wandering in the distance

The teenager saw long arms bear down on him
He whooped and turned tail
The man and the teenager were soon out of sight
Consciousness slipped through the woman's fists

She awakened fully when the sun was down

She didn't need daylight to see her fate
She heard a horse storming towards her rock
The horse had no rider

She rolled into the horse's path
Step on me, crush me, end me
But what if the horse breaks its leg?
She squiggled out of its path

She heard its hoofsteps fade
But felt no regret about her squandered chance
If she was to take that way out
She'd need another form of transportation
© LH Michael

The Ballad of Bushwhack Bill
Chris Wilder

The story I am about to impart unto you is both Right and True. The horrors contained within are those seen with my own very eyes. I do not reckon many will be believin me, but I am in the hopes that some will and might be avoiding a most gruesome fate. Gentlepersons, be they of the fair sex or of youth, or perhaps of a slight way, should forego continuing.

This account is from the area of the town of Fair Views, which is right on the edge of true desert territory. I was a fair constable of the town, which most of the times did not see much in the way of trouble. There was surely always a number of men who were of the rough nature as would be expected in such a locale. Many a folk passed through there as they headed towards the mighty California, and most of my duties involved keeping the peace between them and those of the townsfolk who had issues with their honestys.

Bushwhack Bill was one of these sorts. I do not recall I quite remember where he cames from. And do not be lettin that name worry you none. That was a self-appointed moniker he posted on himself, so as to appear deadly and intimidatin, I reckon. Now that don't mean that Bushwhack Bill was any sort of good fellow. Because he weren't. What he was was lazy. I reckon he could have been quite a handful of outlaw if he put his mind to it. Just could not be bothered to make an effort.

He was involved in all sorts of money makin schemes, none of which were much. He even tried his hand at honest work at times, but the lazy was with that as wells. I figured he could have maybe even kept himself decently in whiskey and victuals with his card playin. He knew his way around a hand of poker, that is for sures. But he would get himself impatient and start a cheating, and then no one would sit at the table with him.

Now at this time, Bushwhack Bill had taken up self-employment by guiding these good folk who were western bound out through the first part of the desert, which was a stretch considered trackless. About three days out there to get them to the dry riverbed and about two days back. He would then spend his earnings about town in drink and whoring, and when finally Big Stan at the saloon or the widower Jones at the hotel stopped his tab, he would look for the next groups of weary travelers who might be thinkin they could use a knowledgeable hand. In that way, he had almost become a respectable businessman.

Now it would an error on my part be if I left you thinking that he was fully reformed. No, he had himself an angle to play. He would negotiate a fair deal price, and he would stick to that. But he had a way of convincin folks that they needed more of his services than they had signed on for. Once out on the desert, he would make available to them for the right price anything from snake deterrent and Indian deterrent and what he called proper desert rope knotting. I can not for any ways tell you how many folks fell for his smooth talk, but I know enough did that he became a bit renowned for it.

Some of the townsfolk, the more honest ones who had concerns about honesty and the reputation of Fair Views, would say unto me, Sir William, how can you be lettin him get on with that? And I would explain to thems that I preferred the Bushwhack Bill who got away with his little bits and kept himself out of real trouble. I would also

tell them that there are folks in this world who could use a little stealin
from, but I do not reckon most of the townsfolk, the honest ones,
understood what I was meaning by that.

Well, I must be going along with the story. It grows late here, and
while my caretakers have certain leniencies towards me, I do not wish
to offend their generosities. There came some days when Bushwhack
Bill had headed out with a family bunch out to the desert. I most often
had some conversing with folks before they set forth onto the sands,
and in some times would give them some fair warnings as to Bushwhack Bill's ways of encouraging monies going from their pockets and
into his. But as the facts be I had not met with this particular family.
I did recall that they had besides the more regular traveling coaches a
wagon with a flatbed that had been boarded over. Now, most folks will
not bother with taking along so much of their belongings but there
are many types of folks about.

I am recallin that it was maybe the third day since they had set forth
when I was hearing quite a carrying on out to the street. I was at the
moment having a relaxation in my office, and I decided to wait before
investigating the ruckus. I did not detect anger in the voices that were
all a hollerin, nor were there indications of violence, such as gunshots.
As it were, Bushwhack Bill came a burstin into my office quite clearly
being upset. I had my deputy Joe secure the door and make sure that
we were having peace in my office and I set about discovering what
Bushwhack Bill was doing, havin returned early from the desert.

Bushwhack Bill took some time to settle and commence tellin me
his tale. I got him to confirm that he had been escortin that one
particular family, and knowin that they could well not yet have reached
the dry riverbed, then where were they? And would you know that
Bushwhack tells me that they all got et up. And I says to Bushwhack
Bill, now Bill, what do you mean they got all et up? Et up by what?

And of course, by et he meant ate. Bushwhack Bill was not well known for his grammars.

Here is where I began to be suspect that this was not one of Bushwhack Bill's notoriety escapades. Because Bushwhack Bill is well-known not to be a man who will use one word when he can spill forth a dozen. I discovered that Bushwhack Bill was havin trouble articulatin his thoughts. I never thought to be seein such a thing. I braced him up with a pair of slugs of whiskey, but not my good malt, mind you, and finally saw some success in gettin him to talk.

Do you know what Bushwhack Bill told me then? He tells me that those good folks got eaten and killed by some feller they had locked up in that flatbed wagon the whole time. Now I get Bushwhack Bill to tell me all this again, and slower this time. And you know he tells me the same story. And he is not all elaboratin and emphasizin as he does in normal days. I tell him that it does not seem likely, that the weather is not being particularly conducive, with it being the desert and a good bit warm, to be hiding in a wagon all the day. And sure enough, Bushwhack Bill agrees with me and says that he knows that no fellow can be hidin in such a fashion but this is what he says did indeed happen.

Now being a well-trained man of the law I know about how to detect things, and I know that I have to have Bushwhack Bill tell me the entire details. This takes some bit of time to accomplish, and I will not here repeat it as he was telling it, for as I mentioned prior, Bushwhack Bill is not a man considered to be gifted in the speaking areas. I will have to relate the tale as if I was the one telling it original. You will have to trust me that I have no interest to slanderin poor Bushwhack Bill; may God have mercy on his soul. I do not reckon many of you will be believin this tale as it be. I must also be remindin you readers that this tale is not for those who are of a faintness. I have been held culpable for too much as it stands, and I will not be held for more.

As Bushwhack Bill told it, the desert foray started plain. He struck a fair deal he says to take the family group as far as the dry riverbed. He thought that the flatbed wagon was an odd sight, but he said he had seen plenty odder. As they rolled over the sands none of the family seemed to go near the flatbed wagon, and Bushwhack Bill figured that if they thought it was not anything of a concern, neither would he. But Bushwhack Bill did admit to being a mite of a bit of curious regardin what was in that wagon.

Here I am thinkin Bushwhack Bill had thoughts of valuables all piled high in that wagon and was entertainin thoughts of getting in there. I am also of a thought that it sure would be nice if I had here one of those fetching young lasses they use at those publishing houses back to the east that can write these things out for a man. I grow aweary from spellin out Bushwhack Bill's name so much.

As Bushwhack Bill told it, he had the family settin up evenin camp in a likely spot, and he was able to at last have some conversin with the patriarch of the family concernin that wagon. This man, who was named Jonas, did admit that there was within the wagon the body of another member of the family. They were bringin him along to bury at the new-to-be-built family plot. When Bushwhack Bill asked about the wagon bein secured with a big old lock, this Jonas tells him that they had heard stories about how the Indians would rob graves. This struck Bushwhack Bill as an odd thing since not only are our Indians hereabouts for most things friendly and peaceable but how would they even know that there was a body to rob in the wagon?

Now a man such as Bushwhack Bill does not get to be still alive without being able to get a tell of a man, and he says that he can tell that this Jonas feller is not right keen on this conversation, so Bushwhack

Bill lays off of it. Here I interrupt him to ask about if he had been gettin the family to agree to his extra services. Bushwhack Bill hemmed and hawed a good bit before admittin that while he had thoughts for that they were such a dour group, and he had made enough by chargin them by the head, and they had a fair good amount of childrens that he had not pursued it much. I made some careful notes of this because chargin by the head seemed like it might be an egregious thing.

Bushwhack Bill says that the night passed just fine, but then as they were breaking camp in the morn this Jonas feller makes a fuss because he says someone has been at that flatbed wagon messin with it, and he is right upset. Bushwhack Bill admits to takin a look at the lock and all since the desert air can make things not work the way they ought to. Well, this Jonas hoots and hollers about it and tells Bushwhack Bill to stay away from the wagon and that he ought not be disrespectin the dead. And Bushwhack Bill tells him that he is sorry and he did not mean no disrespect but quite the opposite and that he figures that any fellers in that wagon are not likely caring at this point no how. I think you agree that this is a right foolish thing to say to grievin folks, and indeed he says they all get in a flutter, and he hears things in talk he ain't never heard before, like that maybe this family is not long from being from the Old Country. Bushwhack Bill says he also sees that this Jonas feller seems to be thinkin that someones was at the wagon by the tracks they left, and Bushwhack Bill knows he left no tracks there at all.

Well, all the yellin and fuss goes on a bit, but Bushwhack Bill finally gets the family movin again. Not much of talkin that day, and Bushwhack Bill says he thinks he can hear someone inside that wagon a time or two, but he cannot get over by it and see if he can hear better. No one in the family seems to notice this, and actually, Bushwhack Bill thinks that maybe they are mostly avoidin that wagon.

The second night they set up camp just fine, and Bushwhack Bill says he pitches his bedroll on the far side from that wagon because he says he wants no part of all this drama. He says he reckons that saved him because when the screaming started during the night, he was safely apart. He says he arose and saw that Hell itself had opened in that camp. He says he saw a big feller he had not seen before, and this feller was all dressed in a Sunday best suit and no shoes and looked not well. Bushwhack Bill said that this feller had one of the old crones of the family in his hands and was hunched over her and was taking bites out of her.

Bushwhack Bill had to stop at his narration here to fortify himself with more of my liquor. I interjected that this fellow must have been insane, and that was why they kept him in that wagon, and that would explain how it was that he could survive the heat since it is well known that the insane can, at times, do things no normal man could accomplish. Bushwhack Bill just shook his head at this and goes on about what he saw that horrible night.

Oh! I am not sure I can rightly continue with this tale. It is a heavy weight on my soul to tell, and I fear what it may do to those who read these passages. However, I think that if I do not put it down now, I never will. On an ordinary evenin I would be sitting in the dark by now, but I have made an agreement with some of the caretakers that they will leave me light this night in exchange for my insight to some of the other inhabitants. My detectin is still powerful.

There is no way I can make this easy for you to read. I do think the best course is to say it and be done. Bushwhack Bill is now well fortified. On a normal occasion, I would think he was overly so, but today it seems to not have much of an effect on him.

He continues with the horrid details. He says there was more to the scene than an insane man. He saw two of the childrens eatin at another crone, and everywhere he looked was blood and bodies and screamin. He says he saw Jonas shootin his brother over and over, but the brother still came up and started on eatin him. I asked Bushwhack Bill what he did to help these folks. I know that Bushwhack Bill keeps his carbine in decent working order since he is not completely without sense.

Bushwhack Bill hangs his head shamefully and admits he did no such thing as help them. He says he got on his horse Jebediah and rode straight back to Fair Views. I asked him if he was looking for a posse, and he says he was not. He only wished to remove himself from that Hellish scene. I had to then give some solid thought on this story of his. Of course, it was outlandish and could not be true as he told it. Men do react funny sometimes when they see violence. Bushwhack Bill was no stranger to a fight but what seems happened at the camp was of a different matter. I figured it might well be true that Bushwhack Bill had been caught stealin or such by them and had fled and concocted this incredible tale to say he was hit with sun poisonin or such. I was also afeared that there had been an insane in that wagon and that somethin had befallen that family. Even with no hardship having struck them, they could be lost in the desert if Bushwhack Bill had left them with lackin direction. I knew that as Constable it was my duty to verify that this family came to no harm.

I might other times have sent some of the other townsfolk since as Constable I should not be leavin too far from the town. This time I knew I would have to go myself. This fantastic story would do well not to be spread around. More so since Willets had been tellin his own tales of Natives performin their pagan rites in his pastures. I put no stock in his tales, but they did have some folks here riled up.

I asked Bushwhack Bill if Jebediah was good for ridin still or if he would need a remount. He paled and flinched at my words. I made clear to him that he was ridin back out there with me. Between my sternness and his shame at havin left women and children in the desert, it was a quick agreement we had. I had Joe go to Bailey's stables to saddle up a pair of good desert horses and make sure they were provisioned adequately for our ride. Bailey was not keen on this as he had seen the condition Jebediah was in when Bushwhack Bill rode back into town. I had to make assurances against my own salary, which would displease Molly without question.

I am pleased to say that we left within the hour. It was quite a hullaballoo in the town. People were concerned about that family, and Bushwhack Bill had spread his story a piece before he made it into my office.

We rode in good time. The sun was dwindlin, and the heat was dwindlin. We drove the horses a good hard bit while we had the good light. The moon was bright that evening, so we could continue through the witching hours. Bushwhack Bill used his guide skills to keep us in the right direction. Our only true fear was a snake bite, but fortune was with us. We approached the camp soon after dawn.

I do believe myself to be a man of some basic learnings. I can use many a word in my vocabulary and can express myself to others with both spoken and the written word. I do not think I can tell you about that camp in any manner or fashion that will be adequate. As we approached, I noted how quiet it was. I noted that there was a lack of carrion birds and that eased my heart. I asked Bushwhack Bill if the camp had moved or if this was the same place. He responded in low tones that it looked just as he had left it.

I reined in before goin in closer. I know not the words to use here. I could tell in some manner right off that the camp was not right. Some inner sense told me this. I found myself loathe to continue but knew that I must. I uncovered my Colt and made sure of its readiness.

The first thing to see was the flatbed wagon. The look of it told me that someone had broken free from inside. The presence of a madman seemed to be true. The camp itself, though spoke of things beyond the atrocities even a madman could perform.

I saw pieces of bodies and chewed bones scattered wide. Much of the blood had dried and been drawn into the sand. I told Bushwhack Bill that animals had been at the bodies, and it was good that there weren't any buzzards or coyotes around now. No tracks is what Bushwhack Bill said to me, and I saw he was right. The only tracks were of the two-legged kind.

It took short minutes to see that nothing living was in the camp. I had hoped that the wagons may have been a refuge for survivors. I estimated the number of bodies to be at least twelve and maybe as many as sixteen. Many of them were in such pieces that a better count would be a grisly affair.

Bushwhack Bill pointed out some foot tracks leadin away from the camp. We followed them with caution. I knew that in a normal time, we would be hollerin out for survivors. We kept silent as we went along the trail. Soon we approached a hollow amongst dunes that had come up around a rocky outcrop. I could hear some faint noise. We dismounted and went forward on foot.

I can hardly close my eyes to this day and not see again what I saw then. There were four figures in that hollow. Three of them crouched over a fourth, a woman who was deceased. The other three were tearing strips of flesh from the legs of the corpse and stuffing them into their mouths. I could see white bone showin just how much they had taken from her.

I cannot tell you what noise I made, but I did make it. The three things, for I cannot bear to call them survivors or even human, looked up at us, and I could see the ravenous hunger in their eyes. One was the madman as described by Bushwhack Bill. His suit was coated to the entirety in blood and sand. The second man was, I determined, the camp leader Jonas. I knew this from Bushwhack Bill's exclamation. The third, and may God forgive me for writin this into words, was a girl of maybe twelve summers.

All three of them were coated on their fronts in blood. I could see how the girl's belly bulged with the flesh of her devoured family. Jonas had pieces missing from parts of him, but I could not see what wound had doomed the girl. The madman looked as if he had been deceased for a longer time. This I judged by the condition and coloration of his bits of skin that were not colored with blood.

The three of them all came towards us. They came forth in an odd way that was part run and part walk. Bushwhack Bill squealed in terror and fell to the ground, crawlin backward as best he could in the sand. I must be honest and say that I also retreated though in a more reserved manner. I raised the Colt and told them to stop. I implored with them and begged. I invoked the law and the Lord. None of the words I used seemed to affect them in any fashion.

The madman was the closest to me, and I felt he had my harm as his goal. I fired the pistol, and the bullet went into his shoulder. The Colt is a powerful weapon, and most men would be knocked down and greatly hurt by such a wound. The madman was slowed down for only a moment. Little blood seemed to come from the bullet hole, and he did not cry out or react otherwise but continued his advance.

I cocked the pistol and fired a second time. My aim was truer, and it was certainly a shot to his heart. To my continuin astonishment, this wound affected him even less than the first. I backed more rapidly away and worked at readying for a third shot. He was close enough now that I could hear his mouth and teeth working in anticipation of rending my flesh. His smell also came to me, but I will not burden you with that description. I fired a third time, but panic was becomin my partner, and my shot was wild.

I was on the cusp of doom. I had only thoughts for this monstrosity that bore down on me. I knew not then where Bushwhack Bill was or how he fared, but I knew that he had been good with his description. This was from Hell.

The madman made a final rush, and I was able to manage one more shot. I cannot claim to have made careful aim. I fired more from reflex and desperation. My bullet struck him, or it, in the forehead. The top of the skull was removed, and the beast dropped to the sand without a word and became still.

I had no time to contemplate or celebrate this victory as I then heard Bushwhack Bill screaming out. I saw that the girl had caught up to him and had laid her teeth into his calf. She was savaging and sawing at his flesh, and his screams were of an animalistic nature. I hurried over to him and kicked the girl, nay the demon, away from him. She tumbled over the sand and, when she stopped, made to come back to attack us again. I took a careful bead and fired into her face.

As her body fell backward, I spied the third one, the man called Jonas, who it seemed had floundered in the sand. I gave a brief prayer on that since if he had kept pace with the madman, I would surely not have lived to write this. I approached him and fired my last cartridge into his skull.

Once the report of my pistol had echoed away, there was a brief moment of silence. This was ended by the moanings of poor Bushwhack Bill. I went to him and performed what aid I could. His calf was truly in dire condition. I told him there was no help for it but for us to return to town as quickly as we could. It would be a job for Dr. Stevens to save that leg. The Dr. was mostly concerned with animals now, but he had seen service with the Army and may have seen similar wounds.

I told Bushwhack Bill that the leg was probably to be lost. He pleaded with me to take it off then and there and was saying he could feel the poison in it. I felt this would be a disastrous action to take and had not an implement to do such a thing in any event. I wrapped it as well as could be done and retrieved the horses. Bushwhack Bill was certain he could ride and had little choice in the matter. We could not double up in the heat and hope to return to Fair Views before he would expire.

There are ways to travel the desert in the heat of the day. We did not follow these ways but made haste. I cannot say how much this might have had an effect on the demise of Bushwhack Bill. We were past halfway back to the town by my reckonin when he pitched from his horse. I do not suspect many of you readers have held a body when the life goes from it. This was not the first time I had done so, and I beg to God each day that it was the last.

Bushwhack Bill had no real words at the end. He had thoughts for them, but they would not come for him. He shuddered and shook and cried a bit, and he passed while I held him. You must understand this part. I am a Lawman and a veteran, and I swear to any and all oaths that man Bushwhack Bill was dead. I composed his body as I was able to and took some time to rest and eat and drink and consider. I had not yet decided if I was to bring his body with me or forego it to gain time to return to the camp with help when Bushwhack Bill got back to his feet.

How can a man be dead and yet alive? I know this not. Some things we are not meant to know in this life but must wait for the Good Lord to tell us once we pass into his glorious realm.

Bushwhack Bill did not stay on his feet. The leg was too damaged to hold him upright. He fell over and began crawling towards me. He had the same look about him as the other things had. I was without direct thought, I believe now. I knew that my Colt was empty as I had neglected to reload it after the camp. I went to the horse Bushwhack Bill had fallen from and took his carbine from across the saddle. I am ashamed to say that I did not even have enough thought to fire it but instead clubbed Bushwhack Bill in the head as he tried to bite me. He fell limp, and I buried him in a shallow grave.

You are likely to be aware of the rest of the story. I returned to Fair Views and had no discretion. I told all of the grisly events I had endured. There was some meager evidence to my tale. My pistol had been emptied, and I had some amount of Bushwhack Bill's blood upon me. It was clear to all that some torment had befallen me.

They say that Bushwhack Bill's grave was empty. They followed his tracks until the sandstorm drove them back to the town. The storm also eradicated most of the Hell camp. Two wagons were found knocked over, but no bodies were ever found.

The magistrate found it likely that I had put Bushwhack Bill in the ground while he was still breathin. A true absurdity. I was given an opportunity at my trial to speak for myself. Before I could conclude the story, the trial was cut short, and I find myself here. The caretakers will not tell me directly, but I believe my trial went on without me. Since I remain here, I cannot think my lawyer prevailed. Now the dawn is upon me again. I can hear the carpenters out there as the gallows go up.

Cemetery Supper

Jeremiah Dylan Cook

June 21, 1898

A single candle flickers on the bedside table as Pete Maxwell shivers under his blankets. The night is hot, but whatever affliction has consumed his body makes it impossible for him to stay warm. He rubs his hands against his chest for heat but recoils in disgust at his flabby skin. The leg injury that had kept him from horseback for a year had also turned his body to dough.

The bedroom door opens, and a breeze of fresh air blows through the stale space. A lantern in the hallway illuminates a tall, gaunt man. Due to the loss of his far sight, Pete is unable to make out more. The stranger steps over the threshold, shuts the door, and sits in the rickety, wooden chair beside his bed. By the light of the lone flame, Pete can make out a black robe, a white collar, and a youthful face devoid of beard or mustache. "You called for last rights?"

Pete manages to stop his teeth from chattering. "Yes."

The priest performs the sign of the cross. "If you are able, we can start with your final confession."

"I'm sure you've heard of Billy the Kid? Or maybe you know him as William H. Bonney?" Pete's shivers subside, but his heart pumps faster as he recalls the horrors of his past.

"I may look young, but I've been around long enough to have heard of Billy the Kid." The priest leans forward in his chair. "In fact, if word around town is to be believed, you had something to do with his demise."

"Damn whisperers don't know anything about it." A coughing fit rips through Pete's body, but he manages to regain control of himself. "They talk about Billy like he was a hero, but I knew the man. He was a monster, pure and simple."

"Is that why you gave his whereabouts to the law? I was told Billy stumbled into your bedroom as you passed information to Sheriff Garrett, and the outlaw paid for his sins with a bullet."

"That's what Garrett wanted people to believe, but the truth about Billy the Kid has haunted me for seventeen years now. Maybe with all your learning in the ways of the lord, you'll be able to make sense of the evil in my tale and give me the peace I need concerning the event."

July 13, 1881

Pete Maxwell hitched his horse, splashed a bit of water on his face, and used his hat to fan his forehead from the setting sun overhead. He surveyed his home with pride. The large structure had originally served as the officers' quarters for old Fort Sumner. His father had purchased the Fort and all the buildings along with it. Pete approached his porch to find shade but instead discovered Billy the Kid.

"Pete, what's it like being thirty-three? I ain't never been thirty-three, and I don't reckon I ever will be." Billy leaned back in a chair with his feet propped on the porch railing. He wore a white shirt with suspenders holding his dusty pants in place. The kid had big ears pushed out by his bowler hat. While most men his age sported some facial hair, he had none.

"Well, everything aches more, but you're also less prone to irrational thinking. The passions of youth hold much less sway. It's kind of sad, though. I sometimes wish I felt more of my old emotions." Pete leaned against a post holding up his porch and smoothed out his mustache with his index finger. He'd chosen a full suit for an earlier trip into civilization, but the layers did not agree with the current heat.

Billy removed his revolver from his holster and clicked back the hammer. "Didn't Jesus die at thirty-three? If that age was good enough for God to die at, what gives you any right to try to outlive the Almighty?"

Sweat started to leak down Pete's brow. "Easy there. Aren't we friends, Billy?"

"Don't be such a chickenshit, Pete. My bullets have better places to be than in you." Billy uncocked the hammer of his gun and slid a bullet from the chamber. "This one has Sheriff Garrett's name on it."

"You don't have to stay here and wait for the Sheriff to find you. Why not head for the hills?"

Billy rechambered his round and stood up. "You'd like that, wouldn't you? You'd have me away from your huge house and your precious Paulita." The kid smiled, revealing sharp, fang-like canines.

"Leave my daughter out of this." Pete moved his hand to the .41 caliber pocket pistol he kept concealed in the waistband behind his back. "I've been nothing but good to you. Especially considering you're on the run from the hanging rope."

"We used to be pals, Pete. Thought you'd appreciate Paulita and me getting close. Wouldn't you want me as a son-in-law?" Billy nonchalantly aimed the pistol at Pete. "Come on now, don't delay with that retort."

"You're free to everything in my house." Pete's hand grasped the pocket pistol's handle. "Except my daughter."

Billy laughed. "Well, make sure you tell her that. I can't help it if she comes up to my room every night looking for lessons on love." The kid holstered his pistol. "I'll be back late. Don't wait up." Billy stepped off the porch and headed toward the cattle corral.

After his father's passing, Pete devoted his time to turning the old Fort into a profitable ranch. Billy the Kid's arrival had, at first, seemed like a blessing. He showed up as an affable young man ready to do hard work. After a few days, the kid's façade dropped, and he stopped helping around the ranch. A few days after that, Pete heard Billy in Paulita's room in the dead of night. Pete wished he'd had the courage to confront the damned ruffian, but the kid's reputation was fierce. He'd recently escaped the state's execution attempt, killing two men in the process.

The radiating light of the sun diminished and bathed the surrounding scrub grass and desert landscape in a golden glow. Night approached. With the darkness would come a refreshing reprieve from the summer warmth. Billy walked past the corral. The cattle mulled about restlessly; some mooed at the passing outlaw. The kid went on walks every twilight and returned after dark. No one knew where he went, but the only thing in Billy's current direction was the cemetery. It contained the dead from old Fort Sumner and those unfortunate souls who'd died since the Maxwell family had taken over.

The cemetery was dark and shaded by some of the few trees that grew in the harsh landscape. It was a perfect place for an ambush. Pete pulled out his pocket pistol and popped open the chamber to confirm the two bullets remained in place, then he stepped off the porch and followed the young man who'd become far too familiar with his daughter.

At the cemetery's edge, Pete crouched behind a tree and observed. Billy the Kid sat amidst the accumulation of hastily assembled wooden crosses enclosed by a simple, picket fence. The few markers that had names were worn away by the elements. In the gloom of dusk, the kid looked much older than his twenty-one years. His hair seemed to shine silver, and wrinkles marred his youthful face. The skin practically seemed to hang off his cheeks. Pete rubbed his eyes and tried to confirm what he thought he'd seen, but the last light of day vanished behind the vast horizon as a cold wind blew across the New Mexico Territory.

In the darkness, the sound of furious digging echoed through the air. Pete's eyes adjusted to the lack of sunlight, and he spotted Billy using the grip end of his revolver to start a hole in one of the graves. Pete drew his pocket pistol and crept forward. The sound of the digging drowned out the sound of his boots on the dusty ground.

The kid dropped his gun and started using his hands to claw the sandy earth. A smell like rotten eggs mixed with sour milk made Pete's stomach churn. Billy pulled out the arm of a recently deceased cattle rustler named Dale. The man had showed up a few weeks back, worked hard for a short time, and died of a presumed heart attack soon after Billy's arrival. Dale wasn't buried with anything but his clothes and boots, and Billy had helped bury the man, so Pete was stumped by the kid's grave robbing.

From behind, Pete stood perplexed as Billy studied Dale's lifeless arm. The skin was mostly intact, except where finger bones protruded from the greying skin of the hand. A worm wiggled free from the flesh near Dale's elbow. Billy bent forward, sniffed once, and ripped into the flesh of the forearm with his teeth.

"What in tarnation?" Pete couldn't stop himself from speaking his mind.

The kid pulled away a grisly hunk of decaying flesh and chewed for a moment. "I knew you were yella, but I didn't know you'd stoop to ambushing a man in the dark. This is my private time." Billy stood up and turned around.

Close up, in the moonlight, Pete's previous observation was confirmed. The youthful visage of Billy the Kid had withered, and now his face resembled a prune. His hands shook slightly and were equally elderly.

"What's wrong with you?"

"Nothing." Billy swallowed the piece of Dale, and all at once his skin seemed to tighten. He didn't look as youthful as he normally did, but now he resembled a middle-aged man with a few lines and darker hair. The kid's hands no longer shook.

Pete squeezed the trigger of the pocket pistol, and his bullet sent Billy tumbling backward. The kid fell and broke the cross erected for Dale. The sound of the shot reverberated through the air. He and his daughter were now freed of the deviant's presence. Pete breathed a sigh of relief.

Dale's lifeless arm rested in the mix of sand and dirt, and Pete kicked earth back onto it. He'd come back in the morning and do a more respectful job of reburying the man's limb. Billy's body lay a few steps away. Pete approached slowly, with his pocket pistol ready to fire a second, final shot. The kid's chest didn't move, and inky blood spread out underneath him. Pete kneeled and looked for where he'd hit the man. A hole smoked in Billy's sternum. Pete glanced up to the kid's face and saw Billy's eyes burst open.

The kid scrambled up and fought with the surprised Pete. Billy's teeth gnashed together as he went to take a bite of Pete's exposed neck. For a horrible moment, Pete thought he was a dead man. He'd arm-wrestled Billy enough times to know the kid was stronger, but to his surprise, Pete managed to keep Billy at bay. He remembered again that this wasn't the same youthful kid he'd talked to earlier. This was a middle-aged version of Billy. Despite his momentary respite from despair, Billy managed to get his teeth around Pete's right earlobe.

The tearing of flesh was all too audible to Pete. The fleshy pulp came away from his head with a plop. The pain triggered reserves of adrenaline, and Pete managed to shove Billy away. The kid swallowed the bit of Pete, and he went from middle-aged to late twenties in a flash. Pete raised his pocket pistol and blew the top of Billy's skull off. Viscera splattered around the cemetery. The kid's eyes rolled back in his head as if looking up to the bits of brain that oozed out of his shattered cranium.

Pete sat back and took in great gulps of air as he clutched his bitten ear. "You damn lunatic."

To Pete's horror, Billy the Kid's mouth responded. "We'll meet again before your end."

"You're not coming back from what my .41 did to you."

"Billy won't be coming back, but I will." The kid's mouth smiled, and the moonlight revealed blood dripping across the white enamel. "You've ruined my vessel, and he was a good one, but I cannot be killed. We'll meet again." The kid's mouth went slack, his jaw dropped, and his tongue rolled out to touch the dirt.

Pete stared down at the body, suspicious of more movement. After several moments of stillness, he returned to his feet. Everything that occurred that night caught up to him in a rush, and he turned to run home, afraid a heart attack would kill him before he reached his front door.

"That's quite a yarn you spin." The priest sat back in his chair after listening intently for the better part of an hour.

Pete had felt some of his energy returning as he'd told his tale. His body no longer shivered, and he managed to keep a bit of warmth now. Something about unburdening had proven cathartic. "The next day, once I'd regained my nerves, I called Sheriff Garrett. I showed him the body, but I didn't tell him the truth. I worried he might gun me down if I told him about the insanity that had occurred the night before. Instead, I told him I'd killed Billy in self-defense. Garrett believed me, but he wanted the credit for dispatching the outlaw. I agreed to go along with his story. I even allowed him to shoot a hole in my home to sell the ruse that he'd surprised Billy in my bedroom."

"Well, I must thank you. This confession has been exceedingly interesting. Most of the time I hear about adultery. I get so tired of people's petty nonsense."

"I didn't think priests could say things like that." Pete shifted uncomfortably as goosebumps ran along his arms.

"Well, who will you tell? You're going to die tonight."

While Pete recognized the truth in the priest's words, the blunt statement of his fate still hurt. "I suppose."

"What do you think you encountered that night?"

"Who knows."

"Come on. Surely you must've tried to figure out what could've taken up residence in Billy?"

"Honestly, I just tried to forget the entire incident. Maybe I imagined the whole thing. Maybe it was a demon. Who knows?" Pete squirmed in his bed.

"Have you ever heard of a Wendigo?"

Pete's shivering returned. "Can't say that I have."

"It's a word the natives came up with for a ravenous spirit. A force that possesses people and imbues them with an insatiable hunger for flesh."

"Sounds like you could be onto something. Can we get on with the other rites now? I don't want to talk about that night anymore."

"Oh, but Pete, I told you we'd meet again. I'm here to finish what I started with your ear." The priest smiled, revealing sharp, fang-like canines.

Pete tried to scream, but the priest covered his mouth.

The Kid

Adam Vine

I never wanted to join no gang
To cross no arid, sanguine plain
To eat no flapjacks for no meal
To put no scalps above my steel.
But I needed money, so I went
South for where the dipper bent
I was just a kid with dandy aim
A steady hand, a love for games.
Those rough men never asked my name
So I became powder, salt, and flame.
Across the thirsting land we rode
Of sand and scrub pine, blood and bone
Hunting scalps for a gov'ment dime
If it had black hair, it sold just fine.
War is a shrub that burns to gold
And men were made for it, I was told
But now I scream and lie awake
By night I fear, and by day I ache.
I was just a kid hunting bushes of gold
I was just a kid, so I was told.

The Snake River Tale

Ann Wuehler

Elk bugled back and forth as I made my way toward the glow of a campfire. Dug's Bar had taken me across the Snake, toward Robinson's Gulch. I had to hope these were friendlies. Mostly not, out here in the Oregon mountains, but I had lost my horse, my sack of pies and bread, and my lone rifle. Damn bear had burst from the brush, almost into my new horse, spooking the ornery beast. Bad luck or the Devil himself had made me fall on my left arm. A clean break, but still broken. I needed to rest, get the bone proper set, and get back to my camp, up toward Sumpter.

My sister Anelia would be making her vinegar pies for the miners up there, but I had decided to try up Hells Canyon way.

Avis and Anelia Brown would continue to sell pies and bread and home remedies as long as the gold boom lasted here in Oregon.

The year 1890 had not been kind so far, but now it seemed I'd have to wait until '91 rolled about to experience even middling luck again.

I could now smell wood smoke, hear the soft burble of men talking, the clank of gold pans, and the rumble of the Snake calling out that it would drown everyone it could, that it held more bones than a boneyard full of cholera victims.

Something told me to turn around, go back. Some little shiver. My sister Anelia called it 'the spooks walking by'. That brush of a ghost's eyes on you. She believed in ha'ants.

Either way, I had a real need to run the other direction. Like a frightened horse at the first sight of a smallish black bear.

Instead, I pushed forward.

Out here, at night, with nothing more than my knife and a broken arm meant trouble. I got a lot closer.

First sight of that camp showed me a single man perched on a once-mighty pine tree, now a broken makeshift seat. He had to be Chinese, with that long, coal black ponytail, the big loose trousers, the sandals, the skin like burned honey. Long black eyes met mine as he turned his head over his wide, skinny shoulder. A rather handsome man, middle years or a bit younger. He peered back at his fire, which had strange colors at its heart. More blue and green than red or yellow. I could smell blood in the very air but could not see a kill hanging up or a carcass of anything nearby. "Sit," he called out, his voice like that of a preacher, low and effortless. "The river's not good company tonight." He spoke English.

I walked toward him, my arm tied to my chest using strips from my old flannel shirt. He did not seem outraged that I wore trousers or had sheared my hair. "You ain't a doc, are ya?"

"No," he said, staring out over the river, where I thought I saw bodies bobbing up and down for a bit. That stench of blood seemed to be his natural odor. I had never encountered a Chinese that smelled of blood unless they'd just butchered something. Same as me or my sister would stink if we just cut a deer into usable hunks. "Are you thirsty? My fire isn't very warm." A flick of those liquid night eyes that held no pupils I could see. Although the only light came from his fire, which did not seem to warm me at all. "But it's not for your kind." A slight smile of such utter sadness that was not meant for me.

I even looked over my own shoulder to see if others had joined us but no, just two strangers on the bank of the Snake. His hand reached up toward his head. His hand lifted a portion of his skull away. He filled that makeshift bone cup from the pot he had over the cold flames, and offered it to me. He watched me as I sat there in icy shock, looking at his head, which now had a sizable bit missing from it. "Have a drink, missus."

I stood, backed away, backed away. "No, oh, no," I said, or something equally foolish. I watched the Chinese man drink from a makeshift cup of his own skull, with strands of his long black hair still attached to it. Blood dribbled down his lips to plop onto the breast of his thin cotton shirt.

"Happened right here. They even came back to make sure they got all our gold." He took another gulp, emptied that vessel of bone, and fit it back into place, like someone doing a puzzle. I noticed there were others here now. I noticed they were all Chinese, some holding those mining pans used to skim the gold out of the local creeks. I noticed they did not speak, their faces scarred and torn from whatever violence had been done to them.

I stood in a place of slaughter and the ghosts wished me gone.

"You're lost. Wait until first light." His fingers burned my good arm, and the rage and sorrow of his eyes burned my heart.

"Seems we're all lost, sir."

The man leaned closer, that stench of blood sickening. I saw what had been done to him, with a knife, with an axe, with the flat of a shovel. Oh, his face whole and peaceful again. "Yes, missus."

A sigh, like wind moving through a ripe wheat field.

I sat by his fire. I slept with my back against that old pine.

Morning light opened my eyes.

No fire pit, no pot hanging over that fire, no company of Chinese miners, and no Chinese man who used his skull to offer drinks to strangers.

Years later, I still wake up smelling blood, hearing the whisper of a man offering me a drink. I yank my covers over my head until the whispering stops.

Omega Forest
Hank Belbin

"Ye needn't think the only folks is the folks hereabouts." — H.P Lovecraft, *The Dunwich Horror*.

Part One
New Mexico Territory. 1850...

The survivors of the cavalry fled north across the salt plains. Ten miles after them, the Comanche pursued. The raid had failed. And now the company was the prey.

East was Fort Apache. West was Tijuana. And south lay the fiery furnace of Sonora desert. Endless and white and dead and shimmering under the sun like a boundless sea of glass. North was the only option. They made for the Coconino forest in search of escape and sanctuary. They were all coated in blood and gore and the black powder from the battle that had carried them wearily across the desert for days now. The ingredients of which were sticky against their tattered uniforms like tar.

The Comanche savages had pursued the survivors relentlessly since Juarez. And they aimed to finish the job before days out. Forty-two of the company's men lay cut down and scalped in the desert wastes some ways back. Now there were only ten more to see to.

The raid was ambushed before any defense could even be mounted. The rattling hail of arrows that had descended onto the unit from the ridge like an unwelcome rain, had sent the calvary into pandemonium. Plumes of gray gunsmoke then echoed in the valley and had carried off into the winds, and the battle raged, but the shots failed to find their targets.

After an hour, those at the back saw that the battle was lost and they were routed. The ten men, under command of Captain Morton, turned on their heels and stole into the shimmering heat of the desert. None of them looked back to see the finale of the nightmare. Men that they knew well were now laid strewn across the sands behind them. They all screamed as the grotesque carnival of savages butchered and danced their way through the company.

But it was not over. Those who had survived and fled across the salt plains had merely lived on only to face a new nightmare. For those men, something far worse awaited them.

Of the men who did escape the ambush, there was Morton—the only surviving officer—Corporal, whose Christian name was not known to any man, Jackson, Hughes, Bill, Lewis, Carson, and Powell.

They rode on for days, away from the massacre, all of them fused to their saddles as if they had merged with beasts and had become an abstraction of the centaurs before them.

It was on the third day that Morton noticed it. Something out there on the prairie behind them, pulsing in the midday heat. On the horizon behind them, a cloud of dust grew. Captain Morton stopped and produced his spyglass and aimed at the cloud. He knew what it was. The Comanche tribe was following them. That much was clear. Morton slammed the spyglass home with the base of his palm and snorted.

"We'll not make camp tonight. We'll leave a fire in the night and ride on," he said. The men about obliged.

Much later, after the sun had set, the trick did not work. The Comanche knew that it was a gambit. They'd ridden past the decoy fire and pursued the remaining cavalry into the twilight all the same. They'd expected the routed to flee south, across the border, but they did not.

The tired survivors rode their horses hard. They whipped and lashed at their horses behinds, desperate to break away from the pursuers. The night was long and cold and dark. They rode on.

And just after dawn, the survivors then saw looming up towards them the deep and brooding forest. A great wall of silhouettes poised there against the tenebrous blue sky of the early morning sun. They believed their salvation was nigh. Yet something else was instead.

Still behind them was the chief and his tribe. However, suddenly, they had lost all compunction to pursue the survivors. They saw their prey and gasped each at what the cavalry in front was about to do.

"Kee!" one of the Comanche shouted.

When the ten survivors came to the fringe of the forest, the Comanche pursuers suddenly halted, as if gripped by something. They snatched and tugged at their reigns ,and the horses skidded in the dust eight hundred meters behind the survivors and the tree line.

All of the tribe were suddenly commandeered by unassailable fear. They had been focused on the mission of dispatching the survivors so much that they had not noticed just where they were pursuing them towards—the dreaded forest. The motionless Comanche leader watched on as Morton and the nine other survivors disappeared into the wall of dark trees. One of the savages mumbled some kind of prayer and shut his eyes to the sight. The chief knew that all who went into that forest never came back out again. There was something else in there. Something old.

They turned around, panic-stricken, and rode quickly back in the direction they'd just come from.

Part Two

Deep in the trees, the men teetered and trotted through in silence. They'd been riding in it for almost an hour. The decaying forest all around was wholly unnatural. Drizzle fell and the trees creaked in the languid breeze. No other sounds apart from the hooves moving through it all. Rows and rows of unmoving pine trees sprawling endlessly before them, bearing down on them, yet no sound. They soon noticed the eerie quiet.

"You hear that?" Bill called out.

"I don't hear nuthin'," Hughes replied after a pause.

"Exactly. Forest this big and not so much as a bird makin' noise. Strange..."

"Keep it down," Morton then barked. "Could be another ambush."

They moved on down gulches and finally stopped at a trickling fetid stream to fill their canteens and tend to their wounds. The ride took most of the morning. Lewis had caught an arrow in his arm during the ambush a few days ago and his shoulder was beginning to fester. His linen shirt was stained brown with pus and blood, and the flies all about swarmed him eagerly. None offered consultation on his injury.

Morton knelt down to the water and considered his reflection in the blade of his bowie knife. He looked ten years older than he was. As he examined his face in the metal though, he caught sight of something. Up on the ridge to his left, something moved. Something big. Too big to be Comanche. Morton snapped his gaze left and up at the ridgeline at the sight. He thought he saw something move in his peripheries. He was sure of it. But peering up there, he saw nothing. Only beams of sunlight slanting through the dead trees and onto him; there was nothing else up there. He frowned, then resigned himself to the task of filling his canteen and shaving his sideburns. The men about him were solemn and filled with dread, like the attendees of some morbid wake. Morton calculated that any further acknowledgment of anything untoward would only panic the men further. He chose not to mention it to his retinue.

Hughes however had already seen something. He stood motionless in the river. The water up to his knees. He stared up absently at the same point on the ridge that the captain was looking at. His eyes were wide with terror and he quivered in his boots.

"Hughes? What you lookin' at, boy?" Corporal snapped, noticing his odd behavior. Hughes did not respond. He just kept staring up at the part of the ridge where the sun straddled the earth.

"Hughes! Fall in line!" Captain Morton barked.

Hughes came back to reality, the tears still fresh in his eyes. He looked up at Morton on his horse. They shared a glance.

"Yessir," Hughes said obediently and shuffled out of the river to collect his personal effects laying on the waxed tarp at the bank.

After a small rest, they mounted and rode on.

The day was almost out and their pace had slowed to a crawl as they navigated over mires and small ravines. When night fell, they stopped and made camp up on a ridge that overlooked the boundless mass of dark trees. They could not see the edge of the forest.

Captain Morton briefed his men and devised a rota for sentry duty. They made a fire and orientated their sleeping bags around it. All of them huddled around the only warmth like a litter of starved puppies waiting for their mother to return.

Jackson had first watch. After taking on some cold coffee, he navigated through the dimness of the forest and stood at a point fifty meters away from the campfire. He then held his rifle loosely and stared off into the brooding night. It was a long shift.

Later, after Jackson's sentry duty was over, he was relieved by Lewis, who took up the exact footprints in the dirt that he had made himself. Jackson then came back to his roll mat and bag of particulars, and saw that the roll mat next to his own was empty. Powell was not there. Jackson frowned and noted that the man's possessions and rifle were still by the fire.

"Where's Powell?" Jackson asked Hughes.

"Gone," Hughes muttered as he spat into the fire. He was sharpening his knife but was not focusing on the task at hand. Instead, he merely rubbed the filthy whetstone up and down the blade with seemingly random motions.

"How long he been gone?"

"Reckon 'bout two hours now. Said he was goin' for a shit. Ain't came back."

Jackson nervously knelt down to Hughes. "You reckon them Indians followed us in here after all?" he whispered.

"I reckon they did," Hughes said and his eyes darkened as he stared into the flames. "There will be blood tonight. I'll take no sleep, you can be sure of that."

Jackson looked away from Hughes and pondered what he meant by such a statement. All the same, he felt something heavy fall into his chest—dread. Hughes stared absently into the fire as if taken by something. He would not say what exactly and didn't speak for the rest of the night. Jackson smoked a cigarette and tried to forget about the whole notion.

It was almost midnight. The men about the fire snoozed and dreamed of seeing the inside of a saloon again. They fantasized about collecting their wages and buying a hot bath, a bottle of whiskey, and a seat at the poker table. The swollen silver moon hung above them all in the black starless sky like a great primordial egg, or like an augury to their fates. The fire cracked and smoldered and no other sounds were heard. Jackson slept and snored softly.

Then, from somewhere out in the twilight, something awoke him. One of the men on sentry screamed. A guttural agonizing screech that echoed through the night...and then nothing.

The men about the fire bolted up in their sleeping bags and reached for their rifles. Cold fear assailed them all like an arctic wind. An icy shiver clawed its way down Jackson's spine. He felt the color drain from his face as he stared out utterly terrified into the silent night beyond the campfire. Something was out there in the dark. They all opened their ears to the wilderness but heard nothing. Just...silence.

None dared to call out for Lewis. Whatever was out there, it had taken him. His screams sounded like choking, then like he was gargling something. Then, nothing but the unnerving widening silence. Jackson's eyes were bulging with terror. He panted and shuddered and tried to take command of his shaking body.

"Son of a bitch," Carson said. "Something has got Lewis!"

"What? A bear?" Jackson asked.

"I reckon. Cain't no Indian produce sounds like that from a man. That boy's been snared by the jaws of a goddamn bear! You heard it on his throat!"

"Shut up, Carson!" It ain't no bear!" Morton shouted. "We got traps all around."

"... Then what the hell is it?"

Morton stood above the cowering party and shook his head, remembering again what he thought he'd seen on that ridge earlier. "I don't know. But that ain't no fuckin' bear."

Some of the horses had broken from their hitchings at the sound and had bolted off into the twilight, all frantic and feral like something driven demented with rabies. No one attempted to reign them in. No one dared to leave the fireside. All were too terrified to even think of moving.

There was no sleep to be had for the rest of the night. The men all sat up in their bags in a circle. They held their rifles outstretched before them as if like a phalanx; gun barrels probing into the darkness all around. All refused to leave their bags nor the glowing side of the campfire as if both would offer protection and insulation from whatever lurked out there beyond the black trees. A juvenile notion that there was safety in the light.

Everyone sat motionless on the freezing ground, like a huddle of terrified rabbits, and they could only hope for the morning and safety in solidarity. None dared imagine what it was. They prayed to see a band of savages running out of the darkness toward them. There would be no fear attached to that. But, deep down, before any explanation had even been offered, they all knew it was something else, something much worse. Hughes was eerily calm throughout the whole ordeal. He simply stared ahead into the heaving darkness, as if awaiting something.

Part Three

Dawn finally crawled around. The men shivered in their spots, the metal of their rifles so cold in their palms, it was gnawing into their skin. The morning was damp and grey. After first light, the men, all haggard and haunted and pale from the night gone, jumped out of their rolls and packed away their possibles. The lines and wrinkles on their greyed and weathered faces ever more prominent. No coffee was made.

Everyone packed and stuffed their possessions into the saddlebags with quick skittish movements, looking all around as they did, like birds nervously checking behind them as they fed. Carson remained at the perimeter of the camp, on sentry, whilst the rest prepared to leave. He fixed his eyes on various points in the trees. In the gloom of the dawn, however, the woods all around blurred and merged into shades of mottled brown. It was hard to distinguish anything at all. There was no movement in that teetering dimness. Not even woodland animals could be heard.

"What you suppose that was last night?" Bill asked the somber group.

"Indians," Hughes replied, lying to himself. "Like I said they would be..."

No one else said anything.

They saddled up quickly and rode on through miles of tall swaying trees, checking frequently over their shoulders as they did. Lewis was not found. Only his rifle remained. Bent into a U shape and tossed into the brush five meters from his sentry point the night before. They moved as one entity, horse and man, men and horses; all locked into a common alliance of survival, no one being separate from another. A covenant of mutual diligence from both creatures. As if the very nature of Lewis's gruesome disappearance had ignited the primal instincts of being prey, long dormant in both man and beast. The sun was low and white and the rays barely filtered through the branches onto them. After another hour they came to a small creek, then a valley.

And Further down that valley, they found Lewis. He had been disemboweled and dismembered, and his head sat in the cavity of his own chest. His dull fish eyes were frozen in their sockets like two orbs of jelly, staring up absently at the clouded grey sky beyond the canopy of trees. Flies buzzed around his desecrated body, and the stench was unbearable for the men. Morton gagged and spat from the side of his horse. The men gawked and stared silently at Lewis's corpse, all too stunned and horrified to speak.

They rode on and no eulogies were said. No one dared to speculate what manner of living thing existed on this earth that could do that to another.

It was late in the afternoon the next day. The men were tired beyond saving. No sleep was had, and they remained unfed. The horses scuttled through the underbrush wearily, as if being led through it all in a trance. The tall grass tickled their underbellies as they stepped and scrabbled over the terrain. The men moved forward, and still the forest kept coming back at them. No matter how far they all moved, it seemed that there was no edge to the trees.

Hughes, at the back of the party, swayed from side to side in his saddle. His eyes rolled around in their sockets and he could not focus on the ride anymore. He was so tired and delirious that he hadn't noticed the party was no longer in front of him and he'd been riding off in the opposite direction for a long time. He could only recall the horrific sight of Lewis back there in the valley. He'd never told anyone what he saw up there on that ridge, but he knew in his heart that *it* had done that to Lewis. The shadow that walked had made a mockery of the man's body, and Hughes wondered who of the party would be next.

It was only after another ten minutes that the party all noticed he was no longer with them. Morton had called for Hughes to come to his side for assistance with the compass, but when there was no response, they all looked over their shoulders for the first time in a while and saw that he was gone.

"Hughes!" Morton bellowed into the trees but was met with no response.

Morton then turned to his second in command. "Corporal, he's fallen behind! Go get him," Captain Morton shouted.

Corporal sat on top of his horse near the front of the party like he'd received a final summons. The prospect of riding back alone turned his stomach. He quivered in his saddle and merely looked back at Captain Morton with doe eyes, like a child.

"Did you not hear me?" Morton snapped.

"I heard you just fine. But I'll not do it," he said as his horse tottered underneath him.

Morton glared at Corporal with blistering red eyes. "He has the second compass...Do it," he snarled.

"...C'ain't no man compel another to tasks he ain't equipped for."

"A higher ranking man can. And you are *equipped* for it."

"In the confines of a regular scenario, I reckon so, but this ain't no regular scenario, sir. I'll not do it. There's something—"

"You will or I will shoot you."

Morton soon produced his Colt revolver and pointed it at Corporal. The party froze in anticipation. Corporal squirmed, but only for a moment.

"Then shoot me, goddammit. And I'll be shut of this," Corporal snarled. "Better than the fate out yonder them trees. You saw what they did to his body! But consider this, you'll have one less soul watching your back if'n you do shoot me dead now. You reckon you can make it out these woods alive on your lonesome?"

Morton locked eyes with Corporal and both stared at each other menacingly. Corporal had begun to slowly reach for his Cattleman revolver, the hand movement slow like a snake's. Morton watched. All about the pair expected blood, but the fight never came to fruition. Morton considered, then slid the hammer up and holstered his revolver once more.

"Bill, you go back and bring him back here," Morton instead said over his shoulder to Bill. Jackson's gaze vacillated between Corporal, Morton, and Bill.

Bill nodded obediently and turned and rode back into the twisted mess of branches and bark. The unit then all watched him silently as his form dwindled against the bleakness of that raw mass of ancient wood.

"That ain't Indians out there. That's something else," Corporal muttered to himself. Jackson pretended he had not heard it.

Later in the day, neither Bill nor Hughes returned. After an hour of waiting, Morton decided that they were not coming back, and they rode on. Night fell with practiced bravado, the overcast, louring clouds smothered and sucked all warmth and comfort from both earth and man. They made camp near a large boulder, and the night was long and uneventful. They sat around the fire and every man stared into the flames, each seeing something unique in the effulgence, as if the flames themselves were extensions of man's hubris unto the world; burning in all directions without a moment's consideration on where to go next.

In the morning, they rose and saddled up and dispatched without admin.

The day was long and monotonous, and Jackson began to wonder if they were merely going in circles. He'd sworn he'd seen that same fallen tree before and that same trickling stream. Time moved forward without definition. But, then...

Five miles north, on a fallen tree, the unit soon found the severed heads of their lost men. Bill, who'd ridden ahead to investigate Hughes' disappearance, Powell, who'd disappeared the night previous, and Hughes himself, who'd fallen behind. All three bloodied heads now sat on the moss-covered tree trunk in front of Morton like some gawky exhibition.

He looked down from his horse at the carnival scene and recognized nothing of the men he once knew from his unit. They were gone, and the husks they'd left behind held nothing anymore. They looked to him like a row of coconuts that one would throw rocks at. A fairground game that people would laugh at. The hacked-off heads nothing more than a pantomime of gore.

Bill's lifeless eye looked up at Morton from there on the tree with an absence that could only now be acknowledged as existence. He once was, and now he was no more. His grayed head perched on the tree trunk with one eye shut and the other lazily, vacantly looking up at his Captain. Powell had no jaw and instead, his head sat on the bark like some grotesque ornament, his face festooned with dried black blood. He had no eyes. They had been scooped out and replaced with dried grass.

"What the hell done that?" Carson mewed.

"Indians," Morton said and no one believed him.

"That ain't no Indian's doin'. Them faces got bite marks on them! You sent Bill off like that, Cap'ain."

"Quiet!" Morton shouted and Carson did.

Morton sighed deeply and shut his eyes to regain some semblance of composure. They rode on in silence. They were down to four men now—Corporal, Carson, Captain Morton, and Jackson.

Later, they found a small river at the base of the valley and set up camp next to it. Corporal sat in the dirt. His knees pulled up to his chest. He stared vacantly into the rolling flames of the campfire, as each man about him did also. Morton watched him from the other side of the yellow blades of fire. Jackson smoked his last cigarette.

"Hughes saw it, didn't he?" Corporal asked Jackson in a low, defeated voice. "I mean, whatever it is out there."

"... I reckon."

"You got a woman?" he then asked strangely.

"No."

"Ever been with one?"

"A whore."

"Where?"

"El Paso."

"I have a wife. Dolores. She's waiting for me..."

Jackson flicked the butt of his cigarette into the fire and struggled to find the right words.

"I'll not wait here any longer for judgment," Corporal said after five minutes. "I'm leaving tonight. One ways or another."

"You go it alone and you die," Jackson replied.

"I'll take my chances. We're as good as dead sitting here anyhow. Whatever that is out there, it ain't of this world. It's hunting us. There are things abroad out here and I'll have no part of them."

With that, Corporal rose silently and unhitched his horse and rode off into the darkness without so much as a word passed. Captain Morton sucked on his pipe and watched him leave and said nothing also. Jackson watched the backs of the horse and Corporal alike steal away into the wall of inky black. Corporal was never seen again.

With the departure, the three survivors then fell in on themselves. The crushing gloom in their souls were heavy against their bodies, like chains of bondage. The fire smoldered and no man rose to furnish it with more wood. All were too taken with the plight to think of anything else.

The remaining three horses had escaped at some point in the small hours of the night. They'd chewed through their bindings and took solace in escape, seemingly seeing more promising refuge in the smothering black out there.

The next day, the men rose, all gray and sullen and beaten. They saw that the horses were gone and could not afford any more than a grunt and a sigh at their passage. They packed their things and walked north. The day was arduous and it carried with it the sense of guilt or some abstraction of survivor's guilt therein. Why, when all others had fallen, did these three stand?

The remaining three then made camp at nightfall with what provisions they had carried with them. They did not eat and instead installed themselves in their bags, all facing outward. They sat and waited and dreamed of home.

The night was heavy and vibrating and was full of strange rustlings. Beyond the meagre glow of the campfire, something was moving around quietly out there. Something big and heavy, but stealthy and taciturn. It was coming closer. Twigs snapped and the earth squirmed under something. All of them heard it. But they refused to acknowledge it just the same. They prayed it was wolves out there on the perimeter, but it was not.

The fire died later and only the oil lamp illuminated the cold dark floor of the forest about them. A small island of light against a sea of black. They sat, waiting on guard, ready for any advance.

It was much further into the night when Jackson's eyelids finally began to sag. He hadn't slept in almost three days and he could not fight it any longer. At some point, he didn't know when, his head slumped forward and he leaned down into his chest. The rifle fell against his head but went unacknowledged. Then, he closed his eyes and everything went quiet.

He awoke later only to hear the shrill screaming of Carson assaulting his ears. A savage jarring scream that filtered through the trees and woke him from his sleep.

"Heeelp!" Carson shouted. "It's got me! Please, help!" He shouted as he was dragged off into blackness.

Jackson bolted up from his slumber and looked around. The spit in his mouth was clumpy and salty. His eyes were swollen with the task of sleep. Jackson looked to his left. On the ground, where Carson was sitting not moments earlier, were drag marks leading off into the grass.

There also were claw marks and clumps of underbrush that had been ripped from their roots.

"Ahhhhhh!" Carson shrieked somewhere back in the forest.

"Goddamn," Jackson gasped in horror. He instinctively reached for his rifle and stood up in the gloom. "What the hell is this?"

Carson's dwindling screams then slithered off into nothingness and his gut-wrenching cries of despair soon vanished. And both Jackson and Morton stood up from their bags and positioned themselves back to back next to the oil lamp, rifles facing out. Neither one of them saw what took Carson.

"Holy Jesus, what is it?" Jackson asked.

"I don't know," Morton replied. "I really don't know." His voice was cracking.

The forest was silent again and the pair stood by the hollow glow of the lamplight with all the loneliness and dread in the world bearing down on them; both men awaiting their turn. Minutes went by like hours and Jackson probed into the pit of his stomach in search of a warmth he might have called hope. The only reassurance he felt was Morton's bulky back pressed against his own. The last two tethered together in an uneasy partnership of survival.

"It's gonna come back," Jackson said.

"I know."

"It's gonna take us next."

They stood together like two stalagmites soldered down to the primal earth below their boots. They waited, and there was nothing. Minutes went by.

"How long you calculate till dawn?" Jackson whispered to Morton after another few minutes. But there was no reply.

"Sir?" Jackson asked.

He turned around and saw that Morton was gone. "Sir?" he asked once more.

Dropping his gaze to the floor, he saw what remained. On the ground by Jackson's feet was a bloodied rifle and Morton's calvary hat, all ripped up.

"My god..." he said as he stared down at all that was left of his captain.

Without even thinking, Jackson turned and ran. He snatched up the oil lamp and panted and screamed as he lurched forward through the woods, away from the scene, away from it all. He ran and ran.

Then, without prelude, he smacked his head on a low-hanging branch and fell into the mud. His body dropped into the mire and he lay there for a pause. His hearing rang like someone was firing an Evans repeater right next to his head. Tingling, nauseating noise that sounded like iron pots being kicked down the stairs.

When he came around again, he sat up blearily in the dirt...and he heard it. Something was coming toward him. Lumbering, heavy footsteps squelching through the marsh. Jackson cautiously stood up. The noise had brought him back to reality, and he took hold of himself once more. He was trembling. He could barely keep a grip on his rifle. He retreated two steps and found his back against a tree, the rough bark prodding through his thin blazer. His eyes darted in all directions, squinting into the shroud, trying to spy the origin of the low steps stalking ever closer to him. He looked right and saw nothing. He looked left and saw only unending blackness. Then he peered forward once more and saw it. He gasped and the rifle fell from his suddenly weakened grip. There in front of him was a giant shadow. This immense black gargoyle that seemed not to have form nor aspect. Just this mass of wet, reeking fur. It had protrusions and antlers spouting from every angle on its behemoth-like body, which moved around like driftwood caught in a tide.

It came closer and leaned down to Jackson. He whimpered. His lips quivered and a tear rolled down his blistered face.

"Please, have mercy," he tried to say, but his voice shook too much for the words to be distinguished.

The breath of the beast was hot and wet and rancid on his face. It smelt like rotting flesh, copper, and stagnant lake water. Its giant damp snout inches from his own. It snorted and steaming strings of saliva hit his face. He held the oil lamp up in the darkness and saw only a massive, slimy, and hairy mouth in front of him—and all the dripping red gore clinging to its flat, square teeth. He screamed, but not for long. It was cut short by the towering goatish beast before him.

Back at the Comanche camp, the chief snapped up from a horrific nightmare. Cold sweat rolled down his face, and he puffed and panted. Somewhere deep in his dreams, he'd seen that all of the survivors who had gone into that forest were now dead. But it was what would happen to them after death that made the chief feel utterly terrified. Their souls would never find rest, and he knew that.

His wife reached up to console him, but it was not warranted. He pushed her away and stared forward at the opening in the teepee, looking past it and out into that ever-expanding blackness of night. Out there, he knew the thing still lingered. He did not see the face that killed them all, nor hear its movements in his nightmare, but only knew its presence as an ancient and evil spirit. It had no name and he knew those men would not be the last to perish in that forest because of it.

The Woman of the Mountain

Daniel Powell

It was raining pretty good by the time Luther Tunsil arrived at the edge of the meadow. It was odd, because the day was otherwise cool and bright—the sun just beginning its descent behind the snow-rimmed summit of Little Elkhorn Mountain.

It was a damned sun shower, of all things.

Of course, the absurdity of the storm wasn't lost on the old cowboy. He studied the tidy little cabin in the distance from beneath a stand of spruce trees, wondering if the witch inside had called up the rain to welcome him to her doorstep.

He slid out of the saddle and rolled a cigarette, content to wait out the storm from beneath a juniper canopy. His breath steamed in the fall air as he put a match to the smoke, and he rubbed Shelby's neck and spoke to her in low, reassuring tones. The cabin had spooked her, and Tunsil had to admit the place gave him a measure of pause as well.

It was picturesque, right down to the thin little ribbon of smoke from the chimney lazing off toward the mountains. It reminded him of something out of a picture book of fairytales—a perfect little oasis in the middle of an unforgiving wilderness. A freshly painted barn stood tall in the distance, and there was a neat little garden and a sturdy stone well. Hurricane Creek meandered through the meadow, sluicing past the property on its southward journey into the Lostine Valley and the townsfolk that had hired him to pay a visit to the woman of the mountain.

Tunsil smoked and waited out the rain. He'd been in the saddle for three days, and the notion of getting Shelby stabled for the night and having a sit beside a warm fire was appealing. It was just a matter of whether or not the people of Joseph were right about the old gal.

When the rain petered out, he took Shelby's reins and started across the meadow. It teemed with switchgrass, fescue, and cold-hardy wild-flowers. Blue bonnets and daisies swayed in the breeze, and there were even a few trilliums dotting the landscape here and there.

Shelby nickered as they approached the cabin. As if on cue, the door snapped open, and a willowy woman stepped out onto the steps.

"Hello, the cabin!" Tunsil called; the woman cocked her head in reply.

"Hello yerself," she replied, not unkindly. She was tall, her hair so blond it was almost white. It fell across her shoulder in a single long braid, and she studied her visitor with her hands on her hips, a wry smile on her face.

Tunsil's heart raced. Here was a beautiful woman—not the hag the sheriff had described.

"You reckon I can rest a spell? Not much out here in the way of shelter."

She nodded. "Horse can stay out yonder. Don't mind Davey and Clyde. They're an ornery pair, but they don't mean nothing by it. C'mon... I'll give you a hand."

She wore cotton trousers, tall black boots, and a denim jacket lined with wool. She met him in the yard, and he was struck once again by her appearance as she took Shelby's reins in a soft, unlined hand.

"Mighty fine place you got here," he said, but she just smiled and nodded toward the barn. They worked in tandem, grooming the burrs from Shelby's flanks while the horse shifted nervously in the furthest stall. Davey, a jet-black steed at least a head taller, studied the horse with unblinking black eyes from his enclosure across the barn. Clyde was a chestnut beauty, and he pawed at the ground and snorted at the intruder.

They finished the chore in companionable silence. When Shelby had been fed and watered, they retreated to the cabin just as the last of the day's light slipped behind the summit of Little Elkhorn. The sky was awash in pink and orange light, and the crisp air filled him with vigor and nervous tension. The woman slipped inside, and he spared the granite peaks a single glance—a shudder trembling his broad shoulders—before following her across the threshold.

"Something to drink?" she said as he hung his coat. The interior was equally delightful, with a quaint little kitchen, a warm hearth, and a cozy sitting room. A cast-iron pot simmered on the little pot-belly stove, the place redolent with the rich aromas of venison and vegetables. She poured herself a tankard of something dark, and he sauntered across the room to the fire, warming his hands at the edge of its crackling flames.

"Be mighty obliged. Been parched a bit out there on the trail."

She set a tankard for him on the table. "No trails to speak of out there, mister...?"

"Tunsil. You can call me Luther."

That wry little grin never left her face, even as she shrugged out of her jacket and sat at the table. "Like I said, no trails to speak of out there. Sherriff Minthorn send you up here?"

Now it was Tunsil's turn to smile. He joined her at the table and took a hefty pull on the tankard. It was beer—some kind of strong, earthy beer. "Reckon so. I was hoping we might have a word."

"A word," she scoffed. Those pretty, unlined hands clasped the tankard before her, and he noticed for the first time that her right eye was blue while her left was green. She had a small, flat nose and a heart-shaped mouth. Straight white teeth. He could tell that she liked to smile. "They want a little more than a word, I think. Speaking of which, you mind stowing those?"

She nodded at his guns, and he felt himself blushing. What kind of a man took shelter in a stranger's house and didn't stow his pistols?

"Those are pretty fancy, Luther. Got silver in 'em?"

He swallowed hard. She had him pegged, all right. He stood and unclipped his belt. Hung them on the peg with his duster.

"This is a fine place," he repeated, attempting to change the subject. "You seem to be doing pretty fine up here."

"I am, and I wish I could just live here in peace. We built it from scratch, you know. Jaime and Ben did the heavy lifting. I put in the garden. Of course, they're gone now, and it's just me up here."

Tunsil was almost finished with the beer, and he felt a warmth in his gut and a tingling in his fingers and toes. Strong drink.

"Ben and Jaime?"

"Son and husband, in that order. But they're gone now. Buried out yonder. Sheriff tell you about that?"

Tunsil shook his head.

"Oh, course not; *they* killed 'em. Jaime first, and then my boy Ben when he went into town to square things for his daddy. Joseph's a hard little town filled with disagreeable people, Luther. Wish they hadn't sent you. Your eyes are too kind for this here work."

"Joseph ain't so bad, from what I can tell. They've sure fallen on some hard times. Said it was your doing, Kate. 'Course, they said a lot of things about you that don't seem to square up."

She tipped him a wink and stood to replenish their drinks. "Let me guess. They called me an old hag? Said I was a witch? Blamed me for the wheat crops?"

"Something like that."

She sipped her drink, then turned her eyes to the table. "Is that what you see, Luther? An old hag?" Her voice was quiet. Calm.

"I reckon they got that one wrong," he said, before starting in his chair and spilling a bit of beer on the table. "What in the...?"

A scrawny tabby cat yowled up at him from beneath the table. The cat had leaned into him, scaring him right down to his mud-splattered boots.

"That's just Jennie," she laughed. "Don't mind her. She's a bit... territorial."

The cat yowled again, shooting the cowboy a glare with bright mustard eyes. She lifted her tail and sauntered out of the room, disappearing into a back bedroom.

"I, uh... no. To answer your question, I don't see that, Kate. You offered me a place at your table and a spot near your fire. Still... the things they said about you."

They sat in silence for a long time, her eyes never blinking. Never leaving his face.

"They say a lot of things," she finally conceded. "Would you have dinner with me, Luther Tunsil? Maybe stay a spell? It's going to get cold tonight, and I don't get much company."

He nodded, and she stood and collected plates, bowls, and silverware from a hutch in the corner. She hummed lightly as she set the table and ladled the bowls full of that rich stew. Tunsil watched her move, her gestures fluid and elegant. It was almost like she floated. She served the stew with thick chunks of sourdough bread, and she set a plate of salty butter on the table between them.

"Eat up. It's fresh venison. Took him myself, not even a week ago. It's more than I can eat, and like I said—we don't get much company up here."

"We?"

"Why, Jenny and I, of course."

Tunsil tucked in, and it was the best meal he'd had in years. The venison was tender and seasoned with sage and rosemary. The bread was soft, the butter rich and creamy.

They ate mostly in silence, speaking occasionally about the coming winter and the progress of the railroad down near Pendleton. People were coming to Oregon—more and more of them every year—although the wheels of progress would never make their way this deep into the hinterlands.

Not in their lifetimes, at least.

When they were finished, Luther helped her clean up, and they retreated to the fireplace. A cold wind buffeted the cabin, whistling down off Little Elkhorn and shaking the timbers and rattling the shakes on the roof.

Luther rolled himself a cigarette.

"You mind if I have one?" Kate said.

"Least I could do."

They smoked for a long time in silence, and then Kate told her story. She told him of an ambitious young Irishman named Jaime. A bright-eyed lass named Kaitlyn. A young couple that had steamed the Atlantic before trekking across America's great expanse.

"My husband staked this land the minute he set eyes on yonder mountains," she said, taking a final drag on her cigarette. She tossed the butt in the fire, and he rolled her another. They were on their third tankards of ale, and he felt himself grow warm, content, and awash with mixed feelings for this strange woman. Could this be the same person the sheriff had said was such a problem? "Wasn't until they came for taxes that we had any real trouble. Can you figure that, Luther? Taxes," she spat. "And us... all the way up here."

"Don't seem right," he agreed. "Can't see a claim on any taxes when you're so far outside of Joseph."

She laughed. "It's human nature, Luther. It happened to us in Ireland, and it happened to us on the trail. People want what others have, and me and Jaime? We had *it all*.

"We had it all, and then they came for it. They came on horses. Came in the middle of the night. Ben was just a seed in my belly back then, but we knew from the start they'd make things hard on us. They jeered me. Insulted my husband. Even vandalized our camp. Back then, we hadn't even started on the cabin yet."

"When abouts was this?"

"Summer of 1871," she replied nonchalantly. "We were pioneers. Some of the first."

Luther started again, doing the math. More than twenty years had passed. He studied her face, and it seemed to shift in the shadows of the dying fire. Her right eye—the blue one—glowed like an icicle. Now, he could see fine lines around her mouth, the corners of her eyes.

Jenny yowled from the corner of the room, her fur standing on edge. She strutted haltingly across the room, then pawed at the door.

"Excuse me," Kate said, and when she stood to let the cat out to do its business, she seemed stooped somehow. Her gait was more of a lurch, and not the least bit like floating.

When she took her seat again and raised her glass, he noticed veins on the backs of her hands. Her fingernails were chipped and yellow—clouded by toil and age.

"I don't understand, Miss Kate," he said, switching to formalities while he calculated how quickly he could get to his guns. "That was more than twenty years ago."

"Aye," she conceded. "Aye. 'Twas, at that. And we paid the taxes. We paid them every year, because by then we had a son. And he was a strong lad, and a *good* lad. We only wanted to keep him safe, and we had enough to get by on. We could afford it, having brought with us some riches from the homelands."

"Ireland?"

"Aye. But it wasn't enough. It was never enough, and they wanted more. And they took it. One year, when Ben and Jaime were off on a hunt, a party of men from Joseph caught me out in the garden. Accused me of things. Called me 'unnatural,' and said they wanted to get to the source."

"The source? I don't follow, Miss Kate."

"The source of our youth. Our vitality. They had me, Mr. Tunsil, and they took from me. It wasn't until Jaime and Ben had returned and found me—beaten and battered, and almost dead—that things set us on the course that has you here, warming yourself at my fire. You, a hired mercenary, sharing *my* fire on the very edge of another Oregon winter."

"I don't under—" he started, but then a gust of wind rocked the cabin and the fire sputtered for a long moment in the hearth. The room went dark for an instant, and Tunsil was stunned to see his host glowing in the gloom. A great shrieking, like a grizzly in the agonies of death, sounded from just outside the front door.

The fire regained its footing, and there *she* was again. A young, beautiful woman with a tankard of beer and a smoldering cigarette.

Only now, she wore a shawl. It crossed her shoulders, her angular beauty now partially hidden beneath a hooded veil.

"Men can be evil," she said, her voice a low purr. Jenny yowled from somewhere in the kitchen. How had the cat got back inside? "Men can be evil, but never my Jaime. Never my Ben."

"Kate, are you...?"

"*Cailleach*," she interjected. "My name is *Cailleach* in the old tongue. You can call me that, Luther. You can call me by my real name."

"Are you," Tunsil started, before clearing his throat. Something was happening to him, and he felt unsure. Felt paralyzed with fear and... and *longing* for the woman before him. "Are you a witch?"

He realized in that moment that he was in over his head. That the stories his mother had told him were real, and that he had been foolish to take the job in the first place. The coins in his jacket amounted to nothing, and his guns were on the other side of the world, for all the good they could do him.

She stood and slid the shawl from her shoulders. Slowly, carefully, she unlaced her shirt and pulled it over her head. Her breasts were firm and high, her tiny ruddy nipples taut in the cool of the cabin air. She stepped out of her britches, standing tall before him—resplendent in her beauty and comfortable in her milky skin. Her hair was the color of the flames in the hearth, and he felt his breath hitch in his chest.

"Do I look like a witch to you?" she purred, and with that she took Luther Tunsil to her bed.

When it was over and she had collected everything she needed, she dressed quickly and wrapped herself in the shawl to guard against the wind.

There was still so far to go.

Blood demanded blood, and she had enough of it now. They'd sent a man to her door, and it was everything that she needed. She saddled the horses. There were three of them now, and that would make it easier for her boys.

When she arrived at their graves, she spilled the cowboy's blood and said the words. Before long, they worked themselves up out of the dirt and they were there with her. Sure, they didn't look like themselves—too many injuries for that.

Too many months in the ground.

But their vitality would be restored in time, and she folded her husband and son into a long embrace. The wind blew, and a soft pattering of dry snow sifted down from the sky like sugar over a cake.

"My boys," she whispered, swiping a tear from her cheek. "My boys."

They mounted their horses and started across the meadow. They had a long way to go, but there was time. Time enough to set things right in the town that had taken so much from them.

Black Blood

WR Platt

Everything turned white. The cavalry detachment appeared ghostly as snow whipped through the arroyo, covering men, horses, and the wagon. Every breath was a frosty cloud of steam that quickly turned to ice, clinging to the soldiers' hats and woolen overcoats.

Sergeant John Caballo spurred his mount to catch up to his commanding officer. He leaned in close to be heard over the wind.

"This storm ain't natural, sir!" he shouted. "We need to find cover before we freeze to death!"

"I agree, Sergeant," shouted Lieutenant Philip Wetherill. "Do you have a suggestion?"

"Just one, sir: ask Red Knife. It's his country. Maybe he knows a place where we can shelter."

Red Knife was their prisoner, a Chiricahua Apache Chieftain riding in the rear of the tarp-covered wagon. Their orders were to transport the old warrior to Fort Davis for relocation to the reservation. Caballo watched the lieutenant work through the problem. Their situation was desperate, but the officer was hesitant to place their fates into the hands of their prisoner.

"You're right," shouted Wetherill. "We got no choice. Let's get out of this wind and see if the old man knows anything."

"Yessir, there's an outcropping just ahead."

Caballo waved his hand to catch the attention of the wagon driver and the mounted soldier. Twice he flashed five fingers spread wide and a closed fist to signal their intention to take a ten-minute break. The men waved back their acknowledgment.

Corporal Willie Candler guided the wagon. Caballo had chosen Candler because of the two years the driver had served with the 9th Cavalry. He was good in a fight, but more importantly, Candler had a way with the mules harnessed to the wagon.

Caballo was more concerned about the teenager bringing up the rear. Private Isaiah Waters had been born into slavery somewhere in East Texas. The kid was raw but eager to prove himself as a recent recruit to the regiment the Apache called "the Buffalo Soldiers."

"Are we lost, Sarge?" asked Candler as he hauled the feed bag from beneath his seat and strapped it to a mule.

"Maybe. Gonna see if Red Knife knows where we are."

"We ain't spending the night here, are we Sarge? It's cold as hell."

"Yeah, Sarge, I didn't think it got this cold in the desert," said Waters, stomping his feet.

Caballo did his best to cheer his soldiers. "Don't worry, kid, I've seen weather way worse than this."

The truth was Caballo had never been this cold in his life. He'd been born in Florida, the only child of a runaway slave and Seminole woman. He and his mother had moved to the Indian Territories north of Texas while he was still a boy. It was there he learned to ride and raid with Mexican bandits. He headed north when the war to end slavery broke out and joined the Union Army. Caballo was a good soldier, but his true value lay in his ability to speak fluent Spanish and a passing familiarity with Athabaskan, the language of the Apache.

He moved to the side of the wagon, unstrapped the tarp, and rolled it to one side. The huge Apache sat quietly, wrapped in a blanket and chained to the wall of the wagon.

Long gray hair hung past his shoulders and was held in place by a faded red bandana. His face was stoic and leathery. Dark, expressionless eyes regarded Caballo. The big man appeared unfazed by the cold.

"*We need your help, Red Knife,*" Caballo addressed the old man in Spanish. "*This storm hit us with no warning. Do you know where we can find shelter?*"

The chief did not move. His eyes held Caballo's. There was no sign of recognition though the two had spoken together many times before.

"*Red Knife! Do you hear me? We need to find shelter.*"

The old man slowly nodded. "*What would my black jailer have me do?*" His voice was a gravelly monotone.

"*We need to find shelter,*" repeated Caballo. "*Can you help us?*"

Red Knife leaned forward until his massive face was inches from the soldier. He looked up and down and back and forth, and then closed his eyes. He spoke as if in a trance. "*My spirit has been before. How did we come here? It is not safe.*"

"*We're lost. Can you find shelter?*"

The old man's eyes suddenly opened. He spoke directly to Caballo. "*I cannot escape in this storm. Release me from these chains and allow me to speak with my ancestors. Perhaps they will find the shelter you seek.*"

Caballo stared at the old man, wondering if there was some Apache mischief at work. "*Wait here,*" he said, and then smiled at the ridiculousness of the statement. The old man was chained to the wagon.

Lieutenant Wetherill stood by his mount, surveying the landscape ahead. A white man, he rarely spoke to the black soldiers he commanded. All of his orders were relayed to the others through Caballo.

Wetherill was known to carry a large silver flask of tequila wherever he went. Caballo could smell the alcohol on the wind as he approached.

"Red Knife wants us to let him out of the irons so he can get his bearings," said Caballo. "He says he's been here in a dream. I think we should let him."

"A dream? What the hell does that mean?"

"It's an Indian thing, sir. I can't explain it, but he's our best chance."

"You think he's up to something?"

"No, not likely in this weather."

"All right, Sergeant, let's humor the old man."

Caballo returned to the wagon where Candler was feeding the mules and Waters stomping his feet.

"Let's get him out."

The three men strode to the rear of the wagon, where Caballo produced a key from inside his tunic. He twisted the lock and the four-foot chain fell from the Apache's ankle.

"You two each take an arm and help him into the middle of the canyon. Let him get a good look around."

Red Knife came to the end of the wagon, still wrapped in his blanket. He moved slowly as the wagon swayed under his weight. The old Apache dwarfed Candler and Waters as they helped him out. Legend held that Red Knife had killed an assortment of more than twenty Comanches, Pawnees, Mexicans, and Americans. Caballo unholstered his pistol and held it at the ready.

Candler and Waters bent their heads beneath Red Knife's shoulders and braced themselves against the wind. The old man faced the blowing snow with his arms spread wide. He closed his eyes and inhaled deeply as if drinking in the world. Pellets of ice and snow stung Caballo's face and hands. He knew the old man felt it too, but Red

Knife seemed to relish the feeling. His gray hair and blanket flowed in the gusts.

The wind died away suddenly and the snow fell in heavy, sodden clumps. Caballo heard it settling on the ground and underbrush. Red Knife opened his eyes and turned to Caballo.

"My black jailer, there is shelter ahead, but we must hurry if we are to arrive before nightfall."

"Where is it?"

"Let me share a seat with your black brother, and I will show you the way."

Wetherill had come to the rear during the wind. Caballo turned to his lieutenant.

"Red Knife says he'll find shelter if he can sit up top with Candler."

The lieutenant looked at the deepening snow, gave a quick nod, and mounted his horse.

"Hell no, Sarge," said Candler. "You sure about this? I don't trust the old man."

"Let's move, soldier. Snow's getting deeper and we're burning daylight."

The mules seemed to understand the urgency as they pulled through the snow. Candler sat on the left side of the wagon next to the big Apache. Caballo rode close by with his hand near his Colt 45. Red Knife called out directions, which Caballo translated.

At dusk, the group made their way into a deep canyon. The south wall was a steep sandstone cliff topped by a mesa. Ironwood and acacia trees lined the bottom of the cliff.

"How much further?" asked Caballo.

Red Knife was slow to answer. The storm had tired him. Caballo could see the weariness in the old Apache's face and stooped shoulders. Instead of answering out loud, the chief raised his right hand and pointed to the sandstone cliff. The sight brought the travelers to a stop.

Thirty feet above them, a cleft appeared in the rockface as if it had been gouged by a gigantic claw. Deep in the recess, buildings made of mud bricks and cut stone were visible. Windows and doorways offered shelter behind stone walls. Stairways connected multiple levels and walls were buttressed with more stone.

"What the hell?" muttered Candler.

"Perfect," said Wetherill. "How do we get up there?"

Before Caballo could translate to Spanish, Red Knife pointed to a spot along the base of the cliff where a circular corral had been built from the same cut stones. A ladder was placed against the cliff and extended to an overhang. The rungs were lashed with braided hemp.

"Is there somebody up there?" demanded Caballo.

Red Knife shrugged.

The troop made their way into the corral. After Waters and Candler had helped him down, Red Knife moved toward the ladder. Caballo stepped in his way and put a hand on the Apache's chest.

"I'll go first. Waters, you follow ten feet behind me, then Red Knife and the Lieutenant. Candler, you cover our rear. If everything is all right, you can get the animals bedded for the night."

"Okay, Sarge."

With his Colt cocked and ready, Caballo made his way up the creaking ladder. Below him, Waters and Wetherill held it steady while

Candler covered the cleft with his Springfield carbine. Red Knife watched impassively.

Caballo crouched at the last rungs and peered over the edge. Nothing moved in the late evening gloom. He sprang up and over the ledge swinging his Colt from side to side. Snow swirled over the rooftops of the deserted ancient ruins. Private Waters came up the ladder and joined him, carbine at his shoulder.

"What is this place, Sarge?"

"Have a look through all these buildings." Caballo motioned with his sidearm. "Report right away if you see anything. And watch your step, Waters, it's getting dark and these rocks are slippery."

Wetherill and Red Knife joined Caballo on the cleft. The old warrior towered over the two soldiers. A ponderosa pine had found enough soil to grow to a modest height. Red Knife tore two dead branches from its trunk and shredded them with his bare hands.

"I want him back in irons," said Wetherill.

"Yessir, but it's not like he's going anywhere."

"A man that big goes wherever he wants."

"Yessir, I'll have Candler bring up the leg irons."

"At least he's got some firewood. Let's get out of this cold."

"Yessir, soon as I check on the men."

Wetherill joined the Apache while Caballo walked to the ladder and leaned over the edge. Below him, Candler had completed the corral by using the wagon as a gate. Three horses and two mules, tied to a mule-string and exhausted, clustered together in the deepest part.

"Willie! You all right?"

"Yeah, Sarge. I'm of a mind to stay down here tonight. This wind is spooking the horses."

"No, it's too damn cold. Come on up."

"I'll be okay, Sarge. I can build a fire back here behind these rocks. The wind ain't too bad and I'll keep an eye on the animals. I'll sentry for you."

"I'm coming down."

Caballo was uneasy about leaving one of his men alone for the night but a big part of what Candler said made sense. The horses and mules would fare better with the Corporal nearby. When Caballo hit the ground, Candler was feeding one of the horses a handful of oats from their stores beneath the wagon seat.

"You sure about this, Willie? It's gonna get colder than a pig's tit out here."

"I'll be fine, Sarge. Got a stack of firewood ready to go. What's going on up top?"

"Red Knife has the Lieutenant spooked. He wants to put the old man back in irons."

"Can't say I blame him. He's one big Indian."

"All right, you stay here. Gimme the irons and a bucket with some jerky and hardtack. We'll take shifts up above and keep an eye on you. I'm going to pull the ladder up so we don't get trapped up there if something happens. You need anything?"

"Some coffee would be nice."

"I'll send Waters with some. Holler if you want anything else."

Once he was back atop the overhang, Caballo pulled the ladder up and laid it a safe distance from the edge. He looked down again on Candler, watching for a moment as the horseman settled their animals for the night.

A fire glowed from the doorway of the dwelling where Wetherill sheltered with Red Knife. Caballo filled the bucket with snow and ducked inside. Red Knife was wrapped in his blanket with his back against the far wall. The Apache took the snow and moved it toward the fire while Caballo shared the hardtack and jerky.

"Where's Candler?" asked Lieutenant Wetherill.

"Corporal Candler is going to stay below with the horses, sir. I thought it was a good idea. We'll need those horses in the morning." Caballo tossed the irons into the corner. Red Knife did not react other than looking from Caballo to Wetherill.

Lieutenant Wetherill stared at Red Knife and took a quick swig from his flask. The smell of cheap tequila hung in the air. "Good idea, Sergeant. The animals know there's something wrong with this place."

Caballo crouched near the fire, removed his gloves, and rubbed the heat into his hands. "What about Private Waters? I sent him to scout the place. Has he come back yet?"

"Not yet." Wetherill kept his eyes fixed on the old Apache.

Caballo stood and put his gloves back on. "I better go find the kid. It'll be nightfall soon. No telling what trouble he might get into." He pulled his blue overcoat tight, adjusted the scarf wrapped around his hat, and strode back outside into the wind.

Waters was at the far end of the cleft, near the last of the stone dwellings. He sat with his back propped against a stone wall with the butt of his carbine on the ground between his knees and the steel barrel pointing straight up. He scrambled to his feet when he heard Caballo crunching through the dirt and snow. Waters flailed with his firearm, cocking the hammer, and pointing the weapon toward Caballo.

"Who goes there?" Waters demanded.

"Stand down, Private Waters, it's Caballo!" The sergeant ducked away from the rifle barrel.

"Sarge? Oh shit, Sarge. I'm sorry, I thought... shit, I don't know what... I thought you were coming for me."

"Relax, Private. Release the hammer on your weapon and calm down. Now, give me a full report."

"I did like you said, Sarge. I did a full sweep and didn't find nothing until I got to that last building. There's something inside. I don't know what to make of it."

"It's okay, Waters. Let's go take a look."

As Caballo walked toward the building the first thing he noticed was the putrid stench of rotting flesh. He was familiar with the odor. It cut right through the wind. But there was another smell. Something gaseous lingered in the background. He advanced slowly to let his eyes adjust. Waters followed a few steps behind.

Caballo stopped at the doorway. The darkness was nearly impenetrable but nothing made a sound. He removed his sidearm from his holster and cocked the hammer.

Slowly, the room's interior began to take shape. It was small with windowless walls that rose a little over six feet. Rocks were strewn about the floor and piled in the corners. Something hung from the ceiling in the center of the room. Caballo took a step forward and kicked a stone. It skittered across the floor and struck another with the unmistakable, hollow sound of bone on bone.

"Step back, Waters, I'm going to light a match."

Caballo reached under his coat, extracted a wooden match from his pants pocket, and struck it against the stone threshold. The flare chased the darkness from the room. Bones were scattered across the floor and piled up to his hips against the walls. Bones from birds, lizards, and mammals. Femurs, tibias, vertebrae, and ribs mixed with skulls and jawbones. Goats, pronghorns, and bison mingled among the rabbits, squirrels, and groundhogs.

Caballo stepped further into the room and a cloud of pale dust coalesced around his boot. He stooped to inspect an enormous skull with impossibly long canines. "What in the hell?" The skull was yellow with age and crumbled to dust in his gloved hand.

The rotting corpse of a coyote hung from its hind feet in the middle of the room with its fur and skin flaking from its body. The dirt floor beneath it was covered with a black sticky substance that was partially covered by a heavy sandstone slab. There were scratches in the dirt where the slab had been moved.

Caballo put his sidearm on the floor and used the last flickers on his match to light another. Between the bones, he could see a passage in the back wall leading down a short flight of stairs into a second chamber.

"Sarge?" Waters' comment was more a question than a statement. He held his Springfield in one hand and a fresh, white human skull in the other. "What's it mean, Sarge?"

"Beats the hell out of me, Waters. Stay there by the door and ready your rifle, but for godsakes, don't shoot me."

Caballo retrieved his Colt and held the match aloft, slowly making his way toward the back passageway. Bones crunched beneath his boots. The dust stung his eyes and fouled his nostrils.

He bent at the waist and stretched the match over the stairway. Two steps down and he was in the chamber. The back half of the room was smooth sandstone formed by wind erosion. The front was constructed with stones by the people who had built the dwellings. Together they formed a rounded dome over a dirt floor. Caballo stood in the only way in or out.

He took a cautious step inside. Near the back wall was a mound of fresh black dirt that rose to his chest. Above it, a faded glyph had been carved into the rock. It showed a body lying beneath a crescent moon with a head that was much too large. Deep scratches had been etched into the face where the eyes should have been.

As the light faded from his match, Caballo made his way from the chamber. Waters stood by the door with his rifle aimed at the passageway. He relaxed as the sergeant emerged.

"What is it, Sarge?"

"Some kind of tomb. C'mon, let's get back to the others."

The two men ran through the wind and snow to the dwelling where the others waited. Red Knife had not moved from his spot. Lieutenant Wetherill sat near the door with the flask on the floor beside him. He rose to confer with Caballo as Waters knelt by the fire.

"Anything to report, Sergeant?" asked Wetherill.

"The good news is we're alone up here, Lieutenant. There's a crypt and a sacrificial altar in one of the houses down at the far end, but there's nobody alive."

"What do you mean, a crypt?"

"Just that, sir. It's a tomb complete with a gravesite and a picture carved into the wall above it."

"Scared the hell out of me," said Waters. "I don't like being up here with all those bones."

"What bones?" asked Wetherill.

"The first room was full of animal bones. I didn't recognize some of their skulls, but it's been a while since anyone was there."

"They weren't all animals, Sarge," said Waters. "That one was a person, same as you or me or old Red Knife there. And it wasn't too old neither."

Wetherill gave Caballo a questioning look. "But you say they're all dead now."

"That's right, sir. There's no one left alive up here."

"All right, that end of the cliff is off-limits. We'll stay here tonight and leave first thing in the morning. What about Candler?"

"I think we should let him be. He's happy to stay with the horses and he'll make sure we have something to ride in the morning."

"So be it. You, me, and Private Waters will take turns on watch."

Waters took the first shift, to be followed by Caballo and Wetherill.

For two hours Caballo drifted in and out of uneasy slumber. Whenever he was on the precipice of sleep, the image carved into the wall flickered in the dim light of his dreams. It filled him with dread. He jumped when a hand shook his shoulder.

Red Knife spoke Spanish in a hushed monotone.

"*I've been watching you, my black jailer. What is it that disturbs your sleep?*"

Caballo leaned on an elbow. The old Apache had moved across the room without disturbing the others. He lay on the floor beside Caballo, close enough to touch him.

"*I've been dreaming about the grave site down the way,*" answered Caballo. "*Most everything down there seemed like it's been there for years, but the dirt around the grave looked and smelled fresh.*"

"*Dreams are messages from the spirit world. My ancestors bade me come here. Tell me about this grave.*"

Red Knife's body tensed with the news of the animal bones in the sacrificial chamber and the mound of dirt in the tomb. A small gasp escaped the old warrior as Caballo described the wall carving.

"*My ancestors have called me to join them, but you should leave this place,*" said Red Knife. "*Now, before it is too late.*"

"*Why?*"

"*Your dream is a warning. You have disturbed the rest of a demon who entered our world long before the Apache. It feeds on the blood of the living and it will come for us.*"

"*A demon?*"

"Yes, the Navajo called them 'ancient enemy.' This place was built by people who wished to hide. Now the demon sleeps in their home."

Caballo stared into the darkened face of the Apache. He could feel the old man's fear.

"Sarge! You awake?" Waters called from the doorway. "There's something happening out here, Sarge."

Caballo got to his feet and wiped the dust from his overcoat. The old man shifted to a cross-legged position and began a low chant. Caballo had heard the Apache death song before.

"What is it?" Caballo adjusted his wide-brimmed hat as he approached the doorway.

"There's a light, Sarge, coming from that room where we found those bones."

The wind whipped across the mesa, curling the snow into swirls and obscuring their vision. The line of stone dwellings receded into the darkness. At the far end, a dim blue light flickered in the night.

"Wake the lieutenant. We got visitors."

The light grew brighter as Waters roused Wetherill. It seemed to gain strength and become more menacing in sync with Red Knife's chanting.

"What's going on, Sergeant?"

Wetherill stepped toward the doorway, adjusting the sidearm and sabre on his hip. Caballo nodded toward the light.

"Red Knife says we woke up a demon and it's going to kill us all."

Wetherill's head pivoted between the Sergeant and the row of dwellings. He stepped outside and peered into the gloom.

"You don't really believe that, do you, Sergeant? The Apaches tell lots of stories about demons and monsters."

As the lieutenant spoke, a dark figure paused in the doorway of the dwelling with the bones. For a moment it was silhouetted by the blue fire. It sniffed the air and then sped across the cleft, faster than a raven in flight, before dissolving into the darkness.

"Did you see that, sir?"

"See what?"

"That shadow. It ran toward the edge and disappeared."

Wetherill stomped the ground with his boots and pulled gloves over his hands. He patted his overcoat as if searching for something in the lining but gave up when he couldn't find it.

"No, Sergeant, I did not see a shadow. I do, however, see the light at the far end, which means someone is up here with us. Obviously, Private Waters did an inadequate job of clearing these buildings." He unsheathed his sabre and drew his Colt from beneath his great coat. "You and I, Sergeant Caballo, will reconnoiter the situation to determine any threats. Waters will stay here with Red Knife."

An audible sigh of relief came from Waters.

"Yessir," said Caballo. "Waters, give me your rifle. You'll have your sidearm if you need it."

Instead of making directly for the light, Wetherill led Caballo by the cleft's edge. The wind screamed across the rocks, threatening to blow them over. They were slow and cautious, using the big rocks for shelter and cover. When they had closed to within fifty feet, they could see the blue flame inside the dwelling, hanging suspended in the air. It was the gas Caballo had smelled, ignited and spewing from a hole in the ground.

Wetherill halted their progress and pointed at a boulder with his sabre to where Caballo was to take a covering position.

Caballo cocked his weapon and aimed at the doorway. Wetherill took two steps forward and stopped. A gut-wrenching shriek of pain and terror cut through the howling wind. It came from the dwelling where their comrades waited. Caballo and Wetherill turned, looking back through the snow.

Something dark came across the rooftops and rock face, moving impossibly fast, crawling over vertical walls like a spider but with the speed of a cougar. The creature blended into the night but there was no mistaking what it carried. The beast dragged Private Waters over stones and ledges. The young man shouted and struggled against the thing that held him to no avail. It carried him as easily as if the soldier were a rag doll.

It dropped to the ground in front of the dwelling and pulled Waters inside. Caballo and Wetherill, frozen in place, watched helplessly as the animal trussed Waters by his feet into the same loop that had held the coyote. The blue flame licked at Waters' uniform. The young man screamed as his clothing burned away.

Wetherill yelled in defiance and charged the entrance with his cavalry sabre ready to strike. The creature heard the shout and spun out the door to meet its attacker. Caballo fired his rifle wildly and missed. The demon met Wetherill head-on. The white man went sprawling, losing his Colt and sword as he fell. The beast was on top of him, swinging its arms and legs in a frenzied attack. Wetherill never had a chance.

Caballo struggled to load another round in the carbine's trap door breech. His fingers trembled and he dropped two shells before sliding one home. By the time he aimed, the creature was dragging the Lieutenant toward the dwelling. Unable to control his tremors, Caballo fired and missed again.

The creature seemed not to notice. It quickly carried Wetherill inside and replaced Waters' burnt corpse in the loop. Caballo fumbled inside his overcoat to extract another cartridge for the carbine. He slid one into the breech, ran to the doorway, and shot the beast in the back of the shoulder as it hunched near the fire.

The demon howled in pain, rolled forward, and somersaulted back onto its feet, facing Caballo. Long dark hair fell around its shoulders. Black fur, caked with mud, covered thick muscles that ran along its arms and legs. A smear of white powder was painted across its black-in-black eyes. It drew back its lips and snarled, showing long, sharp canines.

A quizzical expression came over the creature's face as it reached over its shoulder and inspected the wound. When it brought its hand back, its long fingers were covered in a dark, viscous fluid. The creature rolled the black blood between its thumb and fingers.

Caballo was frozen in place. The creature reminded him of the apes he had seen in picture books. But this was no ape. It stood erect on human legs. Its arms were short and it studied its greasy blood with intelligent eyes. It turned and spoke to Caballo in a language he had never heard.

"*Hagh throm fumg maw?!*" Its voice was deep and clear. There was a question in its words, but it was more a statement of astonishment. "*Fumg maw!*"

The words broke the trance that held Caballo. He released the breech on his rifle and slammed in a new cartridge. Before he could raise the rifle, the demon covered the ground between them and hit him with the strength of a bison. Caballo's head smacked the ground and he felt the air leave his lungs. The beast placed a heavy foot on Caballo's chest and ripped away the carbine, holding it up for inspection.

Lying on his backside, stunned and out of breath, Caballo watched the creature handle the rifle. It studied the trigger mechanism without cocking the hammer and smelled the gunpowder residue in the barrel. There was no fear in the beast, just a desire to comprehend. Gradually, the demon turned its attention back to Caballo.

It bent close to study the black man's face with the same inquisitiveness it displayed with the rifle, running its hand over Caballo's hair and stubbled beard. It extended a single finger and ran it alongside Caballo's temple. When it withdrew the finger, it was covered with red blood from a gash above Caballo's eye. The demon brought the finger to its nose and inhaled. The black eyes within the white smear lit with anticipation. It dipped the finger into its mouth, licked away the blood, and began to laugh.

On the roof behind the demon, Caballo caught sight of Red Knife. The beast was unaware of the old warrior. Red Knife was pouring the liquid from a silver flask over his own body, saturating his hair and robes. When the last drop had found its spot, Red Knife threw the flask onto the ground, where it clattered among the rocks.

The demon looked up instantly, searching for the disturbance. Red Knife dropped behind, looped the iron chain around its body, and drew it tight, pinning the creature's arms to its sides.

The demon surged backward. It slammed the old warrior into the dwelling's wall, but Red Knife held tight. The Apache loudly sang his death chant.

Caballo rose to his knees and brought forth the Colt 45 from under his overcoat. He fired and struck the demon in the chest. The bullet passed right through the creature's body and into Red Knife, but the Apache continued to sing.

Caballo got to his feet and fired again and again. Each shot hit the beast, extracting chunks of fur and flesh. Caballo fired again. The demon staggered as Red Knife pulled it back through the doorway. Another shot and the Apache moved into the blue fire. His tequila-soaked clothing burst into flames. Caballo fired again. The demon and its fiery captor plunged down the stairway into the crypt.

Caballo hurried into the dwelling. He crept forward and peered into the tomb. Red Knife had stopped chanting. Flames still flickered from the dead Apache's robes.

The demon sucked air through the holes in its chest. Caballo leveled his Colt to deliver a headshot. He pulled the trigger and— *click*. The monster moved an arm, rattling the chains that bound it to Red Knife's body. The damn thing seemed to be recovering.

The light faltered. Caballo ran back upstairs to where the gas burned. Using his legs and feet, he pushed the sandstone slab, covered the hole, and extinguished the flame. He reversed his position and pushed the slab away. Methane filled the room. He cut loose the Lieutenant and dragged both bodies outside the dwelling. Then he went looking for his rifle.

He sat in the snow and waited for hours. When he saw movement inside the dwelling, he knew the wait was over.

Caballo fired one shot into the back wall. The spark ignited the gas and the room exploded in a fireball. Tons of sandstone came crashing down. Maybe he imagined it, but he thought he saw the white streaked face of the demon peering from the passageway as the tomb's entrance filled with rock.

Dawn crept over the mesas. Caballo called from the ledge of the cleft for Candler, but there was no answer. He tied the bodies of his mates to a long rope and lowered them over the side. Then he lowered the ladder and climbed down himself.

He found Corporal Candler sitting in the shadows near the makeshift corral. He was dressed in his faded red dungarees and Army-issued pants and boots. Sweat soaked through his shirt and streaked his face.

"You all right, Willie?" The corporal stared at the ground between his knees. "Willie!"

"Oh, hey Sarge." Candler looked past Caballo. "Where are the others?"

Caballo nodded toward the bodies lying at the foot of the cliff. It was hard to believe Candler hadn't noticed them before. "We had a real bad night. I'll tell you about it on the way but you ain't going to believe it."

Candler regarded the bodies of his friends without much emotion. "Yeah, my night was strange too. What about Red Knife?"

"The old man died like a warrior." Caballo took a closer look at Caballo. "You sure you're all right, Willie? You're sweating like a hog and it's close to freezing."

"I'm okay, Sarge. In fact, I feel pretty damn good. It's just the sun. So hot it's making me sweat."

Caballo shook his head in disbelief, but his desire to leave the canyon outweighed other concerns. "Where are the horses, Willie?"

"They run off last night and never came back. They were hobbled but they broke their ropes. I think there was something in my camp, like a cougar or a bear. Whatever it was, it spooked the horses. All we got left is these two mules."

Candler harnessed the mules while Caballo loaded the bodies into the wagon and covered them with the tarp. The sun rose, but the winter chill persisted.

Caballo bundled himself into the overcoat and tightened the scarf that held his hat. He sat in the seat beside Candler who guided the mules as they pulled the wagon from the canyon. Candler wore a light jacket with the collar drawn up. Caballo could see the sweat soaking through Candler's clothing. What he couldn't see were the two puncture wounds on Candlers' neck, oozing black blood.

There Lives a Mountain

Cygnus Perry

There hums a Mountain on the northeast side of town
Some say they see it shiver on dry spring evenings
And on some brief nights, when both sun and moon are down,
The bubbling of sage grouse coats the air in a robe of inky proceed-
ings.
There cries a Mountain with tears that glitter blue and gold
Whose children lurk in tunnels lit by drops of dying sun
Best to keep the windows closed, or so all children are told
For the Mountain's kin eat little, and starvation stops no one.
There lives a Mountain who came to this town one year
No time traveled brings one closer to its wine-hued stony surface
It stays fixed in the distance like stars both far and near.
A mirage on yesterday's horizon—a stain on Earth
But only til the day it vanishes from this empty place.

Stairway to Nowhere
Ben Curl

Every half-mile, a wooden signboard dripping with scarlet beads told me I was heading toward Penumbral Cross. A second signboard, tacked below, informed me that the town was home to "the Famed and Disputed and never-Conquered—Stairway to Nowhere."

I hoped I hadn't stumbled into the northern fringes of Deseret, that land of mad, religious fervor. But that was impossible. Only three days ago, I'd been at the Black Hills, in the heart of the Lakota Territory.

Pausing at a crossroads, I saw little choice but to carry on toward Penumbral Cross, no matter what fools may await me. I'd not eaten for days. Though sorely tempted, I knew better than to sip even a droplet of the red rain that weighed down the broad leaves of the aloe plants.

It was close to town, coming round a ridge, when I saw the Stairway rising from the valley below. The chiseled, crooked steps curled upward around a rugged tower. The small town huddled in its shadow. A black ridgeline, fringed with a violet sunset, stood behind.

The sight of the Stairway, curving in an unfinished arc toward infinity, filled me with wonder. The tower was not exceptionally tall. It could not afford a worthwhile view. Nothing seemed to invite anyone to make the climb—nothing except those steps, which cried out to be used for their universal function.

While I stood gazing, pondering the meaning of it all, a man on horseback drew up beside me.

"Have you come to watch?" He wore a dark purple suit with black stripes, a short-brimmed hat, and a sheathed saber. He did not look at me as he spoke, but toward the unseeable summit of the Stairway, stroking a corner of his sleek mustache, a glimmer in his eye.

"To watch what?" I asked.

"The first man, woman, or beast to do it—to scale the Stairway to Nowhere."

I didn't bother to suppress my laughter. "In the last two hours, I've walked seven hills higher than that piece of rubble."

He cringed as if I'd spat on the hallowed ground of Golgotha. "You truly haven't heard of the Stairway?"

"Never in my forty-three years."

"Countless people, far braver and less stupid than you," he said, "have died trying to reach the last step. Some have made it past the second bend. As far as anyone remembers, no one has ever made it round the third."

Together we stared at the vague crater, where a violet haze engulfed the upper landing.

"I've come here to reach whatever lies beyond the final step," he said. "I've trained ever since the last Ascension Day, when I watched the competitors, one by one, tumble from the steps or vanish into the heights. I was only passing through at that time, but I knew I would return. I've gone from town to town, collecting from loved ones the stories of those who went before, those who failed. I am going to conquer the Stairway and obtain the knowledge of its summit."

"Have at it," I said. "Tell me what eagle droppings and lizard spittle you find. But if you see the Almighty lounging about up there, please do us all a favor and keep your mouth shut, will you?"

He ignored me and fiddled with a locket attached to a wrist chain. "It's said that if you have the boldness to climb to Nowhere, you can go Anywhere."

"All sounds like mystical hogwash. Tell you what." I pointed to the presumptive saloon, a gray-shingled building with a sagging roof over its porch. "I'll watch you do it and vouch for you, if you'll buy me a drink and a pie."

"I don't need you to vouch for me, you wretched Philistine. The whole town will be watching two dawns from now, when Ascension Day begins."

He lingered behind on his horse, his eyes reflecting the violet-fringed crater, while I made my way to town, leaving him to dream his foolish dreams.

"Are you a prince in disguise?"

The sooty-faced child accosted me from the shadows while I staggered out of the saloon and onto the creaking porch, struggling to light a cigarette I'd filched from the auburn-haired man (whom I'd convinced to buy me a piece of pie) who had been sitting beside the bald woman (who had bought me two shots of brandy, against her better judgment.)

"What'd you say?" I asked.

From the dark sockets of his stained face, the boy's blue eyes burned frostier and lonelier than the stars above. "I asked if you're a prince, coming around in those rags pretending like you're one of us. You know, only acting the part of a thief when really you're the king's son, the heir to the salt mines, the magnetic carriage that rides along the silver railway, and all the rest. You know, just seeing what life is really like for the people in the valleys before you make your final decision."

"It seems I've come to a town of mockers." I managed to light the cigarette. "If I were that good of an actor, I'd have a job in a traveling show." I tugged the loose, tattered corners of my jacket. "No, my child, what you see here is genuine filth, earned by my own bad luck and worse choices."

He rested one elbow on the arm rail, looking much older and more disillusioned than he should. "You're saying you're exactly what you seem?"

"I don't know what I seem, but if it's dirty and mean, it's probably not far off the mark."

He leaned both his elbows on the rail and stared at the jagged outline of the black cliffs on the far end of the valley. "This world is rubbish."

The following day, I ambled about town, pursuing what opportunities may exist. Finding a day job in exchange for a few meals usually wasn't hard for me. Finding an incautious wanderer at the outskirts of town was usually far easier.

Penumbral Cross, however, offered nothing. Besides a few meager garden plots and exhausted cows, I couldn't see how the town survived. Wagons came and went from the surrounding hills, but I never saw anything being loaded or unloaded except the grimy people with their wry grins. The dirt of the valley was dry, gray, and chalky. It got in your nose, turning your snot to ash-colored brittle. There was no one with any money or goods to borrow, as far as I could tell.

Eventually, I had some luck helping the townspeople erect a massive, painted signboard in the main intersection. It read, "Ascension Day." The locals shared rhubarb stalks, red beans, and tepid coffee with me.

No sooner had the sign gone up, specks of color began dotting the gray hills. Dust clouds rose from every direction. The travelers arrived.

Some wore gaudy, black-feathered costumes and silver face paint. Others wore plain, gray dresses and wide, sloping hats. Several large buildings, which I had presumed abandoned and condemned, were lit from within, transforming into hotels and brothels.

It was a festival unlike any I'd seen before.

"What's the meaning of all this?" I asked Robbie, the boy who had approached me outside the saloon..

He was sitting cross-legged on a crate outside the tavern, watching a procession of feathered people carry unlit torches in the gray light of the afternoon. "Every town can send up to one contestant to see if they can make it to the top of the Stairway."

"That thing?" I pointed to the winding steps.

"Yes."

The Stairway clasped the darkness of night tight to itself like a vaporous blanket, even in the noon hour. Unlike when I'd first seen it, the cratered top of the tower was now visible. A final series of steps arose from its center, leading to the edge of nothingness.

"The suffocating dust of this valley must have addled everyone's brains," I said.

Per age-old custom, all entrants needed to declare their intentions by sunset. With nothing better to do, I decided to watch. Amid the revelry, it wasn't hard to find loose coins and unattended half-full glasses of ale.

Donovan Dahl, the man with the purple suit whom I'd met upon arrival, was the only one to have declared entry. Sitting back from the crowd, watching him stand alone on that rickety stage like some kind of hero, I chuckled at how far these people had taken their outrageous play. I was getting ready to leave when something said by the speaker at the podium caught my attention—something to the tune of a $100 prize that would be awaiting Mr. Dahl, should he return.

There were precious few seconds before the sun would sink below the black cliffs. The violet band was slinking along the horizon. This wide waste of a world wouldn't give me another chance like this, I realized.

"I declare myself an entrant!"

Lurching to my feet, I dropped the glass mug I had borrowed. The shattering added a dramatic effect that I did not intend but also did not regret.

Members of the crowd gasped. Feathers rustled. Dahl gave me a disdainful and incredulous look as I clambered onto the stage and took my place beside him.

"Wait!" A cry came from the alley. "I'll join too!"

My heart sank and my world spun, watching Robbie run toward me through the rows of spectators, his eyes beaming. I wanted to push him away, off the stage and into the shadows, but before I could, he stepped between Donovan and me and grabbed our hands in his, raising all three of our arms into the air together, to the cheers of the onlookers. Trumpets blared.

"I knew you were more than you seemed," he whispered.

And darkness swallowed the stage.

Everyone in the saloon wanted to buy drinks for Donovan, Robbie, and me. They insisted we choose the songs, despite my and Robbie's complete lack of culture. "It's only right you should hear your favorite melodies tonight," the lank-haired pianist drawled. "I doubt there's any music where you're going."

I asked a girl in the crowd to give me suggestions. She shouted things like, "A Madrigal for A Madwoman," "The Tale of the Lyncsod Who Loved," or "Three Lovers in a Lost Planet's Embrace."

A sullen, Prussian hermit from a nearby cavern, who visited the town yearly on Ascension Eve, told me that last year's fatalities had deterred most others from attempting the climb. A record number of contestants had entered, but the outcome had been more abysmal than usual.

Five jumped to their deaths. Seven were never seen again, except for a few isolated body parts that showed up in random quarters of town in the subsequent months—an earlobe in a butter dish, a kidney in a boot, an eyeball in a jewelry box. All were covered in moss.

The Stairway to Nowhere and the festivities of Ascension Day were all that kept this town alive. It would have been a shame if no one had competed this year. Perhaps it would have signaled the final decline of Penumbral Cross.

Dahl and I were heroes, merely for making the attempt. We had given the people hope that, even should we fail, the life of Penumbral

Cross would carry on as it had done for decades, in the shadow of the Stairway to Nowhere.

The locals expressed both sorrow and pride for the fact that young Robbie had joined us. In any case, there was nothing that could be done. Once an entrant was declared, there was no going back.

When I asked what was to keep someone from repenting of their decision, the hermit told me that a firing squad positioned at the bottom of the Stairway had never failed to make sure that entrants remained faithful to their pledge.

"Don't worry," Robbie said, leaning toward me, tipsy on the few drops of whiskey I'd let him sip, "I'm not afraid to go up them steps, not as long as you're with me. I'm not turning back."

Donovan Dahl kneeled on the chalky slab that formed the lower landing of the Stairway. His eyes were closed, and his mouth was moving. When he arose, the knees of his dark purple pants were gray.

"Who are you talking to?" I asked. "Who do you think is going to help us? God has abandoned this continent, you ass-swine."

"You're so ignorant you don't even know how to blaspheme properly," he said, brushing the dust off his knees and stretching his legs. "I have a respect for things greater than myself—whether I understand them or not. That's what's kept me alive out here. You'd best learn the same, or you won't make it past the first bend."

"We'll see," I said, looking up toward our climb. The darkness that clung to the Stairway thinned, allowing us to see the contours of the angular steps.

Robbie tugged at my elbow and pointed to the eastern hills where the white sun oozed over black mounds.

The crowd went silent as we set off. I heard footsteps shuffling for better views. Then, nothing of the world below could be heard at all. The quality of the air seemed to thicken around us.

Donovan moved at a steady and cautious pace, making his steps land in the dead center of the stairs. I followed close behind with Robbie at my side.

"Should you have your gun out?" Robbie asked.

"I don't know. He doesn't." I pointed at Donovan.

"Of course, I don't," Donovan said. "The challenges of the Stairway are not of a material kind. A silly blunder with a firearm could kill us all."

"Why did they make this pointless tower anyhow?" I asked.

"The people of Penumbral Cross didn't build it. No one did."

"What's that supposed to mean? Someone had to make this thing. A stairway doesn't just appear out of nowhere."

"This one did."

I shook my head and threw a piece of rubble over the edge. We listened but heard no impact. Robbie looked toward me with a pale, screwed-up face.

"It's all just illusions," I said to him. "Do you understand?"

He nodded and bit his lip.

"Come on, let's go," I said.

With every step we took, dark vapors gathered, flying toward us from over the plains, as if a loose cloak were reassembling itself from the shadows.

A long whistling wind arose, then descended, before settling into a constant whir.

"We're past the first bend," Dahl said.

"What does that mean?"

"I wish I knew."

A faint, green light seeped down from the steps above. The threads curled around our feet, nuzzling our ankles.

Robbie kicked at them. The green threads widened like ripples in a pond around him, then contracted once again before sliding past to the shadows below.

"Donovan, what's happening to the steps behind us? I can hardly see them anymore."

"There's no going back once you go up this far."

From a step in front of me, I grabbed a discarded boot. Inside was a stump of a leg, cut clean just above the ankle. Plants that resembled bean sprouts spiraled out of the wound and crawled up the leather. Grimacing, I tossed it underhand to the black fog below. As soon as the boot spun toe-first into the threshold of the dark curtain, the whole thing vanished without a sound.

"Remember what I said?" I grabbed Robbie by the shoulders and stared into his cold blue eyes. "It's still just illusions, dammit. You got that?" A bit of my spit landed on his long eyelashes.

"Yeah . . . yeah . . ." he replied.

Dahl swallowed hard. "We should keep moving. I feel a sense of life here, which should be reassuring, but it's not. It's more horrifying to me, for some reason, than that void behind us. I feel as if we've wandered into the fever dream of an ancient brain. Do you feel it too?"

"Not exactly," I said, watching the green, luminescent filaments spiral downward. "I feel more like we are playthings in a demon's puppet show."

"Two different ways of saying the same thing, perhaps" Donovan said and turned to the steps above. "Shall we?"

We walked in silent rhythm. The atmospheric transformation happened slowly, so gradual and natural that we did not register any surprise. Legions of white pinpoints blossomed all around us in a black expanse. Unfamiliar constellations sprawled above and below. It seemed the tower had grown weightless and was rotating.

"If this is an illusion, I rather like it," Robbie said, his eyes wide.

"Don't get too enamored," I said, pulling out a revolver.

"Why not?"

"Every time the universe has shown me something beautiful, it's just as quickly snatched it away."

"You're always looking for the bad in things, aren't you? That's why you're unhappy."

"I'm unhappy because the world is cruel. Let's not get philosophical about it."

Ahead of us, Dahl was crouching beside a slab. He motioned for us to be quiet and join him.

I couldn't comprehend what was happening in the broad, rimmed crater before us. Somehow, we had reached the summit, where in the center the final steps of the Stairway to Nowhere climbed toward the stars. Eight-foot-high trellises, roughly hewn from a glimmering, metallic ore, formed a wide arc around the steps. Bulging vines writhed along the posts of this odd, starry garden. In the center of this confounding scene, the steps stood alone, unguarded, cold and enticing. I felt an irresistible urge to reach the top step and find out what I would see. It seemed I had forgotten something... something that the Stairway would show me.

Apparently, Dahl felt similar emotions.

"All my life," he said, with a tear welling in one eye, "I've felt this broken world was not the right one for me. I was a knight errant. That's who I was. Yes. That's who I am." He looked up at the innumerable stars and muttered a rapid prayer I couldn't hear. Wiping away his tear, he clasped my shoulder. "I'm sorry, my fellow traveler, but I cannot let you take this moment from me. I was born to be the one who scales the Stairway."

Before I could lurch away, he shoved a dagger into my ribs. I stumbled back against the wall and fired a shot. The bullet ricocheted off the steps and careened out into the void.

He leapt into the crater with Robbie on his heels.

"Cheater!" the boy yelled. "Scoundrel!"

"Leave him be," I shouted, causing a sharp pain to jolt within my lungs.

Dahl bounded across the moon-like declivity with long strides, pulling his saber from its sheath and pointing it forward, his purple coattails streaming behind him like pinions.

"For god's sake, Robbie, don't follow him!" Again, it felt as if my lungs were imploding.

The boy wouldn't listen. Nearing the steps, Dahl turned on him with his saber, raising it high above his head.

"I would not be ashamed to strike you down, child," Dahl said. "Turn back."

Robbie stood his ground, defiant.

"Do you hear me?" Dahl said, his words reverberating off the stony rims of the crater. "I am conquering these steps! I will go Anywhere!"

It was the best shot I'd ever made in my life. In all honesty, my marksmanship wasn't one of my defining traits. And to be even more honest, I wasn't aiming for the hand that held the saber. I was aiming for the violet lapel on his left hand side. Nonetheless, luck was on our side.

The saber jumped out of his hand, clattering on the cold ground. Dahl howled. With one last ferocious outburst, he kicked Robbie in the chest, sending him down. I scrambled forward, across the crater, entering the arc of metallic trellises. The vines seemed to be thrashing with a sudden intensity, and something about their movements—something about the glimpses of figures that resembled wiggling mandrakes—unnerved me.

"I'm coming, Robbie!"

I took another shot. This one missed.

Dahl scowled. "You fool. You won't be the one to reach the summit. You were never here for the right reasons."

With a grin and a hop, he danced up the steps, to the top, and leapt out into nothingness. I fired a shot but missed again. This bullet sailed past, toward a trellis near the rim, from where we heard a hideous shriek return. All the vines and leaves along the circle of trellises rustled, like a snake moving through a bed of reeds.

I hunched beside Robbie and we watched, shivering, for a blast of cold had arisen as soon as Dahl had leapt off the top step. Our eyes were transfixed. He had not fallen to the other side. He had not vanished (as I had expected.) Rather, his body floated in thin air, rotating. His face was frozen in an expression of exultation, stained by a tinge of impending terror.

There seemed to be dark, scarcely visible currents moving around him, like he was suspended in molasses. Momentarily, green filaments, like the ones we had seen earlier, sprouted from these thick currents. These flickering threads entwined his arms, his legs, his head, and every part of his body. They constricted. The one on his left ear wound so tightly that it sliced the appendage clean from his skull. The detached piece of flesh floated out into the starry expanse, twirling end over end.

Cold winds from the stars washed over us. The trellises groaned with the age-old groans of rock. I held Robbie close.

Amid the trellises, the shapes became clearer.

Indistinct human forms, wrapped in vines, moaned, and shook from their mounts. Arms, overgrown with webbed leaves, stretched outward. Eyelids encrusted with pale-green lichen fluttered. Lips, glued together with stems like a series of columns, murmured in vain.

Dahl hovered to a vacant spot in the garden. From out of his shadow, a stalagmite rumbled upward. Two rocky arms sprouted outward, forming a new trellis. There, on this stony cross, the still-breathing body of Dahl was strewn.

My mind was flooding with impossibilities. Reason was failing.

"What does it do with them?" Robbie asked.

"I told you; the universe doesn't give such beautiful visions without a price. You ever heard of a Venus fly-trap?"

"No."

"Well, that's what this is."

"How do we get out? Dahl said we can't go back down the steps."

I took Robbie's hand and walked him over to the mounted body of Dahl. Vines were slithering in and out of his nostrils, his ear, and the hole where the other ear used to be. His mouth, filling with algae, gurgled a prayer that I couldn't make out word for word, but I got the gist.

"Look away," I said to Robbie. "You shouldn't have to see this."

The gunshot echoed back and forth off the cratered walls, before dissipating into the endless silence of space. The vines along Dahl's slumping body shriveled and receded. What was left of him fell to the ground, a discarded and shriveled husk.

"He wasn't right about this Stairway," I said, looking out to the twinkling stars, which made me think of the sinister eyes of an infernal audience gathered around a stage, watching us with glee and derision. "He wasn't right about lots of things."

From what we could tell, there were all sorts of people—young and old, rich and poor —hanging on the trellises. One wore a beaverskin cap; another wore a skirt of beads. Others had never been human at all. I only had eight bullets left. We couldn't spare all of them from their fates. But we did what we could.

Down the darkness of the steps, we had to push with all our strength. There grew in my heart a pervasive fear that I was doing the wrong thing, that I was turning away from my destiny, that I was losing something I would never be able to find again, something I'd left beyond the top step. Robbie sensed it too.

"But maybe you are the prince," he said. "Just like I thought. Maybe it wasn't true then, but it will be once we go through. Once we go past that top step, to the invisible…"

"No, no. It's trying to draw us back in."

And it nearly had me at times. It would have had Robbie, if I hadn't pulled him back. He bit my arm, trying to escape my grasp and run back up the steps.

It was like that predatory thing fed off dreams of glory impossibly obtained. It made sense that it had begun prowling western North America.

In any case, I don't think there ever will be any learning exactly what that Stairway to Nowhere is all about. When we returned to town, the people were shocked. They kept looking at us like they expected us to gouge our own eyes out or turn into ravenous beasts. Their shock turned to horror when the entire tower, Stairway and all, flickered and faded away. One moment it was there; the next, you could see straight through to the black cliffs on the other side of the valley.

I tried hard to persuade the people of Penumbral Cross to pay me the one-hundred dollar prize, given I'd learned what had been up in the crater and had lived to tell about it (and had saved Robbie, to boot). But they were hagglers. No one knew who Robbie's parents were. Moreover, they pointed out that the town now had no future, thanks to me making the Stairway vanish.

In the end, we settled on $10 and a horse.

Since then, I've heard stories about the Stairway to Nowhere showing up in new parts: Manitoba, the Grand Canyon, the crater of former Lake Superior, the Baja Peninsula, New Machu Picchu. But I haven't heard of anyone else climbing up top and making it back down. When people talk about their desire to find out what's up there, I don't warn them anymore. I try not to listen.

I'd have taken Robbie along with me when I left that dry, chalky valley. He was the only person I'd met in a long time who believed there was something good in me.

But, after the Stairway faded, I couldn't find him anywhere. No one saw where he went. So when it was dark, I set off with my new horse, whom I christened *Dull Donovan*, and rode out into the domed expanse of night, where beyond the black ridgeline, shivering among the frosty stars, I saw a pair of blue orbs that burned brighter and lonelier than all the rest—and then they were gone.

About the Authors

 Keith Anthony Baird is the author of *The Jesus Man: A Post-Apocalyptic Tale of Horror* (Novel), *Nexilexicon* (Novel), *And a Dark Horse Dreamt of Nightmares* (Book of Shorts), *This Will Break Every Bone In Your Heart* (Novelette), *Snake Charmer Blues* (Short) and a psychological/horror novella titled *A Seed in a Soil of Sorrow*. His works can be found on Amazon and Audible. His novella, *In the Grimdark Strands of the Spinneret*, is due to be published by Brigids Gate Press in November 2022. The *Diabolica Britannica* horror anthology was his brainchild, in which you'll find his own contribution *Walked a Pale Horse on Celtic Frost*. 2021 saw the launch of his *Diabolica Americana* and *HEX-PERIMENTS* anthologies. When not at his desk writing, you might find him up a mountain, snorkelling on a coral reef with his partner Ann, or having adventures with his grandson. Failing that, it's a good bet he'll be on Twitter. Keith Anthony Baird (@kabauthor) / Twitter

 Richard Beauchamp hails from the verdant hollows and hills of Ozark country. When he isn't spending time in the woods or with his fiance, he can be found in his office, crafting away hells of his own making. His stories can be found in various magazines and anthologies including Gehenna and Hinnom's *2017 Year's Best Body Horror Anthology*, Dark Peninsula Press's *Negative Space: An Anthology of Survival Horror*, and several issues of "Night Terrors" from Scare Street Press. His debut collection *Black Tongue & Other Anomalies* is currently a nominee for the 2022 Splatterpunk Awards for Best Fiction Collection.

Links: Instagram: r_b_author

Facebook: https://www.facebook.com/RichardBeauchampOfficial

Website: richardbeauchampauthor.com

 Hank Belbin is an English author of horror, focusing primarily on cosmic horror and the exploration of darkest corners of humanity. He has published several short stories, all of which are also available as audiobooks, two full length stage plays, and a literary fiction novel. He is currently working on his second novel about a sadistic rural cult in the heart of Dartmoor. He lives in Southampton, England. For more works visit www.hankbelbin.com

Matt Bliss is a construction worker turned speculative fiction writer living in the wild west of Las Vegas, Nevada. He believes there's no such thing as too much coffee and is the proud owner of way too many pets. His short fiction has appeared in MetaStellar, Cosmic Horror Monthly, and The Nosleep Podcast, among other published and forthcoming works. If you can't find him haunting the used book aisle of your local thrift store, you can always find him on Twitter at @MattJBliss.

 Deborah Cardillo is a queer writer living near the Monterey Bay, because she cannot bear to be far from the sea for long. She has an MFA in Writing Popular Fiction from Seton Hill University, of which she is absurdly proud. She talks to crows and sea lions, but they don't talk back. Yet. She lives with too many cats and a singular spouse.

Website: http://deborahcardillo.com/

Jeremiah Dylan Cook is a horror writer whose work has been published by The NoSleep Podcast, Castle Bridge Media, Ghost Orchid Press, The Lovecraft eZine, Hippocampus Press, Necronomicon Press, and Eye Contact: The Literary and Art Magazine of Seton Hill University. He won Purple Wall Stories February 2021 Writing Competition, and the Ligonier Valley Writers 2018 Flash Fiction Contest. While pursuing his bachelor's degree at St. John's University, Jeremiah received the Mario Mezzacappa Memorial Award for Outstanding Achievement in Poetry and Prose. He completed his Master of Fine Arts in Writing Popular Fiction at Seton Hill University. Jeremiah is an affiliate member of the Horror Writers Association, and the Managing Editor of New Pulp Tales. If you are interested in learning more about him, you can visit his website, www.JeremiahDylanCook.com, or find him on Twitter @JeremiahCook1, where he loves to post pictures of his daughter and discuss David Bowie, Resident Evil, and John Langan.

Aristo Couvaras was born to Greek parents in Durban, South Africa. He attended the University of the Witwatersrand, where he obtained a Bachelor of Arts, as well as a Bachelor of Laws. Aristo and his wife live on the island of Cyprus.

His stories have been featured in *Found: An Anthology of Found Footage Horror Stories,* at horrortree.com, Econoclash Review, Things in the Well's anthologies, *Beneath the Waves - Tales from the Deep* and *Trickster's Treats 4,* Critical Blast's anthology, *Gods & Services,* Fantasia Divinity's *Behind Glass Eyes* and Macabre Ladies' *Dark Carnival.*

Aristo can be found on Twitter @AR1sto.

 Jennifer Crow's poetry and fiction have appeared in a number of print and electronic venues over the past quarter-century, including Uncanny Magazine, Strange Horizons, Asimov's Science Fiction, and Analog, where two of her poems were finalists for last year's AnLab reader awards. She's currently at work on a couple of poetry collections and the rough draft of a fantasy novel. Those who'd like to know more about her work can find her on Twitter as @writerjencrow.

Patreon: https://www.patreon.com/poetrycrow

 **Ben Curl** is descended from shamans, sailors, and miscreants of the Artic Circle. He admires the writers Jean Ray, Clark Ashton Smith, and Angela Carter. His stories have appeared in podcast and print in Night Shift Radio, Horror Hill, Underland Arcana, and Dark Horses: The Magazine of Weird Fiction. His western metaphysical mystery "The Pendulum of Mound Junction," is included in *A Fistful of Demons: An Anthology of the Weird West*, available now on Amazon.

 A.L. Davidson (she/they) is a writer who specializes in massive space operas and tiny disturbances. She writes stories about ghosts, grief, isolation, space exploration, eco-horror, queerness, and the human condition. They live with their cat Jukebox in Kansas City.

Website: http://disturbancesbyalycia.weebly.com

Patreon: https://www.patreon.com/AlyciaDavidsonAuthor

Twitter: @MayBMockingbird

Robert DeLeskie writes under the stairs in an old, dark house in Toronto. In addition to penning fiction, he writes and directs spooky stories for paranormal TV series and is a published board game designer. Robert's work has appeared in Aurealis Magazine and Macabre Ladies' *Dark Nature*. Twitter/Instagram: @rdeleskie

 Rachel Horak Dempsey is a writer of dark fiction living in Denver. Her short stories have been published by Shacklebound Books, Brigids Gate Press and Twenty Bellows. She holds a BFA in Drama and English from NYU'S Tisch, a Master's in Journalism from Georgetown and is pursuing an MFA in Creative Writing from Regis. Find her on Twitter and Instagram @rachelsdempsey or blogging at www.rmfw.org/blog.

David A. Elsensohn lives for coaxing language into pleasing arrangements. He makes rather good sandwiches, he's told, and his chili recipe gets appreciative nods from friends.

He has short works published in the *Northridge Review*, *Crack the Spine*, Kazka Press's *California Cantata*, and Flame Tree Publishing's *Chilling Horror Stories*. His story "Trading Ghosts" was a published winner in Writers of the Future #36. His story "Vanni's Choice" was a winner of the NeoVerse Short Story Writing Competition, and published in *Threads: A NeoVerse Anthology*.

Terminally distracted, he lives in Los Angeles with an inspirational wife and the ghost of a curmudgeonly black cat.

 Maxwell I. Gold is a Jewish American multiple award nominated author who writes prose poetry and short stories in cosmic horror and weird fiction with half a decade of writing experience. Three time Rhysling Award nominee, and two time Pushcart Award nominee, find him at www.thewellsoftheweird.com.

KC Grifant is an award-winning Southern Californian author who writes internationally published horror, fantasy, science fiction and weird west stories for podcasts, anthologies and magazines. Her tales have appeared in *Andromeda Spaceways Magazine, Unnerving Magazine, Cosmic Horror Monthly, Dark Matter Magazine*, the British SF Association's *Fission Magazine, Tales to Terrify*, the *Lovecraft eZine*, and many others. In addition to a Weird West novel, MELINDA WEST: MONSTER GUNSLINGER (Brigids Gate Press, Feb 2023), she has also written for dozens of anthologies, including: *Chromophobia; Musings of the Muse; Dancing in the Shadows - A Tribute to Anne Rice; Field Notes from a Nightmare; The One That Got Away; Six Guns Straight From Hell; Shadowy Natures; Beyond the Infinite - Tales from the Outer Reaches*; and the Stoker-nominated *Fright Mare: Women Write Horror*. For details, visit www.KCGrifant.com or @kcgrifant.

Levi Hatch fell in love with writing the minute he first learned to craft individual words in elementary school. Armed with an admittedly unhealthy imagination and two loving parents that willingly subjected themselves to his torturously awkward tales, he has continued to write to this very day. His first ever publication will be his short story *"The Awl"* as it appears in the Timber Ghost Press Anthology *"Along Harrowed Trails."*

Levi now lives in Northern Alberta, Canada with his beautiful wife and young daughter and the three of them own and operate a small cattle ranch. That is until he becomes a rich and world famous author, of course, whereupon he plans to buy his own island in the pacific and retire eating pizza and watching true crime documentaries.

Pedro Iniguez is a speculative fiction writer and painter from Los Angeles, California. His work has appeared in *Nightmare Magazine, Helios Quarterly, Star*Line, Space & Time Magazine*, and *Tiny Nightmares*, among others. He can be found online at Pedroiniguezauthor.com

Samantha Kelly is a current student of the Warwick Writing Programme. She lives in Coventry with her family and a cat named after the Terminator. Her writing can be found in STORGY and Tether's End. She is @SambucaJK on Twitter.

C. H. Lindsay (Charlie) is an award-winning poet & writer, housewife, and book-lover. She currently has short stories and poems in twenty anthologies, with more coming out in the coming months. Her poems have also appeared in several magazines, including *The Leading Edge: A Magazine of Science Fiction and Fantasy, Amazing Stories, Fantasy Magazine, Strange Horizons,* and *Space and Time Magazine.* She is working on four novels, six short stories, and at least two dozen poems, although the numbers are always in flux.

In 2018 she became Al Carlisle's literary executor. She now publishes his true crime under *Carlisle Legacy Books, LLC,* with plans to add more books in the coming years.

She is a member of SFWA, HWA, SFPA, LUW and is a founding member of the Utah Chapter of the Horror Writers Association. Mostly blind, she lives in Utah with her "seeing-eye husband" and one cat (so far).

Native New Yorker **LindaAnn LoSchiavo**, a four time nominee for The Pushcart Prize, has also been nominated for Best of the Net, the Rhysling Award, and

Dwarf Stars. Elgin Award winner "A Route Obscure and Lonely," "Women Who Were Warned," Firecracker Award and IPPY Award nominee "Messengers of the Macabre" [co-written with David Davies], "Apprenticed to the Night" [Beacon Books, 2023], and "Felones de Se: Poems about Suicide" [Ukiyoto Publishing, 2023] are her latest poetry titles. In 2023, her poetry placed as a finalist in Thirty West Publishing's "Fresh Start Contest" and in the 8th annual Stephen DiBiase contest.

 Winston Malone is the creator of The Storyletter, a Substack newsletter dedicated to platforming independent authors, artists, and small businesses. He's an Air Force veteran currently living in SLC, Utah with his dog named Vinnie. He likes to read and write speculative fiction, and has aspirations of opening a coffee shop just for writers.

Substack - Storyletter.substack.com Instagram/Twitter - @thestoryletter

Morgan Melhuish is a writer and educator from West Sussex. His work has recently been published in *Beyond the Veil*, an anthology of queer supernatural love stories, from Ghost Orchid Press and *Annus Horribilis* from Bag of Bones Press. You can find him on Twitter @mmorethanapage.

LH Michael's credits include *Vastarien*, *The NoSleep Podcast*, and anotherealm.com.

Dermott O'Malley is a lover of horror, whiskey, and sometimes, horrible whiskey. He is the author of short stories such as "Thread Count," "Memoirs of a Mute," and "West for Its Own Sake." His stories have been published in various anthologies and magazines.

Cygnus Perry is an undergraduate student at Utah State University. They have lived in Utah since they were in high school where they developed a passion for creative writing. Cygnus loves to explore the natural world and uses it as inspiration for unnatural stories and poems. For Cygnus, writing is the best way to discover the unreal and unbelievable. Follow them on Twitter @perrypianist and on Instagram @perrypurplefingers.

WR Platt is a former advertising exec who loves speculative fiction. His award-winning stories have been published in The Florida Writer Magazine and FWA's recent anthology *Collections #14, Thrills and Chills.*

Daniel Powell teaches a variety of writing and literature courses at Florida State College at Jacksonville. He is an avid long-distance runner and outdoorsman, and he recently earned his doctoral degree at the University of Central Florida. His most recent publication is the thriller novel

Cold on the Mountain, and he lives near the Timucuan Preserve with his wife, Jeanne, and their children, Luke and Lyla. To learn more about Daniel's work, please visit his Author Central page with Amazon.

 Craig E Sawyer is an American writer known for horror, western, sci-fi, and crime, and is a direct descendant of the McCoy family that famously feuded against the Hatfield's over a stolen pig. He has been published by Quill & Crow Publications, Brigid Gates Press, Timber Ghost Press, Shotgun Honey, Weirdbook (Wildside Press), Schlock Publications, Crystal Lake Press, Nightmare Press, Levy-Gardner-Laven Productions, and Skull Dust Press. He is the creator of the horror/adventure comic "The Forbidden Museum," and the RPG sci-fi board game *Escape from Dulce*. Craig traveled much of the United States, eventually settling on the West Coast, and before becoming a writer he worked as a bartender, roofer, carpet weaver, bouncer, and actor. Insta & Twitter: @csawyerwriter

Kathryn Tennison received her MFA in creative writing from Butler University in Indianapolis. She lives in Arkansas with her husband, two cats, and one enormous dog. When she's not writing, she enjoys judging characters in horror movies for making the same decisions that she would probably make in the moment. Her fiction has been published by Bag of Bones Press. Follow her on Twitter: @acaffeinatedkat.

 Emily Ruth Verona is a Pinch Literary Award winner and a Bram Stoker Awards® nominee with work featured in *Under Her Skin*, *Lamplight Magazine*, *Mystery Tribune*, *The Ghastling*, *Coffin Bell*, *The Jewish Book of Horror*, and *Nightmare Magazine*. Her debut thriller, MIDNIGHT ON BEACON STREET, is expected from Harper Perennial in 2024. She lives in New Jersey with a small dog. For more visit www.emilyruthverona.com.

 **Adam Vine** was born in Northern California. By day, he is a senior writer at a game company. He has lived in five countries and visited forty. When he is not writing, he is reading something icky, training Brazilian Jiu Jitsu, or playing the guitar. He lives in Northern California with his wife, Hilary and their highly energetic goldendoodle, Frodo.

Website: www.adamvine.me

 Chris Wilder lives in the Pacific Northwest, enjoying horror, rain, and Star Wars with his wife Christina (an author) and cat Bella (a diva). He can be found on Twitter @neevalovesme. Bella can be found on Instagram @bellawildercat.

Ann Wuehler has written five novels--*Aftermath: Boise, Idaho, Remarkable Women of Brokenheart Lane, House on Clark Boulevard, Oregon Gothic* and the *Adventures of Grumpy Odin and Sexy Jesus*. Her Roxie and Ericka is included in *Well, This is Tense*, from Bag of Bones Press. Sefi and Des is in Brigid Gate's *Musings of the Muses*. Her short story, "Jimmy's Jar Collection", appeared in the *Ghastling's 13*. "The Cherry of Her Lips" appeared in the *War* anthology by Black Hare Press. "The Blackburne Lighthouse" will appear in a gothic horror anthology, in the spring of 2023, by Brigid's Gate. "Pig Bait" was included in the *Gore* anthology, by Poe Boy Publishing, and "Pliers" appeared in *Gore II*. "Prince Charming Finds His Sleeping Beauty" was selected for *That Is All Wrong, Vol. III*. "Annie Helps" made its way into the anthology, *Are You A Robot?* "The Tale of Grenadine" shows up in the Horror Zine's Magazine, *Spring of 2023*.

Website: https://annwuehler.wordpress.com/

If you enjoyed *Along Harrowed Trails*, please consider leaving a review on Amazon or Goodreads. Reviews help the authors and the press.

If you go to www.timberghostpress.com you can sign up for our newsletter so you can stay up-to-date on all our upcoming titles, plus you'll get informed of new horror flash fiction and poetry featured on our site monthly.

Take care and thanks for reading *Along Harrowed Trails*!

-Timber Ghost Press

Made in the USA
Columbia, SC
17 October 2024

44566199R00221